Marius' Mules III:
Gallia Invicta

by S. J. A. Turney

2nd Edition

"Marius' Mules: nickname acquired by the legions after the General Marius made it standard practice for the soldier to carry all of his kit about his person."

For Chris and Mary.

I would like to thank those people instrumental in bringing Marius' Mules 3 to fruition and making it the success it has been, and those who have contributed to the production of the Second Edition, in particular Leni, Jules, Barry, Robin, Kate, Alun, Nick, two Daves, a Garry and a Paul. Also a special thanks to Ben Kane and Anthony Riches, who have greatly encouraged me towards the improvements in this edition.

Cover photos courtesy of Paul and Garry of the Deva Victrix Legio XX. Visit http://www.romantoursuk.com/ to see their excellent work.

Cover design by Dave Slaney.

Many thanks to all three for their skill and generosity.

All internal maps are copyright the author of this work.

Also by S. J. A. Turney:

Continuing the Marius' Mules Series

Marius' Mules I: The Invasion of Gaul (2009)
Marius' Mules II: The Belgae (2010)
Marius' Mules III: Gallia Invicta (2011)
Marius' Mules IV: Conspiracy of Eagles (2012)
Marius' Mules V: Hades Gate (2013)
Marius' Mules VI: Caesar's Vow (2014)
Marius' Mules VII: The Great Revolt (2014)
Marius' Mules VIII: Sons of Taranis (2015)
Marius' Mules IX: Pax Gallica (2016)
Marius' Mules X: Fields of Mars (2017)
Marius' Mules XI: Tides of War (2018)
Marius' Mules XII: Sands of Egypt (2019)

The Praetorian Series

Praetorian – The Great Game (2015)
Praetorian – The Price of Treason (2015)
Praetorian – Eagles of Dacia (2017)
Praetorian – Lions of Rome (2018)

The Damned Emperors (as Simon Turney)

Caligula (2018)
Commodus (2019)

Tales of the Empire

Interregnum (2009)
Ironroot (2010)
Dark Empress (2011)
Insurgency (2016)
Emperor's Bane (2016)
Invasion (2017)
Jade Empire (2017)

The Ottoman Cycle

The Thief's Tale (2013)
The Priest's Tale (2013)
The Assassin's Tale (2014)
The Pasha's Tale (2015)

The Templar Series

Daughter of War (2018)
The Last Emir (2018)
City of God (2019)
The Winter Knight (2019)

Roman Adventures (Children's Roman fiction with Dave Slaney)

Crocodile Legion (2016)
Pirate Legion (2017)

Short story compilations & contributions:

Tales of Ancient Rome vol. 1 (2011)
Tortured Hearts Vol 2 (2012)
Tortured Hearts Vol 3 (2012)
Temporal Tales (2013)
Historical Tales (2013)
A Year of Ravens (2015)
A Song of War (2016)
Rubicon (2019)

For more information visit www.simonturney.com
or follow Simon on:
Facebook Simon Turney Author aka SJATurney (@sjaturney)
Twitter @SJATurney
Instagram simonturney_aka_sjaturney

tis Personae (List of Principal Characters)

mmand Staff:

Gaius Julius Caesar: Politician, general and governor.
Aulus Ingenuus: Commander of Caesar's Praetorian Cohort.
Cita: Chief quartermaster of the army.
Decimus Brutus: Staff officer and favourite of Caesar's family.
Quintus Atius Varus: Commander of the Cavalry.
Quintus Titurius Sabinus: Senior lieutenant of Caesar.
Quintus Tullius Cicero: Staff officer and brother of the great orator.
Titus Labienus: Senior lieutenant of Caesar.

Seventh Legion:

Publius Licinius Crassus: Legate and son of the triumvir Crassus.
Titus Terrasidius: Senior Tribune.
Publius Tertullus: Junior Tribune.
Gaius Pinarius Rusca: Junior Tribune.

Eighth Legion:

Quintus Balbus: Ageing Legate of the Eighth, close friend of Fronto.
Titus Balventius: Primus pilus & veteran of several terms of service.
Aquilius: Training officer, senior centurion and perfectionist.

Ninth Legion:

Publius Sulpicius Rufus: Young Legate of the Ninth.
Marcus Trebius Gallus: Senior Tribune and veteran soldier.
Grattius: primus pilus, once in sole command of the Ninth.

Tenth Legion:

Marcus Falerius Fronto: Legate and confidante of Caesar.
Gaius Tetricus: Military Tribune, expert in military defences.
Servius Fabricius Carbo: Primus Pilus.
Petrosidius: Chief Signifer of the First cohort.

<u>Eleventh Legion:</u>

Aulus Crispus: Legate, former civil servant in Rome.
Quintus Velanius: Senior Tribune.
Titus Silius: Junior Tribune.
'Felix': Primus Pilus, accounted an unlucky man.

<u>Twelfth Legion:</u>

Servius Galba: Legate.
Gaius Volusenus: Junior Tribune.
Publius Sextius Baculus: Primus pilus. A distinguished veteran.

<u>Thirteenth Legion:</u>

Lucius Roscius: Legate and native of Illyricum.
Atenos: Senior centurion and former mercenary.

<u>Fourteenth Legion:</u>

Lucius Munatius Plancus: Legate and former staff officer.
Cantorix: Centurion in the Third cohort.

<u>Other characters:</u>

Faleria the elder: Mother of Fronto and matriarch of the Falerii.
Faleria the younger: sister of Fronto.
Corvinia: Wife of Balbus, legate of the Eighth.
Lucilia: Elder daughter of Balbus.
Balbina: Younger daughter of Balbus.
Galronus: Gaulish officer, commanding auxiliary cavalry under Varus.
Gnaeus Vinicius Priscus: Former primus pilus of the Tenth, assigned camp prefect of the army, convalescing in Rome after serious wounding last year.
Paetus: Former camp prefect, betrayed by Caesar and Clodius. Believed dead, but escaped and at large in Italy.
Publius Clodius Pulcher: Powerful man in Rome, enemy of Caesar and conspirator, responsible for multiple crimes.
Philopater: Clodius' chief enforcer.
Clodia: Sister of Clodius, a devious and dangerous woman.

The maps of Marius' Mules III

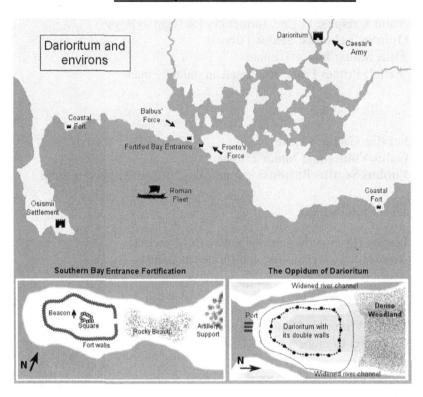

Darioritum and environs

Darioritum — Caesar's Army

Coastal Fort

Balbus' Force

Fortified Bay Entrance — Fronto's Force

Roman Fleet

Coastal Fort

Osismii Settlement

Southern Bay Entrance Fortification

Beacon

Square

Rocky Beach

Artillery Support

Fort walls

N

The Oppidum of Darioritum

Widened river channel

Dense Woodland

Port

Darioritum with its double walls

N

Widened river channel

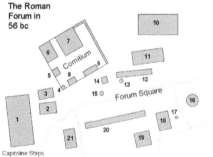

The Roman Forum in 56 bc

Comitium

Forum Square

Capitoline Steps

Key

1   Tabularium (Public records office)
2   Temple of Concord
3   Basilica Opimia
4   Senaculum (Senate's gathering hall)
5   Tullianum (Prison)
6   Basilica Porcia
7   Curia (Senate chamber)
8   Graecostasis (Ambassador's hall)
9   Rostra (Public speaking podium)
10   Macellum Piscarium (Fish market)
11   Basilica Aemilia
12   Shops
13   Shrine of Venus Cloacina
14   Temple of Janus
15   Lacus Curtius (ancient sacred pool)
16   Temple of Vesta
17   Lacus Juturnae (sacred nymphaeum & spring)
18   Temple of the Dioscuri (Castor & Pollux)
19   Basilica Sempronia
20   Shops
21   Temple of Saturn

Gaul, marking major settlements

GERMANIA

Morini   Menapii
• Nemetocenna
BELGICA

Crociatonum
ARMORICA   Unelli Lexovii
Curiosolites   Esubii
Veneti   Vindunum   Cenabum
Darioritum
Corsicum   Turonum   • Vesontio
• Bibracte

Geneva •   Octodurus

Sotiates
Tolosa
AQUITANIA Carcaso
Narbo   Massilia
Spanish Tribes

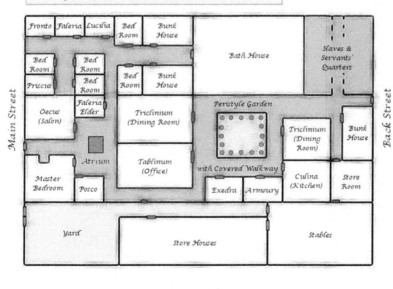

House of the Falerii on the Aventine Hill in Rome

Main Street

Back Street

| Fronto | Faleria | Lucilia | Bed Room | Bunk House | | | Slaves & Servants' Quarters |

Bed Room   Bed Room   Bath House
Priscus   Bed Room   Bed Room   Bunk House

Oecus (Salon)   Faleria Elder   Triclinium (Dining Room)   Peristyle Garden   Triclinium (Dining Room)   Bunk House

Atrium   Tablinum (Office)   with Covered Walkway   Culina (Kitchen)   Store Room

Master Bedroom   Posco   Exedra   Armoury

Yard   Store Houses   Stables

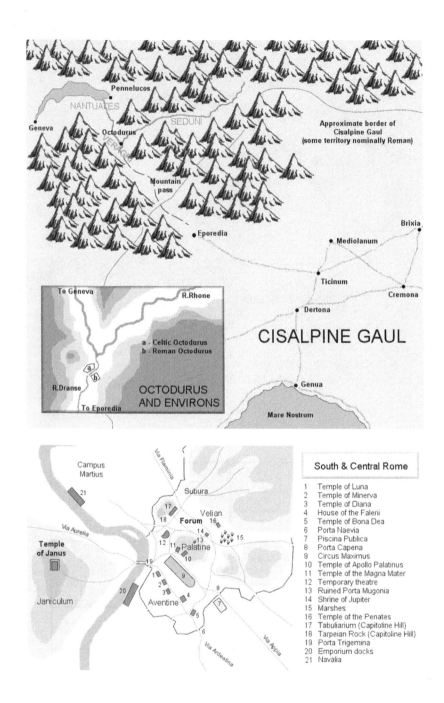

Pennelucos

NANTUATES

Geneva

SEDUNI

Octodurus

VERAG

Mountain
pass

Eporedia

Approximate border of
Cisalpine Gaul
(some territory nominally Roman)

Brixia

Mediolanum

Ticinum

Cremona

To Geneva

R.Rhone

Dertona

a - Celtic Octodurus
b - Roman Octodurus

CISALPINE GAUL

a
b

R.Dranse

To Eporedia

OCTODURUS
AND ENVIRONS

Genua

Mare Nostrum

Campus
Martius

Via Flaminia

21

Subura

17
18

Velian

Forum 16

Via Aurelia

Temple
of Janus

14
12 11 Palatine
10

13

15

19

Janiculum

7
1
2
3
20

9

4

Aventine

5

8

7

6

Via Ardeatina

Via Appia

South & Central Rome

1   Temple of Luna
2   Temple of Minerva
3   Temple of Diana
4   House of the Falerii
5   Temple of Bona Dea
6   Porta Naevia
7   Piscina Publica
8   Porta Capena
9   Circus Maximus
10 Temple of Apollo Palatinus
11 Temple of the Magna Mater
12 Temporary theatre
13 Ruined Porta Mugonia
14 Shrine of Jupiter
15 Marshes
16 Temple of the Penates
17 Tabuliarium (Capitoline Hill)
18 Tarpeian Rock (Capitoline Hill)
19 Porta Trigemina
20 Emporium docks
21 Navalia

Also available online at:
http://simonturney.com/downloads/marius-mules-maps/

PART ONE: GALLIA INVICTA

Chapter 1

(December: Octodurus, in the Alpine passes above Geneva)

It is the third day before the nones of December, and we are feeling the first morsel of security in months. On the orders of the general, I left Titus Labienus and his command at Nemetocenna and brought the depleted Twelfth Legion into the mountains above Cisalpine Gaul, a territory only nominally Roman, plagued with bandits and antagonistic Celts, in order to secure a trade route across the mountains.

Our task has not been an easy one. Indeed, this is the first time I have had the leisure and reason to make report.

Upon arrival in these unforgiving valleys, once we had departed from friendly territory and lost sight of the Geneva Lake, we immediately encountered opposition in the form of the Nantuates. It causes me to shake my head in wonder when I remember that these men were raw recruits less than two years ago, hastily trained and armed for campaigning in the very lands that we once again occupy. Two years of brutal warfare against Gauls, Belgae and Germans have left me with tough, if relatively inexperienced, men at every level, but all too few of them. By the time we had reached Geneva we had lost another fifty men or more of our already woefully understaffed legion to their wounds and the increasing cold of the mountains.

Despite promises of reinforcements from Cisalpine Gaul, we have seen or heard no sign of relief and have carried out the orders to take and hold this vital mercantile pass with a legion so diminished we would not be able to form three complete cohorts, let alone the full ten. Our numbers are down to a little over seven hundred, including my officers, some of whom have only been soldiering for two years, due to the high death toll last year and this small but costly campaign. Even with the cavalry ala that accompanied us, we are terribly reduced.

And yet we have fought on for more than two months. The valiant and rapidly diminishing Twelfth have pushed back and contained the Nantuates, reducing three of their fortresses to ash and rubble, have forced the Seduni back deep into their lands and reduced their

1

strength, and lastly stormed the main strongholds of the Veragri, breaking the greater part of local resistance. Only three days ago did we stop for the first time to take account of our accomplishments.

The three tribes we have subdued here sent emissaries seeking peace and I have never been more pleased to be able to grant a request. Our men were close to breaking through exhaustion, numbing cold and the unsettling odds. But we have agreed terms with them all. The Seduni, who are the most distant of the three, have sent us hostages as a sign of faith. The Nantuates have done the same, but there was something about the way they spoke that has left me unsure of their fidelity and so I settled three centuries of men, which was all I can truly spare, among the Nantuates under a veteran centurion with orders to fortify and keep in contact with riders.

I then brought the rest of the army to the centre of this hornet nest: the town of Octodurus in Veragri territory. Here, we are fortifying our own position and preparing to send out patrols and set up a line of signal stations in both directions across the pass, to the north through our garrison among the Nantuates down to the fort at Pennelucos by the lake and to the south as far as the fort at Eporedia in Cisalpine Gaul.

It is my dearest hope that within a few weeks we will be settled, fortified and beginning to trade and work with the local tribes rather than having to watch them for signs of trouble and increased banditry. When we have signal towers and watch stations we will be in a position to say that the pass is truly safe for merchants, but at this time I would still strongly discourage any civilian from trying the route, even with armed escorts. It will be some weeks at the least before we can claim the pass is safe. Indeed, I still feel uneasy in myself; a sentiment that is echoed among the men, though they try not to show it.

I will make further report when we have the signal system in place and have set up good lines of trade and communication.

While I do not wish to speak out of turn, I would urgently request that emissaries are sent to Caesar in Rome or Illyricum, wherever he may be, with a request for reinforcements. Without them, the Twelfth remains in dire straits throughout this damned winter.

My courier and his escort will need food and shelter upon receipt of this report and will stand by to return to Octodurus with a reply at your earliest convenience.

For the senate and the people of Rome.
Servius Sulpicius Galba, legatus of the Twelfth Legion.

Galba furrowed his brow as he reread the last paragraphs for the fourth time. It was delicate. With the general away involved in politics either in Rome or across the sea, their closest senior contact was the camp prefect of the Tenth's garrison fortress at Cremona. While Galba theoretically outranked the man, Piso was the de facto senior commander in the whole province of Cisalpine Gaul and therefore the immediate step between Galba and the general.

To suggest that the general had been neglectful or deficient in some way in not providing the troops that he had promised almost half a year ago would not be, Galba was sure, a good career move. Still, something had to be done. The Twelfth barely had enough men to keep Octodurus quiet, let alone the entire pass that led from the eastern end of the Geneva Lake all the way across the Alps and down to Eporedia in Roman territory.

With a sigh, he nodded at the last few lines, his mouth turning up at the corner as he noted once again 'For the senate and the people of Rome' when the whole campaign was clearly 'for the glory and purse of the great Caesar'. Fronto may be an outspoken lunatic with plebeian tendencies, but there were times he nailed the general to the wall with a well chosen description.

'Shame *I* couldn't get away with that...'

'I'm sorry sir?'

Galba blinked. He had forgotten the cavalry decurion was there.

'Oh, nothing. Just talking to myself.'

Taking a breath, he snapped the wood-encased tablet shut and sealed it with the wax from one of the three candles that lit the room's murky interior, plunging the seal of the Twelfth's commander into the liquid and watching it harden instantly. For a moment, he frowned down at the mark of the bull with the XII and sighed. If they did not get more men soon, this letter may be the last time the seal was ever used. Shaking the gloomy thoughts from his head, he reached up and passed the tablet to the cavalry officer.

'This goes into the hands of Prefect Piso at Cremona and no other. Do not be fobbed off at the gate with a promise to deliver it. Understand?'

The decurion nodded.

3

'Yes, sir. I have assembled a turma of men for escort. I realise that leaves you with diminished cavalry, sir, but the pass is very dangerous.'

Galba nodded.

'I'm aware of the situation, decurion. One turma of cavalry will hardly make or break our position here. Just get this report to Cremona and don't come back until you have a reply... preferably a good one with an offer of help.'

He smiled at the man. A little encouragement would not go amiss. The valley was still home to many bandits and pockets of resistance that had not surrendered with the main tribes and the journey would be dangerous.

'And make sure they feed you well and soak you in wine when you get there. On my orders, yes?'

The decurion grinned.

'Count on it, sir.'

With a salute, he turned and left the building, tucking the wax tablet away into his tunic. Galba sighed and leaned back in the chair. This room smelled of badly-cured animal skins, burned meat and a tightly-packed family group who had clearly eaten too many vegetables.

Trying not to picture what might be lurking in the dark corners of the room where he had not yet had the courage to prod and examine, Galba stood and turned to follow the trooper through the door.

Outside the house, the street sloped gently down toward the river that cut Octodurus in two. It was the most unusual Celtic settlement Galba had ever seen. No hill fort here, with high walls and a central gathering place at the summit. Here, the Veragri had been at the mercy of the vertiginous landscape. Octodurus lay on almost flat land at the head of a 'Y'-shaped valley, in a commanding position and bisected by a river. The view down the street was truly breathtaking, not for the town itself, but for the enormous mountains that rose up like unassailable walls to either side of the valley and at the spur rising like the prow of an upturned trireme between the valleys.

Climbing those mountains was an epic journey in itself, as the scouts that he had sent up there yesterday had verified when they returned late in the evening, exhausted, scratched and bruised. Since the legion had arrived here two days ago, the town had changed beyond measure. In an effort to preserve a level of reasonable trust and acceptability with the Veragri, Galba had allowed them to keep

4

the lower, flatter half of Octodurus for themselves on the other side of the river, across the single bridge that joined the two halves.

The Twelfth and their cavalry counterpart had taken control of the so-called 'upper' town and evicted the natives, forcing them to take up residence down the valley. The better of the squat stone and timber buildings had been requisitioned as the headquarters, armoury, store, watch office, and the various senior officers' quarters. The town's granary lay on the far side of the river, but the men were busy converting a building on high ground to do the job. The rest of the structures had been divided up among the men as barrack blocks.

The situation was hardly perfect, and it would take days or even weeks before the buildings were clean and comfortable and serviceable as fort structures. Galba glanced back over his shoulder once more, narrowing his eyes at the dark corners of the house with their piles of unknown objects. The idea of burning the damn thing down and building a new one was appealing. It would take weeks just to get rid of the smell in there.

A voice surprisingly close by cleared its throat and Galba grimaced as he jumped a little in a very unprofessional manner. Whipping round to see who had been lurking at the corner of the legate's quarters when they should have been busy working, he was relieved to see the battered and worn figure of Baculus, the primus pilus, sitting on a large half-buried block of stone and tapping his bronze greaves with his vine staff. His helmet lay on the grass beside him.

'In the name of Jupiter's balls, do you have to sneak up on me like that?'

Baculus raised an eyebrow and Galba chortled at himself.

'You startled me. How can a man like *you* be so quiet?'

The primus pilus started pulling himself respectfully to his feet. Galba waved the man back down and wandered across to take a seat facing him on a similar stone nearby.

'Sit, man. You're still supposed to be on light duties at best. The medicus keeps telling me that you're a long way from healthy again and that you're overdoing it. In his opinion you should be back in Rome for the next season recuperating.'

Baculus shrugged.

'Too much to do, sir. And you're already understaffed. Frankly, if I wasn't here, the whole collection of adolescents and near-cripples that pass for the officer class might just collapse into a blubbering heap.'

Galba frowned.

'Harsh, centurion, don't you think?'

Baculus curled his lip and waved his vine staff expansively at the town around them.

'Respectfully, sir, there are four officers left in the legion that I would consider veterans. Apart from myself there's Herculius, who's damn near due for retirement, and Petreius who suffered a blow to the head at that hill fort with the rolling logs last month and keeps forgetting words and misplacing things. There's the one tribune left who's good but exhausted from having to perform the duties of several men. Other than that, the entire officer class is filled with centurions who'd been immunes legionaries with perhaps three years of service in other legions before being drafted across to us, or even green recruits who couldn't have told you one end of a gladius from the other two years ago.'

He sighed and settled back on the rock.

'Don't get me wrong, legate. They're good lads, all of them. They've fought like monsters through this campaign, despite their youth and lack of experience, and they'll do whatever you ask, they're so damn loyal to the banner. They'll be an excellent cadre of officers in time; best I could ask to serve with. But that's at least two or three years of campaigning away yet. They're trying hard, but they've just not got the experience to carry out this sort of operation without older, steadier hands holding them in place.'

Galba nodded and stretched his arms out.

'Good job they have you to advise them, then.'

The two men fell silent for a time, nodding, until finally Baculus raised his face and cast a meaningful glance at his commander.

'I assume you've put a fairly urgent request for men in that report, sir?'

Galba nodded.

'Couched it in the best terms I can, but you know as well as I that, even if we get these reinforcements, they'll be raw and untrained. We'll be very lucky indeed if the command in Cremona can rustle us up a few veterans who are bored of their retired farming lives and feel like taking up the stick again.'

'Indeed. But at least it would give us a little more manpower.'

Silence descended again for a long moment.

6

'How are the works coming on?'

Baculus looked up again at his commander and leaned forward, his hands on the end of the vine staff, standing point down in the turf.

'Getting there. They should be basically ready by noon or midafternoon tomorrow. We've got the ditch and breastworks complete around the west, south and east sides, and the palisade is being produced at the moment. I've got the men working in shifts cutting timber on the valley side and working on construction, and they'll continue through the night. If everything goes according to plan, the gates and palisade should be up not long after first light. I've got them planning towers, lilia, a fortified bridge and various other things as well, though.'

He narrowed his eyes.

'We may have these bastards officially subdued and hostages and all that, but I wouldn't trust any of those carrion-feeding dogs further than I could spit one. I won't be able to relax until I have at least three levels of defence between us and them.'

Galba sighed and leaned back.

'I know what you mean. Things are theoretically quite settled here and yet I just can't shake this impression that something is going on that we don't know about.'

'It's *like that* with Celts, legate. After all, Caesar's conquered them twice, and they still rise up and complain. They just won't stay conquered.'

That last comment drew a throaty laugh from the stocky, barrel-chested legate.

'I wouldn't say that too close to the general.'

Baculus reached down to the hardness on his chest and stroked the shiny phalera and golden corona decorations that hung from the leather.

'You think he'd take these back?' the grizzled veteran grinned. 'I'd hate that, having just become accustomed to the extra weight.'

Galba laughed and scratched his chin.

'We'll see soon enough. At least we'll have the defences up soon.'

Baculus nodded again.

'I wish we still had Calvus or Ruga with us. The few remaining engineers we've got don't have between them half the experience of either of those poor sods. Still, as you said: we'll see soon enough.'

* * * * *

Galba blinked twice and tried to reel in his whirling thoughts. A knocking; heavy and fast. Urgent. Blink. The room was dark. Yes, middle of the night.

Blearily, the legate pushed back his blankets and rubbed his eyes as the hammering on the door began once again.

'All right. I'm coming!'

Pulling down his ruffled tunic and wishing the Gauls had discovered heated floors, or even just *smooth* floors, he shuffled to the entrance and undid the latch, swinging the heavy wooden door open. A legionary barely old enough to shave stood at attention outside, a look of heavy concern weighing down his features.

'What is the meaning of this, soldier?'

The young man looked panicky, but also red-faced and exhausted. He'd been running. Alarms were triggered in Galba's head as he realised this must be one of the perimeter guards, since no one else would have cause to be armed at this time of night. With a snap the blurred fuzziness of waking from a deep sleep evaporated and Galba straightened, his eyes straying to the periphery as he listened.

'Sir… beg to report sir that the Veragri have gone!'

More alarms. The legate's eyes darted to the native settlement on the far side of the river, behind the red-faced legionary.

'Gone? From the town?'

'Yessir.' The legionary was calming down now, and Galba realised the lad was still standing stiffly to attention.

'Stand at ease. Details, man. What's happened?'

'Watch centurion sent me to find you sir. He sent a patrol to check out the town, and it's completely deserted, sir.'

Galba frowned and rubbed his stubbly chin.

'Why in Minerva's name would he be sending out patrols in the middle of the night?'

'Sir?'

Galba shook his head.

'Wait here.'

Leaving the bewildered legionary in the dark road, Galba rushed back into the squat stone building and grabbed his sword belt and boots. Pausing inside the door, he hurriedly pulled the boots on. The night was chilly but dry, much as the last two days had been, and he could get by without his cloak for the sake of a few moments. Strapping on his belt, he strode back out into the night air.

'Take me to the watch centurion.'

The soldier saluted and started to march off at high speed down the road toward the bridge. As they strode forth, Galba peered ahead into the darkness. It may have been dry, but the sky was filled with fast clouds that hid the stars from view, and it was hard to pick out detail at any distance. The bridge was the only area of the camp defences that was still under construction. The old Celtic bridge of heavy wooden piles with no rails had been upgraded, given a new surface and sides, but also incorporated into a new fortified gate system at that end of the camp. It appeared, as he squinted into the darkness, that work was almost complete.

Beyond, past the narrow, swift waters of the Dranse, the settlement of the Veragri lay silent and dark. It would have been eerie, but for the fact that, since the arrival of the Twelfth Legion, the native settlement had been silent and dark every night.

The pair approached the gate and bridge to see a small group of soldiers at the entrance, two of them bearing officer's crests.

'Centurion?'

The men turned and saluted as their legate came to a halt before them.

'Legatus. You've heard the news, sir?'

Galba nodded.

'Tell me what happened.'

'Well, sir' the centurion said, tapping his vine staff idly on his leg, 'one of the lads thought he saw something out there in the fields about an hour ago. We didn't think much of it. Picket guards is always seeing things in the dark, and this was on the other side of the river, way out past the town...'

Galba frowned.

'What did he see?'

'Said he thought he saw maybe a half dozen people running off toward the valley side, sir. Well we watched for another quarter hour or so, sir, but saw nothing more. No one else appeared, and no other guard saw them.'

The irritation was welling up in Galba. Baculus was right. These men were too inexperienced to be commanding a campaign like this.

'And this seemed unimportant enough to go on watching without having any kind of alarm raised?'

9

The centurion flinched.

'Well sir, it was only a few folk and they was running away, not coming toward us; and that's even if he wasn't mistaken about it anyway.'

'Centurion, we are in hostile lands, surrounded by a treacherous bunch who would outnumber us a hundred to one if they all pull together. What else happened?'

'Well, I looked hard at the town and realised that there was no smoke coming from the roofs, and it's quite a cold night, sir. If they was just settled in for the night, they'd be keeping warm sir.'

'And this didn't push you to raise the alarm?'

'I sent a patrol across the bridge to check the town, sir.'

Galba rubbed his temples as he squeezed his eyes shut.

'And they discovered the town was completely deserted. And then you decided to send for me?'

'Yes sir. They must have run away.'

Galba stared at the man. Clearly, he was an idiot. The legate was winding himself up to deliver a tirade when he noticed the startled looks on the faces of the soldiers around them and forced himself to relax, exhaling slowly. The officer class were still very inexperienced, but they were all he had and hauling them over the coals in front of their men would hardly serve to improve matters at this point. He nodded to himself and kept a straight face as he turned to the optio beside them.

'Raise the alarm, but do it quietly. No buccinas or shouting. Just pass the word and get every man awake, dressed, equipped and to the wall as fast as you can.'

The optio saluted and ran off, taking several of the legionaries with him to help spread the word and Galba turned back to the centurion.

'I want a dozen of your fastest men out of their armour and split into groups of three. Send one group down each branch of the valley, past the town. I want a three mile search down there, and then they can report back. The other two groups need to get up the valley sides and to the top of these hills. I want a clear picture of what's going on here.'

'You think there's trouble, sir?'

'You're damn right I think there's trouble. They've not run away; they've no reason to. And if they're not running away that means they're organising; massing somewhere. We could be knee deep in the shit any moment now.'

The centurion nodded, a hunted look about his eyes, and sent one his men to rouse the soldiers of his century and bring them to the gate.

Galba ignored the quiet activity going on around him as the camp burst into silent, eerie life. Instead, he climbed the steps to the rampart by the bridge gate and turned slowly, casting his gaze over their surroundings. The town had emptied under the cover of darkness, and that meant that they were gathering somewhere secretly. There were seven hundred or so left of the Twelfth and at least twice that number of enemies had just left Octodurus. There was no doubt in Galba's mind that the Veragri from the town had met up with a much larger force somewhere. His uneasiness of the last few days seemed to have been well founded.

Squinting, he peered off down first one valley and then the other, straying up the slopes and...

He stopped dead. Silvery moonlight had just, for a fleeting moment, flickered through the fast scudding clouds, and there had been reflections, high up on the hills above the valley. Galba found he was holding his breath. Sharply, he reached out to the legionary nearby, who stood fast, watching the empty settlement across the river.

'Soldier, look up on the hills above us. What can you see?'

The legionary, startled at being addressed directly by his senior commander, turned and cast his own gaze up the vertiginous valley side. There was a long moment of silence and the legionary made some uncertain noises in his throat before finding his voice.

'I can't see anything, sir.'

But he had.

Before the sentence was fully out there was another brief flicker of moonlight and this time they knew what they were looking for. Only one thing could produce that effect; like the myriad points of light as the moon reflected on calm seas, there was a scattering of reflections along the mountain top. Spinning round, already knowing what he'd see, Galba focused on the matching force of glittering men on the opposite side of the valley.

'Shit.'

Ignoring the shocked stare of the legionary as he gawped at the huge force that loomed over them, Galba scoured the camp. The watch centurion was returning to the gate with a dozen men from his century while Baculus, already armoured, strode down the street toward them. As he turned, he spotted the tribune, Volusenus, hurrying out of one of the buildings, strapping on his belt and carrying his helmet. Furrowing his brow, Galba gestured down to the watch commander.

'Belay my earlier orders, centurion... no time for that now. The hills above us are swarming with Celts. Get every man to the walls; we've not got long.'

Shaking his head in irritation, he beckoned to Baculus and Volusenus and the two most senior officers of the Twelfth hurried across the space before the gate and joined their commander on the rampart.

'Bad news, sir, I take it?'

Galba nodded at the tribune.

'They're all over the hills above us. If they charge, they'll be on us in moments. Our only advantage right now is that I've kept the buccinas quiet, and I'm hoping they haven't paid too much attention to all the activity in the camp. Thing is, as you know, we're vastly outnumbered, so I need your opinions. Can we hold out, or is it worth trying an ordered retreat before they attack?'

Baculus shrugged.

'We can hold out for a while, but not forever. There's a lot more Celts around here they can call on and precious little chance of us getting any support. It's a 'gates of fire' situation, legate: glorious, but suicidal.'

Beside him, Volusenus was nodding.

'True, but there is some value in certainty. *Here,* we have the defences, and we know the land. If we pull out, we're essentially marching into the unknown and will likely end up joining battle somewhere much less advantageous. We have no idea how many there are of the enemy or their disposition, and we don't know the territory in any direction well enough to plan ahead. My heart is already running for home, but my head says stay and fight where you know what you're doing.'

The primus pilus raised an eyebrow as he regarded the tribune for a moment and he finally nodded.

'I concur, legate. I don't like it, but he's right.'

Galba sighed. He had reached much the same conclusion, but had hoped for a flash of inspiration from his two veteran officers.

12

'Very well. Then if we're going to stay and do this the old-fashioned way, let's do it properly.'

He turned to the watch centurion, at the gate below, waiting for further orders.

'Have the call to arms delivered from the buccinas, get the cavalry in with the men, have all the spare pila brought out to the walls and get the artillery crews to their weapons. Time to let them know we're aware of them.'

Tribune Volusenus leaned past him, a grin on his face.

'And when you've delivered the order, centurion, take these dozen men of yours across the river and fire the town. Get the whole place blazing as fast as you can and then get back here.'

He turned to the quizzical looks of his peers.

'Less cover for them to hide behind, and it effectively prevents them from attacking on one side until the fire dies down.'

Galba nodded.

'Fortuna and Mars smile on us tonight!'

* * * * *

Baculus stood on the platform above the east gate of Roman Octodurus, surrounded by a centurion, an optio and a number of legionaries, while the ramparts stretched off to left and right, manned by the diminished cohorts of the Twelfth. Galba had taken the south wall and Volusenus the west, leaving the watch centurion to command the bridge entrance, should the enemy try to navigate the blazing streets.

The cavalry had dismounted and were now bolstering the numbers on the ramparts but at this moment, defending the walls of a fort against overwhelming numbers, Baculus wished once more that Pansa and his auxiliary archers were here and not still quartered up in Belgae territory with Labienus.

The walls of the fortification were punctuated with squat towers, each home to one or more of the precious few scorpion bolt throwers left with the Twelfth, while the remaining two ballistae and the single onager, of little use in this situation, were positioned together in the fort's central square.

They were as prepared as the numbers permitted, and Baculus clenched his teeth as he looked back up at the vast swathe of men on the hillside above.

13

Only moments later, a call bleated out from on high: a horrendous honking, followed by a messy metallic crash as the Gauls rapped their weapons on shields, helmets, or anything they could find to make noise.

'Here they come, lads. Hold fast and pray! Pila first, but make them count.'

The Veragri and their allies, the blaring and crashing done with, began to roll down the hillsides from their dizzy heights like a wave crashing toward the beleaguered Roman defenders. Baculus heard a soldier close to him mutter a prayer to Fortuna and nodded approvingly. They could all do with a little luck right now.

Closer they came, racing down the slopes and the defenders of Octodurus watched, patiently and professionally but, as Baculus glanced here and there, he noted that where the men changed their grip on the pila ready to cast, there were a number of shaky arms.

'Ready…'

He concentrated on the enemy force that had reached the valley floor and picked up speed now they had to pay less attention to their footing. Most of them were unarmoured, much like any other Celtic force he had seen. The majority of those few with breastplates, mail shirts or helmets were in the front row: nobles and powerful warriors among the tribe, displaying their wealth through attire and their valour through the position at the front.

Unfortunately for them, like so many other Celtic charges Baculus had faced, the veterans knew how to break the morale of a force like that.

'Artillery: aim for anyone wearing bronze. Same goes for every pilum you throw.'

A little bit closer…

'Artillery: loose!'

A chorus of sharp cracks from the five towers along the wall mingled with those of the others around the far sides of the defences as the outnumbered Romans faced the attack on all sides. The initial volley of eight shots peppered the front line of charging Celts, each blow picking out one of the armoured nobles, punching through the protective bronze and killing or mortally wounding the man, throwing him back among the charge.

Such, however, was the blood lust of the Veragri that the loss of a few nobles failed to even slow the charge. Baculus watched them come on, judging the distance from the wall and counting under his breath. Briefly he glanced up at the towers, just in time to catch the second volley as it began, hammering into the bronze-clad nobles. He nodded as he counted; the third volley would coincide nicely.

The primus pilus waited patiently, counting down and, as the line of charging barbarians finally reached a good range, he raised and dropped his arm, shouting a command to release. The order went unheard over the roar of charging Celts, but the men had been waiting for the gesture and, as the scorpions released their third volley, two hundred pila soared out over the wooden palisade and swooped down like a deadly hail into the front lines of the Veragri.

The effect was impressive. Eight bolts at a time, no matter how well placed, hardly drew the attention of the frothing, frenzied barbarians. Two hundred pila punching through the line was, however, an entirely different matter.

The bodies of the initial targets collapsed to the ground, causing a number of their comrades to trip and fall across them. The front ranks of the Veragri slowed in uncertainty as a fresh line of iron tips appeared over the parapet, awaiting the order.

'Release!'

The second volley of pila flew forth from the battlements and plunged into the seething ranks of the Veragri. Chaos ensued as many of the ordinary warriors on the front lines attempted to push their way back through the crowd to flee the deadly hail of pila.

'Arm and release spares at will and then prepare for melee!'

The reserves and support staff below the turf and timber defences passed the few remaining cached pila up to their compatriots on the walls. Baculus watched as roughly every other man received an extra shot and cast it as soon as he could before settling into a defensive position with gladius and shield.

There was an eerie pause as the front line of the Veragri shuffled around, punctuated occasionally by the shot of one of the scorpions as the engineers loosed down into the mass. Baculus tensed. Something would happen any moment now. He had known this to be the breaking point of some weaker assaults, but the Veragri had been planning this for a while, knew they outnumbered the Twelfth tremendously, and were slowly becoming aware that the rain of missiles had all but stopped.

'Steady, lads…'

The strange silence, somehow made all the more oppressive by the distant sounds of battle on other fronts, was broken by a stone, flung with amazing accuracy and power by some hidden arm among the barbarian crowd. The missile crested the wooden parapet, catching one of the legionaries square in the forehead with enough force to knock him from the walkway and send him tumbling down the earth slope within. Instantly one of the reserves stepped up and took his place while a capsarius rushed to help the fallen man. All along the wall, helmets sunk a little to meet shields coming up, closing the gap through which a stone could strike.

And then suddenly the Celtic army answered the Roman artillery with a volley of their own. Hundreds of iron darts and sharp rocks began to arc up from the crowd, aimed at the defenders on the wall. Baculus ducked back behind his shield as he watched the projectiles strike home in increasing numbers. Here and there one would manage a lucky blow between the shields, helmets and wooden palisade and the location would be marked with a shriek and a crack of bone. Baculus leaned back in time to see two men topple from the parapet and down the interior slope of the rampart, either unconscious or dead.

A quick glance upward showed that the towers were out of effective enemy missile range, the few shots aimed at them bouncing off the timber or falling short. Over the enemy onslaught, the engineers kept up their steady pace with the scorpions. Another glance at the mass of Veragri confirmed that the artillery were picking off more targets every heartbeat than the Celts could manage with their darts and rocks, but the Twelfth would be unable to withstand the attrition rate for long.

He realised with irritation that even the support staff and reserves were in danger, as missiles that crossed the parapet without striking home were falling among those inside the fort. Something would have to be done soon, or the reserves would end up buried in a pile of rocks.

'Reserves and support staff…' he shouted down inside, attracting the attention of everyone he could. 'Gather all the fallen missiles you can and get up into those towers where you can throw them back!'

There was a pause for only a moment, while the more nervous of the men within weighed up the chances of being struck by one of these projectiles while gathering them if he left the safety of his shield. Then the interior of the camp burst into life, men grabbing baskets and sacks and beginning to fill them with darts and stones.

Baculus turned back to the enemy, trying to ignore the occasional cry of pain from behind where one of the support staff was caught in the open by a falling stone. The men on the wall had given up hope, if that was an appropriate word, of being able to take on the enemy with swords and had closed up in small pockets with their shields raised, forming mini testudos that effectively protected them from almost any angle.

Baculus was impressed. He knew there were still a few veterans among the men, but that kind of quick thinking was what saved armies. Keeping himself covered as best he could, he watched tensely as bags and baskets were hauled up the towers on ropes that were used for rearming the artillery from the ground. The hail of projectiles was beginning to slow. Soon the enemy would run out of missiles, both purpose-made and hastily-gathered, and the assault would begin in earnest. At that point it would come down to pure numbers. The Roman army was the most effective force the world had known. *Gods* would tremble before the legions, but the simple fact was that no army, no matter how good, could fight odds like this for long.

Men were now hurrying up the ladders and to the towers. As the primus pilus watched, two were caught mid-climb by stray weapons and thrown clear into the fort's interior, but more arrived on the raised platforms every moment and, without waiting for the order from a superior, they began to cast the waste projectiles back among the enemy.

Once again, the Celtic lines faltered under this fresh barrage and slowly the missile shots from both sides diminished and tailed off to the occasional lob, while the 'thunk' of scorpion bolts continued unabated.

'This is it, lads. Break your testudos now and get ready. I don't want to see any of you fighting cleanly or being fair. If you see Gallic flesh, stab it, hack it, kick it or bite it. I don't care what you do, just keep them off the ramparts.'

There was a trickle of nervous laughter along the palisade as men resumed the traditional stance of the legionary line, shields presented, and blades hefted at the ready.

'Remember, we're eagles, not sparrows! If the Twelfth are destined for Elysium today, we're going to swim there in a river of barbarian blood!'

17

A roar ran down the line, triggering a similar response from the enemy thirty paces away and the whole mass suddenly broke into a screaming run, bearing down on the walls with their handful of Roman defenders.

'Here we go!'

* * * * *

'Sun's coming up!'

'Thank you for stating the bloody obvious, Sep!'

Baculus took the opportunity between exhausted sword thrusts to glance down the line at the source of the banter. Once again, it reminded him of a truly veteran unit, where even hard pressed and in constant bloody danger, the troops could find something to laugh at. Off down the wide valley, past the pillars of smoke and the smouldering remains of the native settlement, the first glimmers of morning were showing between the mountainous spurs. A welcome sight, even in the circumstances.

His attention was drawn back to the present situation as one of the barbarians still seething below the parapet threw himself up to the top, hooking an arm over the palisade while trying to swing wildly with the sword in the other. The situation, grave at the onset, was becoming more and more perilous all the time. The centuries defending this wall had suffered almost a fifty per cent casualty rate and, though they had only ever lost control of small sections of rampart very briefly before regaining them, the incursions were becoming more frequent and harder to repel. The end was close.

Unable to step back far enough to stab effectively at this latest interloper, Baculus swept his sword out to the side and head-butted the man with every ounce of his remaining strength. The helmet's iron ridge smashed into the barbarian's face, shattering bone and loosing him from the wall to fall back among his companions. The primus pilus blinked away the spattered blood that had sprayed across the helmet's front and raised his blade to strike as something grabbed at his arm.

His arm swept wild as he realised the hand grasping him was a Roman, and the blow fell into empty air.

'You bloody idiot. I nearly cut your arm off!'

The soldier, his eyes wide, shrank back.

18

'Sorry sir. I couldn't get your attention. Legate Galba sent for you. Wants you to meet him at the headquarters, sir.'

Baculus growled at the man and then nodded.

'Well since you're nice and clean and fresh, step up here and take my place. Don't let one of those shit-eating dogs across my wall.'

The legionary nodded meekly and stepped up to the rampart, drawing his sword and settling his shield in front of him. Paying the lad no further attention, Baculus dropped from the parapet and slid down the grassy bank of the rampart to the ground. A quick glance back told him that, despite his fears, the Twelfth was still miraculously holding the walls, though for how much longer remained to be seen. Squaring his shoulders he set off at a quick march toward the squat stone building that served as Galba's headquarters. No matter how dire the situation, a centurion should not move at an unseemly run.

A moment later, he rounded a corner to face the building, its usual guard stripped to help man the walls. No man was being excused today, even the legate's bodyguard, as Baculus was pleased to note. The door stood open, and the primus pilus entered, allowing his eyes to adjust to the dim glow within, darker than the pre-dawn light outside despite the guttering candles. As he strode into the room, the legate and tribune Volusenus looked up from the table and a hastily prepared model of their immediate surroundings formed from the various small pieces of clutter they had gathered.

'Ah, Baculus. Come and join us, quickly.'

'Sir.'

The primus pilus, aware that this was a gathering of desperate minds rather than a situation for high etiquette, strode over, dropped his shield and helmet and sank into one of the two spare seats around the table.

'We were just trying to find a way out of this mess, Publius.'

'Unsuccessfully, I might add' agreed Volusenus quietly.

Baculus nodded as he examined the makeshift model.

'We're certainly in the shit, legate. The enemy has all but filled in the ditches, the piles of bodies are giving them a ramp to reach the palisade top, and we're out of missiles. My lads are down to about half strength and the wall will go within the hour. I can't imagine either of you are managing to fare any better?'

He was greeted with silent nods.

19

'Then frankly, we're bollocksed. We're trapped here. We must number maybe four hundred by now and, though we're killing them in droves, there are still quite a few thousand out there. Once they get inside the walls, we're done for.'

Galba shrugged.

'Then we either fight on like this and fall, however heroically, to the barbarians, or we have to find a means to get away.'

The tribune rubbed his eyes wearily.

'The only thing for it is to try and buy ourselves a little time somehow and then make a break through the south gate, out up the valley and back toward Cisalpine Gaul. I don't like running, but it's better than extermination and losing the eagle.'

Galba shook his head.

'No chance from the south. The Veragri pushed a cart up against it just over a quarter hour ago and lit it. My men are trying to stop the spreading fire, but the chances are that gate will be ablaze any time now and will fall soon.'

Baculus shrugged.

'Then we have an obvious choice. Our walls are all heavily under attack, but the bridge across to the town still stands.'

Galba raised an eyebrow.

'You are aware, I suppose, that that bridge leads to the north, deeper into enemy territory.'

'Indeed, sir, but beyond that lies Geneva and friendly tribes like the Allobroges. We might be able to make it, so long as we can get out of here.'

Volusenus frowned as he examined the makeshift model.

'We might be able to take them by surprise… if we timed it right?'

'Explain?'

'Well,' the tribune said, furrowing his brow as his gaze swept back and forth across the model, 'we don't care about holding the walls, just about getting the men out as fast as possible, yes?'

He was greeted by nods from his fellow officers.

'We don't want to stay here now, so everything is disposable. Also, we'll need to travel as light as possible to outrun them until we're a long way from here. So…'

He gestured around the model walls and then pointed to the centre.

'We've still got the siege weapons, and we've got pitch. What would the barbarians do if we set fire to our own walls?'

Galba blinked.

'I expect they'd laugh, once they were able to believe it. Why would we do that?'

Volusenus shrugged.

'We can't hold them much longer, and we need to buy some time while the enemy can't cross them. If they're on fire, the barbarians will have to hold back at least for a while. They'll be in a state of confusion. We can add to that by madly firing the ballistae and the onager into their ranks.'

'But what good does it do?'

'While they're milling about in confusion, we form the men up into testudos and break out of the north gate, across the bridge. The enemy are thin over there, and the river will prevent the rest from joining them without following us over the bridge which, of course, they can't do because of the blazing walls. Then it comes down to discipline, the ability of the men, and a little bit of luck. Once we're clear of the barbarians, we do a triple time and head northwest as fast as Mercury himself.'

Baculus frowned as he stared at the model.

'It has merit, but there were a mass of barbarians on the hills on that side of the valley as well as this. Will they not be waiting for us in the open across the river? I'd assumed only the river and the bridge were stopping them from taking the north gate easily.'

Volusenus shook his head.

'We watched them from the west gate as they first charged. Once they realised we'd fired the town, and they couldn't get in that way, they spent a good hour and a half crossing the river to join in the attack. Had to put together rafts. Might piss them off a bit when they realise they have to do it again.'

The legate leaned back in his seat.

'It's a mad plan... absolutely *barking* mad. Even Fronto would think twice before doing this, but then, I really can't see any other way. Can we *do it*, tribune?'

Volusenus grinned.

'Given the alternatives, I'll have to say yes.'

'Then lets get back out there and start passing the orders down.'

* * * * *

21

Baculus mopped his forehead and then replaced his helmet.

'Are we set?'

The wounded legionary with the empty pitch bucket nodded and gave a weary half-salute, being careful to avoid the medical padding at his temple. The primus pilus turned and peered into the early light. Someone by the south gate was waving a torch. Reaching down, he lit one of his own from the brazier that burned at the top of the sloping rampart and as it burst into life, passed it to the legionary.

'Wave that like you're at the races.'

The man did so, and Baculus squinted off across the camp once more. A hundred tense heartbeats followed until he finally saw the twinkle of a torch being waved across at the west gate.

'Fire!' he bellowed and, as the dozen men standing ready with blazing torches stepped up to the rampart, in a precision manoeuvre as beautiful as any parade ground exercise, the beleaguered legionaries defending the walls stepped back, disengaging the barbarians and feeding between the torches, retreating down the bank in an orderly withdrawal. Barely had they left the walkway and stepped onto the grass slope before the torches of those men that had stepped forward connected with the pitch that had been liberally spread on as many of the wooden surfaces as possible.

The victorious cries of the Veragri as they began to clamber across the palisade in pursuit of the fleeing defenders turned in short order to panicked screams as the timber defences around them caught like dry tinder and leapt into roaring flames. Many of the front line of the barbarian attack were unable to pull back from the flames, the crowd behind driving them on, and blazing figures dotted the ramparts, screaming and floundering, as the Roman lines reached the bottom of the slope and, turning at Baculus' orders, reformed quickly and ran in perfect order along the street toward the fort's centre.

At the call of a buccina from somewhere in the heart of the camp, Baculus and his men split into lines and hugged the buildings at the sides of the street as they ran. Overhead, a half dozen rocks, each larger than a balled fist, arced across the heavens toward the mass of barbarians beyond the walls. The chances of one falling this far short were very small, but Baculus had lost enough men for one day and motioned the centurions around him to keep close to cover.

A roar of dismay arose behind them outside the fort, as the artillery attack of the Roman defenders began to take its toll on the mass of enemy milling around in confusion below the blazing walls.

As they approached the central square where the siege weapons kept up as speedy a barrage as they could manage, Baculus spotted the men from the other walls, pouring in good order from different roads and into the space, where they converged, creating larger units and moving toward the northern street.

With a quick gesture, the primus pilus passed down the order to continue on to the north gate, while he marched at speed from the advancing column toward the onager and its crew. As he reached the engineers, they finished winching the machine and stepped back. Baculus waited patiently until they loosed the shot, launching a collection of small but deadly rocks away toward the distant unseen attackers. As the crewman reached for the next in the pile of ammunition, the primus pilus waved his vine staff.

'Forget that now. Cut the cables, get your gear together, gather the ballista crews and fall in with the rest of the men. Time to go.'

Leaving the men to their work, Baculus strode back, picking up his pace yet more in order to catch up with his unit. As they marched off down the street toward the north gate and the bridge that would take them to relative safety, he spotted legate Galba striding out alongside another column and angled across to join him.

'Centurion.' The commander looked tired and drawn.

'Sir. All went off rather nicely, I thought.'

The legate shook his head.

'We're not out of it quite yet, Baculus.'

The primus pilus nodded.

'Perhaps, sir, but we're on our way. We'll be out in no time and then heading down for friendly territory. Mind if I ask, sir, what we do then?'

Galba nodded.

'I've been thinking about that. Caesar promised us extra recruits that we never got. He's going to be a little put out by what happened up here, but even *he* can't push the matter, given our numbers and situation. Even Scipio would have pulled out of there. So we're going to go stay among our allies in Gaul, and I'm going to start recruiting myself on Caesar's behalf. Then I'll send another report to the general.'

'What do you think the general's plans are for the coming summer, sir?'

Galba shrugged.

'That all depends on what's happened to him in Rome, Crassus in Armorica and Labienus and the Belgae. I can see this being a problem season for us, Publius. Once we've replaced some of the losses, and I've sent off a report, we'll march off up to Vindunum, training the recruits while we move, and joining the main force there. At least there we can make use of their stores and armourers to rebuild the Twelfth.'

Baculus nodded as they approached the gate. The massing Roman force within, added to the burning of the camp, had struck the smaller force of Veragri among the charred ruins on the opposite bank with uncertainty and, far from gathering to prevent the legion leaving, they had skirted away out of reach to the east and west, watching warily.

'Been a hell of a winter, legate.'

'That it has, Baculus... that it has.'

Chapter 2

(Ianuarius: The Andean oppidum of Vindunum in northwestern Gaul)

'Have you made an example among the locals?'

The tribune sighed inwardly but was careful to keep his expression neutral. He'd managed to avoid much direct contact with Crassus, but word got around.

'With respect, legate, we've made an occasional example, but it really is no good. They simply don't have the grain to spare and no amount of beating is going to make more grain grow.'

He winced, aware that he could have overstepped the mark there. Crassus may be only one of several legates with a command at Vindunum, but Caesar's orders had been clear. Crassus was in overall command of the army in this region over the winter months. There were many rumours as to the reason for the extra power granted to the man, but the most common was that Caesar needed to tighten the bonds between himself and the legate's father in Rome.

Crassus stared at him, silent, those piercing eyes boring into his skull.

'Also, legate, the Gauls are a proud people. If you push them hard, they don't bend, sir; they break. I and the other officers are walking a fine line between keeping them subjugated and trying not to fan the flames of revolt. The failure of the Belgae's revolt last year may have settled things for now, but they will only take so much.'

'I fear you forget your place, tribune...'

Gallus, senior tribune of the Ninth, ground his teeth, irked at such a rebuke from the commander of a different legion. A complaint to legate Rufus would be no use; Rufus was as powerless as he to put the influential Crassus in his place.

'I mean no disrespect, sir...'

Somewhere deep within, Gallus laughed at his own words.

'...It's just that the Andes have been nothing but accommodating and helpful. Given that we have effectively displaced them and tithed their stores during a fairly harsh winter, I feel we should be rewarding them, rather than punishing them. Perhaps we can send to Caesar and request that extra supplies be sent up from Narbonensis?'

Crassus swept a hand angrily through the air.

25

'I have conquered Armorica with *one* legion, tribune! Imagine that! While the rest of the army was bogged down with the Belgae, the Seventh *alone* pacified the whole of the north west! Do you think I am about to crawl to Caesar with my tail between my legs and beg for some extra supper?'

Again, Gallus had to bite his tongue. He'd seen first hand the results of Crassus' conquest. Pacification by near-genocide. The mass burial pits were still visited by weeping relatives all up and down these lands. Still, the winter would soon be over and then his own legate would return, along with the general and the rest of the staff. Things would change then.

'What are your orders, sir?'

Crassus glared at him for some time and finally slid from his chair and stood, reaching out to the table and swiping his crimson cloak from the surface, fastening it around his shoulders.

'Come with me.'

Gallus nodded and, turning, followed the legate out of the headquarters. The air outside was cloying and unpleasant. A fog had settled earlier in the week and seemed to be set in for the duration, lifting only briefly during the height of the day before descending once again to wrap them in its damp embrace as the sun sank. The unpleasant weather was affecting the mood of the army, who had weathered the crisp cold winter reasonably well, but this damp fog was a whole different matter. It soaked into the clothes and made even the flesh feel soggy and cold, it cut down visibility and shut out the welcome gaze of the sun.

The headquarters had been converted from the house of the Andean chief at Vindunum during the Seventh's campaign last year. Indeed, the Seventh and their allied legions occupied the entire Gallic oppidum and the surrounding territory on this side of the river, the surviving population having been evicted to the far bank where they had set up makeshift huts to survive the winter. The *pax Romana* as demonstrated by the great Crassus.

Still grinding his teeth, Gallus strode out into the street behind the young commander as he glanced left and right. There were the standard legionary guards on duty outside the headquarters, as well as the granary and other stores, but here in the hub of Roman command, the higher proportion of the sparse figures visible bore the crests and plumes of officers.

'You!'

Gallus frowned as Crassus gestured to two tribunes standing huddled against the cold and studying a wax tablet. The tribunes looked up, and Gallus vaguely recognised them from meetings and dice games. Men of the Eleventh, if he remembered correctly.

The two tribunes turned and saluted the legate, standing at attention.

'Identify yourselves.'

'Quintus Velanius, tribunus laticlavius of the Eleventh, sir.'

'Titus Silius, tribunus angusticlavius of the Eleventh, legate.'

Crassus nodded.

'Come with me.'

The two men exchanged anxious glances and, as they fell into step with Gallus at the legate's heel, they looked around at him questioningly. Gallus shook his head and made a face suggesting they should stay quiet.

The three tribunes pulled their cloaks tighter around them against the numbing fog and traipsed on down the street toward the former centre of the oppidum. As they entered the main square, once more Crassus waved an arm at a man with a tribune's plume.

'Terrasidius? Join us.'

The tribune, one of the junior, or 'angusticlavius' tribunes of the Seventh, turned and came to attention, saluting, before striding toward them. As the five men converged, Crassus gestured to one of the buildings around the square, converted for use as an office for the clerks of the various legions and the camp prefect, nominally Priscus, ex-primus pilus of the Tenth, but who was convalescing in Rome with his commander during the winter.

The small group approached, and Terrasidius stepped out ahead to open the door and stand aside politely until the others had entered, closing it behind him as he joined them. This building had clearly been a shop or a tavern before being commandeered by the Seventh. Three clerks worked studiously at desks in the large open room.

'Find something to do outside' Crassus said flatly.

The clerks looked up in alarm and saluted hurriedly before gathering their tablets and styluses in their arms and leaving the room in haste, making their way out of the front door and into the damp, depressing square outside.

'Right.'

Crassus turned to the four tribunes as he leaned back against a desk and folded his arms.

27

'Tribune Gallus here informs me that we are being too harsh on the Andes here; that we cannot demand any more grain or supplies from them, or we may push them into open revolt.'

Gallus' teeth continued to grind in irritation but, as the other three officers glanced across at him, he noted the sympathy and understanding in their eyes.

'So' the legate continued circling his neck to the sound of bones clicking. 'What are the options?'

He fell silent, but none of the tribunes fell into the trap. Crassus nodded to himself.

'One: we banish the Andes altogether and send them to leech off one of the other tribes in this benighted land, while we commandeer their remaining stocks. Certainly the easiest option, and their own stores should see the army through until spring, when we will move again.'

Gallus noted the almost despairing looks on his peers and pinched the bridge of his nose, trying desperately not to comment.

'Two: We send to Narbonensis or Cisalpine Gaul in Caesar's name for extra supplies. Of course, it would be more than a month before anything gets to us, and we run the risk or putting forth the appearance that the better part of seven of Rome's elite legions cannot even gather enough supplies to keep themselves fed.'

He peered at the tribunes and allowed his gaze to rest on Gallus.

'Or three: we extend our demands to other tribes. At the risk of testing tribune Gallus' 'bend-or-break' theory, we procure every ounce of provision we need from the various tribes we have conquered.'

One of the tribunes cleared his throat, but said nothing.

'No opinions, gentlemen?'

Velanius of the Eleventh scratched his chin. Gallus noted that he winced in anticipation as he opened his mouth.

'It has been a harsh and freezing winter, legate. Most of the tribes will be in a similar state. I'm not at all sure how much they will be able to spare. Back down on the coast of the Mare Nostrum, however, where it's been warmer…'

His voice tailed off, and he fell uncomfortably silent.

'Since the lot of you seem to be so concerned about the tender feelings of these pointless barbarians, it strikes me that I could hardly find any better men to send.'

Straightening, he strode across to the wall, where a map was pinned to the timber, giving the locations of the local tribes and settlements, along with the disposition of the various scouts and spies. He examined the map for some time while the tribunes watched unhappily. Finally, he tapped his fingers on the vellum.

'There you go: Gallus, you'll take a detachment of cavalry as a bodyguard and go to the Curiosolitae. Their capital is some turd hole near the north coast. We checked it out briefly last year, and it was hardly worth our attention, but there's good farmland around them. You should be able to get fully half of what we need from them. I would suggest you threaten them with the heel of the Roman boot, but you can use your charm if you prefer.'

Ignoring the rising colour in Gallus' face, he turned to the others, his finger sliding down the map and coming to rest on the jagged lines of the southern coast of the peninsula.

'The Venati are somewhat fractious and spread out and will be more difficult to deal with. We're not even sure where their centre is, so you two' he gestured at Velanius and Silius, 'will need to take two turmae of cavalry and go find them and draw supplies from them. I'm not expecting them to have much grain but, from what I read, they're fishers, so you may be able to procure us stocks of seafood.'

Lastly, his finger strayed up and right, deeper inland and back toward better-known territory and came to rest somewhere around forty or fifty miles north of Vindunum.

'Terrasidius? You can take a detachment to the Esubii. They should be nice and easy to deal with and will have surplus grain stocks if I'm not mistaken.'

The legate fell quiet, still regarding the map, his chin cupped in a hand. The tribunes stood in uncomfortable silence, shuffling their feet. After a pregnant pause, Crassus turned, an expression of feigned surprise on his face.

'Are you still here?'

Without waiting for further admonishment, the tribunes turned and made their way out of the building and out of sight of the legate. As they left the relative comfort of the low, dark interior and stepped out into the grey cloth of mist, they kept walking until they were at the far side of the square and safely out of earshot of both the office window and any other human being.

'Arsehole!'

The other three turned in surprise at Gallus' outburst, but understanding quickly flooded their expressions.

'He really has *no* idea just how much of the time we spend trying to smooth over relations with the Gauls after he wanders around Armorica kicking them out of the way. It's almost as though he *wants* them to revolt.'

Velanius nodded unhappily.

'The Venati are an argumentative bunch. They fight for fun in their village squares; I've seen it – bare knuckle fighting until they're lying comatose just to work up an appetite for dinner. I have absolutely no idea how I'm going to approach them and broach the idea that they should give us a sizeable chunk of their fish. I have a horrible feeling about this.'

Gallus' grim expression revealed his own thoughts on the matter quite clearly. He turned and rounded on Terrasidius.

'See how he favours his own legion? Cushy job you got there, asking for a handout from a friendly tribe that's almost drowning in excess grain.'

The tribune from the Seventh shrugged.

'You can call it favour if you like and, yes I get the easy tribe, but when we start moving in spring, you'll head back to your own legates and get on with it. I'll still be wandering around behind my illustrious leader, trying to remove the stick from his arse!'

Gallus stared at the tribune for a moment and burst out laughing.

'Fair enough. He won't be expecting us to leave until the morning. Too late in the day to set out now. Anyone else here fancy a drink? There's two taverns in this shithole that they left in service, and I know which one doesn't spit in the beer for Romans!'

The three men nodded, relieved to have their thoughts turned from the task ahead, and strode off toward the tavern with its friendly warmth.

* * * * *

'This had better be the right place; I'm truly sick of getting the runaround with these people.'

Tribune Velanius nodded miserably, shrinking deeper into the crimson wool cloak as his horse plodded slowly through the bone-soaking drizzle.

30

'You know how some sailors say that the seas go on to the north and west to the end of the world and then irrigate the Elysian fields?'

Silius eyed him suspiciously.

'Yes. You do know you can't irrigate *anything* with sea water?'

'Well you can quite bloody believe it! The further north we get from Rome the wetter, colder and more miserable it gets. If it weren't for all the cliffs and rocks, I'd say it would be hard to tell where the land ends and the sea begins in this place.'

His companion gave a small laugh and turned to look at the cavalry escort. One of the outriders was returning.

'Now we'll find out.'

The pair drew their steeds to a halt and sat in the miserable rain as the cavalry trooper approached and reined in.

'Sir' the trooper said, giving a half bow in the saddle, 'there's a sizeable settlement up ahead on a spur of rock above the sea. It's a lot bigger than any of the other villages we've seen. I think we've found our town.'

'Good. Form up an honour guard. Let's do this properly.'

As the cavalry settled into lines of twelve men to either side with a small van- and rearguard, the two tribunes held their breath as they approached the crest of the hill. They still had no idea how they would go about their mission, but the time seemed finally to be upon them when they would have to decide.

Slowly they rode to the top of the hill in a stately procession. Beyond, the open countryside, dotted with copses, stretched out, swooping down and then up to the now all too familiar line of jagged cliffs and coves that formed the coast of north western Gaul. In the centre of the view, a headland stood proud, rising higher than those to either side. Ramparts protected the landward side, while cliffs formed the defence of the rest, with jagged rocks and heaving seas below. Within the walls, a typical Gaulish town lay, squat and grey-brown with random, curving streets. Smoke rose from a multitude of roofs, warming the occupants and warding off the chill rain.

'Even that place is starting to look good when you've been on horseback in the rain for so damn long.'

Velanius pointed down at the near side of the town.

'Will you look at that!'

'What?'

'The approach. It would take Neptune and Mars working together to take that place!'

Silius peered through the rain, trying to pick out more detail and, as he did, he understood his companion's fascination. The town was all but impossible to access from the sea, given the steep cliffs and the fact that the whole headland was surrounded by partially submerged rocks. But the land approach was no better. The walls were as thick and high and impressive as any they had seen these past two years in Gaul, but to even *reach* the walls, an attacker would have to descend the slope to sea level, crossing a narrow causeway that stood perhaps a hundred paces wide.

'That would be a killing zone if they had archers on those towers.'

Velanius shook his head.

'Better than that. It's still a fairly low tide right now. That causeway will be underwater a lot of the time, and those nasty rocks will be hidden just below the waves. This place isn't a town, it's a damn fortress.'

As they descended the slope, the seaward dip and its tidal causeway disappeared from view. The first of a number of small copses rose up to either side of the road, granting blessed, if momentary, relief from the worst of the bleak drizzle that seemed to travel horizontally in this country.

'I'd be willing to come to some very favourable terms if they'll just supply me with a towel, a warm hearth and a bowl of broth!'

Silius laughed again.

'Don't start on about your stomach again. I spent most of yesterday listening to you banging on about it.'

Velanius opened his mouth to deliver a stinging retort, but instead his mouth formed into a shocked 'O' while his eyes widened. Behind his companion and the line of miserable cavalry troopers, a vague figure appeared like a ghost between the boles of the trees, a long spear thrusting out ahead. The tribune had not even the time to call a warning before the spear caught the nearest rider just under the ribs on his left side, plunging in deep through his torso, to emerge at the opposite collar bone. The shocked rider opened his mouth to scream, and a gobbet of blood was all that issued as he toppled from the horse.

Velanius was aware that he'd shouted something, though he could not remember what it was in the sudden confusion. They had no chance, and that was clear from the outset. There must be dozens of men lining the sides of the road, hidden in the trees, each armed

32

with a long thrusting spear. Almost the entire cavalry guard died in the first few moments of this brutal and well orchestrated attack.

'Ride!' bellowed Silius, jerking his knees to guide his beast around the falling horses and men to either side.

Velanius needed no further urging. The escort lines beside them were gone, horses and men alike on the ground, flailing in a growing lake of blood as the Gaulish spearmen stepped out of the eaves and finished their victims off with repeated stabs of those wide, leaf-shaped spear heads.

Both ahead and behind, more attackers had emerged with their spears held out before them, blocking the road in both directions.

'Shit, Silius, we're trapped.'

'Jump them. Have you never jumped a horse?'

The men from the woods to the side had finished off the escort, while those both ahead and behind moved in on the van- and rearguard. Time was up; any more delay and they would merely be caught between those same spearmen. With a last gestured to Velanius, Silius kicked his horse into speed and began to race toward the front doors of the trap ahead, grasping the mane. The four troopers that formed the vanguard were clearly in trouble. Two were already down, and one was fighting to control his wounded horse.

As Silius, with Velanius close by, raced toward the scene, they saw the struggling trooper caught simultaneously by two spear thrusts that lifted him bodily from the saddle and vaulted him across and down to the turf.

The sound of pounding hooves attracted his precious attention, and he was as surprised as he was relieved to see one of the rearguard troopers pulling alongside at a run, apparently with the same idea of escape.

Silius had been a rider from a young age, spending time on the family estate outside Aquinum exploring the countryside on one or other of his father's horses. Seeing the distance left to ride and the height of the blockade, as the Gauls began to pay attention to the three men bearing down on them, he adjusted his posture, kicked as much extra speed as he possibly could and prepared himself.

The Gauls were well aware of what was happening and equally prepared to stop it. Silius was the first to reach them, leaping his steed high over the men. He closed his eyes and made silent vows to Fortuna as his horse sailed through the open space, the steed of the cavalry trooper close by to his left and behind.

33

When his mount's hooves touched the earth beyond the Gauls, his heart soared, relief flooding through him, boosted all the more by the sound of the trooper's horse reaching the ground once more.

The screech behind them told all too well of Velanius' failure. A fair weather rider with little experience at the jump, the other tribune had left it too late. As he coasted low over the Gauls, several spears plunged into the steed, killing it before it even hit the ground.

Silius, already racing away from the scene with the one remaining cavalry trooper, afforded himself only a quick, sad glance back to see that Velanius had been thrown clear and had hit the ground hard, likely breaking bones with possibly fatal results. Several of the Gauls were running toward the heap that was the senior tribune of the Eleventh Legion.

Silius offered up a silent prayer for his friend as he concentrated on the terrain ahead. They would have to ride like never before to get out of Veneti territory. This was a coordinated attack, which meant that those villages and farmers they had spoken to, enquiring of the tribe's capital, had been betraying their presence and plans to an unseen enemy.

He would have to tell Crassus...

His thoughts exploded into slivers of painful flashing light as a heavy stone cracked against his skull, knocking the sense from him and throwing him clear from the horse that, panicked by the melee and noise, ran on heedless of its rider.

Silius lay for a moment on the grass, stunned and confused. He reached around to the back of his head, and his hand came away slick with blood. Not a good sign.

His wits began to return rapidly, but not before he realised he was done for. Figures were approaching, brandishing spears and swords: Celts. Silius craned his neck painfully and could just make out the distant, retreating figure of the cavalry soldier, fleeing the scene. At least word might get back to Crassus of this betrayal. Silius closed his eyes, painfully. The question was: what would Crassus do in response? The man's only answer to trouble was the tip of a sword, which meant that Silius would be likely used as an example by the tribesmen.

He opened his eyes again and tried to roll onto his side to rise, but a heavy skin boot pressed against his chest and pushed him back to the ground. A Celtic warrior, missing a number of teeth and with patterns painted across his cheeks, grinned down at him and said something in his guttural language, gesturing with the spear point to emphasise his incomprehensible words.

Silius slumped back. Hopefully this grinning lunatic would make it quick.

A groan caught his attention, and he turned his head slightly to see two more of the Gauls dragging Velanius across to him by the shoulders, his feet trailing in the wet grass. At least he must be alive. Silius would have company while he died.

The senior tribune was dumped, unceremoniously, next to him, and tried to rise slowly until another foot pressed against his back and pushed him to the ground. Velanius exhaled another groan and turned his head to look at his companion.

'I think we might be in trouble, Titus.'

'This depends upon your friends' a voice above said in passable Latin with a thick Gallic accent.

Silius turned back to look up in surprise, as did his fellow tribune. A new figure had joined the Gaulish warriors around them. His charcoal grey robes were decorated with animal images and strange designs, while his straggly beard appeared to have small bones tied in among the braids. The man held a long sword of the Celtic style, etched with further arcane designs.

'Druids? Great. Just when I thought we'd struck rock bottom.'

The heavy-set druid shook his head, like a disapproving father.

'The world is so much more complex and wondrous than you blindfolded Romans ever deem possible, and the people in it so varied and astounding. You, just as almost every other Roman I have ever met, have the manners of a goat.'

He turned to the warrior beside him and issued a command. As two of the Gauls disappeared on some unknown task, the druid leaned over them.

'We shall have to teach you a few manners if you are to enjoy the hospitality of Crosicum. The chief is less jovial than I and may take offence.'

Silius glared at their captor as the two warriors returned with a fishing net that they threw over the two Romans and pulled tight. Velanius tried to struggle out of the way, but a broken arm seemed to be giving him great trouble. Silius shook his head. They were at the mercy of this man now and trying to escape at this point was futile.

Craning his head and rising as far as the restraining net would allow, now that the foot had been removed from his chest, he followed the line of the huge fishing net and saw that it was attached to a rope which in turn led off to the saddle of a horse. With a heavy heart, he turned to his friend.

'Brace yourself, Quintus. We're in for a rough journey.'

* * * * *

Decimus Brutus, staff officer and friend of the Julii, leaned against the outside wall of the headquarters along with Varus, the cavalry commander, and Felix, primus pilus of the Eleventh, passing a skin of wine back and forth. Leaning to the side, he pressed his ear to the door once more.

Within, he could still hear Crassus raging, amid the sound of things being thrown.

'Always a professional, eh?'

Felix grinned at him.

'Not entirely unexpected, though. That trooper's news was bad enough, but add to that the lack of any communication from Gallus or Terrasidius over the last two weeks and it begins to look like our good commander has made more than a mere tactical error. All this on top of the news that Galba and the Twelfth are on the way to restock from our stores. He's having a bad day.'

Varus nodded.

'I've lost a few good men this week, if all the grain gathering missions have fallen foul of such Gaulish atrocity.'

'It's worse than that' Brutus frowned. 'This is the first sign of insurrection. It may not be a full blown rebellion yet, but that all depends on how we handle it. And you know damn well what Crassus will do. He can't afford any blemishes on his precious reputation.'

'Should we go back in and see if we can calm him down? It's been an hour. He can't have much furniture left intact in there.'

Brutus shook his head and pointed down the road toward the main square.

'I'm not sure that's an option.'

A small party had entered the street below and were making their way up the hill toward the headquarters. A group of legionaries surrounded two men who led their horses on foot. The Gaulish warrior was no surprise, his bronze torc and mail shirt marking him as a noble. The grey robed druid by his side was, however, a different matter.

'Varus? Be a good fellow and go in to tell Crassus that he has company.'

Unhappily, the cavalry commander stepped across to the door, opened it gingerly and stepped inside. Ignoring the muted sounds of arguing voices from within, Brutus narrowed his eyes at the approaching party. A druid meant something important. This could be the opportunity they were looking for to smooth the matter over and avoid any further unpleasantness.

As the party came to the crest of the sloping street, the door beside them opened, and Crassus emerged, head high and crimson cloak settled on his shoulders. Varus appeared at his shoulder, looking peeved. The only sign of the legate's outburst and fury was the slightly wild look about his eyes.

The soldiers stopped in the street, saluted the officers and spread out to the sides, remaining alert. The two Celts, accompanied by the watch centurion, stepped forward. The centurion saluted and addressed Crassus directly.

'Sir, these two arrived at the gate seeking counsel with yourself. They have left their sizeable escort across the river and offered up their weapons as a gesture of goodwill.'

Crassus glared at the centurion and then shifted his obvious displeasure to the two Gauls.

'You are far from welcome here, and *your* presence in particular offends me, druid.'

The stocky, impressive man smiled a crooked smile.

'A sentiment echoed by the whole of Gaul toward yourself, Roman. However, I am not here to bandy insults, but rather to offer you an opportunity; some might say your *only* opportunity to keep your skins and your honour intact.'

Crassus' wild eyes flashed dangerously.

'You dare to threaten me in my own camp?'

His voice had a high pitched tone that the officers recognised. Varus had moved forward next to the legate and Felix, and Brutus joined him, reaching a position where they could prevent anything untoward happening.

The druid shrugged.

'You are invaders and, while many of our kin advocate a policy of fighting you until the last of us breathes and bleeds out, we are not all so short sighted. We have the chance to coexist and avoid the bloodshed that others see as inevitable.'

Crassus continued to glare silently as the druid continued.

'Despite the arrogance of your sending collectors out to take the food from our children's mouths to feed your hateful army, we are willing to negotiate terms.'

'*Negotiate?*'

Crassus' voice had risen another notch, and the warning signs were there for all to see.

'Yes, Roman. Last year when you beat the armies we sent out, you took many of our sons and daughters as hostages. Now we have done the same with your officers. Send our people back to us in peace and we will consider sending you the supplies you so desperately need as well as those men we have. Send our people back and we will extend to you the same courtesy.'

Crassus had gone pale, and Brutus noted Varus' hand hovering near the man's elbow, ready to restrain him if necessary. The druid shrugged again.

'You will never subdue the Armorican tribes by force, but you may yet do it through respect and care. It is your choice, Roman.'

Falling silent, the man folded his arms and stood quietly, watching the expressions racing around Crassus' face.

The legate pointed at the watch centurion.

'Have these two thrown in the stockade and send word to the provost to execute one hostage in ten.'

Varus grasped Crassus' elbow and reached across to whisper something to him, but the legate wrenched his arm free and turned his back on the visitors, opening the headquarters' door and entering, allowing it to slam behind him.

As the centurion and his men surrounded the two Gauls, Varus, Felix and Brutus exchanged worried looks.

'This is a major cock up of a situation' Felix said flatly.

'Understatement of the year' added Varus.

Brutus glanced back to catch the expressions of the two Gauls as they were pushed away down the street. There was no fear there; just defiance.

'Go with them and make sure they're treated well and for Gods' sake don't let the centurion carry out that execution order or we burn our last bridge. I have to talk to Crassus.'

* * * * *

'You did *what*?' Crassus screeched.

Brutus gripped the back of the chair behind which he stood, his knuckles whitening as he tried to restrain his temper.

'I stopped your execution order.'

The fire of anger danced in Crassus eyes and, for a moment, Brutus wondered just how far this man could be pushed before he did something truly dangerous.

'I would remind you, Brutus, that you are under my command at this time. Without Caesar's countermanding orders, what I say goes here, and I can not and *will* not have my orders disobeyed and countermanded by my lessers!'

Brutus ground his teeth and took several deep breaths before he trusted himself to open his mouth again.

'What's done is done, Crassus. I have stopped the order, and if you change it again, you'll look either indecisive or idiotic, so leave it be.'

Crassus' eyes took on that dangerous sparkle again, and Brutus continued while he had the chance.

'Look, Crassus… there is an opportunity here to build a bridge and try to get things settled in Gaul. All you need to do is grant their paltry request. The hostages were a good idea when the war was just concluding last year, but we won't need them if we can conclude a proper alliance with the tribes. If you just aggravate them, however, things could flare up here again, and we'll end up in the same situation as we were when the Belgae revolted last year. That almost cost us the Twelfth Legion!'

'No, Brutus. The reason last year caused *you* all so much trouble is that you left it too long. You let it build into a proper rebellion, and you all paid the price by having to put it down again. I conquered *this* land myself with just one legion, and I will instil peace the same way. If they want to rebel, then let them. We are already in their lands and ready to put them down.'

Brutus shook his head.

'That's not a clever approach…'

'Be *quiet*!'

Brutus blinked. Crassus may temporarily outrank him in this particular place and time, but there was no less nobility, power and rank behind Brutus than the commander.

'Speak to me like that again, Crassus, and when you leave this building it will be with a limp; do I make myself clear?' Brutus hissed through clenched teeth.

It was Crassus' turn to blink in surprise. Brutus was, to Crassus' mind, one of those soft, boyish officers, who had come out to war like a child on an outing, wanting to see how things were done. Brutus had nothing really to gain from his command, while he, as son of the great Marcus Licinius Crassus, needed to stamp his coins with victory slogans. He needed the prestige. Money was half the battle in Rome these days, but without patrician blood, no matter how rich and how influential a man was, people always looked at you as though you were in some way lacking. Military victory and a triumph was the way round that.

'Listen, Brutus. You don't need this victory, but I do. It's as simple as that. I can't have this taken away from me. I *won't* have this taken away from me!'

Brutus raised his eyebrows; it was like dealing with a petulant child.

'You had a victory last year, and you'll have the opportunity for others. Now is a time for conciliation.'

'No. We're past that. I will stand on their neck until they *beg* to go to Rome in chains.'

Inwardly, Brutus sighed. There would be no persuading the commander, and he could see that now. He would have one last try and then have to take matters into his own hands.

'At least inform Caesar. Let him have his say. It is, after all, his army; paid for with his money.'

Crassus narrowed his eyes.

'And have Caesar pull my backside out of the flames? Or worse still, blame me for this fiasco and remove me from command? Hardly, Brutus. Mark my words: I shall have this fledgling revolution stamped out within the month and will inform Caesar of events only when I have them firmly under control once more. Now you've done enough damage for the day. Don't you have anything better to do? I have to think.'

Brutus glared at him for a moment, stood and, saluting in the most half-hearted fashion possible, turned and left the room, taking care to allow the door to shut quietly. Slamming doors and stamping feet in a childish tantrum was best left to the great Imperator Crassus.

Angrily, he marched on down the street toward the north gate, where the prisoner stockade lay. He could see it from the slope; a mini camp in itself, with its own palisade, divided into sections and surrounded by defences and guards. The number of Gauls in there seemed to grow every time he looked, and every one of them would be a nobleman of one local tribe or another.

At the bottom of the hill, just inside the decumana gate, Varus and Felix were returning from delivering the prisoners. Brutus waved at them until he got their attention, and then pointed to a small, almost hidden garden off the main street. As soon as he was sure they had seen, he strode off down that side passage and into the peaceful tranquillity of the Celtic garden.

Unlike the ordered rows and graceful arcs of a Roman garden, this small, irregularly-shaped space was a muddle of jumbled shrubs, flower beds and fruit trees, with a small pond and a rustic seating area. It was in no way an organised formal garden and should be a mess, yet it had been created with such an instinctive knowledge of nature that everything fitted perfectly, blending in with the features around it to such an extent that, when taken as a whole, the effect was charming and relaxing.

That was what Brutus needed a little of right now: charming and relaxing. Crassus was neither.

He was just musing over what benefits Rome could reap through the infusion of a little Gaulish thinking when Varus and Felix rounded the corner and entered the garden. Brutus beckoned to them.

'Have a seat. I think we have a problem.'

Varus nodded as he strode across and collapsed onto one of the benches.

'I didn't think you'd have much luck with Crassus. He's a stony faced and stony hearted imbecile.'

Brutus shook his head sadly.

'No, he's far worse than that, Varus. He's a six year old with an inferiority complex. His daddy is rich and powerful, and all his peers are more noble than him. He's desperate to be better than the rest of us. I think your argument with him back near the Rhine after the Ariovistus affair made him realise that being one of the nobiles was no replacement for a noble lineage. He will lead us into the wolf's mouth and watch the whole army burn rather than admit he can't manage something.'

Felix nodded sourly.

41

'I can quite believe it. I served under his father fifteen years ago when that Thracian dog Spartacus was roaming around Italia with his gladiators and slaves. The old bastard had two legions decimated for cowardice, because they lost the field to Spartacus. He was a nasty piece of work and clearly the apple has not fallen far from the tree.'

'The question then' Brutus sighed 'is what we can do about it?'

Felix shrugged.

'He's the commander. If he wants to take the legions to crush the local tribes, we can hardly say no, no matter how much we might disagree. One of the prime requisites for being a primus pilus is obedience to the chain of command.'

Brutus stared at the grass.

'It's a delicate situation. I've pushed about as far as I dare and there's no way I can stop Crassus from carrying out his little punitive war.'

He straightened and flexed his shoulders.

'But I can put a little cushion in place for us to fall back on. Its possible Crassus is right, I suppose. He might be able to nip any insurrection in the bud and solve it all before it becomes a major problem. I very much doubt that's the case, but I can't ignore the possibility...'

Varus and Felix turned their expectant faces on him.

'But I can give him a month to try, and I can use that time to get things ready in the event he fails.'

'Like what?' asked Varus suspiciously.

'Well firstly, I have to send a letter. I need to make Caesar aware of what's happening.'

Felix shook his head.

'That's just going to land you knee deep in the shit. When Crassus finds out, he'll have you cut to ribbons for going behind his back and, to an extent he'll be justified. It's damn near mutiny.'

'Not quite. I shall write my monthly letter to my mother; she likes to be kept informed of my activity and also that of the general. They're friends, you see. The Julii and the Junii go back a way, and Caesar is actually a distant cousin. I shall 'accidentally' drop a few hints about what Crassus is doing. You can guarantee that within a week of mother getting hold of the letter, Caesar will know everything.'

Varus shook his head.

42

'That's a dangerous game you're playing, Brutus. And anyway, what if Caesar's not in Rome, but in Cisalpine Gaul or Illyricum or somewhere else?'

'Then she'll make sure that word gets to him. She knows Fronto's mother quite well, and Fronto's in Rome at the moment with Priscus and Crispus. Word will get back.'

Felix smiled a curious smile.

'Priscus and Crispus. Every time anyone says that it sounds like two characters from a Plautus comedy to me!'

'Anyway' Brutus went on, sparing a glare for the primus pilus by his side 'on a serious note, the next thing we need to do is anticipate the trouble we're going to be in when Crassus fails.'

'You thinking of raising your own legions, Brutus? I'm not sure the general would approve of that.'

'Not exactly. That would be even closer to mutiny, but the tribes we're dealing with here are sailors born and bred. The Veneti almost live at sea, and all these tribes centre around coastal fortresses and towns. What we need is naval support; to have access to the tribes by land and sea. If Crassus pushes us into open war, we'll be at a serious disadvantage otherwise, and I doubt he'll even think about the possibility of naval action.'

Varus frowned at him.

'I don't know much about the navy, but is it feasible to get the nearest fleet all the way from Italia to here in time to help?'

'Probably not. Plus I have no authority over them and even Caesar would have to apply to the senate for control of them. No. But we can build a fleet and man it ourselves in plenty of time.'

Felix laughed.

'Madness. How are you going to build the fleet without Crassus knowing? You'll need to use the legions and Crassus will find out what you're up to in no time. Then there's *manning* the ships, even if you got them built. How many sailors do you know?'

Brutus smiled at the primus pilus.

'We can start constructing a fleet at Turonum. It's only a day's march from here, with a mercantile harbour on the Loire, which has naval access all the way to the sea. I'm sure we can siphon a few of the men away from the army to work on them. So long as we can get a few engineers who know what they're doing, we can recruit the locals to do a lot of the basic labour. I can organise remuneration for them; the Junii are not short of a few denarii as I'm sure you're

43

aware. As for the crew, we'll have to send to Narbo. The province is Caesar's anyway, and the whole land is full of fishermen and sea traders, so we shouldn't have any problems raising up a crew from there.'

He turned to Varus and grinned.

'If I supply you with the appropriate letters and finance, can you organise a few discreet cavalry officers to ride to Narbo and put things into motion?'

Varus shrugged.

'If *you're* taking the responsibility for this, I can provide whatever you need.'

Nodding, Brutus turned to Felix.

'And how about engineers? Think you can spare a few good men from the Eleventh?'

The primus pilus grinned.

'You mean give them the option of continuing to dig latrines for the camp or go help design and build a navy away from our illustrious commander? They'll bite my hand off.'

'Good' Brutus nodded. 'And Galba's coming any day now with the Twelfth. We can probably rely on some men from him, since Crassus has no idea about the Twelfth's strength as it is.'

He stood, stretching.

'And I think that later I might swing by the headquarters of the Tenth. I don't know their new primus pilus very well, but people say he's got his head screwed on right, and if Fronto trusts him, then it's worth seeing if he can spare a few men.'

He rolled his shoulders a couple of times and then smiled.

'Well, I shall see you fellows later on, at the tavern? I have to go write a letter home.'

Chapter 3

(Februarius: Rome. The house of the Falerii on the Aventine)

'Not long now, Gnaeus, and the general will be back.'

Priscus sighed and looked at Fronto over the top of the cup.

'I can't imagine why anyone would want to spend the winter in Illyricum. From what I hear, the whole place is just mountains, goats and toothless women.'

Crispus frowned disapprovingly.

'Ah, now Gnaeus, that's hardly fair. Illyricum is an ancient region with a rich history and a distinct culture.'

'Bollocks. It's a vaguely Greek toilet that never achieved anything notable other than becoming Roman. Name me one great person or thing that ever came from Illyricum.'

Crispus fell silent and frowned, his head angling slightly. There was a long moment's silence.

'See? Goats, mountains and toothless women.'

Crispus shrugged with a laugh.

'I simply cannot find an argument; no fault in your logic.'

Priscus grinned.

'Anyway, I'll be pleased when Caesar *does* come back, cause he'll drag you two off onto the next mad war he's planned, and I'll finally be free of people calling me 'leftie' and making jokes about me being limp.'

Fronto nodded, his face suddenly sombre. His former primus pilus was putting a brave face on things, and he knew it well. Priscus would be smarting over the situation. His combat career was over and, while he might settle into the role of camp prefect in time, he was on a year's enforced convalescence and was forbidden from joining the legions until the general's personal surgeon decided otherwise.

The three men, along with Galronus of the Remi, had returned to Rome before the winter set in. Crispus had been to visit his family for a while, and the other three had descended upon Fronto's family townhouse, causing his sister to fuss and complain about the lack of warning. Priscus had stayed with them, given that he had no surviving family, and the winter months had been among the most relaxed and interesting that Fronto could remember.

Every day saw something new. The three Romans showed Galronus the delights of the great city and introduced him to expensive wine and racing in the Circus Maximus, following which the Belgic auxiliary officer had begun his descent into the world of gambling, racing and late night tavern visits. Fronto's sister Faleria had initially taken a fancy to the striking foreigner, but the lustre had soon worn off when she realised that Galronus was more like her brother than she'd originally imagined and she now treated him with the same loving contempt.

Priscus left the house rarely to begin with, unsure of his ability to walk any sustained distance. The first few months, however, had seen a tremendous change as his leg strengthened. He still limped, his foot angled uncomfortably inwards, and occasionally had to stop and rest against something, but Fronto was convinced, with great relief, that by the end of his convalescence, his old friend would be mobile, if uncomfortable. As Priscus put a brave face on his injuries, so did his companions help by turning the horrific wounds of the previous year into a source of endless humorous jibes.

'I'm sort of getting used to being back home and not facing screaming Gauls and biting women and having to take a shit in a bucket while the latrines are being dug. I have to admit I'm starting to dread the call in spring.'

Crispus turned to look at Fronto, frowning.

'You fool nobody Marcus. If *I* said such a thing, you would believe me. You, however, have a vine staff for a spine. I have watched you many times, and you're only truly happy when you stand facing a screaming enemy with a sword in your hand.'

Fronto winced.

'Don't say things like that near Faleria. She already has enough ammunition for making my life difficult without you providing a character reference!'

Priscus slugged down the last of his wine.

'Where is Galronus, anyway? I thought we were going to the Circus Flaminius for the camel racing?'

'I imagine he's only just now waking up with a thick head in the bed chamber of some delightful young lady in the subura. He'll be here in plenty of time. He's never late for the first race, you know that.'

Priscus opened his mouth to reply but was interrupted when the door opened with a polite knock. The shiny, wrinkled, olive pate of Posco, the house's chief slave, poked round the door.

'Master Marcus? There are *visitors* for you. I have shown them into the atrium.'

Fronto frowned. He and Posco had known one another long enough that he knew the little Greek's signals; the two were far more friends than master and slave these days and Posco rarely even told Fronto about his visitors, dealing with the various irritating issues himself without bothering his master. The stress he laid on the word 'visitors', however, meant that these particular people were out of the ordinary.

'Would you like them *shown through* or to meet them there?'

Fronto frowned.

'I think you should lead them on in, thank you, Posco.'

With a nod, the little man exited the room and shut the door.

'Visitors?' Priscus raised an eyebrow. 'Can't be the general. He won't be back here for a few weeks. Who then?'

Fronto shrugged.

'We're about to find out.'

The three waited a few moments, listening intently. A number of voices out in the corridor became gradually louder. Posco and three others. One had a deep and rich voice, one somewhat miscellaneous. The third...

'That's Cicero!'

Fronto turned to Crispus.

'You sure?'

'I know that voice. Heard it often enough in camp.'

The pair fell silent as the footsteps reached the far side of the door and stopped. Posco swung the portal open and stepped through with a slight bow.

'Masters Marcus Caelius Rufus, Quintus Tullius Cicero, and Marcus Tullius Cicero.'

Fronto stared.

Quintus he was familiar with from the last two years of campaigning, Marcus Caelius Rufus was prominent enough to be a household name as praetor, tribune and public speaker. *Marcus* Cicero was something of a surprise: the great orator was not the most favourable advocate of Caesar and deigning to visit one of the general's senior officers seemed out of character.

'Gentlemen? To what do we owe this pleasure?'

The elder Cicero brother shot questioning glances at Crispus and Priscus and then let his gaze fall on Fronto.

'What we have to say, Fronto, is rather private.'

Fronto raised his brow.

'Unless you're here to tell me that you slept with my sister or something, these two can stay. Even then, since they've met Faleria...'

Cicero frowned meaningfully at Fronto, but his younger brother tapped his shoulder.

'I know them, Marcus. I've fought alongside them. Trust Fronto; he knows what he's doing.'

Fronto's stomach began to churn. Politics. This had the stink of politics all over it.

'Come on, then. What brings three such eminent folk to my house?'

He gestured to the various spare couches and seats in the room and the three men filed in and sat. Cicero manoeuvred his toga into a more comfortable position.

'I was, to be frank, rather hoping that Caesar would be here. I hear rumours that he is returning to Rome from Illyricum.'

Fronto shrugged noncommittally and Cicero steepled his fingers, gazing over the tips and addressing his host in that deep and rich tone.

'It seems that a viper has arisen in Rome these years past.'

Fronto laughed.

'A single one? A nest, I would have said.'

The orator glowered at him but otherwise ignored the comment.

'This particular viper has struck time and again and is causing troubles for the more reasonable men in Rome. I fear we have mutual enemies.'

Fronto laughed.

'All *my* enemies are wild, hairy men that paint their faces and run around naked trying to kill Romans. A bit like the senate, but with better hygiene.'

Crispus shot him a warning glance, but once more, to his credit, Cicero ignored the comment.

'Publius Clodius Pulcher. The man forced my exile two years ago, and it is only through the judicious use of contacts and influence that I secured my recall. My brother here had his house burned down last year by one of Clodius' gangs, merely, I fear, for being associated with me. Young Caelius here is, however, in slightly more serious trouble. He used to be an associate of Clodius you see but, following a somewhat scandalous affair with the snake's sister, he finds himself at the sharp end of Clodius' fangs. I won't go into the details at this point, but suffice it to say that he stands accused of murder, attempted murder, accepting payment for murder, assault, civil disturbance and wilful damage to property.'

Fronto gave a noncommittal shrug.

'So one of Clodius' friends tries to knock up his sister and falls foul of them. Politicians are always doing things like this, and if he's one of Clodius' cronies, why in the name of Fortuna should any of us give a shit? *Particularly* you two. And why come to me anyway?'

Cicero nodded.

'It is a good question. Caelius here has a great deal of inside knowledge of the activities and associates of Clodius and his sister that could be used in the right circumstances to bring the viper down. Can you see the value of *that*?'

Fronto nodded.

'Fair enough. You save Caelius, and you can use him to bring Clodius down. Why *me* though?'

The orator glanced across at his brother and nodded. The young staff officer leaned forward.

'Quite simply, Fronto, we had nowhere else to turn. We all have a mutual enemy that we share with Caesar. We were hoping he would be here, but I told Caelius and my brother that you were the man we needed. You see, my brother is going to defend Caelius in court and make Clodius and his sister look like fools. The problem is that Clodius has eyes and knives everywhere. Anyone remotely involved in the politics of the city cannot be trusted, and nor can anyone with mercenary tendencies.'

Crispus narrowed his eyes.

'You ask a lot master Cicero. I agree that Fronto is probably the only man in Rome you can say without fear of falsehood is completely free of any possibility of influence from Clodius, but to involve him is to drop him in the centre of what is, to all intents and purposes, a war between gangs and villains. You are asking him to bodyguard a man that, shortly, could become the most wanted man in Rome.'

Fronto grinned.

49

'*Now* it's starting to sound more like fun.'

Crispus turned to look in surprise at his friend.

'Well' Fronto said, rubbing his hands, 'it was all starting to sound political and boring, but if you're talking about giving a quick knee in the happy sack to a bunch of villains round the back of the temple of Janus, then count me in.'

Priscus laughed out loud.

'If you're fighting gangs, you'll need a gang of your own. We'll have to gather together a few of the less delicate types we know in the city. Fortunately, I know quite a few.'

Fronto nodded and turned to the visitors, his eyes narrowing.

'For young Cicero, here, who leads a good reserve charge and had our back at Vesontio, I would happily do whatever I can to help. And for you too, master Cicero. But I want to state for the record that I don't trust anyone who's ever had anything to do with that Clodius character and from what I see nobody ever gets themselves truly free of him. We'll help you, but if you turn on us afterwards I'll see to it that my friend Galronus gets to show us some of the less savoury Belgic practices using you as a subject. Fair?'

Caelius Rufus, his face straight and stony, nodded quietly.

'Right then. How's this going to work? I presume you'll need Caelius around a lot to go through trial stuff?'

Cicero pursed his lips.

'Make sure nothing happens to him, keep him either here or in some location you deem safe, and I will visit from time to time as I need to speak with him on the subject of his defence.' He turned back to his brother. 'You are sure this is a good idea?'

The younger Cicero nodded.

'There's nobody in Rome that I'd rely on more for something like this.'

Fronto leaned back in his seat and grinned at Caelius.

'Do you like to gamble?'

Cicero stopped in the middle of rising and arranging his toga.

'The idea is to keep him *safe* from Clodius. Surely you can't be thinking of taking him to the games?'

Another answering grin from Fronto.

'I'm most at home in the sweaty armpit of the city, and I'll get a few friends along with us. Clodius seems to have a habit of burning down people's houses anyway, so I think it might just be a little safer to be out in a public place.'

He turned to Priscus.

'Now about trustworthy thugs, Gnaeus: any names leap to mind?'

* * * * *

A narrowed eye peered through the balustrade and blinked as dust fell across it. Down below and across the roofs, small as ants, the figures of Fronto, Priscus and their small group strode along the paving beside the Circus Maximus.

The past two weeks had been fascinating viewing with all manner of interesting events. Firstly, some very highly influential politicians had visited them at Fronto's house, including the great lawyer Cicero. Then things had settled into an odd routine. The ex-tribune Caelius had joined Fronto and his cronies, along with this growing gang of what could only be described as 'heavies' and the small and very odd party frequented games, drinking pits, gambling houses and more in the seedier districts of the city. Oh that was hardly surprising for Fronto and Priscus, and even for Crispus these days, but for Caelius? And with what appeared to be one of the Belgae nobles hanging around with them too?

Their shadow had observed them almost continually for a fortnight and had seen no less than four close calls where arguments and insults with other groups almost exploded into full street warfare. For the first week, he'd been perplexed. The situation was well and truly baffling. Fronto and his compatriots spending their winter break taking noblemen and foreigners into the most dangerous parts of Rome and starting fights?

Then he'd made a few enquiries, spoken to some people, and learned of the upcoming trial and its connection to Clodius. Piecing that together with Caelius, the Ciceros and Caesar's men, he could well assume that the solid Fronto had been chosen as an appropriate guardian for the accused.

Close behind, someone cleared their throat meaningfully.

Paetus turned sharply, but the noise was innocently directed at someone else and nobody was paying him any attention. The ordinary folk of Rome passed by along the walkway at the southern edge of the Palatine, beneath the hallowed portico of the great Temple of Apollo Palatinus. Once again Paetus chided himself for lurking like some mischievous child. He was free and in no danger of being recognised.

Standing, he brushed off the dark blue tunic that seemed to have picked up so much dust. Down below, Fronto and his group approached a street salesman and his cart stacked with bread, cheese and other nourishing basics. The games today would be big. The great Sicilian charioteer Fuscus was to run the first and third races today, but Apollodorus of Nikopolis had also drawn the third race and, while the man had nowhere near as many victories under his belt as Fuscus, he was tipped by all the gambling dens as the man to watch. People had come two days' ride to watch the races today.

And in the midst of this, Paetus moved unseen.

Getting away from the slave train during the winter had been ridiculously easy. It had been mostly a matter of timing. He'd waited until they had almost reached Russellae, only a couple of days from Rome, and had then given himself a deep cut on his leg. Periodically, he would prise the wound open so that it bled profusely and take a mouthful of tinny crimson liquid, waiting until he was near one of the guards to cough it back out. A day and a half of feigning such critical illness almost did for him for real, as the continual reopening of the wound left him feeling dizzy and light headed and stumbling as he walked.

But the ruse had been successful. The morning they rose after their stop at Russellae on the way to the markets of Rome, Paetus repeated the blood-coughing procedure with a great flourish, the illness being made all the more realistic by his now pallid, rubbery features. As he coughed a mouthful of blood over the boot of one of the guards, he collapsed as though in a faint. The guard used his muckied boot a couple of times on Paetus' ribs and the Roman 'slave' felt at least two bones crack, but kept himself as still as death, ignoring the pounding.

'Chalk up another!' the guard shouted to his mate and, as the slaves were roped together once more and began to move, two of the soldiers picked up Paetus by the limbs and flung him unceremoniously into the ditch near the road for the carrion feeders to work on.

Once the slave train had gone, Paetus picked himself up and began the long and painful trip to the city. His ribs still gave him trouble now, over two months later, but he would have taken the punishment tenfold to find himself in the position he was now.

While his family were gone to the Elysian fields, his home still stood, after a fashion. The building had been burgled and ransacked repeatedly since falling empty. It had been claimed by the state upon confirmation of Paetus' death and would be demolished to make way for something else, but public works were a slow business in Rome and Paetus had found the boarded-up shell of his house standing forlornly, reminding him of what Clodius and Caesar had ripped away from him.

It had taken him less than an hour to locate and retrieve the hidden stash of coins, buried in an amphora beneath the dining room floor for a time when it would be needed. It was hardly wealth beyond the dreams of avarice, but would give him funding for the best part of a year for food and lodging in Rome if he used it carefully.

And so he had become someone new. He'd decided to call himself Plautus, for humour value, but had stayed so alone the past two months that the only person who had asked for his name was the lowlife landlord who rented him his basic room on the Caelian Hill. A shave, a haircut and a trip to the baths had turned him from a Gaulish vagrant into a Roman once more, and a few shrewd purchases in the markets had dressed him like one again.

It had taken him a few weeks to organise everything and then he had begun his task. His room was full of wax tablets that detailed the daily movements and activities of Publius Clodius Pulcher and his cronies. It had come as a surprise to learn that Fronto had come back to Rome for the winter, as the legate of the Tenth had a notorious love of provincial dives and tried to avoid prolonged contact with his family. But that knowledge had given him his first chance to learn more of Caesar's activity, since the general seemed to be wintering in the provinces.

Paetus was a patient man, given to forward planning and care and, although eager to set about righting the wrongs that certain unscrupulous demagogues had perpetrated upon himself and others, he recognised that acting rashly would likely bring his revenge to a brief and very unsatisfactory conclusion. It could take years to do it right.

He leaned back, thinking to himself, pondering the near future. He would have to use some of his finances to arrange an income. Perhaps the buying and selling of goods? He had enough experience in military logistics, after all.

53

His attention was attracted sharply by the mention of Fronto's name nearby. He almost spun around to look, but managed to stop himself in time.

'Which one is Fronto?' a deep voice asked.

'See the one that's dragging his leg and lurching a little and the one with the green tunic? Fronto's the one between them, but all of them are dangerous, even the Gaul behind them. Try not to get tangled with them. Leave the thugs to get them out of the way. A common street fight, as you see every day the races are on. Fronto will likely be expecting something, but he won't have time to react to everything. Just make sure you're quick and not seen.'

Paetus smiled to himself. He appeared to be centre stage in this little production entirely by chance. The two men fell silent, but Paetus, his ears sharp, listened to their footsteps as they strode away along the path. The former prefect gave one last glance down from the rail, to the road by the circus, where Fronto and his companions were busy gnawing their way through a hearty breakfast as they strode along.

Allowing enough time for the men to have moved off, Paetus turned to look at the back of the two men who were now making their way down the Scalae Caci toward the circus. The figure on the left was familiar enough to him: Philopater, the gaunt Egyptian with the hook nose who 'arranged' things for Clodius. Paetus had met him a number of times, not always in the best of circumstances. The other man he did not know, but he had the bearing of a veteran soldier and, contrary to the law, the shape of a pugio scabbard bulged at the belt beneath his tunic. A killer then, either professional, or at least a well-trained amateur.

As they reached the grand façade of the temple of Cybele, Philopater nodded to his companion and then veered off to the right, past the temple and back toward the forum. The second man continued on down the slope toward the circus, and Paetus was briefly torn between the need to follow the Egyptian and find out what else he was up to, or to see how events played out down below.

The first race was still over an hour away, and the illustrious family names of Marcus Falerius Fronto and Marcus Caelius Rufus would guarantee them a good spot, even if they arrived late. The small group were making for a tavern at the foot of the path, where it met the main road that led down to the Aemilian bridge across the Tiber. The figure ahead picked up speed. The streets down there

54

were crowded enough that a clever man could inflict damage and escape unnoticed; especially when they had a distraction...

Paetus looked behind Fronto's group and spotted the dozen thugs moving through the crowd behind them, carrying heavy lengths of wood. Fronto, as always, was out ahead with his friends, letting the hired help bumble along behind, largely unprotected.

'No help this time, Fronto. When Clodius' thugs leap on your own, you'll fall foul of a well placed blade.'

Though he was bright enough not to voice his thoughts aloud, Paetus found himself hurrying. He would have to do something. Not only was Fronto just about the only man that had proved to be sympathetic to Paetus' plight, he was also apparently involved in a plan to cause Clodius trouble. The situation was good for Paetus, so long as this killer did not get his knife in Fronto or Caelius.

Paetus frowned as he descended. Everything he did these days was prepared far in advance, but now he found himself in a corner with no time to plan; just to choose a path and take it. To help Fronto could possibly lead to him being noticed, but to not do so was to likely condemn the man to an assassin's knife.

The killer was already reaching the stretch where the path levelled out, Paetus still several dozen steps behind him. He watched in anger as the man reached up under his tunic and drew the knife ready to act. The thugs had all but caught up with the back end of the small group. No time left. Decide!

Paetus clenched his teeth and shook his head. He could not attack the man; it would be too ridiculously obvious. Reaching down to the side of the path, he picked up a weighty stone. Was his throw good enough? He *used* to be good, certainly, but that was a long time ago.

A scream below announced that the action had begun. The group of thugs sent by Clodius had jumped on Fronto's men and had taken the first two down with the initial blow. Already they had erupted into a confused tussle. The hairy Gaul behind the noblemen turned instantly and leapt into the fray among the hired help. Paetus clearly heard Fronto's shout, tuned to it as he was from years of campaigning with the man.

'Priscus and Crispus? Get Caelius away to safety!'

Paetus faltered for a moment. Fronto was turning back to join the Gaul in attacking the thugs. Priscus and the legate of the Eleventh grasped Caelius and propelled him from the action, to somewhere presumed safe. Paetus watched as the killer bore down directly on the three approaching men.

With a sigh, he hefted the rock.

'Apollo guide my hand.'

Ignoring the strange looks he received from the various others on the path, he drew back his arm and cast the stone with as much force as he could while maintaining a level of accuracy.

Priscus was looking back at the gang fight going on behind him and Crispus was looking at the nobleman he was helping along the street. The assassin whipped the freed blade from beneath his tunic and, brandishing it, pushed a startled woman out of the way, already lunging with a swipe aimed straight for Caelius' neck.

It would have been an instant kill, had the thrown rock not connected with the man's head and thrown him back into the crowd. The knife leapt, glittering, into the air before descending in an arc down to the ground.

Biting his lip, Paetus turned and began to hurry back up the sloping path, trying to appear as unremarkable as possible. Perhaps he still had time to catch up with Philopater before he became lost in the crowd at the forum.

As the figure of Paetus disappeared up the slope, the fight was already under control and swinging back in favour of Fronto's men. Priscus and Crispus had pushed Caelius beneath the arch of the tavern doorway before Priscus lurched back through the crowd, grunting at the pain his crippled leg gave him, only to find the would-be assassin had vanished. He turned to locate Fronto, irritation gnawing at him, only to see the legate staring up at the Scalae Caci leading up to the Palatine with a curious look on his face.

'What's up with you?'

'I honestly don't know. Must be seeing things!'

'Well let's get back to the house. I think we can safely say my appetite for violent sports is sated for the day!'

Fronto nodded and turned to gather his hirelings, finding it hard to tear his gaze away from the slope.

'No. Couldn't have been.'

* * * * *

Fronto blinked. Cicero he had been expecting, but his companion? The elder Crassus carried with him a gravitas that instinctively made one want to bow. It was no wonder this man had held such pivotal roles in Roman government for the last fifteen years; no wonder that Caesar seemed to be bending over backward to keep Crassus sweet. The man's heavy brow and serious gaze turned back from conversation with Cicero and settled on Caelius Rufus and the small group accompanying him at the bottom of the steps.

'The date for the trial has been set' Cicero announced, as he left the staircase of the curia and alighted in the forum once more. 'We have been most fortunate, not the least because of the political weight that our friend here carries.'

Caelius, between Fronto and Crispus, nodded with a mix of eagerness and fear. He had succumbed recently to bouts of mad depression, contemplating the seriousness of his situation, and Fronto was starting to worry about the man.

Crassus nodded toward his companion.

'Cicero is too generous with his praise. The Clodii pushed for as early a trial as the senate would allow, since their evidence is vague and tenebrous at best. Far better would it be for them to push the accusations before we have a chance to put together a solid defence.'

'We?' Caelius frowned.

'Yes' Cicero smiled. 'Crassus here has agreed to stand as co-advocate for your trial. The good news is that we have persuaded the senate that an early trial would likely lead to misrepresentation and false information. We have managed not only to get the date set back to the beginning of Aprilis, giving us over a month to put your case together, but also to have the proceedings moved to the privacy of the Basilica Aemilia which will be closed for the session, rather than a public trial.'

Fronto frowned and cast his gaze around the square casually, heaving a sigh of relief as he spotted Galronus, arms folded, leaning on the inscribed panel above the lacus Curtius, three of the hired hands close by. Priscus stood on the steps of the temple of Concord, his eyes continually strafing the forum for anything out of the ordinary, a small party of men at his shoulders.

'You'd best make the case tighter than a Greek's arse' he stated emphatically. 'Someone is very definitely out to remove Caelius from the picture. We've stopped half a dozen attempts on his life in the past two weeks. Another month? His chances diminish with each week, so make that time count.'

57

Crassus nodded in a vague recognition to Fronto. The legate could not remember when he'd met the man before, but clearly Crassus recognised him.

'Keep him safe. The continued situation here appears to be driving a wedge between Clodius and his sister, and a disorganised opposition is always to be commended.' The statesman narrowed his eyes at Fronto. 'Do you have any idea when Caesar plans to return to Rome or what his plans are?'

Fronto paused for just a moment, contemplating whether it would be prudent to disseminate such information.

'The general should be here in weeks at the latest. I've no idea what his plans are from there, but campaigning season's almost here and knowing the old bas... knowing the general, he'll have engineered some incursion by ice monsters from the north or some such for us to go and fight for the glory of... Rome.'

Crassus gave him a curious lopsided smile.

'Caesar *told* me that you were outspoken. He seems to think this is a merit rather than a flaw and perhaps he is correct. Still, the fact remains that it is more than possible you will be off to ravage your 'ice monsters' before the trial actually begins. Have you given any thought to continued protection for the defendant here should you have to leave and join your legion?'

Fronto frowned. The thought had not occurred to him. For the first time in years, he'd wintered in Rome and had found that he'd actually enjoyed himself; particularly in the past few weeks with the added entertainment of villains to kick. He'd hardly spared a thought for the Tenth. Beside him, Crispus cleared his throat.

'I daresay that our favourite convalescing camp prefect would be more than adequate for the task. He is to stay in Rome on enforced leave, and I suspect would welcome the distraction.'

Fronto grinned.

'Aye, Priscus knows what he's doing; Caelius'll be in good hands.'

Cicero and Crassus shared a glance and nodded.

'Very well,' Crassus smiled, 'you just keep on doing what you're doing, and we shall begin putting the case together in detail. Cicero here has gathered copious notes, details and depositions over the past fortnight, and we should have everything we need, though we may drop in from time to time when questions arise that only Caelius here can answer.'

Cicero changed hands with the tablets he was carrying and opened his mouth to speak, but then closed it sharply, a cloud falling across his face as he looked back up the steps.

Fronto turned to follow his gaze. The prosecution party had appeared at the entrance to the curia and begun to make its way down to the comitium where they stood. The legate spared a moment to take in everything he could of his enemy. He wasn't sure what he'd expected from Clodius, but for some reason his mind had padded the man out with a rotund, sweaty form, dripping in jewellery and excess, piggy eyes greedily searching out his next vice. This mental image could hardly have been further from the truth.

Clodius was a handsome man of middle height, with neat black hair and high cheekbones, his form slim and athletic and attire suited to an austere public event. The man was, quite simply, stylish. Behind him stood the tall, olive figure of his 'facilitator', Philopater. Fronto had met the man a couple of times and had taken enough of a dislike to him that he had to restrain himself on sight. The other prosecutors had separated from the pair as they emerged and, without any exchange, had veered off to the left away from the gathering. As Clodius and his man approached, however, a new figure appeared at the doorway and stepped light and fast down the stairs to catch up with them.

Clodia was *stunning*. Her ebony tresses, pinned elegantly and woven around a diadem of silver filigree, surrounded a pale face that would make Venus green with envy. Her small and delicate form, dressed in a stola of midnight blue, seemed lithe and dextrous and almost glided down the steps. Fronto found that he was staring and wrenched his gaze away to glance at Caelius. He could quite see how the man had fallen for her charms.

Caelius' downcast and miserable features had filled for a moment with a golden light as his eyes fell on her and, in that single moment, Fronto realised just how dangerous this woman could be.

'My dearest Cicero' Clodius announced as he reached the bottom of the steps, his sister catching up with them there. He held out his hands and clasped Cicero's grudgingly proffered arm. 'You spoke well in there; almost destroyed our case before it was even presented. I am, as ever, in awe of your oratory.'

Cicero smiled with a rictus and inclined his head slightly.

'Your prosecutors supply the ammunition. I merely use it.'

59

Anger flashed for a moment in Clodius' eyes, but he forced it down and continued to smile.

'And Crassus. To have your illustrious presence gracing the court is always a joy.'

Fronto glowered at the man. Clodius was plainly the kind of man that Fronto hated most in the world: a devious thug, hiding behind a mask of civility. His attention was drawn once more to the figure now standing at the man's side. Clodia smiled her most devastating smile at him and licked her lips. He tore his gaze quickly away from her and realised that Philopater was also watching him. What was it with these people?

Clodius nodded respectfully at Caelius.

'I am so sorry that events have come to this point. You have been like a brother to me. But then' he smiled sadly 'my brother would have known better than to sleep with my sister, wouldn't he?'

Caelius flinched, and Fronto cleared his throat.

'I'm a soldier, not a politician, and all this feigned civility is in danger of forcing my breakfast to make a reappearance and my sword arm's beginning to itch. If we're all done posturing, could we go our separate ways?'

Clodius laughed.

'You would be this Fronto I keep hearing of. Caesar must be a truly patient and forgiving man. But you are absolutely correct: let's dispense with the pleasantries. My sister has a habit of involving herself in difficult and sticky situations. I would just as rather this whole affair had not occurred. Rest assured, Caelius, that, despite the best efforts of your two noble advocates, we *will* win the case and then you will be executed and your family will suffer grave dishonour.'

He smiled at Caelius rather unpleasantly.

'You could, of course, save us all the trouble, and take the honourable way out. I give you my word that no further motion will be made against your name if you remove the need for the trial.'

Clodia glared at her brother, but he ignored her. Fronto tried to ignore the fact that the woman's gaze kept coming to rest on him, while the burning eyes of the Egyptian continued to bore into his skull.

Something clicked in his head in that moment. He'd been wondering why Clodius should be trying so hard to remove Caelius from the picture when it was *he* who pushed the trial in the first place, but the answer was obvious now. His sister was the source of the accusation and Clodius would rather have disassociated himself from the whole potentially-destructive matter had he the choice. Clodius was trying to make the problem go away in any way he could. Now Fronto *really* hated the man.

In a moment of insight that he would rather not have had, Fronto realised that it was a damn good job that this man and Caesar were enemies. Were they together, they could rule the world within a year with their unscrupulous methods. He flashed his teeth in an almost-smile at Clodius.

'I'd just as rather he didn't fall on his sword quite yet. He's staying with me and the mess would be appalling.'

Clodius frowned for a moment and then laughed.

'Very well. I have important matters to attend to. Philopater? Come!'

He bowed and, turning, strode away across the forum. The hook-nosed Egyptian nodded toward Fronto and made a strange sign with three fingers pointing at his own eyes and then at Fronto. The legate's lip curled.

'See you soon.'

He watched Philopater until the man turned his back and then nodded to Crispus.

'Get Caelius back to the house and gather Galronus and Priscus and come meet me at the Taverna Arabia in an hour or so. We need to step up our routine if Caelius is going to live long enough to be tried. If young Cicero is at the house, bring him too. He said he'd be dropping by.'

Crispus nodded and turned to the small gang of men he currently commanded, gesturing them on and marching them back toward the Aventine. Cicero and Crassus let their gaze rest on Fronto for a while and finally Caesar's patron pursed his lips.

'I am aware of your reputation, Fronto. With the current evidence, we can walk this trial through the way we want it. Leave matters in the hands of the lawyers and don't do anything stupid that might give our opponents ammunition to use against us.'

Fronto grinned.

'Trust me!'

Crassus shook his head and muttered something to the elder Cicero that Fronto did not hear before the pair turned and strode away across the forum. Fronto watched them go, silently voicing his

61

opinion of lawyers and politicians alike. Men like these had built the republic, yes, but then it was men like these that would destroy it too.

He almost jumped as he turned to leave and saw the startling green-blue eyes of Clodia locked on him. She had been so silent he'd forgotten she was there again.

'Can I help you?' he asked, with an audible trace of irritation.

'It would appear that my brother has left me to your tender care. It would be unseemly and dangerous for a lady to return home through the streets of the city without an escort.'

There was an unspoken command in the words, masquerading as a request. Fronto gritted his teeth. This woman was far too dangerous to be around, but to refuse her request would be…

He couldn't actually see any *reason* why he shouldn't just turn and leave her here. She was, after all, one of the opposition and probably planning to use him in some wicked way. And yet, as he turned, he realised he was already holding his arm out to her. She took it with a full-lipped, knee-trembling smile. Fronto swallowed nervously as he looked her in the face.

'Where are you headed?'

'Actually, I have no plans. I should be home for the evening meal, but perhaps we should go somewhere to talk? A tavern perhaps?'

Fronto smiled, heaving a sigh of relief. Now he was heading for familiar territory: women that wanted to use him.

'I don't think that's a very good idea. You see, I'm pretty sure that men usually fall over their tongue when they talk to you and would happily knife their grandmother to spend a night with you but, while you're very attractive, I'm quite used to dangerous women. I still limp slightly after an encounter with a German woman. I really don't fancy being the next man to have to defend himself in court because you've changed your fickle mind.'

Clodia flashed an angry glance at him.

'I had you measured as a better man than this, Marcus Falerius Fronto. You have an opportunity with me to gain a little advantage over my brother, and I strongly suggest you take it. He and I are siblings; we are not friends.'

Fronto smiled unpleasantly.

'That's as maybe, but I leave politics in the hands of politicians and if I'm going to spend time with vicious women, I prefer ones that bite to ones that corrupt from within.'

Withdrawing his arm, he nodded at her.

'I suspect you can safely make your own way home, lady Clodia, and I also believe that if I have to spend any more time listening to your lies, I might have to go to the baths on the way home to wash the stink of corruption off me. Good afternoon.'

He turned his back on her furious features and strode off.

'Walk very carefully, Fronto' she shouted after him. 'My brother is not the *only* one with friends in low places.'

Fronto sighed. Why was it that every woman he ever met wanted to either use him, or change him, or both? His sister pictured him as a future consul, Balbus' wife, Corvinia, had contemplated marrying him off to her daughter, Longinus' widow had seen him as a replacement for her husband, and that Belgic woman last year...

He suddenly realised he'd never even known *her* name. Shaking his head, he drew his thoughts back to the immediate situation.

The next month was going to be interesting. Tense... but interesting.

Chapter 4

(Martius: Rome. The house of the Falerii on the Aventine)

Fronto rubbed his head vigorously with the towel. He'd only been outside for less than quarter of an hour, but the rain was so torrential that it felt as though he'd done several lengths of the pool at the baths.

'All this for bloody breakfast!'

Priscus, sitting warm and dry on the small seat by the altar to the lares and penates in the vestibule, laughed.

'Well if you wouldn't wind your sister up so much, life would be much easier for you.'

Fronto glared at his friend but, in truth, Priscus was absolutely right. He'd been very hung over this morning, and Faleria had rubbed him up the wrong way, causing him to become increasingly unhelpful and childish. In the end, she had thrown up her arms and told him he could sit and simmer until he'd changed his attitude. Fronto had been happy at the time to see her go, but it was almost a quarter of an hour later before he realised that she had accompanied her mother and taken the slaves with her. Fronto was alone in the house with Priscus and Caelius and no amount of exploring the working area of the house had turned up bread, butter, cheese or milk.

Shunning the remains of the unfinished wine and something grey on a stick he'd bought from a street vendor on the way home last night and had not been able to face since, he'd eventually come to the conclusion that if they wanted to eat, he was going to have to brave the rain and go to the bakery two streets down toward the Porta Capena.

Shaking wildly like a dog after a dip in the river, Fronto grunted, picked up his soggy shopping and nodded at the altar on the way past.

'Let's go get breakf...'

He was interrupted by a knock at the door behind him and for a moment continued walking before realising that nobody would be opening it for him. He grinned. This was more like being back in Gaul: uncomfortably damp, getting hungry and having to do everything for himself. Throwing the wet shopping bag to Priscus, he turned on his heel and walked to the door, flinging it open, trying his best to mimic the humble stance of a house slave.

'Can I 'elps thee, master?'

The wet and disgruntled face of Gaius Julius Caesar, Proconsul of Cisalpine and Transalpine Gaul and of Illyricum, glared down at him, half a dozen togate figures gathered around behind him.

'If this is supposed to be funny, Fronto, you're far from the mark, as usual.'

Fronto rolled his eyes. Bloody typical.

'You've chosen a nice day to visit, Caesar' he said, straightening. 'I *wondered* where all this sudden rain came from. You must have brought it with you from Illyricum.'

'Is there any danger of you inviting us in out of the downpour?' the general asked, his eyes beginning to narrow in irritation.

'By all means, general. I'd invite you all for breakfast, but I have a single loaf of bread, some cheese that may well be out of date, an amphora of wine with things floating in it and something dead and sticky on a stick. You might be better not taking me up on the offer.'

The general glared at Fronto as he strode in past him and removed the crimson cloak, raking fingers through his thinning hair and discarding droplets of water to the marble floor. Behind him, the men in togas shrugged off their own cloaks and used them to rub their heads. They may be dressed as Roman gentlemen, but Fronto knew the bearing of a soldier when he saw it. He did not know these men; Caesar must have brought new blood in from Illyricum. They all looked vaguely Greek. Except.

'I know you from somewhere.'

The man bowed his head, a crown of shiny skin showing through the curly brown hair.

'Appius Coruncanius Mamurra. We've met a few times, Fronto. Your sister invites me to her socials. Admittedly I'm often late, and the last time I attended, you and your friends were already in the garden, peeing in the fountain.'

Fronto cast his eyes downward. Damn it. This was why he was more comfortable in the field. He nodded.

'Mamurra. I've heard Tetricus talk of you. Famous engineer, right?'

The man bowed again, and Fronto tried not to stare at the shiny pink circle in the middle of the man's hair.

'I have been known to build the odd thing, yes.'

65

Fronto grinned at Caesar.

'You've something in line for the campaigning season then?'

Caesar, having wrung most of the water from his clothing, pinched the bridge of his nose.

'Not exactly, Fronto. Shall we go and sit down to talk?'

Fronto shrugged.

'By all means, but we should go to the triclinium, there's a guest in the main room sleeping off the effects of last night. Galronus is around somewhere; possibly in the garden face down. Shall I fetch him?'

Caesar shook his head.

'Not so important. It's you and Priscus I'm here to see.'

Shivering in the cold, damp air, he turned to follow Fronto into the dining room. The general stopped to nod at Priscus with a measure of respect and familiarity. The Camp-Prefect-in-waiting gave a small bow in return and then followed the group in, limping with a rhythmic grunt.

Once the party were all seated, Caesar stretched and locked Fronto with a searching gaze.

'I've only been back in the city for a few hours and already I hear the most astounding rumours about your activities, Fronto. My niece is very well informed. I look forward to hearing all about it, but first let me give you a 'heads up' as they say.'

Fronto nodded. All business; something had unsettled the general.

'A message reached me a few weeks ago at Salona, courtesy of Brutus' mother Sempronia here in the city. It would appear that young Crassus, busy wintering away in northwestern Gaul, is about to cause a Gallic uprising; or possibly he has already done so.'

Fronto groaned.

'I was really beginning to hope we'd settled things in Gaul. Every year we go there, have to sort some arrogant bastard out and then you announce that Gaul is conquered again... until the next rebel pops up.'

Caesar nodded grimly.

'It is very much as you say and, I have to admit, it's starting to make me look bad in the eyes of the senate. I cannot keep pronouncing Gaul conquered and then having to go back and sort the damn place out again forever. But it's a little... delicate. I have a great deal tied up in my alliance with his father; as much as I do with

Pompey, if not more. I cannot simply remove the runt and send him running back to daddy. So, sadly, we're going to have to go and make sure this revolt either doesn't happen at all, or fails to become noteworthy back home.'

Fronto sighed and reached across to Priscus, motioning for him to pass the bread and cheese. As he did so, Fronto shrugged.

'I've sort of been expecting the call to arms, anyway. It's a few weeks earlier than I expected, but still...'

Caesar shook his head and then reached out speculatively for the loaf of bread that Fronto had finished with and was about to discard.

'May I? Don't panic over the call, though, as I'm not planning to head out for a few weeks yet. There are things I need to do in Rome: I have to see Crassus and Pompey, and spend a little time with Atia and her family. I have to renew a few acquaintances, and pass on my gratitude to Sempronia. It was she who knew to send the message from her son on to Illyricum. Besides, half the staff officers and legates will need to be informed and gathered. I believe Crispus is here somewhere?'

Priscus nodded.

'He's returned to staying at his family's house on the Esquiline, general. I think he's sick of waking up with a bad head.'

Fronto hurriedly chewed through his mouthful, speaking with a mouth packed with bread and cheese and dropping crumbs onto the floor.

'If Crassus is causing that much shit, shouldn't we get back as fast as possible?'

Caesar shook his head.

'Gaul may be important, but it's only *one* of my worries at the moment. Besides, young Brutus seems to be keeping things in order, with the help of some of the veterans. He's even gone as far as building a fleet on the Loire to prepare to deal with the coastal tribes.'

Fronto nodded appreciatively.

'He does think ahead, that one. Clever lad.'

'So...' the general said, pulling himself up a little in his seat, 'what's this I hear about you getting involved with half the criminals and politicians of Rome?'

Fronto took another bite of cheese and shrugged.

'Your friend Clodius is messing with things. Him and his sister, anyway. They've taken Caelius to court, and Cicero and Crassus are defending him. Well...' he added with a grin, 'they're defending him in *court*. Me and Priscus and a bunch of lads with stout wooden clubs are defending him everywhere else. It's him that's asleep on the couch in the other room.'

'Indeed' Caesar nodded. 'I'd heard that he was involved. You *do* know, I presume, that Caelius Rufus is one of the names on a list I have of people that work for Clodius and cannot be trusted and will need to be dealt with in due course?'

Fronto chuckled mirthlessly.

'I think if he was still in Clodius' pocket there would be considerably fewer knife-wielding maniacs out to gut him in the street. You might find that Caelius is one of the most useful people you could meet in the near future, so long as Cicero and Crassus can keep him away from execution.'

He looked up at Caesar from beneath lowered brows.

'So long as you do right by him and don't send him the way you did with Paetus, that is.'

The general's features hardened.

'Paetus was a fool and a tool; nothing more. Don't start getting sentimental over people you feel sorry for Fronto. There are too many of them for comfort.'

Fronto glowered for a moment, but let the matter pass.

'You might want to speak to both Crassus and Cicero as soon as possible' he added. 'I'm just playing bodyguard, but the pair of them know what's happening in more detail. They seem quite positive that they can destroy Clodius' case.'

'Fair enough' the general nodded. 'The trial is set at the start of Aprilis, yes? I think we can delay our departure until after that. I would rather like to be around for the event. Where are your mother and sister, by the way? I was hoping to pay my respects while I was here.'

Fronto leaned back.

'Mother wanted to go shopping this morning, and Faleria felt the pressing need to be a long way away from me. In her defence, I *did* smell like a dead bear this morning.' He sniffed his tunic and winced. 'And the rain hasn't helped much. Now I smell like a *soggy* dead bear.'

Two of the new officers exchanged quiet words in Greek.

'Don't you know it's rude to do that?' Fronto glared at them.

'I am dreadfully sorry, legatus. I was led to believe that you were not a man to stand on ceremony.'

Fronto glared.

'Not with people I know. *You* I wouldn't know from Socrates!'

Priscus grinned uncomfortably through the tension that hung in the air.

'The legate is suffering with a bad head this morning and is quick to anger. I suggest you stick to good honest Latin for now. Fair?'

The toga-clad Illyrian nodded hastily.

'Good.' The former primus pilus of the Tenth turned to Caesar. 'I expect I know the answer, general, but does the call up include me on the roster? It's getting quite dangerous in Rome at the moment. I might just be safer in Gaul.'

Caesar smiled.

'I've already appointed a temporary camp prefect for the season to hold the position for you, Priscus. You rest for a few months more yet. I'm sure there will be plenty of action for you to come back to when you're fully recuperated.'

Fronto smiled as he saw the Greek-speaking fellow with the attitude in the corner go white at the mention of Priscus' name. He laughed.

'Let me guess? That fellow over there's your temporary camp prefect?'

Caesar nodded, his face betraying no emotion.

'Ha. No wonder you went pale. Hey Priscus... meet the man who's covering for you.'

Priscus smiled at the Greek-speaking man.

'You'd better not screw my legions up for me before I'm ready to take over.'

The man gulped and nodded.

'And a word of advice? Speak Latin. If you start to spout your fancy Greek around the legions, someone like Balventius will bury you up to the waist in the latrines... face down!'

Fronto grinned wolfishly, and Caesar gave him a weary smile.

'Well this has all been very pleasant but, in the absence of your family to visit, I fear that's all that need be said at this time. I'll be at my home for the next few days when I'm not with friends. Find me there if you need to speak to me, or leave a message.'

Fronto nodded and he and Priscus rose with the visitors, escorting them back into the vestibule and to the front door. As the men adjusted their togas and cloaks, readying for the torrential rain outside, Fronto stepped past them and opened the door. Caesar peered out into the deluge and gestured to his host.

'Are you aware you're being observed, Fronto?'

Fronto leaned past him and squinted into the rain. On the far side of the street, lurking in the shadows beneath the wall and shrubbery that surrounded the garden opposite, a young woman in ragged clothes crouched, her eyes locked on the house's door.

Fronto nodded wearily.

'Don't let the vagrant clothes fool you. She's one of Clodia's servants. I've seen her shadowing me in the forum. Looks like they've started watching the house now. That woman is beginning to become a powerful pain in the arse.'

Caesar frowned.

'You'll have to do something about her, of course.'

Fronto nodded with a cheeky grin.

'Absolutely. She looks starving. Priscus? Go ask her if she'd like some breakfast.'

As Priscus laughed and threw a cloak over his head, Caesar shook his head in exasperation.

'Should I live a thousand lifetimes, I swear I will never understand you, Fronto.'

Without waiting for a reply, the general, along with his escort, strode out of the door and hunched his shoulders against the rain as they turned and made their way down the street, past the humorous tableau of Priscus offering bread to the bewildered spy.

* * * * *

The first day of the trial of Marcus Caelius Rufus ended without pomp or ceremony, reminding Paetus of the adjournment of a meeting, with the various attendees gathering up their notes and shuffling them before filing out silently to go about their own business for the evening. The public were not admitted to the basilica during this private session, of course, yet Paetus had spent his youth around the forum and knew, like many others raised within its boundaries, how to get a personal view of these private matters.

70

The eastern end of the top step of the temple of Castor and Pollux, for example, beneath the ornamental colonnade, gave a partial view of the interior of the Basilica Aemilia through one of its high windows. Much of the interior was still hidden from view, and there was no hope of listening in, of course, but to keep an eye on things, the point of view was unrivalled.

Paetus, grateful for a break from the incessant rain, had spent his day here quietly and undisturbed, other than having to shoo a couple of children away when he'd returned from purchasing his lunch. His position gave him a clear view of the open space where the advocates and prosecutors strode about, espousing their views. Apart from Crassus and Cicero and Caelius himself, the respected senator Gaius Coponius and Clodius' pet praetor Quintus Fufius Calenus both took turns to give their own, probably spurious, evidence, along with many less notable noblemen.

And finally, with the outcome still hanging in the balance, the trial had ended for the day, the doors were unlocked, and the basilica began to empty. Paetus watched carefully as the togate figures emerged; a studious man could tell a lot from facial expressions and body language.

Many of the men involved in the case bore the stony, serious gaze of the career lawyer. Such a high profile trial brought most of the legal minds in Rome out of the woodwork, whether they were required or not.

Then Cicero and Crassus appeared, and Paetus sighed with relief. Crassus was known for his stony features anyway, but the chuckle he gave at some unheard comment of the smiling Cicero spoke volumes about the direction the trial was taking. Paetus' conclusion was confirmed twice more, principally as Caelius appeared at the door to be greeted instantly by Fronto and Priscus who had been sitting on the marble steps outside. Briefly his eyes flicked across to the Gaul – Galronus he was called apparently – and Crispus, each leading a small gang of men and closing on the emerging group protectively.

Caelius' grin threatened to separate the top of his head from his body. And then Clodius and his sister emerged, followed by a gaggle of family and assorted cronies. The man had a face like thunder and gesticulated wildly as he argued with Clodia, whose own features raged between fury and helpless despair. Paetus nodded to himself. Good. Anything that might go wrong for Clodius was a step toward his own revenge.

71

The argument between the siblings reached a crescendo when Clodius drew back his hand and gave his sister a ringing slap across the cheek, causing her to stagger, the colour draining from her already porcelain face. Paetus almost chuckled at the sight, particularly given that the pair were still in full view of many of their courtroom opposition.

Turning his back on her, Clodius gestured to his followers and strode off into the city. Clodia stood for a time, the colour slowly returning to her cheeks as the shock turned into low, burning anger. After a brief discussion with the two advocates, Fronto, Priscus and Caelius turned and made their way across the square, past the temple where Paetus stood, and heading toward the circus and home. As they moved out into the open space their hired hands, in two groups led by Crispus and Galronus, appeared from among the crowd where they had been lurking, watching for trouble, and gathered as a protective unit around the defendant. Paetus smiled. Even in the winter months, back in Rome and in civilian clothes, Fronto could not shake the habit or appearance of a soldier. No wonder he'd never made a go of it in politics. The man was like a ballista: direct and to the point and as military as they came.

The silent observer was smiling at the mental picture of Fronto addressing the senate when unexpected movement caught his eye. The temple of Castor was, apart from himself, emptying. Most of the people beneath the colonnade were here for the same reason as he: to get the best possible view of a trial that involved some of Rome's greatest men. However, now that the basilica was emptying, most of the interested onlookers had descended to try and get close to the parties involved. Indeed, even most of the beggars had also descended, smelling the wealth as it passed.

One figure, however, was moving against the human tide. Clodia, in her finery, cut a graceful figure; hardly subtle in any way, drawing appreciative and hungry glances from the men around her as she climbed the steps to the far side of the temple portico where Paetus stood. The former prefect watched her with interest, his eyes narrowing. She cast her gaze around the temple façade as she reached the top step and he slumped against the column in the manner of a drunk. Her eyes passed across him, barely noting his presence, a testament to how much he had changed in the last year, given that he had met Clodia at social occasions in Rome a number of times in the old days when his wife had been...

Paetus shook away the morbid thoughts. This was no time for a descent into misery. There was something suspicious about Clodia's stance and the way she checked out her surroundings, and the former prefect tensed.

Reaching into her stola, Clodia withdrew an iron object around half a foot long that must have been very uncomfortable to secrete in such a way. Paetus frowned at the item. He'd seen them before in the supplies of some of the Greek-speaking auxiliary units that fought with him under Valerius at Zela a decade earlier: plumbata – a throwing dart, heavy and deadly.

He was already moving before he'd made his decision. After his potentially disastrous move to prevent Caelius' assassination weeks ago, he was now committed to the path; besides, it was the *right* thing to do. Would Caelius ever know of his silent guardian, Paetus wondered as he stepped up behind Clodia, who was testing the weight of the heavy dart while judging the distance to the laughing figure of Caelius, striding across the forum?

Clenching his teeth and with a single glance to make sure that no one of consequence was paying attention to them, Paetus grasped the wrist of her throwing arm with one hand while the other came around from behind her head and clamped across her mouth. As she uttered a stifled squawk, Paetus lifted her bodily off her feet with ease and stepped back into the shadows of the colonnade. Without pausing there to give her time to regain her senses and fight back, he retreated into the temple doorway with her. The interior, dim and shady after the overcast but bright light of the forum, was austere and quiet.

Paetus cast his glance around and noted the two figures in the centre of the open space. A junior priest in his white robes was explaining something to a plebeian in a depressing grey tunic. The two looked up in surprise as Paetus and the thrashing woman entered the building and stepped aside from the bright square of the door.

'You two: out!' Paetus barked and, to illustrate his command, he jerked his chin toward the door. The citizen took one look at the tableau and ran from the room. The priest, on the other hand, approached the door and held his hands out in a soothing fashion, turning to face the pair. He opened his mouth to speak just as he noticed the deadly weapon clutched in the woman's white hand, the circulation cut off by her assailant's grip. The priest changed his mind hurriedly, closed his mouth and scuttled out of the door, making frightened sounds.

Finally, Clodia seemed to calm down, her breathing settling just as she brought her foot down hard on Paetus' own, expecting him to screech and release her. His grip on her wrist tightened as he took his other hand from her mouth. She gasped at the pain in her arm, and her spasming fingers lost their grip of the plumbata dart, which fell into her assailant's outstretched hand. With a grim smile, he let go of her wrist and weighed the dart in his hand.

'That would have been exceptionally unwise, Clodia.'

She glared at him.

'A spoiled girl' he declared, 'stamping her feet and throwing things because she is not getting her own way.'

'Who are you?'

Paetus smiled. She really did not recognise him, even face to face and a foot apart.

'I am a child of Mars, watching over the wellbeing of Marcus Caelius Rufus and his companions.' He pursed his lips and then smiled humourlessly. 'In time, I will become an agent of Nemesis, but for now, Caelius is in my care. I see that the results of the trial appear to be swinging against you. Your petty and personal accusations against an innocent man for your own vain glory are driving your brother ever further away from you and serve no purpose for either of you. You have lost the case, as tomorrow will make clear to you. Let the matter drop and move on with your corrupt and stained life and forget you ever heard the name Marcus Caelius Rufus.'

Clodia glared at him, and her lip curled into a snarl.

'*Nobody* tells me what to do, you piece of refuse. Not my brother; not Caelius; not even Mars himself. When I find out who you are, be on your guard, as I shall add your name to the list below his.'

Paetus smiled, though with clenched teeth the effect was far more frightening than it should have been. Clodia drew a nervous breath as her attacker dropped the dart and grasped her at the shoulders, his hands gathering a bunch of her stola as he lifted her from the floor once again and swung her round to press her against the temple wall, knocking the wind out of her.

'You have *no idea*, girl; simply no idea. I have been through Hades and back, dragging my feet in the fire of the underworld. I have fought armies, been tortured *and killed*. I am Mars becoming Nemesis! I have endured more than a human *can* endure and still I survive. Do not presume to threaten me, and mark my words: stay silent and out of the way. Every step you take into the public light brings you one step closer to my grip, and I offer only this one warning.'

To punctuate his point, he shook her so that her head snapped back with a crack against the tufa wall of the temple's interior. As he stepped back to let her go, she slumped, becoming limp in his grip as she passed out.

Silently, he chided himself. He'd become incensed and had taken things too far, even using part of the speech he was saving for the day he had his hands on her brother. He'd meant to merely warn her off but had ended the encounter by threatening her, claiming a divine duty, and knocking her unconscious against a temple wall. Still, there was little doubt in his mind she *would* remember this.

Gently, he allowed the woman in his arms to slump to the floor, where he left her propped against the wall. There was no blood on the tufa or her head, so he'd not hit her that hard; she would wake soon enough. Collecting the heavy dart from the floor, he returned to her unconscious form and dropped the weapon in her lap. She might have trouble explaining the possession of a weapon in the forum. He was sure she would talk her way out of it, but the embarrassment would filter back to Clodius too.

Taking a deep breath, Paetus stood and left the temple. There was no sign of the priest near the steps. Perhaps he had gone to Pontifex Maximus to report the defilement of his temple. Wherever he may be, Paetus was pleased to have the time to leave the podium and head back to his lodgings to ponder on the outcome of the day.

* * * * *

Fronto frowned at Priscus.

'Do you ever see dead people?'

The former primus pilus of the Tenth grinned.

'Have you any idea what a stupid question that is, given our profession.'

Fronto's frown deepened for a moment in confusion before he realised what his friend was talking about and shook his head irritably.

'Don't be an idiot. You know exactly what I mean. A long time ago I used to see my father from time to time...' he glanced sidelong

75

at Priscus. '*After* he died, before you make any more smart remarks. I remember seeing him here and there. I've never had much use for Gods and priests…'

He turned his eyes upwards apologetically.

'Apart from Nemesis and Fortuna, of course… But there are times that make me question either my beliefs or my sanity.'

Priscus made a face.

'What the hell are you talking about? I swear the longer we stay out of combat, the weirder you get.'

Fronto sighed.

'The spirits of the departed. Mother always said that the manes and the lemures were real; that the manes appeared to give you advice and support when you needed it, and the lemures stalked those who were responsible for their deaths. She thought she saw my father several times too, so she was pleased that I did, but she always assured me, even when I was young, that the restless dead would have no cause to haunt me, cause I was a good boy.'

Priscus rolled his eyes; it was going to be one of *those* conversations.

'You can get quite peculiar and depressing sometimes, Marcus.'

Fronto glared at him.

'Don't you believe in *anything*?'

'Steel.' Priscus answered flatly. 'And cake. And wine, and women, and the inability for dice to ever come up right for me, and that politicians should be automatically denied the right to serve with the military.'

Fronto stared at him for a moment and then laughed.

'Fair enough; particularly to that last. But the thing is that, although I don't sacrifice or do much in the way of libations or praying, that idea has been at the heart of everything I've done since I hit adulthood. Looking back, I can't think of a single occasion where I've deliberately caused harm to someone who didn't deserve it.'

He paused and grinned.

'Plenty of harm to those who *did* deserve it, mind you.'

His face became serious again.

'Thing is, Gnaeus, that I keep seeing someone that simply can't be here, and they're always watching me. It's starting to make my spine itch and my scalp crawl. And while I can't say I'm directly and personally responsible for hurting them, I'm still serving and supporting a certain general who *is* directly responsible.'

Priscus narrowed his eyes.

'Who are you talking about?'

'Never mind' Fronto sighed, spotting the door of his family home up ahead in the quiet street. 'I'm just starting to feel like a man at the circus, watching the quadrigae racing out of the starting gate and realising too late that he's backed the wrong driver.'

Again, his companion pursed his lips.

'You saying you're not going to go back with the general?'

Fronto shook his head, but Priscus noted something uncertain about the manner of the legate of the Tenth.

'No; not that. I'm needed with the Tenth, and they deserve a commander who knows them. But the general is starting to wear on my nerves. The more I look at Pompey and Crassus, the more I think that *they're* the future that Rome deserves and that Caesar is a new Sulla in the making, ready to march his men into Rome and...'

He shrugged.

'I'm in service with the general, but it's more through acknowledgement of our history together than anything else; I certainly don't need his patronage and we don't owe him money or anything. I *will* head out when he issues the call, but I think the time of me keeping my mouth shut and playing along is just about at an end.'

Priscus turned to look back at the assorted group behind them: a well known politician with a good history, a Gaulish nobleman, a young legate, and a bunch of hired muscle. Hardly the legion he was used to having at his shoulder.

'At least you get to *go* back. I'll be staying *here* for the duration. Try not to start another civil war when you disagree with him, though. Caesar may be powerful, and a great orator, but try and remember that your opinion carries a lot of weight with the centurionate and the more impressionable officers, so be careful.'

Fronto smiled.

'Aren't I *always* careful, Gnaeus?'

'Are you *ever*?'

* * * * *

Fronto rolled the dice again on the marble step.

77

'Shit.'

Grumbling, he fished in his pocket and withdrew two more coins, slapping them irritably down on the step in front of Galronus. The Remi chief grinned.

'You get worse at dice when you are tense.'

'And your Latin gets suspiciously better when you're winning. I constantly fear that you're hustling me, Galronus.'

The Belgic nobleman laughed and gathered up the dice, raising a questioning eyebrow at Fronto.

'Go on then. One more.'

Beside them, leaning against the column, Crispus sighed and adjusted his toga.

'Have you ever considered stopping playing games before you run out of coin? No one has been on a losing streak like this since the Carthaginians.'

Fronto shot an irritable glance up at his friend.

'I notice *you* never put your hand in your pocket!'

'And that is why there is still money in it. Can you not see that Galronus is better at this than you; as well as luckier, of course.'

'Shut up.'

Crispus smiled benignly. He had enjoyed his winter in the city. The previous year, Fronto had shown him the delights of Tarraco, but there really was no place like Rome. It would be sad in a way to return to the legions, but then life there was rarely dull either, particularly with Fronto around. He wondered briefly how Felix was doing in his absence.

A few bony clicks and a sigh announced a further emptying of Fronto's pocket. Galronus stretched.

'Enough. I can hardly walk with all your coins as it is.'

Fronto glowered at him and examined the dice suspiciously before handing them back to the Gaul.

Crispus smiled again. There was something *about* Fronto. He was a catalyst in the best sense of the word; a force that brought everyone to his level. Last year he had taken Crispus, a serious and fairly naïve young officer, and had taken him under his wing, opening his mind to a number of surprising experiences. The result had been astounding: Crispus had returned to the Eleventh a stronger, more commanding legate with a better understanding of the men who followed him. The life experience Fronto had pushed at him had been invaluable.

And in the same way as Fronto had brought Crispus down to a practical level last year, he had taken Galronus and done something similar with him. The Remi chief was already intelligent and honourable for sure but, in just a few months, Fronto had shown him the very best and the very worst that the city and its people had to offer, and the Gaul had come away with a new view of Rome. He had confided in Crispus a few nights ago after a party, while Fronto lay draped across a couch, drooling, that he had never truly understood why Rome considered itself civilised and everyone else 'less' in some way. And yet now, when he returned to the Remi after Caesar's campaigns were concluded, he would miss the comforts he had discovered...

... *if* he decided to return to the Remi.

There was a click from the door behind them and the wooden portal swung open. Fronto scrambled to his feet with Galronus and joined Crispus as they backed away behind the columns and out of the way of the basilica's main exit.

The first person to emerge was Gnaeus Domitius Calvinus, the judge presiding over the trial. Fronto examined the man's face for any clue, but he was unreadable. Behind him came a number of lawyers and clerks while Fronto tapped his foot impatiently.

It seemed hours as togate men with serious expressions left the basilica before the first face they recognised appeared. Cicero and Crassus stood side by side at the shoulders of Caelius, who wore an ecstatic grin. Fronto sighed with relief. Caelius turned toward them as Crassus and Cicero, deep in conversation, veered off on their own errands.

'Acquitted on all counts' the relieved politician announced with a smile. He grasped Fronto by the arms happily. 'Marcus, you should have seen it. Cicero pulled the pair of them to pieces; not just Clodia, but her brother too. They looked like idiots; and not *just* idiots. They looked like *vicious and greedy* idiots. The expression on Clodia's face! I thought she was going to explode.'

Fronto smiled.

'Very good. Now stop jumping around like a six year old with a new toy... you're far from out of danger. Indeed, if I'm not mistaken, now that they have no legal recourse to taking you down, we should be ever more on the lookout for hidden knives, poisoned mushrooms and perhaps the odd incendiary building.'

Caelius' face fell.

79

'I hadn't thought about that. I'm not going to be safe for a long time, am I?'

'Not while Clodia's around. It's just possible that her brother will forget about you; consider dealing with you more trouble than it's worth. After all, it was his sister that started all this, not him. But he *can* be a vengeful sack of dog vomit, that man, so I wouldn't be too sure.'

'Then what do we do?'

Fronto shrugged.

'I've had the muster order from the general. Start of next week Crispus, Galronus and I head to Ostia with him and his staff and take ship for Gaul. However, my sister has invited Priscus to stay at our house and he's got the brains, experience, money and men to keep you safe. Be very nice to him and stay close. We'll be back here as soon as either the campaigning season ends or Caesar considers the Gauls subdued, whichever happens first.'

Caelius nodded nervously, his eyes darting around the crowd as though assassins were already lurking there which, of course, they very well could be.

'It may be better for all concerned if I return to Interamna Praetutianorum. We've a large estate there, and I could stay out of the city for a while; let things die down?'

Fronto shook his head.

'You're safer here. Out in the countryside accidents could happen even easier... fewer bystanders too. In the city you have lots of witnesses. Besides, Priscus needs to keep his eye on Clodius. That man has his finger in a lot of pies and sooner or later he's going to burn it. Stay here, but keep close to Priscus and do whatever he says.'

Caelius nodded and stepped away from the moving crowd of chattering lawyers to stand with Fronto and his friends as Clodius and his sister emerged from the doorway, their faces grim. As the pair reached the top step, close to Fronto, the man stopped, his sister almost running into his back in surprise.

'Fronto? And your pack of dogs too. Where's the lame one?'

Fronto grinned wolfishly.

'Somewhere close by. Where he can see every move you and your pals make. Had a bad day?'

Clodius shrugged.

'You win some, and you lose some. In spite of what you think, this is not an overwhelmingly important matter to me. I have other, more significant things to think about.'

Fronto's grin remained in place.

'I can imagine. A few houses to burn down? Some women and kids to knife? The odd kneecap to break? That sort of thing?'

Clodius' expression flickered for a moment and settled into an ironic smile.

'Something like that, yes. On a grander scale, but yes. If you ever feel the need to abandon that declining has been that can't keep Gaul quiet, feel free to come and see me. I can always use a few good men.'

Fronto's teeth clenched, and he spoke through them in a low hiss.

'I shall continue to smile for the look of the thing, since we're in public. If we ever meet in private, however, I might have to explain to you in great detail just how little I think of you. In the meantime, since I see no sign of your pet Egyptian catamite, I have to assume that he's busy sharpening some knives, or treating some mushrooms, so I think we will take our leave and go celebrate somewhere where I can't see your dog's-arse ugly face.'

Turning his back on the rigidly-fixed smile of Clodius, Fronto grabbed Caelius and Galronus, strolling down the steps to join the small band of hired mercenaries below.

Clodius scratched his chin.

'That man interests me; fascinates me, really. He is part thug and part orator, part vagrant and part patrician, part hero and part villain. I was very seriously thinking of having both Fronto and Caelius killed tonight, but it may just be both more prudent and a great deal more fun to let him be and see how this develops.'

Clodia stared at her brother.

'You *can't* just let this end here?'

He turned and regarded her with a sneer.

'*I* cannot? What has this got to do with me other than a rather imprudent attempt to help my sex-crazed and idiotic sister take her revenge on an ex lover?'

Clodia stared for a moment and then, bringing her arm back, delivered a slap that would have stung Clodius' cheek had he not raised his own arm to block the blow. His teeth clenched, he grasped her wrist and pulled her around in front of him.

'You stupid *bitch*. I am up to my neck in plots and plans that have taken years to put in place, with some of the most powerful men in Rome playing roles, some unaware even that they are doing so. I am standing on the top of a rickety tower built of my own machinations, and I leave you to your own devices for a few months and you pull the base of the tower out from under me. I need public exposure and humiliation right now as much as I need a knife in the gut and what do you do? Launch mad accusations at a high profile young politician with powerful friends. Congratulations on making us both figures of public derision!'

He let go of her wrist and pushed her back away from him.

'But you *will* deal with him? For *me*?' Clodia's voice had almost become a whimper. Her brother turned his angry gaze on her.

'You will disappear from view. I don't want to see your face until the next time I send for you, and if I hear anything about your exploits from an outside source, I may well re-task Philopater with a new target. Do you understand?'

Clodia blinked.

'You're just going to let him *go*?'

'You've lost, Clodia, and I will expend no further money or effort to try and salvage your tattered reputation. Now get out of my sight.'

Without a parting glance at her, Clodius turned and strode purposefully off down the steps. Behind him, Crispus straightened by the column beside which he lurked and waited for the broken and dejected figure of Clodia to shuffle off across the square. The basilica had emptied, and the last of those involved had descended and disappeared in the forum. Crispus smiled to himself as he stepped out into the open and gazed off after the retreating figure of Clodius, now on the other side of the square.

'And *you* interest *me*, Clodius Pulcher. Just what plots and plans *are* you hatching?'

With a grin, he set off to catch up with the others. Priscus would certainly have something to do this summer other than babysitting, after all.

Chapter 5

(Aprilis: Approaching Vindinium in northwestern Gaul)

Fronto sighed as the mounted party crested the hill and the oppidum with its legionary camps appeared, sprawled around the low hill beside the river.

It had not been a long journey by the standards of some he had taken, but had still been more than two weeks in all. The general and his staff and senior officers, accompanied by Aulus Ingenuus and the general's praetorian guard had embarked on a small transport vessel at the navalia, the military port on the Campus Martius, and had taken a couple of hours to Ostia, where they had transferred to one of the triremes of the fleet for the two day journey to Massilia.

By the time the ship had put to sea, the miserable grey drizzle that had once more set in had grown to a full blown deluge. Fronto had looked nervously out at the crashing waves and asked tentatively whether the captain really thought the sea was safe enough, but the man had merely laughed at him and told him that they would put to port for storms, but not for a bit of rain.

Never the world's best sailor, Fronto had lurched miserably from foot to foot as the Argus bounced from wave to wave, trying to ignore the smell of the cooked pork and bread dipped in spicy sauce that the others were tucking into for lunch.

The only thing that made the miserable two days bearable for Fronto was the fact that he managed to hold onto his stomach's contents for the duration, while Galronus, who had never before stepped aboard a ship, had turned a worry grey-green colour in the first quarter of an hour and had made sounds like a dying goose for the whole journey.

Finally, blessedly, the ship put in at Massilia just as, to Fronto's intense irritation, the clouds dispersed and gave way to an unseasonably bright and warm day. The officers had led their horses up from the Argus, along the dock and up the slope, to turn and watch the ship pull back out into a freshly calm and placid open sea for its return journey.

The sixteen officers and two dozen cavalry troopers, armed against the bands of thugs and robbers known to operate in the dirty streets of this great port, and followed by the dozen carts that contained their campaigning gear, had made their way slowly from the coast up the slope toward the area of exclusive villas owned by some of the more affluent, yet discerning, Roman nobles. Few men born in the great city itself would choose such a site for a country residence, but those who valued their privacy and solitude, while maintaining close access to a major crossroads, could hardly do better.

Fronto had nodded appreciatively. He'd been promising to visit here for the last couple of years when he was off duty and free, but had never seemed to have the time. He'd not pictured himself turning up among a group of senior officers with the general himself, though. The view was quite stunning, with the villa they were here to visit sprawling over the crest of the hill, giving a massive panorama of the city below and the coast for several miles in either direction with its coves and rocks and sapphire sea.

More welcome even than the sun and the breathtaking scenery was the figure of Quintus Balbus, commander of the Eighth Legion, standing by the gate at the entrance to his villa. Balbus looked, as always, every inch the Roman legate, his cuirass polished to a mirror shine, the protective Medusa head leering out from the chest, his crimson cloak freshly cleaned and pressed, draped about his shoulders, and his plumed helmet beneath his arm. Despite the commander's advanced years, his limbs were muscular and powerful; the result of two years of strenuous exercise during the Gallic campaigns.

Behind the grinning officer, his wife Corvinia stood, a warm, if disapproving, smile aimed directly at Fronto while she held her two girls back respectfully. In the two years since Fronto had last met them, the eldest had begun her transformation to womanhood with remarkable results. Fronto sighed. Here we go again: women. Corvinia had wanted to mother him and marry him off, whereas Lucilia, the elder daughter, had clearly seen him as a prospective catch.

But much to Corvinia's disappointment, the general had no plans for a social visit, and there was barely time to exchange pleasantries before Balbus' horse was brought round by a slave, and the legate hauled himself up to join the column riding back to the legions.

The next fortnight had been a steady ride across country, up the Rhone valley, past the various small outposts set up by Cita's men to deal with the ever increasing supply train that ran from Roman territory through the lands of the Allobroges and on into deeper Gaul. They had passed the oppidum of Vienna, stopped for a happy night at Bibracte, where they had recounted the tales of the Helvetii and the happy time they had spent there two years ago, and had then followed the line of the river Loire half way toward the west coast before cutting across the land and striking northwest for the legions' winter base.

And now, as the roiling black clouds threatened yet another torrential downpour, the officers and their escort were finally within sight of Vindunum. The former town of the Andes rose on the southeast bank of the river on a bluff, with heavy walls and squat buildings of a traditional Gaulish nature. Around the town each legion, from the Seventh to the Fourteenth, had its own fortified camp, close enough to throw things between the ramparts; too close for defence, so clearly for show and to keep the legions separated.

Fronto leaned across toward Balbus and his mount sidestepped irritably as the first drops of the next shower began to patter on his face. Though he was no fan of riding in general, he had to admit he missed Bucephalus. *This* beast was disobedient to say the least and Longinus' old horse had received the best training the Roman cavalry had to offer. He jerked his mount straight, wondering whether Bucephalus would be quartered in the camp of the Tenth.

'Some of the camps are empty. That's got to be a bad sign.'

Balbus nodded.

'The question is: where are they and what are they up to? Is Crassus already having to batter the tribes into submission?'

On the other side of the older legate, Crispus turned and shrugged.

'They could simply be on manoeuvres. What concerns me is the size of the camp for the Twelfth.'

Fronto frowned and scanned the settlement. Crispus was right. Each legion had its standards up and, as the riders approached, they could see that the Twelfth was in a worryingly reduced state, occupying less than a quarter of the space of any other legion.

He cleared his throat.

'Caesar?'

The general glanced round at the three legates close behind him.

'Yes?'

'You planning a meeting of the senior officers once we're in camp, I presume?'

85

Caesar nodded and stretched in his saddle.

'Later on. Possibly even in the morning. First I need to speak to Crassus, then to visit the baths and my quarters and refresh myself. I sent my body slave and the bulk of my baggage on a few weeks early, but it will take me several hours, I fear, to drive this damp chill from my bones.'

Fronto nodded emphatically. The dismal conditions on the journey once they had left the south coast and the sunshine behind had made them all yearn for the warmth and cleanliness of a good bathhouse. His faint smile sliding into a grin, Fronto leaned closer to Balbus and lowered his voice.

'That gives us a good few hours and possibly even the whole night to change into something more comfortable, find a bar, and drink until we can't see one another.'

The general, without even turning his head, replied 'Be sober enough to attend a meeting should I call it, Marcus. I don't want you falling over in front of the new staff officers.'

Fronto glowered at the back of the general's head and winked at Balbus, who smiled benignly, like a father who has given up trying to train his wayward child and was riding the crest of a wave.

The column moved slowly on. Fronto had spent most of the journey in close company with Balbus, Crispus, Galronus and Cicero, while the various new additions to Caesar's staff kept to themselves at the rear, often retreating into Greek for their hushed conversations.

'I suggest we report in with our legions, clean ourselves up, and then head into town and find a passable watering hole. Shall we meet in the central square in... say an hour?'

Crispus sighed.

'I suspect it will take me almost an hour just to get clean and dry and rake the knots out of my hair. Can we say two?'

Fronto grumbled a grudging acknowledgement and turned back to the camps ahead. The Tenth appeared to be quartered next to the river, close to the northern walls of the oppidum, and he peered at the ordered lines of tents within the ramparts, in some way hoping to find minor fault, given the absence of both he and Priscus. Nothing appeared to be amiss at first glance, however, and Fronto rolled his shoulders before turning to his companions.

'Well I'm going to go and see what's been happening. See you all shortly.'

As the others waved their temporary farewells and the baggage cart carrying his gear veered away from the column and followed him, Fronto kicked his horse to speed and rode through the increasing rain, down past the northern edge of the oppidum's walls and to the gatehouse of the Tenth. As he approached, he was surprised and perversely pleased to note that no call went up announcing the return of the legion's commander. He prepared himself for a tirade against the guard at the gate as he slowed his beast on approach, but noted at the last moment that his new primus pilus, Servius Fabricius Carbo, stood in the centre with his chubby arms folded and a wide grin on his shiny pink face.

As he reined in the horse and dismounted, Fronto's unreasonable irritation and anger melted away. The journey, with its inclement weather, horrible waves, disobedient horses and enforced proximity to the general had contrived to plunge him into a disgruntled mood as he approached but, as he had found to his irritation last year, something about Carbo defused such moods easily.

He took a deep breath, ready to shout and the primus pilus tapped the top of his head.

'One of the great benefits of losing my hair at a frighteningly early age is that I never get soggy and waterlogged in the rain. Perhaps I can offer you something in the way of a towel and a wooden mug of something nasty enough that it eats through bronze?'

Fronto caught his deep breath, eyed the man before him, and let the air out slowly, taking the residual anger with it.

'You been taking a peek into my mind, Carbo?'

As he led his horse forward, one of the soldiers at the gate rushed out to take the reins and Carbo turned to address the other.

'Pass the call that the legate has returned.'

Fronto sighed and glanced upwards, his eyes flickering in the falling rain.

'I am piss wet through, and it feels like I've been sleeping on a bag of helmets for the last few weeks. I'm looking forward to getting my tent set up. Do you have somewhere in the meantime I can dry off?'

He stepped in through the gate and Carbo nodded, still smiling.

'I've had a tent set up for you. It's not got all your personal gear in yet, of course, but I had it stocked with food, drink, towels, sheets and blankets and four spare sets of clothes that I'm fairly sure are your size.'

87

Fronto blinked.

'You knew we were imminent?'

Carbo nodded seriously.

'Yesterday the Tenth's augur saw a pigeon and a duck flying in the same direction, with a swallow going the other way. He said you'd be back before dark and would be wet and in need of a drink.'

Fronto stared at the earnest pink face and boggled.

'He did?'

Carbo burst out laughed.

'No, of course he didn't! One of the outrider scouts saw your column two days ago and reported in. But to be honest, I had the tent stocked weeks ago, 'cause I assumed you'd be here soon.'

Fronto grinned at the man, astounded that in the years he'd commanded the Tenth, he'd never noticed this man playing second fiddle to Priscus. But then, only legates who were not doing their job properly had time to get to know every officer in the legion who did not report directly to him. Still, given how smoothly this man had slid into the role of senior command, it was perhaps time he started to pay more attention to the lesser centurions.

'Well if you can cope with hanging around while I quickly towel myself dry and change, I could do with a bit of a 'catch up', given what I've been hearing. Then I fully intend to find a bar and get merrily slammed. Two weeks of best behaviour en route with the general has me itching to get involved in a little debauchery.'

Carbo laughed.

'Your needs have been anticipated, Marcus. The cavalry commander, Varus, along with legate Brutus and the primus pilus of the Eleventh, dropped by a few hours ago and asked me to tell you where they were. I gather the senior officers have been frequenting a particular tavern in the centre where most of the rank and file go...'

He lowered his voice conspiratorially.

'I suspect that's because it's the only place they can go where they know legate Crassus won't be, since he is apparently repelled by the scent of plebeians.'

Fronto laughed.

'Sounds good; in fact it sounds like *just* my kind of place. And I expect you, as my second in command, to join me. It would be only right, after all.'

Carbo shrugged.

'You mean put off the latrine roster til later on in order to sink a few mugs of local beer? I think I can manage that, yes.'

Fronto's grin widened.

'Right. In the meantime, while I get changed, tell me everything that's happened; and I don't just mean the official version, but all the dirty and slanderous stuff and the rumours too.'

* * * * *

Fronto leaned back in the low chair, sliding his mug onto the table, looked over his shoulder at the three legionaries sharing a bawdy joke about a Syrian woman with one leg, and smiled sweetly.

'Here's a deal for you: You three piss off over the other end of the bar and stop anyone coming within earshot for the next half hour and the rest of your drinks are on me. Deal?'

The affirmative comments were almost lost among the kerfuffle and scraping as the three men greedily gathered their gear from the floor around them and shuffled off along the bar, grinning and nodding respectfully at the legate as they went.

'Good,' he announced once the officers were safely alone at the dingiest end of the bar. 'Now we can talk properly.'

He smiled at the faces gathered around the table, some of whom he had not seen in almost half a year. Varus and Brutus had a haunted look, the stress of the winter command telling plainly on their faces. Felix seemed to have weathered the shit-storm better, though the centurionate were notoriously hardy. Now, with Galba, Crispus, Rufus, Balbus, Cicero, Carbo and Sabinus, the core of what Fronto considered the professional officers were all present in one place for the same time in a long while. His thoughts briefly flashed to thoughts of Labienus, still camped out east in Belgae lands.

'Right. I expect we're all heard titbits since we arrived back in camp, but it's time we got a few things clarified.'

There was a chorus of nods and grumbling agreement around the table.

'Alright. These tribes in the area. Carbo tells me that Crassus has been less than successful in keeping them calm and under control.'

'I believe I used the words 'almighty cock up', actually' Carbo nodded.

Varus grumbled as he leaned across the table.

89

'Rather than trying to mollify them or come to terms, he seems to have abandoned any hope of getting our hostages back. Instead, he's taking whatever crops he can from them, commandeering their cattle and goods and burning down the settlements afterwards. He seems to think that eventually they'll just give up and accept it. My scouts tell me a whole different story.'

Fronto shook his head.

'Scorched earth never works. We're here to make this place part of Rome, not to turn it into an ash-strewn wasteland. What's the point in conquering a place if you've murdered the population?'

Galba nodded sadly.

'Indeed. Every legion is sending six cohorts out in two groups of three on 'loot and burn' missions. They go out for a week in some direction and if they come back without enough loot Crassus has those units given the shittiest jobs in Vindunum until their next opportunity. More than half the army is out of camp at any one time, marching around the country, taking and burning. The Twelfth have been omitted from the roster, since our veterans make up less than a cohort.'

Balbus frowned.

'Balventius tells me that you've been hogging the workshops, knocking out weapons and armour like madmen.'

Galba grinned at the older legate.

'I may have used the general's name without permission to drum up new recruits among our Gallic allies on the way back from the Alps. When they're fully trained, we'll be back up to over half strength, even if most of them are greener than the forests they came from.'

'Where are they then?' Fronto interjected, leaning forward. 'The camp of the Tenth is basically almost empty.'

Galba laughed and leaned back, taking a swig of imported wine.

'I sent them to Brutus' shipyards at Turonum on the Loire. They're alternating training with construction work, and it keeps Crassus in the dark about both our true strength and Brutus' little project.'

'How's that coming?'

Brutus leaned forward.

'We're nearly done, to be honest. The fleet's just having the final touches added. What we're missing at the moment is the crews, but I am informed they're on their way up from Narbo and should be here

90

any time. We'll be ready before Crassus has managed to recall his legions.'

Fronto laughed nastily.

'*His* legions! Things might change a little now that Caesar's back. The general may be a politician who doesn't give much thought for the locals, but he *does* have a better than elementary grasp of tactics and enough common sense to go only so far with them. Better than Crassus, anyway.'

The table fell silent, a reaction that often greeted Fronto when he began to espouse his opinions of the great Caesar, and particularly after a few beverages.

'Anyway,' Fronto went on, glancing at Varus, 'you say your scouts have told you more?'

The cavalry commander nodded unhappily.

'The tales I hear sound more like a nation gearing up for war than a beaten people trying not to starve to death. The Veneti have retreated to their fortresses on the coast which, I am informed, are almost impregnable. When the legions get to their inland settlements to impound their animals and grain, they're finding the people are already gone and have taken everything with them. They're stocking up for a siege and leaving nothing for us to take. It's starting to get to Crassus.'

'I can imagine. Are we just talking about this Veneti tribe then?'

The look on Varus face answered Fronto's question before he opened his mouth.

'There are tribes all over Armorica doing the same. But even that's not even the main worry. Some of my outriders caught a messenger riding east. He was taking a message to the Belgae, urging both them and the Germans to rise up and drive us out of Gaul. Crassus has turned the small issue this started as into a catastrophe. We could very well be looking at an uprising all over the north.'

Crispus sighed.

'This land is somewhat like a lumpy sleeping pallet.'

He looked around at the confused faces of the others and spread his hands.

'You cannot sleep comfortably, so you have to flatten out the lump, but then a lump forms somewhere else. No matter what you do, there will always be a new lump forming somewhere. And the more you play with it, trying to make it comfortable, the more lumps you have until, in the end, there is nothing else for it but to discard the pallet and begin again with a new one.'

'*That's* a depressing picture' Galba sighed.

'So' Fronto grumbled, 'we may be looking at more than just these tribes?'

Varus cleared his throat meaningfully.

'I have it on good authority that their messengers also went south to the Pyrenees and the tribes around there and into Spain, and even by boat across to Britannia. The more we hear, the more it sounds like we're about to be crushed between armies from all over the place. Who the hell knows *what* we could be facing if the Celts in Britannia cross the water.'

Balbus leaned back, his expression bleak.

'If all this is accurate then it would appear we are already beyond hope of negotiation. We are at war; we just haven't moved yet.'

Varus nodded and took another slug of wine.

'Well then, gentlemen' Fronto announced, slapping his mug on the table. 'It's no use us sitting here wishing things were different. We've got to get things moving. We should go see the general and start pushing.'

A chuckle caught his attention, and he peered across the table at Sabinus.

'You're being uncharacteristically quiet?'

Sabinus shook his head wearily.

'I have had three months of trying to argue and gainsay Crassus with the man talking down to me and over the top of me. I'm exhausted Marcus. But it's nice to have you back. Nothing stirs the army up like having you around!'

Fronto smiled.

'Then let's get stirring. Time to go see the general.'

As he stood, he turned to Carbo. The primus pilus nodded.

'I know. Head back to camp and get the men on a first alert.'

Fronto nodded.

'That and more.' He turned to Varus. 'Can you send riders out looking for the wandering cohorts and give them the recall order?'

Varus shrugged.

'I can do it; I just don't have the authority.'

'I'll take responsibility. Just get the men back here.'

As Varus nodded, he turned back to his primus pilus.

92

'When the rest of Tenth make it back to camp, stop anyone else leaving. There'll be no more of this pointless burning.'

He turned back and threw the last of the wine down his throat, wiping his mouth with the back of his hand and smearing deep red across his chin.

'Right. Let's go ruin Crassus' day.'

* * * * *

Two of Crassus' legionaries, polished and straight, stood at the closed door of the headquarters building. As Fronto and his group of officers approached, they crossed their pila over the doorway.

'Sorry sir. The legate is in a meeting with the general. No one is allowed in at the moment.'

Fronto glared at the man.

'Have you any idea just how many senior officers there are here? Get out of the way.'

The legionary had the decency to look nervous and apologetic.

'I have my orders from both the legate and the general, sir and, with respect, the general outranks all of us. If I let you past I'll be cleaning latrines until winter comes again.'

Fronto stepped uncomfortably close to the man and grinned through bared teeth, the fumes of freshly-imbibed wine washing over the man's face and making him gag.

'You know who I am and the sort of thing I get up to. Crassus might have you emptying latrines, but if you don't open that door, I will snap that pilum in half, stick the sharp bit up your arse and use you to mop the latrines. Do I make myself clear?'

The man held out defiantly, if nervously, for a moment longer until his companion buckled under the legate's glare and stepped out of the way. Suddenly alone in front of an angry officer, the legionary stepped aside and averted his gaze.

'Good choice' Fronto growled as he swung the door open and stepped inside.

The building was divided into four rooms with a central corridor that connected each of them with the front door. Most were likely given over to office space, but the room to the immediate right had its door closed, from behind which Fronto could hear muffled conversation. The irritation of the guards outside still driving him, he

93

reached for the handle and swung the door open without knocking, striding through purposefully.

Crassus, his back to the door, had apparently not noticed and continued addressing Caesar while the general looked up in surprise.

'…and we estimate that the lack of supplies will push the Veneti into submission within the month.'

'That's not what I hear' Fronto barked, the other officers filing in behind him. Caesar furrowed his brow.

'I believe I left instructions we were not to be disturbed, Fronto? I was planning to call a meeting first thing in the morning and give you time to pickle your brain in the meantime, since it seems to be your hobby.'

Crassus spluttered as he turned. Fronto grinned at him with no humour at all.

'It sounds to me like you handled the situation badly and you've all but pushed the local tribes into full rebellion.'

Crassus shook his head.

'Totally untrue. Wherever the legions go we are encountering no resistance.'

'That' Fronto snapped 'is because the tribesmen are gathering for war in their coastal fortresses while they send to Germany, Spain and Britannia for help.'

'Preposterous' Crassus spluttered.

Caesar, behind him, leaned forward in his chair.

'You have conflicting information, Fronto?'

'And from a number of trustworthy sources in your own army, general. The Veneti are all but ready to go to war, and it looks like they have incited other tribes to the northwest, the southwest, back toward Germany and even across the water in Britannia. If they haven't killed the hostages they took, it'll only be because they're holding on to them in case they need them later.'

Crassus shook his head.

'That is a stalemate. They will never execute the hostages, as I have one of their chieftains and a druid in custody myself.'

Balbus, near the door, made a grumbling noise.

'Yet you have written off any hope of getting *our* men back. You think they couldn't have done the same?'

Fronto glared at Crassus while he addressed the general.

94

'We have to move straight away, Caesar, before this shitty situation becomes a disaster and we lose our foothold in Gaul altogether. 'All Gaul is conquered', remember?'

The general stared at him for a moment and then, nodding, stood, placing his hands on the large map on the table before him.

Then we have to decide on how we move now. We have less than half the army here, the rest being out on food gathering missions.' He looked up at Brutus. 'What's the state of the fleet?'

Crassus blinked.

'Fleet? What fleet?'

Brutus ignored him and scratched his chin.

'A few days from operational, Caesar. A little rigging, some more sails, and the crews are imminent. Once the ships are ready, we can leave them to the new crews with just a skeleton staff and Galba can have the rest of the Twelfth back, preparing to move.'

Crassus turned to look in confusion at Brutus and then Galba.

'*What* rest of the Twelfth? *What* fleet? What in the name of Minerva are you talking about?'

Caesar ignored the legate and nodded.

'Very well. The fleet was a good idea. Moreover, it was *your* idea, Brutus, so I'm putting them under your command. Draw marines from the stronger legions who can spare the men, particularly the Ninth, and then head for Turonum. As soon as the ships are finished and the crews arrive, send Galba's men back to him and get the fleet underway. Take them downstream to the sea and stay there until the legions arrive. Use the intervening time to get a little training and practice in. Are you happy with all that?'

Brutus nodded, his face straight.

'I'm no experienced admiral, Caesar, but I know the basics. We'll be there and ready.'

'Good. Where is Varus?'

Fronto smiled nastily at the astonished face of legate Crassus.

'I asked him to get riders sent out to the legions with the recall order.'

Crassus opened his mouth to argue but, behind him Caesar overrode him.

'Good. When he's back, tell him to take half the cavalry and a few of the fastest moving foot auxiliary units and move across country as fast as they can to meet up with Labienus at Nemetocenna. The last report I had from Labienus a few months ago seemed to indicate that things were going exceptionally well there. He seems to be well on his way to Romanising the Belgae already and, with the cavalry reinforcements, he should be able to keep things settled and safe over there and hopefully keep the Germans on the other side of the Rhine.'

Fronto nodded approvingly. Labienus was, most certainly, the man for the job. With him watching their back, Fronto felt reasonably secure.

'So are we going to concentrate the rest of the forces on Armorica and hope the example we make keeps the Spanish and the British out of it?'

Caesar waggled his hand in a noncommittal fashion.

'Partially. There's very little we can do at the moment about Britannia. We just have to hope that either they decide against interference, or they take so long preparing that we have dealt with the situation before they can land in Gaul. Spain is a different matter.'

Fronto nodded. He had personal experience of the Celtic and Iberian tribes across the Pyrenees. They were as hardy as the Gauls but less inclined to settle and negotiate, a fact that had contributed greatly to the heavy-handed and brutal tactics Caesar had employed there years ago when Fronto had commanded the Ninth.

'We need something like the Labienus situation down there.'

'No' Caesar disagreed, shaking his head. 'This is different. What we need with the Pyrenean tribes is to frighten them into submission. They've no real experience or appreciation of Roman culture, despite being so close to Narbo. They won't be talked out of action, and we need to put a stop to them getting involved and also to seal the passes over the mountains and stop the Spanish tribes helping them.'

Sabinus, near the back of the room, frowned.

'Sounds like we're in danger of splitting the army and spreading it a little too thin for comfort, Caesar?'

The general nodded, rubbing his temple.

'We can't spare too many men, for certain.'

Sabinus cleared his throat.

'If you want me to take a legion or two and deal with it, sir?'

Caesar shook his head, examining the map by his hand.

'No. I shall be sending you, Crassus.'

The room fell silent, many faces quickly registering both surprise and disapproval. The tense quiet was broken when Crassus, finding his voice for the first time since the conversation began, turned to the general.

'Sir?'

The general glowered at him.

'You took a peaceful situation up here and turned it into a war. You are a good commander for punitive campaigns, Crassus, but to be frank, you are just too brutal in your methods to administer a freshly-conquered land.'

Fronto almost laughed aloud. To be considered 'too brutal' by the man who had ordered the execution of an entire captive tribe not long after they had first ever marched into this country said a great deal.

Crassus was nodding, though, as though the general had complimented him.

'You want their spirit and their will to resist crushed?'

The general smiled.

'I see you have the picture. Can you repeat your success of last year?'

Crassus nodded, an unpleasant smile creeping across his face.

'I shall take the Seventh and seal off the southwest completely, general.'

'Good. You will need to be highly manoeuvrable in the foothills of the Pyrenees, so I'm sending the rest of the cavalry with you.'

Crispus leaned close to Fronto and whispered in his ear 'That'll please Varus!'

Fronto nodded slightly and spoke from the corner of his mouth.

'Question is: will he go with them to Labienus where he won't have to deal with Crassus, or would he rather go south and keep his eye on his men?'

He became aware that Caesar was glaring at him.

'Sorry sir. Go on.'

The general took a deep breath and then focused on Sabinus, standing at the back of the room.

'Are you still up for a command, Sabinus?'

'Of course, general.'

'Good. I'm giving you the weaker legions, I'm afraid. Take the Twelfth, who are still busy training and reequipping, the Fourteenth who are still very green and a little... Gallic... if you get my drift, and most of the Ninth.' He scanned the room for the legates of those legions and spotted Rufus near the door.

97

'Sabinus acts with the full authority of praetor over the three legions, while you'll each maintain command of your individual legions. However, I require three cohorts of the Ninth to join the navy as marines. The Ninth had experience of naval combat near Saguntum a few years ago, so they may be useful.'

Rufus saluted, his expression neutral.

Sabinus frowned. 'What am I to do then, General?'

'You'll take the Ninth, Tenth and Fourteenth up toward the north coast. Do whatever you have to in order to keep those tribes from marching south and joining the Veneti. Keep the peace if you can; keep them subdued if not.'

Sabinus nodded.

'Good,' the general said, leaning back. 'That means the rest of you are with me. The Eighth, Tenth, Eleventh, and Thirteenth will be moving against the Veneti, backed by Brutus' fleet. I intend to put this situation in order as fast as possible. I need to be back in Rome in the autumn, and I don't want to drag this out.'

Balbus cleared his throat.

'We can move as soon as the roving cohorts return, general, but are we leaving a garrison here? We could be in danger of letting the locals rise up behind us, given how I hear they've been treated during the winter.' He cast a quick glance at Crassus, who glared back balefully at the veiled accusation.

The general rubbed his chin thoughtfully and then pinched the bridge of his nose.

'I was trying to avoid it. We can't really spare the men.'

'There is another solution...'

They turned to Crispus, who was smiling, a twinkle in his eye.

'Yes?'

'The Labienus solution? We are, after all, trying to Romanise the land and enforce the pax Romana? A little trust given goes a long way to receiving more in return.'

Caesar frowned. 'What are you suggesting?'

Crispus smiled.

'No caretaker garrison. We speak to their leaders, who have been dispossessed and moved across the river. We thank them for their help and support. We tell them that we are moving on and apologise for inconveniencing them. When we leave, we leave them some of our surplus supplies... we don't have many, but Cita has more coming in from the south. They will have their oppidum back, but we have cleaned it, strengthened it, constructed an aqueduct channel from the springs to the north, and stockpiled goods. To give it back to them might go some way to repairing our somewhat tattered reputation and make our task easier?'

Fronto laughed.

'He's quite right, Caesar. We need to stop burning bridges and build the occasional one.'

The general took another deep breath and straightened.

'Very well. You all know what to do. Let's start clearing Vindunum up and getting the troops onto a war footing. Most of you are dismissed, with the exceptions of Crassus, Sabinus and Brutus. We have further plans to hammer out, so I'll need you to stay behind.'

He looked up at Fronto as the rest began to file out.

'And when you see Varus, send him to see me.'

Fronto nodded with satisfaction. He'd been getting soft back in Rome with all that easy living. It felt good to be back in the saddle... figuratively speaking, he added mentally, rubbing his still saddlesore rump as he left the room.

* * * * *

It had taken four days for the various vexillations of legionaries to be recalled and to arrive at Vindunum, and then a full two days further to take down the defences of the various camps surrounding the oppidum and prepare to move out. The downside of having such a large army quartered in one place for so long was the extent of the roots they put down in that time and how long it took to pull them up and move on.

The almost constant drizzle of the preceding week had finally let up, brightening the atmosphere of the soldiers working in the soggy conditions to demolish ramparts and pack gear. Still, the next week had, instead, threatened the advance of yet worse weather. The winds had become so strong that taking down the tents had required every man available, and huge sheets of leather wafting away down the river valley were not an uncommon sight for a while. Then, once the horrendous winds had disappeared late yesterday, they had been replaced by Jupiter's own clouds, roiling and threatening thunder and lightning.

It was not, Fronto had to admit, an auspicious start to a campaign. He wasn't feeling uneasy about it, though, as he increasingly had with last year's foray against the Belgae, and the haruspices had found nothing untoward in the goat they disembowelled before departing. It was just the weather that put funny thoughts in one's head.

They had departed Vindunum in the battering winds and numbing cold, saying their farewells to Sabinus and Varus and their companions as the officers prepared to travel north and east to keep the peace while the bulk of the army dealt with the Veneti. Crassus had taken the Seventh and his cavalry detachment with no fond goodbyes, though Galronus, who commanded part of the cavalry, had dropped in to bid farewell to Fronto and his friends.

And then the worst part of any campaign: the travelling. The four legions, with their auxiliary support and supply train had set off southwest from Vindunum for the hundred mile journey to the mouth of the Loire. Each day the legions managed perhaps fifteen miles, given the interminable pace set by the wagons with their oxen, and yet each day it felt as though they had marched forty miles, with the constant cold and the battering of the forceful winds.

Fronto rode Bucephalus once more, at the head of the Tenth, grateful not to be traipsing through the soggy, muddy turf. The beautiful black steed was steady and calm, though clearly miserable in the unpleasant cold and windy conditions. Even Carbo, marching along behind him with his helmet hanging from his shoulder, had taken to wrapping his scarf around his hairless cranium to keep the numbing cold away.

Where had the lovely Gaulish summers of the last two years gone, Fronto wondered? It was almost as though the land itself was turning against them. But finally, early on the afternoon of the seventh day out of Vindunum, the army had crested a low rise and the Atlantic Ocean stretched out before them, the great wide mouth of the Loire feeding into it.

Likely on a hot summer's day the sight would be magnificent, the water a stunning turquoise and the coast visible for dozens of miles in either direction. With the black and grey clouds glowering above them, however, the water looked dark and forbidding and the waves began to make Fronto feel uneasy even standing on dry land and watching them.

The army had paused there for a time, watching with fascination the numerous ships of Brutus' fleet manoeuvring in the bay. It seemed to Fronto as he watched that they bobbed around barely under control, like those toy ships he and his sister had made of parchment when they were children and raced down the channel of the Aqua Appia where it surfaced near their home. He was unbelievably thankful that he was not currently on board one of them.

And then the legions had separated as they descended to the coast to make camp, likely for several days. The officers, along with the general and his praetorian cavalry, however, had ridden ahead down to the water's edge, where temporary ramparts contained the tents and support wagons of the fleet crews and their marines.

As they reined in outside the command tent in the open muster area, Fronto handed the reins of Bucephalus to one of the Marines and turned to look at his fellow officers. Each of them, once they dismounted, spent a few moments stamping their feet and bringing life back to their frozen appendages. Fronto looked up apprehensively as a deep rumble some miles away caught his attention.

'Let's get inside, general, before Neptune pisses on us.'

Caesar, weary from the journey and as cold as his men, nodded silently and strode through into the tent. Inside, several men in dark tunics with their cloaks tightly wrapped around them stood at a large central table with Brutus. Fronto almost sighed as the warmth from the four braziers that heated the tent hit him like a wall of comfort. The small hole in the roof issued smoke as though the place were on fire and the upper regions of the headquarters were invisible through the murk. And yet, down below, where the men gathered, the warmth was far more important than the smoky conditions.

As the general entered, with Fronto and Cicero at his shoulders, the others behind and Ingenuus' troopers creating a protective cordon outside the tent, the occupants turned to see who had entered and came suddenly to attention. Brutus, poring over the map, looked up and straightened wearily, saluting the general.

Caesar waved aside the pleasantries, and Fronto noted with concern the pale, haggard look of the young staff officer and the dark circles beneath his eyes that told of stress, overwork and lack of good sleep.

'The army is here and ready to set up camp' the general stated. 'I don't mean to rush you, Decimus, but I need to know the status of the fleet before I can plan our first move. We'll call a full meeting in the morning when the legions are settled, but what can you tell me quickly?'

Brutus sighed and stood back from the table, flicking one of the little model triremes onto its side.

'I'm afraid it's not good, general. We've got a lot of good sailors and some experienced officers who've taken part in naval battles and after six days of training and manoeuvres they have uniformly come to the opinion that the Veneti could trounce us in the blink of an eye.'

Caesar frowned.

'What is the problem? You have a good number of solid triremes and quinqueremes; perhaps a hundred of them, with fresh sailors and experienced officers and marines.'

Brutus nodded.

'Yes, general. But conditions out there are nothing like anything they've ever dealt with before. We're used to the Mare Nostrum. No Roman fleet has ever operated beyond the Pillars of Hercules, and we just had no idea what to expect. The Atlantic Ocean is, if you'll pardon the pun, a whole different pot of fish.'

'The sea is different?' Caesar asked dubiously.

Brutus sighed.

'The Mare Nostrum is like a still, glassy pond compared with this. We've lost one quinquereme, and two triremes in the last three days and all we've been doing is practicing. The waves and currents out there could capsize an *island* if it were small enough. We strike out forward but, despite the best efforts of the oarsmen and the captains, most of the time the ships go more sideways than forward. We keep having very unpleasant collisions. And with the weather the way it is, there's simply no way we can rely on the wind. The first attempt to unfurl the sails almost lost us a quarter of the fleet as they were thrown around the bay.'

He waved his hand dismissively at the map on the table.

'I can't see how the Veneti can manage in these conditions. Their ships must be totally different to ours. I feel like the first Roman sailor to meet the Carthaginian navy.'

Caesar frowned.

'How could they be so *different*?'

Brutus shrugged unhappily.

'Well for a start, they have to be a *lot* stronger and heavier. Out there it feels like we've been thrown into the cloaca maxima on a leaf. We've little control over the ships and only stronger construction and a lot more weight would counteract that. Then they must have a much shallower hull. I don't know whether you've seen the rocks around this coast, but there are shelves of them hidden just below the waves most of the time. We can't even get within striking distance of the coast in most places.'

To illustrate his displeasure, he leaned across the table, gathered the small models of the fleet and put them in a pile in the mouth of the Loire on the map.

'*That's* the operational ability of the fleet, general. We could use them as a bridge I suppose?'

'Are you telling me that the fleet is effectively *useless*?'

Brutus sighed again and rubbed his eyes wearily.

'Not exactly, but we are totally at the mercy of conditions beyond our control, Caesar. The weather... well frankly, the weather is shit, sir, as I'm sure you've noticed. If the wind would die down and the sun would come out, then the sea would calm and we might have a totally different situation. Once summer actually arrives, we might be able to do something, but until the weather changes, I wouldn't give a bent denarius for the chances of any ship making it as far up the coast as the next navigable harbour.'

The general grumbled and rubbed his face irritably.

'The Veneti are a people that are heavily dependent upon the sea. I need to take the legions against them and put them in their place, but my ability to do that is greatly hampered without support from your ships. I have been working on my next move based on the principle that we would have naval support.'

Brutus shook his head, exasperated.

'I know, general. I had been labouring under the same illusion, but we simply could not have prepared for this. No Roman ship has ever tried to operate in these waters, and we could not have known. All I can say is that as soon as the weather breaks, we can try again, but every time I send a ship out more than a few dozen lengths I'm putting it in danger of sinking.'

Again the general grumbled before straightening.

'Very well. We'll have to go back to relying on the legions. But I want you to stay here and keep working at this, Decimus. Practice. Try to change things. Try new ideas and nontraditional tactics. Quite

103

simply, find a way to make this work and get the fleet involved as soon as possible.'

Brutus sighed.

'It raises logistical issues too, Caesar. If we suddenly find we have a nice day and can sail, how will we know where you are?'

Fronto leaned forward.

'Signals.'

'Sorry?'

The legate looked at the general and shrugged.

'The Veneti have retreated to their coastal fortresses, right? So that means the army is only going to be operating close to the coast anyway. We have no reason to go inland. So we set up a number of small scout units that stay on the cliffs and beaches near the army who can signal the fleet if Brutus arrives. They can pass messages back and forth and, well let's face it, we're going to need scouts on the coast keeping an eye on any moves the Veneti make at sea anyway.'

Caesar nodded, still clearly unsatisfied by the situation.

'I suppose that's workable. Brutus? Keep working here and get this fleet operational. As soon as you can move, travel up the coast and watch for the signals.'

Brutus nodded, and Fronto smiled at him.

'And for the love of Fortuna, get some sleep. You're exhausted.'

Brutus smiled a weak smile back at him and gave a half-hearted nod.

'Well, Caesar' Fronto said, straightening, 'it looks like the legions are going to have to march on the Veneti. Perhaps we should call a meeting of the legates, tribunes and senior centurions. And we need to get some scouts out there to locate the fortresses and check the terrain and situation for us.'

Caesar nodded and turned back to the door.

'Cicero? Gather the officers and prepare a meeting. Send me a message when they're ready. We'll meet in the command tent once it's up.'

As the staff officer nodded and turned to leave, Caesar turned to Fronto.

'Marcus, I am tired and somewhat peeved, and I may need someone to vent at. Come with me.'

Fronto nodded, rolling his eyes as the general turned away, making a silent motion to the praetorian trooper at the door, suggesting that the delivery of an amphora of wine to Caesar's tent in the immediate future might be a good career move.

As they left the tent, Jupiter and Neptune met with a resounding crash, and the downpour began in earnest.

Chapter 6

(Maius: The Veneti fortress of Corsicum on the west coast of Gaul)

Tetricus shook his head.

'It's a joke. He can't be serious?'

Fronto nodded glumly.

'He's very serious. This whole situation has him wound tighter than a ballista. I honestly think that at this point he'd sacrifice a legion to get his hands on Corsicum.'

The tribune and artillery engineer continued to shake his head in disbelief. Just as they'd expected since they left Brutus and his fleet wallowing in both waves and misery, traipsing through the torrential rain and accompanied by regular storms, every settlement they reached had been abandoned and anything of use or value had been stripped and taken away. They had wandered a few miles inland, examining the situation, but had returned to the coast the next day and finally located, only ten miles or so from Brutus' anchorage, the first major stronghold of the tribe.

He just could not stop shaking his head.

The fortress of Corsicum stood on a huge rock that jutted out into the sea, like a lesser copy of one of the Pillars of Hercules. The only land approach was a causeway perhaps two hundred and fifty paces wide that stood almost at sea level and was swampy and treacherous. Above the approach loomed the heavy walls of the stronghold, the towers topped with Gauls watching intently as the might of Rome began an orderly descent of the opposite slope toward the causeway.

Fronto had tried to argue Caesar out of launching a full attack, given the obviously strong defensive capability of the Veneti. He had no doubt, given the mettle of the men in the four legions that accompanied them, that they would *take* the fortress at the end of the day, but the casualties could be appalling.

Tetricus swung his gaze out past the high cliffs of Corsicum to the roiling sea beyond, trying to think of a solution. The rocks out there formed a platform just beneath the waves that would make it impossible for the fleet to approach, even were they here.

He ran his hands through his hair, brushing the excess water from his head.

'At the very least we could have pounded the walls first?'
Fronto grumbled next to him.

'We've got limited time to get across that causeway before the tide cuts the place off. Caesar's determined to take the fortress without having to camp and perform a protracted siege. I have to admit the idea of sitting here in the pouring rain for days battering at the place is not entirely appealing, but I don't think throwing men away is a valid solution.'

The young engineer sighed and shivered in the cold, wet air, pulling his cloak around him and totally failing to produce any extra warmth. He turned to look at his handiwork. On the promontory facing the fortress, a 'dolmen', as the locals called it, had been dismantled by the engineers. They had been dubious about doing so, through some strange Gallic superstitions, but the site was just too useful to leave for the dead of millennia past, and the stones had been taken down and rearranged to form a perfect artillery platform where, even now, the engineers were beginning to set up their machines. Caesar had not given the order, but Tetricus had consulted Fronto and they had decided that the time would come when it was needed.

'In about a half hour the artillery will be ready to start firing' Tetricus said, flatly.

'In about a half hour the ground down there will be thick with dead Romans.'

The pair stood glumly watching as the ranks of marching soldiers reached the bottom of the slope and began to trudge their way through the marshy ground toward the well-defended Veneti fortress ahead.

'This is going to be a massacre. I can't believe the general ordered it.' Tetricus turned back to Fronto. 'And I can't believe that you agreed to put the Tenth in the front line of the attack. Wouldn't it have been fairer to march the legions in columns, so that the front line is evenly distributed?'

Fronto turned his head slightly and winked.

'Thinking ahead, that's all.'

'What?' Tetricus frowned.

'When it all goes to shit and the legions are stopped, someone is going to have to call for the army to fall back. The order won't come from command, since Caesar's adamant, but there are a dozen or more veteran centurions down there who'll decide it's too much of a waste and will put their own head on the block to save the men.'

107

Tetricus nodded slowly.

'And you want that to be the Tenth?'

'Carbo knows what he's doing, and I can argue Caesar into letting it slide, given the absurdity of the whole thing. I'd rather that came down to me than some other poor sod who's not expecting it.'

Tetricus nodded as he watched the legions sloshing along the approach.

Down below, Servius Fabricius Carbo glanced left and right at the advancing ranks of the Tenth. From perhaps fifty paces behind him he heard his optio yelling in a parade ground voice:

'Get your arse back into that line, Falco, or I will stick my foot so far up it you can taste the boot!'

Carbo smiled to himself. For the first month or so since he'd taken over as primus pilus, the optio had treated him with care, as though he had to protect this new commander from his own men. Time, however, had brought him the respect of the first century and the optio had fallen back into his accustomed role, making the life of his men troublesome wherever needed.

Turning back to look ahead, he sized up the approach.

'Prepare to receive missiles. Shields ready.'

Two of the men close by shared a nervous glance and Carbo smiled at them.

'They're not Apollo with his bow, lads; they're just a few dozen hairy misfits with rocks. Don't let 'em get to you.'

But the truth was entirely different, and Carbo knew it. The Veneti up there on the walls would have slings, spears, probably bows and maybe even fire arrows, since he was sure he'd seen smoke being suppressed by the incessant rain. The next few moments were going to be a march into sheer hell, and their only hope was to keep themselves as covered as possible and pray fervently. At least, until *he'd* had enough, anyway.

'Incoming! Raise shields.'

Next to him, one of the soldiers frowned.

'I don't see anything, sir?'

'Get your shield up.'

As the soldier lifted his shield into the most protective position, covering most of his front, his eyes peering over the top, a sling shot rapped on the wood and leather and fell to the floor in front of him.

And then, suddenly, hell broke loose.

The Veneti launched everything they had as individuals rather than in ordered units, and sling stones, lead bullets, arrows, rocks and spears fell from the walls in a hail. Carbo gritted his teeth, listening to the shouts and shrieks of the men who were too slow, too unprotected, or just too plain unlucky, and were felled by the onslaught.

The ground began to slope upward as they battled on against the constant hail of missiles, men toppling out of the line, only to be replaced by the soldier from the rank behind. Despite the change of terrain and the difficulty of maintaining a solid line while marching up a slope, Carbo still welcomed the end of the wet, sloshy ground below as his boots finally found dry land.

There was a deep and loud groan from above and the primus pilus frowned for a moment, cocking his head to one side and listening intently. A clunk and another groan.

'First Cohort: Form two columns on the flanks!'

Without comment or question, nearly a thousand men forming the advancing ranks of the legions split into two groups, angling away from each other, so that the single line of two hundred men became two columns, each with a front line of fifty, a wide gap opening in the centre. Carbo just had to hope that the other cohorts and legions had realised what was up.

Just as the trap was sprung, Carbo glanced back to note with satisfaction that the other senior centurions had followed suit and that the front ranks of the Eighth behind then were copying the manoeuvre.

A cry of angry disappointment rose from the walls above as a huge tree trunk rolled through the now-open gate in the walls and hurtled down the slope toward the attackers, neatly descending into the gap between the two advancing columns and rolling inoffensively to a halt in the marshy ground below without having touched a single man.

Carbo nodded in satisfaction. If they had oiled the hinges on those gates, that could have been so much worse. In his early days with the military, he'd acquired the nickname 'the augur' due to his innate sense of self preservation and his uncanny knack of being prepared just ahead of any unexpected event. Carbo himself knew that it came entirely down to using the senses the Gods had gifted him with, combined with experience and a sprinkling of common sense.

And common sense and acute hearing had just saved the First Cohort. Above, the gates were shut once more, hurriedly, and the missile shots increased, accompanied by savage cries.

'Single line... lock shields!'

In a perfect reverse of their earlier manoeuvre, the Tenth Legion closed ranks once more, though the formation would be no help in taking those walls in the circumstances. The time was almost upon them, now.

As the legion trudged slowly up the slope, men occasionally falling out of the line with a squawk, Carbo narrowed his eyes and cast his gaze across the ranks of men. There were very few places in the cohort where the line was five men thick, and as often as not it had thinned to three rather than four. He'd lost a fifth of his men already, and they were still two hundred paces from the walls up an ever increasing gradient. The First Cohort would be gone before a Roman hand touched the wall.

'Pass the word back. Sound the retreat! Orderly, mind you...'

The signifer, Petrosidius, three men along from him, grinned and waved the standard as somewhere back by the optio the buccina called out the retreat order. Carbo could almost feel the relief, not just from the men around him, but also from the legions following them up, who took up and relayed the call with telling speed.

The First Cohort slowed to a halt, their shields still up against the battering missiles falling on them from above, and began carefully to step back down the slope, maintaining the forward defensive wall.

'We're going to get bollocked, sir.'

Carbo smiled at the man who had spoken.

'I don't think you need worry, lad. The legate'll look after us.'

Fronto, high on the promontory above, watched and nodded with satisfaction. Shame they'd had to waste so many damn men before retreating, but at least they could show Caesar how stupid the idea was. Tetricus laughed.

'You were right, Marcus.'

'I know. I'm going to see Caesar. You get that artillery up and running. As soon as I've talked some sense into the old man, I'll get the other legions' engineers up to join in.'

Tetricus nodded and jogged off toward the makeshift artillery platform while Fronto turned and set his sights on the hastily-erected headquarters tent that held a commanding view of the enemy stronghold. The general emerged from the tent as he watched, waving his arms angrily at three of the staff officers that lurked outside in the torrential rain.

The hawk-nosed general was still laying into the innocent officers a short while later as Fronto approached, and one of the men meekly raised his finger and pointed at Fronto. Caesar turned to him, his face red and angry, his eye flickering dangerously.

'I want the man who ordered that call to be stripped naked and flung down onto the rocks, and the musician who made it will follow him.'

Fronto shook his head.

'No you don't.'

'*What*?' The eye flickered faster.

'With respect, Caesar, those two men just saved you thousands of men. Remember last year? Plancus marching on the walls of Noviodunum? Throwing men away like mad until you relented and let us do it properly? Don't turn into a Plancus, general.'

'I...'

The flickering in his eye stopped, and the general's face took on a strange and almost frightened look.

'Fronto... the tent...'

The legate frowned and stepped forward, grabbing the general's arm, just as his legs started to give way. The officers stared at them.

'Don't read anything into it, lads. He's exhausted.'

Without sparing them another glance, he steered the general toward the command tent and entered without ceremony. The tent was empty other than a table and seat.

'What's happened?'

The general was starting to shake slightly, his brow pallid and sweaty.

'I'm fine... Fronto.'

He leaned over the table, his face hidden in the darkness.

'Just... exhausted, like you said.'

Fronto narrowed his eyes.

'You're *ill*.'

'No. I'm fine... Get out. You deal with it how... however you feel.'

Fronto's frown deepened as he watched Caesar slump slightly.

'Get *out*!'

111

With a shrug, Fronto turned his back on the general and strode from the tent. The old man had looked like death was closing in on him, and the expression on his face had only added to the impression. The legate had this nagging feeling that he would deal with the retreat and go back in only to find the great Caesar dead on the floor in a pool of his own bile.

Perhaps the world would breathe a sigh of relief if that happened.

Fronto gritted his teeth as he emerged into the rain and looked at the three officers, their faces full of concern.

'As soon as the legions are back, send the officers to me and have the engineers report to Tetricus.'

One of the officers opened his mouth to object to this clear command from a man who was, in theory, at *most* a peer, if not a lesser officer, but his throat dried up as he saw Fronto's face.

'At once, legate.'

* * * * *

'Caesar?'

'Fronto? Come in.'

The legate shrugged, casting a quick look around at the view outside the tent. The rain had died down to an intermittent drizzle that was almost worse than the downpour, but the change had made the work of the engineers easier and visibility was greatly improved. Straightening his shoulders, he ducked into the tent, allowing the flap to fall back behind him.

The general sat at his table in the cavernous, largely empty tent, a studious look on his face; no sign of his recent indisposition showing.

'I'd offer you a seat, Fronto, but I only have the one, for now. I'm rather hoping not to have to unpack. What is the news?'

The legate shook his head.

'Oh no. I'll give you a full report in a moment, but first I want you to level with me. There's something wrong, and I don't want to come in to report one morning to find you draped over your table bleeding out. I wouldn't know how to proceed.'

Caesar gave a knowing smile.

'I rather think you know *exactly* how you'd proceed. In fact, I'll be most surprised if you haven't already planned for the eventuality. But no... I'm in no danger of dropping dead.'

112

'Then what's wrong?'

Caesar fixed him with a searching glare and sagged in the chair.

'Just an illness, Fronto. I caught something in Illyricum that's taking a little more shaking off than normal.'

'With respect, Caesar, that's a pile of crap. I've known you a long time, and I've never seen you do that. You were in the middle of building up a real argument with me, and I know how much we both enjoy *that*... and then you petered out and almost collapsed. Whatever this is, it's big enough that you're trying to hide it, even from those closest to you.'

The general glared at him.

'This subject is not open for discussion, Marcus. Leave it be.'

Fronto gave a vicious grin.

'Well we were headed for an argument about the attack, so let's just have an argument about this instead.'

He ignored the warning glance again.

'Whatever it is, we're in wet, boring, north west Gaul, a long way from the jackals in the senate that are always sniffing around you for a weakness. Out here it's just you and your army. You need to be straight with me, 'cause it worries me. I've not seen you...'

The legate paused and frowned thoughtfully.

'But that's not true, is it? I *have* seen you like that before.'

The general still had not spoken, and Fronto nodded as his thoughts stretched back.

'Vesontio last year... before we moved against the Belgae. You virtually pushed me away and disappeared on your own, complaining about the smell or something. That was the same thing, wasn't it?'

'Fronto, you might sometimes be too bright for your own good. How can you have recall like that when you pickle your brain so often?'

Fronto brushed the comment aside, frowning.

'It's a preservative. Come on... you've got to trust me. I know something's up, and you'd be better off giving me the truth than letting me speculate.'

Caesar sighed and sagged again.

'I *do* have an affliction that strikes from time to time. It's not lethal; just inconvenient and I would rather like to keep it from the rest of the men. You and I know that it's men, not strange forces, that control the future of the world, but there are a lot of intelligent men out there who cling to ridiculous superstitions, let alone the average soldier.'

Fronto nodded.

'They could see it as some sort of curse?'

'Exactly. A mark of divine disfavour or some such.

'How many people know about this?'

Caesar shrugged.

'My body slave, some select few of my family… and a merchant in the forum holitorium who will die a very wealthy man so long as he keeps his mouth shut.'

The general smiled.

'But since *you* now know, I may need your help from time to time in keeping this quiet.'

'Does it happen often?'

Caesar frowned.

'Rarely more than a couple of times a year, really.'

Fronto sighed and leaned against the leather of the tent wall.

'So what is it? Give me the details and I'll know what to do the next time that happens, rather than making feeble excuses to the men and leaving you on your own in the tent to ride it through.'

The general nodded quietly.

'I'm not entirely sure, Marcus. It only started a couple of years ago, about the time we first left for Gaul. I've discounted the possibility of a connection; men like you and I look at plain fact, rather than superstition, as I said.'

Fronto pursed his lips.

'And you've not seen a physician?'

Caesar smiled.

'In fact I have seen several, Marcus. One of the main reasons for my wintering in Illyricum this year was to be safely away from Rome for a while, somewhere where I could investigate this without my enemies getting wind. Illyricum is home to a number of physicians who follow the Greek medical traditions; very smart men. Unfortunately, just like their democracies, the medical profession are plagued by differing opinions and the inability to reach a unified conclusion.'

'And?' Fronto prompted.

'The most common theory is that I have what they call the 'falling sickness'. That's the worst case, I suspect, since the stigma it carries means that revealing it could be political suicide. But even if that is the case, it needn't be a real problem. I've heard it said, after all, that Alexander of Macedon had the same problem, and he built a vast empire.'

'And died very young if I remember rightly' Fronto added flatly.

'Something from which, I fear, I am quite safe.'

Fronto sighed.

'There are other possibilities?'

Caesar nodded. 'I will not speculate, Marcus. Whatever it is, it appears to be periodically debilitating rather than life threatening. But if you see me starting to get hazy and confused, or if I appear to be hearing or seeing things that aren't there, find an excuse and get me somewhere private urgently.'

'Then what?' Fronto asked with genuine concern.

'I may lose consciousness. I may shake and spasm for a while. The symptoms, I understand, are quite varied and interesting...' the general smiled '...though I am never in the right frame of mind at the time to record what it is that's happening. It might be very useful the next time it happens if you could note the progression, so that I can approach the physicians with the details the next time I return to Salona.'

Fronto nodded seriously.

'Somehow it doesn't surprise me that you share traits with Alexander. Alright, general. I'll keep this quiet and my eyes open. In the meantime, we need to deal with the current situation. I realise that I overstepped my bounds by allowing the Tenth to call the retreat but, as I'm sure you're aware, I've always considered it more important to do what you *needed* done than what you *wanted* done.'

Caesar shook his head slowly.

'You were, of course, quite correct, and I would normally recognise that myself. You've known me since my earlier commands, Fronto. You know I'm not the sort of man to throw troops away on foolish errands.'

Fronto nodded. 'That's what took everyone by surprise, sir. Is it the illness?'

Caesar shook his head sadly.

'Nothing to blame this on but lack of adequate thought. The past few months have been extremely draining and aggravating, Marcus. Those in Rome who have influence are beginning to array themselves against me; the senate and even the people, who have ever been my greatest advocates, are beginning to question my actions, since Gaul will not accept the eagle; the elder Crassus seems to be genuinely affectionate toward me while his son undermines everything I do here; Pompey keeps placing minor obstacles in my way and even Cicero is starting to speak out against me. Everything feels like it is pressing on me and I'm on the verge of snapping under it all.'

Fronto smiled sympathetically. He could understand the weight of politics. It was a contributory factor to his own avoidance of it.

'You need the campaign over as fast as possible. We all know that, general, but cutting corners will only cause you trouble in the end. Let the legions do their jobs properly, and we'll have this over in no time.'

'I hope you're right, Marcus. I really do. Alright, then; let's have the update.'

Fronto stepped away from the tent wall and stood before the table.

'Alright. Well I've sorted things outside. We lost maybe four hundred men, but it could have been a lot worse. I'm allowing tents to be set up, but nothing else. No fortifications or suchlike. We don't want to get involved in a protracted siege, as you said, but the men need to keep dry when they're off duty, or the whole army's going to come down with something.'

'You still expect to be able to resolve this quickly, then?'

Fronto shrugged.

'A lot of that depends on factors outside our control, Caesar, but we hope so. Tetricus has the artillery of four legions finding their range right now. If you listen hard, you can hear them.'

'I thought that was just my head' the general said with a small laugh.

'Tetricus reckons that he can topple those towers and flatten that gate in about half a day with the full weight of the artillery. And there's free stone knocking around here for ammunition, so that's no worry.'

The general nodded.

'So by the next low tide, we might be able to manage?'

Fronto nodded.

'I'd have hated to be down there when the tide came in. It's not like standing on the beach at Antium and watching the line slowly licking toward you. With the storms and the choppy sea, the tide came in here in about quarter of an hour. It was like watching a dam burst.'

Caesar nodded wearily.

'We might need to repair the morale damage of that first attack. Perhaps if I march with the men? Always boosts morale when the officers take a risk.'

Fronto nodded.

'And you'll also be pleased to hear that our scouts have reported sighting Brutus' fleet a few miles away. Looks like he's taken advantage of the lull and come out to meet us.'

'Very good. That could give us an edge.'

'Perhaps'. Fronto looked less certain.

The general sighed.

* * * * *

Fronto strode up the slope at the head of the army in the gentle drizzle. The Tenth, having led the first, abortive attack, had been given the honour of being the first legion through the breach. The walls had crumbled swiftly under Tetricus' constant deadly barrage, and the Gauls lining it had fled after the first few shots found their range. Despite the stone, timber and packed earth of the ramparts, the artillery of four legions made swift work of them, reducing the gate to rubble and toppling the towers more than an hour before the tide had receded enough to allow troops to cross the causeway.

As soon as the water level dropped, the general gave the order and the legions marched before even the artillery had ceased. The general, resplendent in his red cloak and gleaming cuirass, joined the vanguard as they crossed the gap and began to climb the incline toward the shattered walls.

The broken defences reached toward the boiling clouds like stumps of sawn trees, small sections of wall at full height, interspersed with rubble, spreading down the hill. As the legion approached the walls, Fronto glanced across in the other direction to Carbo, marching strong at the head of the Tenth. The man was already looking at him and, as the two men's eyes met, Carbo nodded, sharing an unspoken thought, and addressed the legion in a steady voice.

'Be prepared, now, lads. Anything could await us up here.'

117

Fronto nodded quietly to himself, imagining the traps the Veneti could have set up behind the broken walls. It had been many hours now since the last figure had dared climb the walls to look at the attackers, and the quiet was eerie. He hefted his sword.

'Secure the walls' Carbo barked as they crossed the rubble, slowing their pace accordingly. Two centurions began shouting out orders, and a century peeled off the column in either direction as they reached the line of the defences, rounding the shattered wall carefully, not knowing what to expect. Fronto and Caesar continued alongside Carbo and the front line of the First Cohort and passed between the remains of the gate and into the fortress of the Veneti. As the two centuries rushed along the line and into position, checking the defences for any traps or lurking Gauls, the bulk of the army marched on up the slope and into the centre of the large headland stronghold.

This was far from the usual Gaulish oppidum or settlement with which Fronto was familiar. Rather than the unplanned, rambling streets of a Gaulish town, with trees rising from the roadside for summer shade and gardens in front of each house, this was a utilitarian arrangement, designed purely to protect a people from harm. There was no subtlety or joy in the layout, with squat, dark buildings for shelter all gathered close around a square at the highest point, with bare, windowless facades facing the outside, one end of the central square given over to granaries and storehouses.

'So where the hell are they?' Fronto asked no one in particular as they crested the hill and approached the silent, strangely deserted-looking buildings.

The general, beside him, bore a puzzled frown.

'Perhaps they hide within?'

Fronto shook his head.

'I don't think so, general. These people aren't the sort to cower without even trying to fight. But the question does remain: where are they?'

Again, Carbo barked out orders to his men and two centuries split off the main group as they approached the square and began to check out the buildings surrounding it. Behind the Tenth, the Eighth crested the hill, Balbus leading his men fast to catch up with the front line. Farther back, Crispus had split the Eleventh and sent them in two groups around the lower edges of the headland, above the cliffs, to meet up at the far end. The Fourteenth had played rearguard, remaining with the artillery for their protection.

Fronto and the general watched with growing unease as the legionaries of the First Cohort entered and exited the buildings, shrugging, nonplussed at the strangely deserted fortress.

'Is it possible that we were mistaken?' Caesar frowned. 'That this is not a principal fortress, and there were only a few dozen men here on the walls after all and they're hiding somewhere. A distraction? A decoy?'

Again Fronto shook his head.

'No. This is a major fortress, and if you look at the mud here you can see hundreds of tracks. The ground's been churned up recently by a *lot* of people. They've got to be here somewhere. Perhaps there's something down near the cliffs? A cave system or something? I've heard tell that they do that in the east; occupy cave systems. If so, Crispus' men will find them soon enough.'

They suddenly became aware of shouting. Squinting into the fine mist of rain, Fronto spotted an optio waving from the edge of the grassy slope ahead, toward the sea; one of Crispus' men from the Eleventh. The man waved both arms above his head and then pointed out to sea. Fronto felt his heart sink. Somehow, he knew what had happened. Gesturing at Carbo, he beckoned the general and the three men strode speedily between the storehouses and across the grassy headland toward the man.

They saw it before they caught up with the optio, as soon as they reached the area where the ground began to fall away down toward the cliffs. Ships. Dozens of dark, heavy ships, their huge rectangular sails unfurling as they watched, were making their way out toward the open sea, hundreds of jeering Gauls lining the rails and gesturing up at the Romans in the empty fortress.

Caesar, next to Fronto, stopped in his tracks, grinding his teeth in angry frustration.

'No.'

Fronto looked across at him.

'Brutus and the fleet can get them. Look… the triremes are already moving.'

The three men watched intently as other officers joined them at their vantage point. Behind them, three legions spread out across the stronghold, searching every inch.

Fronto found that he, too, had his teeth clenched as he watched the sea below. Despite the fact that the storm had died to a gentle drizzle, the sea still rose and fell dangerously, huge waves crashing against the rocks where they breached the surface. The Veneti galleys were moving slowly as yet, a mere hundred paces from the cliffs, their sails only just beginning to catch the wind, whereas Brutus' ships, powered by banks of oars, were already tearing at high speed toward them.

'They can't get away' Fronto noted as he watched. 'There's not enough time.'

Caesar nodded as he continued to peer down into the roiling waves in intent silence. Beside them, Carbo made a strange rumbling noise. Fronto turned, frowning, to look at his primus pilus. The man was shaking his head.

'What's up?'

Carbo unstrapped his helmet and, removing it, mopped his brow.

'It's not going to work. If the commander doesn't pull his fleet back, they're in trouble.'

'What?'

But instead of explaining, Carbo merely pointed to the lead trireme as it put on an extra burst of speed, bearing down on the escaping Veneti fleet. Fronto turned back to it and peered down.

'I don't see...'

He fell silent as he watched the trireme meet the submerged rock shelf that surrounded the headland. There was a series of cracks and crunches as the oars hit rocks and shattered, followed by an almighty bang as the hull connected with the undulating shelf beneath the jagged pinnacles.

He watched in horror as the trireme foundered on the rocks, water rushing in through the broken hull. The crew panicked and began to abandon the ship, some diving blindly onto the rocks. Behind them, the rest of the fleet veered away sharply.

Fronto stared. 'How is that possible?'

Carbo shrugged.

'It's all about draft, sir. The hulls of the triremes are too deep beneath the surface to cross these rocks, and the oars are no use there.'

'But how do the Veneti do it then?'

'Their ships must be designed differently. A lower draft so that their ships can cross the rocks in safety. And if you look, sir, they've a much wider beam too.'

'Beam?' Fronto began to feel as though he was being toyed with.

'Yes sir. The beam is the width of the ship. Ours are deeper underwater and narrower in the beam. Theirs have a shallow draft, which allows them to approach the coast easily, but that would make them less stable at sea, so they've counteracted that with a wide beam so that they remain the right way up even in strong waves. Quite clever really. They've adapted their shipbuilding style to the conditions they live in.'

As they watched, the Veneti fleet was already leaving the rocky area beyond the cliffs and making for open sea, their sails billowing.

'It's not over yet' Caesar noted, watching as the Roman fleet, now carefully avoiding the rocks, began to head out to sea.

Again, Carbo shook his head sadly.

'They're actually moving faster than our ships at the moment. Once they get out into those heavy waves our triremes will be in extreme danger. They'll capsize and break up in those conditions. If commander Brutus doesn't turn them back before they're half a mile out, we'll lose the fleet.'

Fronto frowned at his senior centurion.

'You seem to know a lot about this?'

'I wasn't always a soldier, sir. I grew up in Ancona. My dad was a shipbuilder, sir.'

Fronto raised his eyebrow. This man never failed to surprise him.

'What's the answer then, Carbo? How do we stop them?'

The primus pilus sighed, his shoulders drooping.

'I'm not entirely sure that we can, sir. Catching them's possible, but it's a matter of surprising them and trapping them in a harbour with deep enough water that we can get our own ships to them, while they can't escape past us.'

Fronto nodded and suddenly became aware that the general was at his shoulder, paying close attention.

'Go on, centurion' the general said. 'You say we could catch them, but that is not enough?'

Carbo scratched his head. 'I'm not sure, sir. The thing is, even from this far away you can see the difference in size and construction of the ships. Their hulls are much higher and thicker than ours; they have to be to withstand the conditions of the sea here.'

121

'So?' Fronto prodded.

'Well sir... if their ships are, say, six feet higher at deck level than ours how would we get a boarding ramp across to them? There's no realistic way of doing it, which renders boarding impossible. That, in turn, means the marines are useless and can't get aboard the enemy.'

'Then we sink them and pick them out of the water.'

Again, Carbo shook his head.

'Solid oak. Very thick hull. I doubt our rams would go through it. If one of our fleet hit their ships at ramming speed, I would give even chances that it would be our trireme that sank and not them.'

Caesar's teeth began to grind again.

'Are you suggesting that the fleet is unlikely to catch the enemy and effectively powerless to deal with them even if they did?'

Carbo nodded.

'Unless the commander can come up with something that helps turn the odds his way.'

The three men raised their eyes to the distance once more. The Veneti fleet were already out among the choppy waves, and Brutus' fleet, having begun to buck and roll with the sea, had slowed their pursuit.

Caesar turned his angry gaze to Fronto.

'Get the legions back to the mainland, dismantle the artillery and, when Brutus puts in an appearance, tell him to get out there and track them. I don't care how he does it, but I want to know where that Veneti fleet goes, so that when they land we can deal with them properly.'

Fronto nodded and turned to Carbo.

'You heard the general. Get the Tenth on the move.'

'Yessir.'

Fronto gazed out once more at the distant, retreating sails of the Veneti. He had engaged defiant people before who had fought until the last man stood, and had dealt with tribes who had surrendered in order to preserve their culture. He'd never dealt with a tribe that refused to engage them and simply slipped out of the back door when the might of Rome came knocking. This was going to be problematical.

Chapter 7

(Maius: Off the coast of Gaul some five miles north of Corsicum)

Brutus pinched the bridge of his nose as the trierarch's fierce gaze bored into him.

'Just do it.'

'As you say, commander.'

The ship's captain turned his piercing blue eyes away from the staff officer back to his second on deck, periodically calling out the timing for the oarsmen.

'Signal the fleet to move into bull horns formation and as soon as the ships are in position, give me attack speed.'

'Aye, sir'

The trierarch turned back to Brutus and glared. The young officer had chosen the *Aurora* as his flagship solely because it had been the first trireme to be completed and the first he had sailed on. He was beginning to regret choosing one with such a headstrong and outspoken captain and, while he knew that he had the authority to shut the man up, remove him from command, or even have him disciplined, he had not the heart, since he knew with every ounce of his being that the man was absolutely right.

'You are aware, commander, that this is inviting disaster?'

Brutus nodded unhappily.

'Sadly, captain, I have my orders and therefore so do you. Whatever else we do and whatever the result, we have to try.'

The comment did nothing to lift the disapproval from the man's gaze as the other ships in the fleet pulled into a flattened crescent shape some three or four vessels deep.

'Execute the plan.'

Brutus took a deep breath. It was a long shot, for certain. In fact, it was several long shots and made him nervous just thinking about it, particularly given that it was a plan of his own devising. Still, none of the experienced naval officers could come up with a better solution.

The 'horns' of the bull on the outer points of the crescents were formed of the quinqueremes, the heaviest warships in the fleet. Their initial task was to sweep in as pincers and to take the edge of the

123

Veneti fleet, effectively sealing them in and, hopefully, given their size and weight, to sink a few with the rams. While this happened, the rest of the fleet would close, the rear lines spreading out to encircle the enemy.

Brutus found that he was uttering a silent prayer to Juno, the family's patron deity. The Veneti fleet, almost twice as many vessels as his own, drifted along at a gentle speed as though they had not a care in the world, and it was both frustrating and worrying. The Veneti were clearly a clever and resourceful people and to let Brutus' fleet descend on them was extremely out of character. Was it a trap somehow? He could not see how. They were too far from the headlands for the Veneti to have hidden surprises, while trying to stay close enough to land to avoid the worst of the seas, even in this soggy lull in the weather.

It was foolish and worrying.

During his last meeting with Caesar, which had not gone well, he'd managed to argue himself into a corner. When Fronto had passed on his orders to track the Veneti, he'd been to see the general to point out that the job could be done just as effectively by scouts on the cliffs without endangering the ships. Caesar had rounded on him angrily, asking what use the ships *were* then, and by the time he'd left the tent, his new orders were to launch an attack.

The fleet closed on the Veneti, and he swallowed nervously. If they could get the Veneti pinned they might stand a chance, the crews had spent the previous evening constructing platforms at the prow in order to raise the height of the 'corvus' boarding bridge and therefore overcome the difference in deck height. It looked uncomfortably precarious to Brutus, but no other solution had leapt to mind.

Glancing to left and right from his commanding position, he watched the horns of the bull closing on the Veneti and something caught his attention. The enemy fleet had thinned out at the periphery. In fact, as he scanned the Gaulish mass, the entire fleet had thinned. A huge proportion of the fleet of ships had begun to break away, altering their huge leather sails to fill with the billowing wind and picking up speed, heading for the coast.

Even as he watched, more and more clumps of vessels began to pick up speed and move away. It was like watching patches of ice breaking away in a fast stream, and the truly irritating thing was that, despite the Roman ships moving at attack speed, the Veneti vessels were fleeing the scene even faster.

He frowned.

Why, then, had they clearly left a few of their fleet at the mercy of the Romans. As more and more of the enemy broke away, it became obvious that they had left six... no... eight ships with their sails sagging, waiting to be overcome. What strange trap was this? Could the vessels be about to be fired? Disease ridden by design? Something was wrong.

He was about to begin shouting, giving the order to call off the attack, when he realised that there were still Veneti standing at the rails of the ships. Why would they leave their own men?

Brutus was without answer as the quinqueremes on the flanks closed on the two outer enemy vessels that remained, drifting alone as the rest of the fleet swept away from them.

Unable to find a convincing reason to halt the attack, he watched, mystified, as the engagement, such as it was, began. The quinquereme on the left flank; the *Celerimus*, he believed, swept forth with a final surge and a roar from the ranks of rowers, and ploughed into the side of their target vessel.

Brutus shook his head, realising what had happened before the scene fully unfolded. The trierarch of the Roman vessel had done nothing wrong, but the Veneti had allowed their ship to drift just slightly, putting it at a slight angle. The ram on the Roman vessel slammed into the heavy oak hull but, rather than punching through and disabling the enemy, the ships came to a mutual halt with a resounding crash and men and goods were thrown around the decks. The ram had broken timbers, but had then glanced off and slid along the hull harmlessly, leaving the boarding bridge pointing out to open sea.

The enemy crew were laughing at them, Brutus realised, as the Gauls raised their sail and began to gather the wind to move away. Silently, he willed the captain of the Celerimus to pull the disaster around and, as he watched, the quinquereme changed angle and tried to face the enemy ship long enough to drop the corvus, which was already manned. There was, he realised, no chance of this happening successfully. The oarsmen had begun to row, trying to manoeuvre the heavy Roman vessel, but it just took too long to pick up speed in the circumstances, while the swift Veneti ship that had been their target began to open the distance between them, disappearing toward the land with a bulging sail and laughing crew.

Brutus felt the pain behind his eyes coming back and pinched the bridge of his nose again.

'Signal the fleet to break off.'

He opened his eyes again, already knowing what he was going to see and dreading it.

Sure enough, two other Roman vessels had closed on the enemy, one on the opposite flank and one close by in the centre of the formation. As they lunged forward, trying to ram and with the corvus swinging and ready to drop, the Veneti ships shifted their sails, caught the wind, and swiftly moved out of the way.

There was no trap. Quite simply, the Veneti had known from the start that they were safe from the Roman fleet, but were testing not only the tactics of their hated oppressors, but also their abilities. The answer was almost embarrassing. Without something new, nothing in the arsenal of Roman naval experience was going to be able to make a dent on the Veneti fleet. The Gauls were toying with them, batting them on the nose and then dancing out of reach.

He turned to catch the accusing glare of the trierarch.

'Yes, I know. Signal the fleet to follow them. When they put to shore, we need to find a useable harbour somewhere nearby and keep a squadron at a time out there, making sure the Veneti stay still. As soon as they're ashore and we've got them under surveillance, I'm heading back to the general to report.'

The captain nodded quietly, and Brutus ground his teeth. Caesar was unlikely to be sympathetic.

* * * * *

Brutus sighed as the general let his glare slip slowly away. Caesar had said nothing, but his expression had said more than the harshest words.

'Very well... We are in the same position as we were before we marched on Corsicum. The only advantages we have this time are that we know what their tactics are likely to be, and the fleet is there and will be able to at least *try* and hold the enemy fleet in.

'Weather allowing' Brutus added quietly, unwilling to raise his eyes to meet the general's sharp glance.

'Solutions, gentlemen. We now know the situation of this next fortress. It is similar to the last, but with narrower coves opening to the sea on either side of the headland. Is there some way we can speed up the whole procedure and not be at the mercy of nature and her damn tides?'

Tetricus cleared his throat next to Fronto.

'We can stop the legions out of sight of the fortress, general; assemble as much of the artillery as possible so that it will require considerably less time to put them in position and find the range. If we then send scouts ahead as we start to move, they can locate a good place for an artillery platform and direct the engineers there. If we do it right, we can have the artillery pounding the enemy in a fraction of the normal time. The surprise could give us an edge and buy us time.'

The general nodded slowly and appreciatively.

'Surprise is clearly important. If they have too much time to plan, we could end up with a repeat of Corsicum, or worse. We shall keep the legions from moving into sight until we are ready. Let's keep them guessing and off guard. What else?'

Balbus frowned.

'Tetricus? Can you split your attack when you're set up and drop some of your shots into the centre of the fortress?'

'I can, but won't it be a waste of shots we could be directing against the walls?'

Balbus smiled and scratched his bald head.

'If we're trying to prevent them from having too much time and leisure to plan, the confusion created by being under random shots across the place could be useful.'

Caesar nodded again.

'Do it. Next?'

'Dams.'

The general turned his head to the voice off in the recess of the command tent. Mamurra, the engineer who had joined the staff in the spring, stepped into the circle of light.

'We know how deep the tide comes in over these causeways. It's not deep; just enough to prevent any kind of land attack. If, as you say, the apertures to the sea to either side are relatively narrow, we can dam them enough to hold back the tide, and that would give you the freedom to work your attack any way you wish.'

127

Caesar frowned and leaned forward across the table, the stylus in his hand tapping on the surface.

'Wouldn't that take a long time?'

Mamurra shook his head.

'Not with, what, four legions available to us. Given complete control, along with a few good engineers and perhaps a legion of men, I can have serviceable dams in position in an hour or two. It'll take longer than that to flatten the walls, so we should have the time.'

Caesar frowned at the engineer for a while and then nodded and faced the others again.

'Surprise, artillery prepared in advance, a fleet anchored in the bay beyond, the sea held back with dams. Anything else we can do?'

There was an uncomfortable silence and, after a pause, the general smiled and sat back.

'Then at least it's an improvement on the last attack. We'll move out in the morning. Have the word given to the officers. The Eighth, Ninth and Tenth cohorts from each legion are hereby assigned to Mamurra to construct his dams. They can separate out now, excused all other duties, and start quarrying the stone and loading it into carts to save time when we arrive.'

'General?'

Caesar turned again to see the interim camp prefect wearing a quizzical expression. Fronto glowered at the Illyrian officer. The man had kept carefully quiet and out of Fronto's way since the day they had spoken in Fronto's own house, which was just as well, since the mere sight of him was enough to make the legate want to break the man's nose.

'Yes?' Caesar said quietly.

'General, the Tenth cohort is currently assigned to camp construction, maintenance and deconstruction. How will I take down the camp and prepare to move?'

Caesar rolled his eyes.

'Good grief, man. The assignments to camp are all transitory. Any cohort can do the job. You have the authority; just draw some other men and get the job done.'

The man shrank back out of sight, and Fronto smiled menacingly to himself as the general stood and stretched.

'Then everything is settled. Let's get prepared and put and end to this uprising.'

128

* * * * *

'Respectfully, legate, I'm going to have to request that you get your arse to the back and take up the traditional role of looking good and urging the men on.'

Fronto blinked at Carbo.

'Sod off.'

'Now, now, sir. I know that Priscus let you charge into the enemy next to him, and I'm slighting neither your ability nor your bravery, but it's my job to lead these buggers into a fight, and not yours.'

'Fine. Your request has been duly noted and declined. Care to disobey your commanding officer?'

The pink faced centurion next him smiled and winked.

'Then don't get in the way, eh, sir?'

Fronto opened his mouth to bark a sharp reply, but the primus pilus turned his head away and shouted across to the signifer some twenty paces away.

'As soon as you see the Eighth move, signal the advance.'

Petrosidius nodded, keeping his gaze on the standards of the Eighth off to their right. Ten paces behind the officers, the Tenth Legion shuffled their feet in agitation, itching to be off. Fronto faced forward once more, looking at the path before them.

It had certainly been a whirlwind preparation. Only two hours ago had the first Roman scout crested the hill in sight of the Veneti stronghold and in that short time Mamurra's men had constructed what looked, to Fronto, like a very unstable dam on either side of the headland, holding the sea back from the causeway. Certainly they appeared to have the odd small leak, rivulets of seawater trickling down the inner face. The plan had extra merit that had occurred to them after the meeting. With the tide in, when the legions attacked, Brutus' fleet would be able to get closer to land.

Fronto's gaze passed across the mass of artillery on the headland keeping up a constant barrage, though having now shifted from the ruined walls to pounding the interior. This fortress was smaller and less well-defended than Corsicum and had succumbed to the assault remarkably quickly.

His eyes followed the missiles as they arced up from the onagers and once again he focused on the brooding sky. He just hoped in the name of every god he could think of that the weather would hold off until after the attack. The grass underfoot was faintly damp, but 'faintly damp' was as dry as it had been in weeks. The sky above, however, boiled with black, grey and white clouds, promising storm conditions and torrential rain, likely with lightning and thunder. Not, he grumbled to himself, good conditions to be marching up a slope and wearing bronze.

A buccina call rang out from the Eighth, and Petrosidius waved the standard, triggering calls from the Tenth's own musicians.

The legions moved off and a grin split Fronto's face. It felt good to be marching into a fight again.

The three officers slowed their pace slightly until the First Cohort reached them and then slid in among the men, taking their place in the front line. The smile on Fronto's face widened for only a moment, and was then rudely removed as the men around him pushed, shoved and jostled suddenly, falling back into military precision moments later and leaving the legate two rows back from the front.

Fronto issued a low growl, glaring ahead, and an apologetic voice spoke up from next to him.

'Sorry sir. Orders of the primus pilus.'

For a moment the legate was tempted to argue, but knew it would be fruitless. The Tenth respected their commander, Fronto knew, as much as *he* respected *them*, but the legate was often just a voice from high up, whereas a senior centurion was the man that put you to digging in shit for months at a time when he was unhappy with you. Fronto had no chance against *that* kind of threat.

Settling into his position in the third line, Fronto continued with the steady march as they descended the slope and reached the causeway at the bottom. His eyes strayed to his left, where he could see one of Mamurra's dams, the other out of sight beyond the promontory. His mind immediately furnished him with vivid images of a dam exploding inwards, rocks tumbling this way and that, releasing the structural internal timber beams to rush toward the panicked Tenth Legion on the crest of a deadly wave. Fronto squeezed his eyes shut and forced the picture away but, when he opened them again, he could not look too closely at the dam without his knees taking on a very unmanly tremble.

The legions marched on across the causeway. By this time, the ground they trod would normally by under at least six feet of water.

Pictures in his mind again.

Damn it.

Or dam it, anyway…

Fronto smiled to himself. The ground beneath his feet squelched unpleasantly, and he sank a fingerwidth or two into the murk with each step.

The moments passed with the unpleasant sound of thousands of squelching feet and the dull clunk of armour and weapons that were becoming a martyr to rust in the conditions this summer.

The legate sighed with relief as his feet confirmed they had finally reached the upward slope that led to the walls and almost smiled until he realised that the rumbling he was hearing was not now the constant barrage of the artillery. The shooting had ceased to allow the legions room to manoeuvre, and so the low grumble he could now hear was thunder.

'Shit.'

'Problem, sir?'

Fronto glanced at the man next to him. He'd not meant to say it out loud.

'Just the weather.'

'I always try to stand next to someone taller if it's thundering and I'm wearing armour, sir' the man replied with a grin. Fronto laughed for a moment and scanned the ranks around him, noting with wry humour that he stood half a head taller than any man close to him.

'Great. Just great!'

The slope ahead was much easier than that of Corsicum. Just as the stronghold was only perhaps a quarter of the size, with less powerful walls, so the cliffs were lower and the promontory less pronounced. Wearily the men of the Tenth slogged up the incline toward the smashed walls that had protected the fortress proper.

Carbo, ahead and to his right, barked out commands as they moved.

'We take the left. First century: peel off as we reach the walls and secure to the left before working your way round the edge of the cliffs. Once we near the crest, I want the rest of the First Cohort to start spreading down the hill and then swing round at higher speed, like a closing gate, making sure we clear the whole surface. I don't want to miss anyone.'

There were shouts of acknowledgement from the appropriate centurions and Fronto grinned. It was *this* that granted command ability. Oh, some of it was natural talent, such as in the case of the general, but far too many legates and tribunes stood at the back, slapping each other on the shoulder and watching happily as their men fought the battle. Only when you understood the men themselves, the abilities and responsibilities of the centurionate, and how everything fitted together in the actual fight, could you hope to direct a legion effectively. It was his appreciation of the situation his men were in that had given Fronto all his experience. He and the Tenth had made a name for themselves together.

His attention was brought back to the immediate situation as there was a shriek from ahead.

He focused, startled, as the line staggered to a halt, a figure missing.

'Lilia?'

Sure enough, as the legion began to move again, more cautiously, Fronto looked down with sympathy at the man who, two rows ahead of him, had discovered the first hidden pit with its sharpened stake.

The man writhed in the hole, the point of the stake through his thigh, the bone shattered. Once the legions were ahead and out of the way, the capsarii following up would find him and take him back to the makeshift camp, but the man's leg was ruined, along with his career. Fronto swallowed sadly and raised his eyes again.

Then, thankfully, they were past and the man was out of sight, though the occasional shriek from left and right announced the location of another deadly trap. Fronto grimaced as he kept his gaze straight ahead, locked on the walls. For just a moment, he wondered how a tribe they had never fought had adopted Roman defensive methods, but it had not taken him long to realise that Crassus had spent last summer suppressing these people. They had picked up Crassus' tricks.

A moment later the front ranks reached the line of the fallen walls, slowing once more as they stumbled over the rubble and into the stronghold itself. The first century set off along the line of jagged stone, only to discover that the deep grass here had been left deliberately long to hide the brambles and thorns that had been left there in a tangled mass.

Moments later the rest of the attacking force encountered the same conditions. The defending Veneti had clearly, as they left the walls, traversed narrow channels through the brambles, before disappearing into the interior.

Fronto gave an involuntary yelp as a thorn wrenched a long jagged cut across his shin, raking through his breeches with little trouble. Fortunately, the entire advancing Roman force, which had slowed to a virtual crawl, were mostly grumbling or shouting at the tearing and jabbing brambles.

If seemed like hours, dragging, wading and stomping through the painful undergrowth before the legions reached short grass and heaved a sigh of relief, examining their arms, legs and feet. To a man, the Eighth and Tenth legions had been scratched and raked, drawing blood in dozens of places. Hardly a great defensive measure by the standards of the Roman army but, Fronto had to admit, innovative and simple. The thorns had irritated and pained the legions and slowed their advance considerably.

Setting their sights on the square at the top of the gentle slope, the Tenth moved on, men fanning out down the hill and searching out any hiding places. The eerie quiet was all too familiar to Fronto and his spirits fell.

The Tenth reached the top of the hill to find, just as he'd expected, a deserted square, surrounded by apparently empty buildings. Irritably, he wrestled with his chin strap and removed his helmet, letting it fall unceremoniously to the floor with a dull thud.

'These people are seriously starting to piss me off.'

He spotted the heavy figure of Balbus, legate of the Eighth, striding across the square toward him from the right. The older officer, bald and tired-looking, had also removed his helmet and carried it under his arm.

A rumble of thunder announced the coming storm just as the first swathe of pounding rain began to fall, battering Fronto's scalp and further darkening his mood.

'Campaigning in this bloody place is like drowning in depression. I am starting to take an intense dislike to the Veneti.'

Balbus shrugged.

'It *is* irritating, I'll grant you, but you can hardly blame them, really. What would *you* do?'

'I'd migrate to a country with better bloody weather for a start.'

The older man laughed and pulled his crimson scarf tighter around his neck.

'Come on. Let's go see what's happening.'

Knowing exactly what he was going to find, Fronto nodded irritably, leaving his discarded helmet where it had fallen, and strode off with his opposite number toward the sea. The slope was gentler than at Corsicum and the cliffs lower, and they were, but a few moments from the top when Fronto blinked as he took in the situation.

'Bloody hell, Quintus! We're still in with a chance!'

Below, Brutus' fleet sat like a dreadful wall of timber in a wide crescent out in the bay, safely away from the rocky shelf, but close enough to cut off any route to the open sea and close enough to flee to their safe harbour at short notice when the storm began to churn the sea too much.

The Veneti fleet wallowed close to the cliff below, almost close enough to drop rocks on.

'They must still be boarding.'

Balbus nodded, his brow furrowed.

'But how did they get down there? The cliffs are too steep. There can't be a path!'

Fronto swung his head this way and that and spotted the primus pilus directing some of his men.

'Carbo! Spread the men out. Start looking for hidden paths or tunnel entrances or some such. There's a secret way down to the water.'

Carbo turned with a grin and saluted, marching away with his men, while Fronto turned his own grin on Balbus.

'We might just have them by the short and curlies, Quintus.'

The older legate nodded and turned back toward the gathered structures at the crest.

'I'll get Balventius to search the buildings thoroughly. Could be there.'

Fronto nodded and punched one hand into the flat of the other with deep satisfaction.

'Got you, you bastards.'

* * * * *

'Here, sir!'

Fronto's head whipped round at the shout. A legionary was gesticulating from a rock near the grassy cliff edge. Slapping Balbus on the shoulder to get his attention, he jogged off down the slope.

'You got something?'

'Think so, sir. Looks like a tunnel.'

134

Fronto hurried down to the rock, blinking the water out of his eyes. The smooth boulder rose from the grass some ten feet from the edge of the cliff and the far side concealed what did appear to be an entrance to a passageway some five feet tall and just wide enough for a man.

'If this is the way they left, they couldn't have taken all their gear through there.'

Balbus, behind him, nodded.

'But if they were prepared with enough time to spare, they could have lowered everything down the cliff before they left. Balventius has put out the call. The Eighth are on the way across.'

Fronto nodded, but was already levering his way down into the gap.

'Then they can follow us down. No time to waste.'

Balbus grinned.

'Crazy as ever, Marcus.'

Stepping into the tunnel and straightening as much as he could, Fronto drew his sword and gestured to the legionary.

'You're not one of mine?'

'No sir. Legionary Capito, sir, of the Eleventh legion, Third cohort, century of Pictor.'

'Well, legionary Capito' Fronto grinned 'time to lead the charge. Come on, but you'll have to leave your shield; I don't think there's room.'

Balbus examined the entrance speculatively.

'I'm not sure I'm going to fit through there either. I can only assume there are no fat Veneti!'

Fronto laughed.

'Stay there, Quintus, and send your men down behind us once they're ready.'

Even as he stepped into the passageway, Fronto could hear the men marching across the hill toward them. He examined the passageway ahead, descending steeply into the darkness. As the legionary clambered into the tunnel behind him, Fronto clicked his tongue irritably.

'No time to get torches and light them. We're going to have to go down in the dark.'

The legionary shuddered.

'Best watch your head, sir.'

Fronto nodded and turned back to the tunnel.

135

The first half dozen steps were easy enough, despite the wet and slippery rock beneath his feet, as there was a touch of daylight still filtering through from behind. As they descended though, the light faded, leaving an oppressive gloom. No matter how hard he squinted, Fronto could hardly make out the passageway ahead and had to move at a ridiculously slow pace, feeling his way as he went.

Ten more steps. A scraping of his cuirass on the wall and a grazed elbow. Yes, it would have been almost impossible to get down here with helmet and shield.

Eight more steps...

Thump.

Fronto almost struck out with his sword before he realised that what he had bumped into was solid rock. Capito walked into the back of him and apologised profusely.

'Shh.'

Feeling around, Fronto tried to determine where the passage went from here. This couldn't be a dead end, could it? It could just be for storage? It...'

His hand disappeared into dark space. The passage turned to the left. Fronto nodded. Of course, it would have to turn back on itself, or it would come out two thirds way up the cliff. Taking a deep breath, he stepped into the space, feeling for more. Yes. It only went a few feet and then turned left again. Nodding with satisfaction, convinced now that this was the route the enemy had taken, Fronto explored with his hands. The passageway seemed to be opening out at this point, much wider and more spacious. Perhaps this was now a natural passage they were in? It was so hard to tell in this stygian darkness.

A few more steps brought him to the next turn and, as he carefully edged round, he was surprised by a yellow glow. Perhaps fifty feet down the long, straight passageway, a lamp flickered on a ledge, illuminating the tunnel. The light was low and small, but felt like the glare of the sun after the darkness behind him. Fronto smiled as he realised that this part of the tunnel was quite wide and high for most of its length.

He paused, blinking. The light had, of course, ruined his night vision, resulting in purple and yellow blotches dancing around in his eyes no matter how much he blinked and squeezed his eyes shut. Why would they leave a light to help...

It was only that sudden thought that saved his life.

The Veneti warrior who had been lurking in the darkness behind a section of jutting wall, his back to the light source and fully attuned to the dark, lunged forward with his blade aimed resolutely for Fronto's neck. The legate was already moving to the side as the man leapt, the blade connecting instead with the shoulder section of his cuirass and scything through the fasteners. The shoulder piece flapped loose as the sword ripped on through it, deprived of a solid target, and the point hammered home into the wall of the tunnel.

With a breath of relief, Fronto stepped to his left twice, away from the blow, trying to get the flickering of the lamp out of his vision so that he could see better. There was a clunk and a shifting of weight as the front and back pieces of his cuirass separated at the shoulder, becoming instantly irritating and uncomfortable.

The Gaul was hauling his blade back for a second blow, though the long Celtic weapon was unwieldy in the confined space. The well-designed gladius in Fronto's hand, however, was subject to no such restrictions. Unwilling to allow the man enough time to make another careful blow, Fronto stabbed with his sword repeatedly into the rough area of the Gaul, the dancing blotches in his eyes making targeting difficult. Still, given the closeness, at least three of his six sharp lunges connected and he heard a gasp and a gurgle.

Stepping back, he tried to focus. Slowly his vision cleared as he saw the body of the Veneti warrior crumple to the floor. Lucky... very lucky.

Fronto turned to the legionary behind him.

'Try not to look at the light. Keep your eyes low.'

Stopping for a moment to try and adjust his shoulder, he fidgeted at it irritably and gave up in disgust. The shoulder piece was ruined. A job for the armourers next time they had a moment. They did not have time now...

Back and above, he could hear the legionaries pouring into the tunnel, making a noise like a hundred iron plates being dropped into a well. So much for sneaky...

Gesturing to Capito, he moved on downwards. The way was easier, but they moved warily, watching for more hidden figures to left and right. After what seemed like an eternity, they reached the lamp and Fronto gratefully turned left to peer down the next corridor, putting his back to the dancing light.

For the second time in a few short moments he cheated death as he felt a hand grasp the broken backplate of his cuirass and haul him away from the corner. He toppled backward, caught surprised and off-balance, and landed on Capito whose hand was wrapped tightly around the bronze plate.

The arrow that would have struck Fronto square, and very definitely fatally, in the head sailed past and hit the passage wall with a crack. Fronto blinked.

'Sorry sir' Capito breathed. 'Heard the bow string stretch.'

'Crap, you have good hearing. Thanks!'

'What now, sir?'

Fronto smiled.

'If they're there to shoot at us, it means they haven't left yet. Hang on.'

Standing, the legate stepped forward gingerly to the corner and peered round the very edge, squinting. The next length of passage, perhaps forty feet long, was lit by dim reflected daylight. The end of the tunnel was sealed with some sort of gate, through which the light filtered. Outside was some sort of wide cavernous opening at sea level. The smell of brine and the distant noise of waves confirmed it. This was the end of it.

He could see two figures moving behind the gate, in some sort of undergrowth. There was the tell-tale stretch of a bow string again, and he stepped back.

'Could be a bit troublesome getting down there without being shot.'

The legionary nodded.

'Not much we can do, sir.'

Fronto grumbled. He refused to get this close and be stopped by a damn gate. Behind, the first men of the Eighth legion rounded the corner and moved down to join them. A voice called out.

'Legate Fronto?'

'Yes.'

'Centurion Hosidius of the Eighth. What can we do to help?'

'Anyone back there brought a shield?'

Hosidius paused for a moment and then relayed the question back through his men. There was a murmur of argument back a way and then a voice piped up.

'Got a signifer's shield, sir. Quite small and round, though.'

Fronto shook his head irritably.

'It'll have to do. Pass it forward.'

There was a moment of grumbling and muttered complaints as the bulky shield was passed with difficulty along the passage. Eventually an unseen hand passed it to Fronto, and he took the item and looked down at it. A circle of red wood and leather perhaps two and a half feet across, emblazoned with the golden bull. Hardly what he really wanted, but apparently the best thing on offer. Fronto turned to Capito.

'As soon as I start to run, get along behind me. Stay close. If I fall, take the shield and keep running. We need to get to that gate and secure it, so that we can get to their ships.'

Capito nodded nervously, and Fronto grinned.

'Don't worry. Fortuna's a personal friend.'

Without waiting further, the legate took a deep breath, raised the shield, and turned the corner, breaking immediately into a run. He felt the bronze strip at the edge of the shield grating along the rock sides of the tunnel as he ran, but was more concerned about the possibility that, though much of his bulk hunched over behind the shield, a well placed shot could still put an arrow through his thigh.

And yet there was no stretch and no twang. He ran on, but began to falter. Something was wrong. Why were they not at least *trying* to shoot at him?

Smoke.

His nostril hair curled, and he came to a halt, Capito bumping into him again, and risked lowering the shield for a moment.

It had struck him as odd when he first looked down here that there should be undergrowth by the gate in a sea cave. Undergrowth, no...but carefully prepared and dried faggots and bundles of perfectly combustible foliage stacked against the gate? Now *that* made sense. Fresh flames leapt up among the sticks as he watched, and the entrance to the tunnel began to fill with dense smoke.

'Shit!'

Turning, he pushed Capito and yelled up the passageway.

'Retreat! They're smoking us out!'

The silence from further up the tunnel erupted into panicked movement as half a century of men turned as fast as they could and began to scramble back up the passageway toward the stronghold above.

The tunnel acted, just as the Veneti had obviously planned, just like the draw hole in the roof of a hut, funnelling the smoke into the

139

passageway and drawing it up toward the boulder entrance on the cliff top.

Fronto coughed as the first cloud of grey, roiling smoke wafted past him.

As fast as they could, they ran back to the corner with its lamp. Already Hosidius had moved his men up to the next bend.

Ignoring the jagged rock walls tearing at their arms as they ran, Fronto and Capito charged up the slope, the passageway thickening every moment with heavy black fumes.

Another corner; and another. And suddenly they were at the back of a column of legionaries desperately clambering through the opening and out into the air.

Fronto coughed raspingly and next to him Capito burst into a fit of choking. Around them the drawn fumes filled the passage, blackening everything and blocking out the light. Everything went dark as men coughed and struggled.

And suddenly an arm grasped his wrist. Fronto squinted into the smoke to see a centurion's chest harness, adorned with phalera and other decorations. The back of the hand around his arm was crisscrossed with scars.

'Come on, sir. Out of there.'

Fronto sighed with relief as Balventius hauled him out of the entrance and all but threw him back on to the grass before reaching in to retrieve Capito.

Fronto fell back with immeasurable relief, relishing for a moment the heavy rain battering his skin and washing the black dust from his face. He wiped his forehead and eyes and sat up. A huge column of smoke issued from the tunnel entrance, pushing up into the sky like a signal. His euphoria at the sudden breathable air and dull light waned once more as he descended into a racking cough that was matched by a crack of thunder from above.

As the fit subsided, he became aware than another figure had crouched next to him. He squinted up into the rain to see the shiny face of Carbo, his primus pilus, frowning down at him.

'Dangerous, sir. Moments like that are why you have underlings.'

Fronto sighed.

'There wasn't time. What's happening?'

Carbo shrugged unhappily.

'They're leaving, sir. They're just flitting across the rock shelf as though they're on wheels. Our fleet can't pursue them, 'cause they just can't get close enough. We can watch where they go, but we can't follow.'

Fronto growled.

'These people are *really* starting to piss me off, Carbo.'

Chapter 8

(Iunius: temporary camp on the Armorican coast)

Fronto pushed the tent flap open and made his way out into the dusk, shivering against the cold. Grumbling to himself, he traipsed through the wet grass and across the hilltop to the thicker undergrowth near the cliff's edge. The interim camp prefect, whose name Fronto had now learned was Draco, had planned their camp so well that the nearest latrines for the officers of the Tenth was more than halfway across the length of the fortress. Consequently, those officers had taken to going near the cliff edge for their business, at least when there were no high winds.

Fronto found the spot nice and easily. A helpful centurion had spelled out 'Draco' with small stones for the officers to piss on; a nice touch in Fronto's opinion. Hoisting the front of his breeches down, he began to relieve himself with a sigh, grateful for a rare dry evening, even if everything underfoot was still wet through.

His eyes strayed from the rocky name near his feet, across the thick grass and to the bay below, passing across the white-flecked waves and to the next headland, which had, until this afternoon, been one of the most powerful of the Veneti strongholds. He sighed again.

For a month now the legions had been marching up and down the coast, even inland a way to chase yet more shadows that dissipated as soon as the Roman army got close. A whole month of besieging fortresses and chasing elusive bands of warriors and what did the army have to show for their efforts? Nothing. Not a single captive.

Every time the army came close to trapping the Veneti, the Gauls found new and ever more inventive ways to slip out from under their enemy and make it to safety once again. Five more fortresses had fallen in the few weeks after that smoky tunnel had demonstrated to him just how prepared the enemy were. Five more fortresses, and still not a single solid victory.

The moment that had brought him close to breaking point had been when they realised that the Veneti that had fled from the latest conquest had doubled back on them and made their way down to one of the strongholds the legions had already taken once. It was like... it was like trying to nail the sea to a tree; like trying to catch fog in a net. One thing Fronto knew for certain was that Caesar was close to the end of his tether and, when they finally caught the Veneti, Fronto would not have been among their number for all the gold and wine in the world. The last time Caesar had had this much trouble, near Numantia in Spain, the general had repaid the locals with genocide.

His gaze rested for a long moment on the shattered remains of the headland stronghold, its buildings pulled down, walls dropped into the sea, the thicker areas of vegetation fired and still showing from this distance as columns of smoke, and the grass salted to ruin it for generations to come... if there were to *be* any future generations, that was.

Fronto sighed again and pulled up the front of his breeches, fastening the drawstring. Before he turned away, he made sure to spit once on Draco's name, a habit rapidly becoming a tradition in the Tenth. Glancing quickly at the sky, which threatened heavy rain again through the night, he strode back across to Tetricus' tent. The warm glow and murmur of good-natured conversation from within welcomed him.

Pulling the tent flap back, he entered once more and made his way across to his seat among the cushions on the floor.

'I just don't see what he expects us to do?'

Brutus gestured irritably with one arm before swigging from the cup in the other.

'I mean...' he paused, rubbing his eyes, 'the simple fact is that our ships can't go out to sea to follow them in those choppy conditions, and they can't get close enough to land to follow them along the coast. All we can do is keep watch. Even when we do get near them, they're both faster and higher than us.'

Tetricus shrugged.

'Then you're going to have to find a way to bring them to your level. To even the odds a little.'

'Easier said than done, my friend.'

Tetricus nodded.

'The time will come. In the meantime, how many of these damn strongholds do we have to take before we can pin them down?'

Fronto sat heavily and reached for his own wine.

'I have to admit I am heartily sick of Armorica. For a few days when I got to Vindunum I was actually glad to get out of Rome and back into the field. For the life of me I cannot fathom why!'

Balventius and Carbo shared a look and then the primus pilus of the Eighth smiled.

143

'It could be worse.'

'How?'

'You could be with one of the other armies.'

Fronto frowned, and Balventius spread his hands wide.

'You could be with Labienus suffering the worst of both worlds. He has the climate of Gaul and the boredom of no action. He's just digging aqueducts and teaching the locals the value of Rome while his boots fill with rain.'

Carbo nodded and leaned across in front of him.

'Or you could be with Crassus... actually, that's enough on its own. You could be with Crassus!'

Fronto chuckled.

'I wonder how everyone else is getting on?'

He leaned back and took another swig.

'Remember the last couple of years? Those times we sat in that nice little tavern in Bibracte?' He grinned meaningfully at Balbus. 'Or that charming little place in Vesontio where you broke my nose? I can't remember there being rain. All I remember when I think back is warm sunshine, bees and the smell of wildflowers.'

Carbo snorted.

'That's because you went to Spain for the winter. You should have seen the conditions at Vesontio in November. It was like camping in the bottom of a latrine.'

Fronto shrugged with a laugh.

'Fair enough. It's just this constant rain is beginning to wear my patience away, particularly when combined with our inability to nail the Veneti down. It just feels like we're wasting our time out here while the Gods piss on us for fun. The only time it stops raining is when the bloody thunder clouds need time to gather to give us yet another storm.'

Brutus nodded.

'But that can't go on forever. At least if the weather clears up the fleet might have more of a chance to prove itself. We've been sat pretty much port-bound for the last fortnight.'

Balbus smiled and leaned forward.

'We need a plan. We need to trap the Veneti and their fleet in the same place with no means of escape. If we can do that, we can force a conclusion to all this.'

He reached up and thumped himself a couple of times gently on the chest before wincing and sliding his unfinished cup of wine back onto the low table.

'You alright?' Fronto asked, his brow furrowing.

'Just heartburn. It's this cheap and nasty wine, and the quantity of it, of course.'

Tetricus raised his eyebrow.

'Cheap and nasty? You have no idea how much I had to pay Cita to get that. It's some of his special reserve store.'

Balbus grinned at him.

'Still tastes like a gladiator's sandal!'

'You're just sore because you haven't won a game of dice in three days.'

Fronto leaned back with his wine and let the ensuing good-natured argument wash over him like a warm bath, soaking him in comfort. Grimacing for a moment, he shifted his supporting weight to his right arm. His left had made an almost full recovery after the spear wound last year, but prolonged pressure still made it ache painfully.

Funny how many things had changed in just over two years. When they were chasing the Helvetii, the people in this tent would have been so different, with Priscus, Velius, Longinus and others. No Carbo or Brutus in those days, though. The seasons changed and, along with them, so did the people around him, but the central fact never changed: these were the core of people that made Caesar's army what it was.

He smiled sadly at the recollection of friends gone and currently absent and realised, with surprise, that events had taken such a turn that he'd never had the opportunity to review the situation of promotions within the Tenth's centurionate. Clearly Carbo had settled into the role of primus pilus comfortably, and Fronto was hardly about to put *that* under review. The permanently happy-looking Carbo had a strange and yet infectious sense of humour and a wicked mind for practical jokes, as Fronto was starting to discover after the third night in a row of waking with a start next to a frog that sat staring silently at him.

But the need for a training officer had slipped his mind, perhaps due to the pain that thoughts of Velius still brought. He frowned and noticed that Carbo was watching him intently across the tent, past the laughing and arguing officers.

145

'Carbo? Mind if I pick your brain for a moment?'

The centurion smiled and shuffled across the carpeted floor until he sat close to the legate.

'By all means. You'll have to find it first, of course...'

Fronto laughed quietly.

'Have you thought about how we fill Velius' place?'

Carbo nodded.

'I assumed this would come up some time, but I didn't want to push anything. I've had the job shared between the three most capable centurions in the Tenth as an interim measure, but I also have a shortlist of three candidates I was going to put to you.'

Fronto shook his head in exasperation.

'You've been prepared all this time? Why did you not speak to me, or even just sort it yourself?'

Carbo smiled.

'Velius was your friend. The time wasn't right yet. Now, it clearly is. And it's not my place to assign promotions in the centurionate; that has to come from you or a tribune.'

Again, Fronto laughed.

'You promoted *yourself*!'

'That was different. Anyway, I've three men in mind, as I said. I've not approached any of them, but the position's likely to appeal to them all and, well... without wanting to blow our own buccina, the Tenth has a good reputation. People are always watching for transfer opportunities. You may have noticed we're rarely far below full strength. We've had almost a hundred inward transfers in the past month. I think it's starting to piss the other legates off, but it's good for us.'

Fronto nodded.

'Go on then. Who've you got down?'

Carbo counted them off on his fingers.

'Well they're all from outside the Tenth. Nobody truly fits the bill here. Firstly, there's Aquilius. He's the obvious choice, given his experience.'

'Aquilius?' Fronto's brow furrowed. 'But he's already a chief training officer in the Eighth. Why would he change?'

Something unreadable passed across Carbo's face for a moment; fleeting and then gone, chased away by a smile.

'We can offer him an identical role in the Tenth, with the same rank, position and pay. You see, Aquilius is a perfectionist. Not like the hard bugger Velius was, but a real professional, and I suspect he'd be excited to get a chance to get his teeth into the Tenth. He's got the Eighth just how he wants them, and there's no challenge there any more. He might not accept, but I've a feeling he would.'

Fronto shook his head.

'Perhaps, but I'd rather not strip a good man from Balbus' legion if I can avoid it. Who else have you got?'

'Well there's a man called Bassianus in the Eleventh that I've been watching for a while too. He's no experience as a chief training officer, but he's done more than his fair share of training and drilling, and he's a long term veteran with a reputation for being hard as a whore's heart. He actually served with the Ninth in Spain under your command a long time ago.'

Fronto nodded appreciatively.

'Don't recognise the name, but then it's been a long time. You think he can do the job?'

'I wouldn't recommend someone who couldn't' Carbo grinned.

'Alright. So who's the third?'

Carbo's smile widened disturbingly.

'You'll love this.'

'What?'

'A centurion called Atenos.'

'That's not even a *Roman name*?' Fronto frowned.

'No. Atenos is a Gaul from the Thirteenth Legion. He's my outside chance, just in case, but I can't help thinking that, even though he appears at first to be the least appropriate, he might just be the best choice.'

Fronto shook his head and waved his arm.

'No, no, no. Any Gaulish centurion in the Thirteenth is a lower ranking one, you know that. All the senior roles were given to Roman veterans. Hell, *all* the centurions were Roman veterans until they started dying off. That means that this Atenos only has a year behind the eagle. He's practically still one of the enemy!'

Carbo laughed.

'Bollocks. He's signed on for the full term, taken the oath and served with distinction for a year. Besides, you've not queried his experience.'

Fronto barked a laugh.

'*What* experience? Ten years of fighting naked and covered in paint and then a year with the legions?'

147

Carbo's grin became a little defensive.

'Hardly. Atenos has a long and distinguished military history... as a mercenary, I'll grant you, but it all counts.'

Fronto blinked.

'A mercenary?'

Yes. When his people were displaced by the Helvetii about fifteen years ago, he went south and signed on with any army that would pay and feed him. He may have fought with the slaves, though he denies it, but he definitely served with Pompey's fleets against the pirates, then turned and fought with the King of Pontus against Pompey and then joined him again when he marched on Jerusalem. Quite a pedigree.'

Fronto stared at his chief centurion.

'Carbo, the man's fought *against* us as often as he's fought *for* us. Are you mad?'

The primus pilus shrugged.

'It's your decision. But think what a man with all that varied experience could bring to the Tenth if he were given the opportunity to train them?'

Fronto shook his head.

'You *are* mad. But I'll have a look at them all and give you my opinions in a few days.'

'Good. Gives you something to get your teeth into and stop you moping around.'

Fronto glared at Carbo, but that grin was just too infectious to stay irritated at.

* * * * *

The legate of the Tenth looked up once more at the sulky grey sky. Last night it had delivered yet another torrential downpour, accompanied by crashes, flashes and grumbles and it looked very much like things were gearing up for a repeat performance tonight. He performed a quick calculation on his fingers as he walked.

By his reckoning, they had been campaigning again for just over eighty days, and dredging his memory as deeply as he could, he could only recall eight days that had not involved rain of some kind and those eight had, instead, been filled with high winds and freezing cold. What had happened to this country? Not for the first time this

148

year, he found himself wondering why Rome would actually *want* this place at all.

Turning his thoughts away from the depressing weather, he instead set his sights on the man standing by the rocks close to the cliff edge. There was the sound of men working nearby, hammering stone with their picks.

Fronto was not sure what he was expecting from centurion Atenos but, whatever it was, it wasn't this. The centurion stood in a traditional Roman pose, vine staff in hand and the other arm behind his back as he rocked gently back and forth on his heels. Fronto could not see his face, as the man had his back to the approaching legate, but he was an impressive enough sight from the rear. Clearly a head taller than anyone Fronto even knew, the man was a virtual giant, probably six and a half feet tall, or even more, though thin and lithe, rather than bulky. His yellow hair was coarse and longer than tradition held, but lacking the traditional braids of the Gaulish. His concessions to Roman equipment were otherwise total.

A stick cracked under Fronto's foot, and the man turned sharply.

His face was strong and proud, with high cheekbones and a tidy moustache. Fronto was surprised to note, given the man's short service history, the four phalera and single torc hanging from the man's harness. He must have had an eventful year.

'Morning' he said, as casually as possible, cursing his dubious talents at duplicity.

The centurion saluted.

'Good morning, Legate Fronto. You're a long way from the Tenth?'

Fronto nodded, unable to come up with a convincing reason for his presence. Instead, he ignored the comment and nodded toward the five legionaries who repeatedly smashed at a flat, heavy rock perilously close to the edge of the cliff.

'Mind if I ask?'

The centurion nodded.

'Sick of having to cross the camp for a crap, sir. Decided to build a proper latrine here. Got 'em cutting bum-holes in the rock.'

Fronto looked confused for a moment.

'Can't they just crouch over the pit like everyone else?'

The Gaul turned to face him, a strange smile on his face.

'No pit. Going to have it perched over the edge. Sea will take it all away... no smell and no mucking out.'

Fronto stared.

'You're actually going to sit on a home-made bench, bare-arsed and leaning out over the cliff for a *crap*?'

The centurion nodded.

'Perfectly safe, sir. Rock solid, you might say. Even had our engineers' approval. I've offered the lads first try, since it's all their own effort, but they gave me the same look as you did. Looks like I might have my very own latrine.'

There was nothing Fronto could do but continue to stare at the man incredulously, his eyes sliding first to the seat the men were manufacturing, and then to the precipitous drop into the sea. He shuddered.

'Well there's no denying the bravery of the centurionate. That's for sure.'

The man laughed.

'So if you're not here for a crap, sir, mind if I ask why you *are* here?'

Fronto ground his teeth. He was no good at this subtlety.

'You were pointed out by one of my officers as a man to watch. Frankly, I was intrigued… and I think I still am.'

The centurion raised an eyebrow.

'You on the hunt for transfers, sir?'

Fronto shook his head, not in answer to the question, but in fascination.

'Perhaps. From what I've been told, I'd guess you were one of the Aedui? Or the Lingones?'

Atenos shook his head.

'Close, though, sir… for a Roman. One of the Leuci actually originally.'

Fronto nodded thoughtfully. He knew the name, of course, but could not have placed the tribe without a map.

'You speak Latin flawlessly, without even a trace of an accent. But from what I hear of your past, that's perhaps not a surprise.'

The huge Gaul smiled down at him. The longer Fronto stood next to him, the smaller he felt. It was like being at the bottom of a well.

'My Latin is good, legate. My Greek has a strange twang, I've been told, reminiscent of a Galatian. My Persian is barely comprehensible, but I know how to talk to barmen and dancing girls.'

150

Fronto stared.

'Persian?'

'Spent a year in Commagene when I got my honesta missio after that business in Judea. Strange place over there, though; and all the sand, rock and dust make a man homesick for some good, honest wet grass.'

Fronto laughed.

'Then you've done well! I've never seen wetter grass than this stupendous Gaulish summer.'

The man nodded and fell silent; a silence that remained for a long moment, backed only by the hammering of picks on stone.

'You've been a busy man prior to joining the Thirteenth... fighting for all sorts of different people, if I hear correctly?'

Atenos shrugged.

'A man has to make a living, sir. I'd have signed on with the legions a decade ago if it were legal, but I'm not a citizen. Happy now, though, since Caesar found a way around that particular rule.'

The legate's eyes narrowed.

'Really? Even though we're here fighting your fellow Gauls?'

Atenos shrugged again.

'Not *my* fellows, sir. Never even been this far west. Still...' he turned a searching gaze on Fronto '... if you're trying to find a subtle way to enquire as to my loyalty, remember that I'm a centurion in the Thirteenth, and my legion is a proud one; bound to be, since most of us are Gauls. I hear that you are a man of the legions; people say you're one of the *men*. If that's the case, could I respectfully ask you to get to the point?'

Fronto nodded quietly.

'I'm on the lookout for a chief training officer. Your name was one of three that my primus pilus supplied.'

'I'm quite happy where I am, sir.'

Fronto smiled slyly.

'I've not offered you it, yet. I've plenty to think on first.'

Atenos smiled at him.

'Who are your other choices?'

'Aquilius from the Eighth and Bassianus from the Eleventh.'

The huge Gaul scratched his chin.

'Take Bassianus.'

Fronto frowned up at him.

'I've already spoken to both of them. Why not Aquilius? He's eminently qualified, and my primus pilus thinks he'd accept.'

'I'm sure he'd accept, but choose Bassianus. I've watched Aquilius work while we were in winter quarters. He's too straight and proper for the Tenth. He'll end up resenting the chaos your lads live in, and your men will learn to hate him. It's a problem best avoided from the start.'

'You think the Tenth are chaotic?'

Again, Atenos laughed.

'In the best possible sense of the word, but yes; of *course* they are, sir. Not in battle, mind. I'm not saying they're not disciplined, and even the general himself acknowledges that the Tenth are the best of his legions. Chaos *works* for you, and it works well. It wouldn't work with Aquilius there. Steer clear.'

The big man looked down at Fronto's scowl.

'Bassianus is a good man. His men are always tired and dirty but smiling. That means he keeps them working and training hard, but fairly and with appropriate reward. He's your man.'

Fronto stepped back. His neck was beginning to ache in this conversation.

'You could be right. I'd certainly rather have someone who works *with* the lads, rather than just *working* them.'

Atenos laughed again.

'Glad to be of help, legate. Feel free to drop by any time you feel like having a death-defying crap.'

Fronto could not help but return the laugh and nodded in a casual fashion as he turned and strode away across the grass, his arms folded.

The big Gaul was right. Bassianus was almost certainly the man for the job but, as he walked back toward the tents of the Tenth Legion, Fronto could not shake off the feeling that passing over the possibility of the hulking Gaul might be a mistake. He was clever enough and clearly brave, but what Fronto had not expected was the man's matter-of-fact and almost eerily acute assessment of the other centurions on the list. That kind of mind was what *made* a good training officer.

The legate was still thinking hard on the situation, unsure how to proceed, as he approached his command tent and raised his head in surprise to see two men standing by the door flap.

'Can I help?'

The two men saluted. One was one of the duty centurions that Fronto vaguely recognised; the other was a nondescript Roman male in plain tunic, breeches and cloak, sweating and steaming from a hard ride.

'Sir! Courier arrived for you just now.'

Fronto frowned at the men and then nodded.

'Very well.' He gestured to the courier. 'Come on in; thank you centurion.'

As the officer left to return to duty, Fronto pushed aside his tent flap, grateful once again to enter the comfort of his own little world as he heard the first few drops of fresh rain hit the leather.

'So... a courier?'

The man bowed.

'Yes, legate Fronto. I bring a missive from Gnaeus Vinicius Priscus in Rome. He tasked me to deliver it into your hands and no other.'

Fronto looked up, surprised.

'Priscus? Well, well.'

He held out his hand, and the courier reached into his tunic, took out a wax-sealed tube and passed it over.

'Could I respectfully request a bunk for the night and perhaps some food? It has been a long journey and master Priscus felt sure you would want me to wait and take a return message.'

Fronto nodded and waved a hand vaguely at the door while he examined the tube in his hands.

'Find an officer somewhere out there and tell him you've got my go ahead for whatever it is you need.'

He waited as the man nodded respectfully and left the tent, and then eagerly broke the seal at the end of the tube, sliding the scroll out and flattening it on the table before picking it up to read. He smiled at Priscus' spiderlike writing. He was hardly a master scribe.

Marcus.

I hope you are well, and everything goes to plan out there. If not I shall want to know why from that Illyrian goat herder that is doing my job. I am sorry that I have not written sooner, but you know how much I hate writing, and the courier costs an arm and a leg – feeble joke there, so ignore it.

153

Matters in Rome continue to descend into trouble. I have managed to gather a pretty impressive group of spies, thugs and borderline criminals here, and they are starting to produce results. You would be surprised at some of these results, too.

I have had people following Clodius, as well as his sister and that Egyptian catamite. Each has turned up interesting news. Clodius, if you can believe this, has been visiting the house of Pompey, and not during normal visiting hours. We have seen him in disguise in the middle of the night, slipping out of Pompey's town house. You might want to pass that on to the general.

Clodia is particularly interesting. She was making a nuisance of herself for a few weeks after you left, showing Clodius up and trying to pin wrongdoings on a number of our acquaintances with no luck. Then, suddenly, she vanished. No one has seen or heard from her in well over a month now. I am personally of the opinion that her brother just got sick of her, stuck her in the gut and dropped her in the Tiber, but it is interesting nonetheless.

And then there's Philopater. He has been distributing quite a sum of coinage to several families in Rome, all plebeian. I have done a little prying and was rather surprised to find who some of those families were. Three names I recognised and can identify at this stage are Tarautas, Fulcinius, and Volcatius, all of whom are senior veterans in the Eleventh legion and who you might want to have a little word with.

On the home news, I remain at your mother's house, with a strong armed guard. Your mother and sister are both well and are planning to send you gifts soon if you are staying in Gaul for the season. I may have dropped myself in it when I enquired as to why your sister still lives at home at her age. Me and my mouth. I am so sorry; I never knew. I have trod carefully around her since then, but you know Faleria. She does not even know what a grudge is. Things will be fine.

I hunger for news of what is happening out there and I told the courier to do a little prying around and find out a few choice titbits for me. Feel free to use him to send a reply.

And that has exhausted both my news and my stylus hand. Now I go to raid your ever-depleting stock of good Campanian wine.

Be safe and Fortuna watch over you.

Gnaeus

Fronto smiled as he dropped the scroll back to the table. Interesting and somewhat worrying news, but just to hear from the man was a joy in itself.

'Time to stir up the shit again…'

* * * * *

Crispus frowned at Fronto as he buckled the cuirass at his side.

'Why *my* legion?'

Fronto exchanged an uncomfortable glance with Balbus by his side and looked a little apologetic as he replied.

'Well the way we see it is that when they signed on, Caesar probably had six legions. The Seventh, Eighth, Ninth and Tenth were all veteran legions with long term experienced commanders. If they had an agenda of their own, they would be trying to lay low. The Eleventh and Twelfth were new and with… untried commanders.'

He shifted uneasily, but Crispus nodded professionally.

'Don't feel embarrassed, Marcus. When I took command of the Eleventh, I hardly knew one end of a gladius from the other. I was used to putting stylus to tablet in Rome. I was the obvious choice for them, I have to admit.'

He shrugged the armour into place comfortably and reached for his belt and scabbard.

'But what are they here for? They must have been with the legion for more than a year now. Are they waiting to carry out some diabolical plan, or is it already in motion, wheels turning unseen beneath our feet?'

Fronto and Balbus made uncertain noises but said nothing.

'Very well. I think it's time we went to see the three. I had them taken to the headquarters tent. Until we know what we're dealing with here, I thought it best to avoid the gossip that would arise inevitably from having them imprisoned in the stockade.'

'We thought we'd best see your legion's clerks first. Find out whatever we can of them?'

Crispus smiled at the other legates.

'Unnecessary. There are few men in my legion of optio rank or above that I can't detail for you.'

'How can you have time to get to know all your officers?' Fronto asked, his brow lowering. 'I've had Carbo serving under me for

155

years, and I'm not even sure I'd met him until Priscus went out of the picture.'

Crispus' smile widened.

'That, Marcus, is because you are, despite all appearances, a tremendously private person. I have noticed that you only open up to a few close friends. I make a point of finding out everything I can about my officers.'

Balbus scratched his bald head.

'So what do you know about them?'

'Fulcinius is the more senior of the three. He's the Eleventh's quartermaster. He's meticulous, and I would have *thought* absolutely incorruptible. I have been told before that he has refused to bend the rules even for tribunes, though perhaps that is because he has been hiding something. He has a wife and two children; had a brother too, but lost him in Armenia a few years ago. They served out there together under Pompey.'

Again, Fronto and Balbus shared a look, and the legate of the Tenth formed the name 'Pompey' on his lips silently. Balbus nodded.

'What about the others?'

'Tarautas is the chief centurion of the Third cohort. First man in his family to go into the military, if I remember correctly. He has a huge family at Rome and in Antium. His uncle is a lanista in Antium with an impressive stable of gladiators. In fact, in his first few months with the Eleventh, we had a small problem with Tarautas, who was running an illicit ring of fighting competitions for money.'

Balbus watched Crispus fasten the cloak to his shoulders and tilted his head, a suspicious look crossing his face.

'Tarautas? Was he by any chance also a veteran of Pompey's Syrian legions?'

Crispus stopped as he was reaching for his helmet and frowned.

'I believe he was. Got his honesta missio around six or seven years ago. You believe there is a link with Pompey?'

Fronto flattened his hands in a suppressing motion and shushed him.

'That's not a thing to go saying out loud; not without a whole barrow load of proof, anyway.'

Crispus nodded silently.

'Volcatius was in Syria too. He's the signifer for the Second century of the First Cohort. Three men in high position in my legion, and all with loyalties that lie elsewhere. That vexes me rather a lot.'

He slapped his fist into the palm of his hand.

'A signifer, a chief centurion and a quartermaster.'

Fronto nodded.

'Could be more too, and in other legions. These are just three names that Priscus recognised from a list of many.'

Crispus sighed as he made final adjustments to his armour before turning and opening the flap of his tent. Water dripped, cold and unpleasant, from every point and edge in the camp, the aftermath of the latest dramatic downpour; more likely the intermission before the next act. The headquarters tent stood only thirty paces away, four duty legionaries on guard at the entrance.

He strode out with a military gait, Fronto and Balbus at his heels, both similarly attired. As the three legates crossed the open space to the command tent, the four legionaries snapped sharply to attention.

'Any trouble?' Crispus asked as they approached.

'Quiet as a mouse, sir' the soldier replied. 'Not a peep.'

'Good. Dismissed. Go get some food.'

The legionaries saluted and walked off toward the centre of camp.

'Is that a good idea' Fronto asked quietly.

'You think they might attack us? What could they gain? No, I think this had best be a professional, very private, and reasonable exchange.'

Fronto frowned.

'I hope *they* think so too.'

Crispus gave a dark half-smile as he reached out for the tent flap and strode into the dim interior, the other two officers close on his heel.

The command tent was the largest in the camp, filled, as anyone who knew Crispus would expect, with tables, chairs, maps, cupboards full of tablets and racks full of scrolls. Two braziers supplied the warmth in the room and, along with two oil lamps, also supplied the light.

The interior was therefore dark and gloomy, even with the flap opened, and it took a moment for their eyes to become accustomed to the change.

'Oh shit.'

Crispus and Balbus could only nod, echoing Fronto's sentiments.

The bodies of three men in tunics and breeches lay in a heap in the centre of the room close to the table. The floor around them pooled with fresh blood and rivulets of the stuff ran down their alabaster faces and limbs, matching the tunic's crimson.

Balbus shook his head and pinched his nose.

'That's just *ridiculous*! We hadn't even spoken to them yet. They couldn't have known what we were going to do!'

'Idiots' Fronto agreed. 'No interrogations. Just bodies. That's just stupid.'

Crispus stepped forward, frowning, and examined the pile.

'I don't think so, gentlemen.'

'What?'

The young legate shrugged.

'These are all senior officers. If they were going to take the noble route, tradition is to use your sword, and each would do it themselves. At least one of them still has his sword sheathed. This was done with a pugio or some other short dagger. And they are in a pile. Why would they, even as they died, throw themselves on each other in a heap?'

Fronto blinked.

'They didn't kill themselves?'

'I very much doubt it. This was done by someone else, and it was done recently, quickly, professionally and must have taken them by surprise.'

Balbus nodded.

'If they never even drew their swords.'

'More than that. There must have been at least three of them. One assailant couldn't have dealt with all three that quickly.'

Fronto slapped his head.

'Did you recognise the legionaries on guard?'

Crispus blinked and stared at Fronto.

'No. I don't know many of the rank and file, I'm afraid. I never even thought to look.'

Fronto grumbled.

'They said it had been quiet. They would have heard any sort of struggle and, that being the case, I think we just walked straight past the culprits and passed the time of day with them. They must have only just been leaving the tent when we arrived.'

Balbus gestured at Fronto.

'You go and see Caesar about this. I'll help try and sort this out.'

The legate of the Tenth gave them a quick nod and then, turning, left the tent and hurried through the rows of ordered tents and out of the section of the camp allotted to the Eleventh.

The general's command tent was a hive of activity as Fronto arrived and nodded suspiciously at the legionaries on guard by the entrance. As he reached for the door, the flap opened and Brutus emerged, looking gaunt and tired, as was so often the case these days.

'What sort of mood is he in?'

'Changeable' the young officer replied. 'Step lightly.'

'Not likely, I'm afraid' Fronto sighed.

Patting the other man on the shoulder in a comradely fashion, Fronto stepped through the door into the tent. Cicero and Cita, the chief quartermaster, sat opposite the general in deep discussion.

'Apologies for the rude interruption,' Fronto announced from the entrance 'but I need to speak to the general in private on an urgent matter.'

The two officers threw a questioning look at Caesar, who nodded. Fronto waited patiently as they stood, saluted, and turned to leave, before he approached the table and placed his hands on it.

He quickly glanced over his shoulder to make sure they were alone, and the tent flap was lowered.

'How much do you trust Pompey Magnus?'

Caesar leaned forward.

'Strange question. Why should you ask?'

Fronto shrugged. 'How much?'

'Beyond any reasonable doubt. We are close allies, along with Crassus. Fronto, he's been my son-in-law for the past three years. I ask again why you should ask?'

The legate rubbed his eyes.

'Evidence is beginning to point toward something involving Pompey. It's all circumstantial, I grant you, but it's pretty compelling, nonetheless.'

'Explain.'

'I just received a letter from Priscus. He's been following Clodius and... well see for yourself.'

Reaching into his tunic, Fronto withdrew the crumpled parchment and tossed it onto the table before the general. Caesar raised an eyebrow and then unrolled the scroll and began to read. Fronto stood for a moment, watching a series of interesting expressions crossing the general's face until he sat back and raised his face again, proffering the scroll. Fronto took it.

'Well?' he prompted.

'There's another explanation. Either Priscus is mistaken, or Pompey is doing something for our mutual benefit. Most likely Priscus is mistaken, though. It is common knowledge in Rome just how much Pompey dislikes Clodius. I am much more concerned about the fact that Clodius has managed to slip more men into my legions. The infection continues to spread despite our efforts. Have you had the three apprehended yet?'

Fronto cleared his throat uncomfortably.

'After a fashion. They went for a stroll in the Elysian fields this afternoon. Looks like someone didn't want them to speak to us.'

Caesar shook his head irritably.

'Not a great help. Now we are back to square one unless Priscus can unearth the rest of these names for us.'

Fronto shifted uneasily.

'What would you say, Caesar, if I were to point out that the three men in question had all served with Pompey in Syria and Armenia in the last decade and had received their honesta missio about six years ago?'

The general frowned.

'There are *thousands* of veterans of Pompey's army still floating around, Fronto. You know veteran soldiers; many of them sicken quickly of the quiet life and sign up at the next opportunity. I think that reading conspiracy into it is reaching a little. Again, it is circumstantial at best.'

'With respect, Caesar, while you may be right, ignoring this could be a huge mistake. If there *is* more to this than you believe, something is festering just below the surface of the army and involves both Clodius and Pompey.'

The general sat silent for a moment and finally nodded.

'Agreed. But there is little we can do about it for now. I assume you will be replying to Priscus? Please ask him to send on any further information as and when he tracks it down and continue to do the excellent job he appears to be doing. I will make my gratitude felt when I next see him.'

Fronto nodded.

'And' the general gestured with a raised finger, 'I have been thinking on our situation here with the Veneti. I believe there may be a solution. We need to settle this region swiftly and get back to Rome. Pass the word among the officers to attend a staff meeting here at dawn.'

Fronto smiled and nodded again as he turned and strode toward the doorway.

'Your help is, as always, immeasurable and gratefully received' the general called after him.

Smiling to himself grimly, Fronto stepped out into the late afternoon on this, the last day of Iunius, and looked up in surprise to see a patch of blue sky opening up between the clouds.

'Let that be an end to it...'

Chapter 9

(Quintilis: temporary camp on the Armorican coast)

'Everyone is here, Caesar.'

The general nodded and rose to stand behind the table, leaning forward, his hands on the surface.

'Very well, gentlemen. The purpose of this meeting is to find a way to break the Veneti. Our strategy so far has been somewhat inadequate. However, the summer is wearing on, and my presence is required elsewhere as soon as things are settled in Gaul, and we need to end this decisively, and soon. So, the first order of the meeting, I would say, is to go through what we have achieved, what resources we have available, and the disposition and likely strategy of the enemy. Then we can decide how to go about dealing with them.'

Sighing glumly, Brutus gestured and stood.

'As I'm sure you're all aware, the fleet has been less than effective during the campaign so far. We have been hampered by our inability to deal with the rocky shores, our inability to make it far out into the sea while racked with bad weather, and our general inferiority to the Gallic fleet in terms of both strength and speed.'

Galba gestured to him.

'Is the upshot of this that the fleet are to be effectively reduced to the task of scouting?'

'Not quite,' Brutus shook his head. 'We have various possible solutions, but the problem is that we need to be able to get our hands on their ships to try them. And since they can outrun us in most conditions, unless it's completely becalmed, we need to trap them for that.' He smiled wanly.

'Mind you, it looks like the weather might be breaking, though I'd hate to tempt the fates about that. If the winds and storms would die down, our range of operation would increase tremendously and, conversely, the enemy, who rely solely on the wind in their sails, might be put at a disadvantage.'

He folded his arms.

'So, in fact, the upshot is that it all depends on the weather. I'm making a libation every morning with the best wine and fruit I can find to every god I can think of, and I suggest everyone else does the same. If things improve, the fleet will finally be able to play its part.'

Caesar nodded professionally.

'Very well. Here is my assessment of our achievements:'

Fronto readied himself for a stormy moment, but the general maintained his composure and his voice was clear and steady.

'I have thought long and hard on the subject, and I am convinced now that we have been far from ineffective. We have continually driven the Veneti to the northwest, reducing the fortresses and settlements as we progress. It has felt as though we are chasing an elusive foe and that they are always a step ahead of us. However, an objective look at the situation allows one to draw an entirely different conclusion.'

He waved a hand across the map he was leaning upon.

'We have pushed them into a corner, and they are running out of places to flee to. We have removed their control over nine tenths of their entire territory. If the fleet is able to act as a cordon, they can prevent the Veneti from fleeing past us again to the south but, even if they did, they have no defensible fortresses there now. They are almost at the limit of their territory to the northwest, where the Osismii live and, while the Osismii are currently their allies, I suspect the alliance will become rather shaky if that tribe suddenly has to play host to the whole displaced mass of the Veneti.'

He tapped the map decisively.

'That means that the Veneti are running out of both room and time. Sooner or later we will trap them and destroy them, but until that happens we should continue to squeeze them against their allies until the alliance becomes strained and breaks. To that end, I feel we need to find plausible victories of the variety that will break their spirit. Symbolic victories.'

The room fell silent.

'Ideas, gentlemen?'

Cicero stood and gestured at the map on the table.

'May I, general?'

'By all means.'

The officer stepped forward, his crimson cloak swaying around his calves as he leaned over the map. He studied it for a moment and then smiled.

'Darioritum, general?'

Caesar frowned as he looked down.

163

'Darioritum is inland. We have it on good authority that the Veneti have abandoned their landlocked towns in favour of their coastal escape routes.'

Cicero nodded.

'Yes, sir. In almost all cases that has proved to be true. However, with respect, there are several things that need taking into account with Darioritum.'

Caesar narrowed his eyes as he gazed down. Now, Fronto, Balbus and Brutus were on their feet approaching the table with interest.

'Firstly, Caesar, this map is not accurate' Cicero continued. 'I have spent time speaking to some of the less reticent captives of Crassus' campaign last year and, in return for a little lenience, they can be very talkative. The map shows Darioritum some six or seven miles from the sea. In actual fact, the oppidum is by a large gulf or saltwater lake that has an opening to the sea. Two spits of land reach out like the horns of a bull. Darioritum is, essentially, by the sea. Moreover, it is also, according to two different sources I have questioned, considered the capital of the tribe, or the nearest approximation they *have* to a capital.'

Caesar nodded slowly, scratching his chin.

'A symbolic victory indeed.'

Cicero smiled at the general.

'Given its importance and location, it is almost certainly occupied, even if only by a small retainer force. *That*, I would suggest, is the victory you're seeking, Caesar.'

The general smiled.

'An exceptional suggestion, master Cicero. Moreover, it gives us an even greater opportunity. Brutus?'

The fleet commander frowned.

'We can cordon off the south, Caesar and, given the right weather, possibly even engage.'

The general smiled wolfishly.

'You are thinking too small, Brutus. Think on what Cicero just told us.'

There was a moment's silence and suddenly a grin split Brutus' face.

'An enclosed bay. The horns of a bull, you said?'

'Indeed.'

Brutus laughed.

164

'If the army can lure the fleet into the bay, we can seal them in and deal with them at our leisure.'

'And what would draw the fleet in more than having to evacuate their capital?'

Fronto became aware that most of the other officers had stood and approached the table, the entire officer corps now trying to see the map. Brutus cleared his throat.

'Can we get a more accurate map of the situation around Darioritum?'

Fronto shrugged.

'Easily. Send some cavalry scouts from the Gallic wings to go and check out the lie of the land. They can bring us more accurate details. And, of course, if the weather stays kind, you can send a couple of ships up there to get a look at the coast.'

Caesar sighed with satisfaction and stood straight.

'I think, gentlemen, that we have a workable strategy here. We must not, however, rush into early action. If this is to be the point at which we break the Veneti, things need to happen in perfect order with no ghastly mistakes.'

Fronto frowned down at the map, trying to picture the large bay with its surrounding horns.

'You realise, Caesar, that those two promontories that seal in the bay will have Veneti fortresses on them. We've not yet encountered a defensible headland without one and they must have a way to control the entrance.'

The general frowned and looked back down at the map.

'I do believe you are right, Fronto. The scouts can confirm their presence, but they are almost certainly there and occupied.'

Balbus ran his finger along the coastline on the map thoughtfully.

'They will need to be secured before any attempt by the fleet to get into the bay and deal with the enemy ships. In fact that will have to be the first move in the whole plan.'

Caesar smiled.

'Indeed. Shall I take that as you volunteering for the task, legate?'

Balbus nodded without looking up, still intent on the map.

'The Eighth would deem it an honour, Caesar.'

'So would the Tenth' Fronto cut in. Both the other men looked up at him.

165

'Well, these strongholds could be only a few hundred paces apart, but getting to them will require miles and miles of marching. Both will have to fall at the same time to attacks from opposite directions. That's a job for two separate forces.'

Caesar shook his head vehemently.

'No. I cannot spare fully half my army to take two peripheral forts.'

'With respect, general, these would hardly be peripheral. I realise that until we have seen the bay, this is all speculation, but if what we surmise is really the case, those forts will be key to controlling the bay and therefore destroying the fleet.'

He smiled.

'But we're not talking about two legions anyway, are we?' He glanced across at Balbus, who shook his head.

'This would have to be subtle, general. We'd have to control the entrance to the bay before your main attack begins, or we risk giving their fleet time to organise and escape. For subtlety we'd only want a small force.'

'And engineers' Fronto added. 'Once we have control of the forts, we'd have to try and get artillery set up to help seal off the bay.'

Caesar nodded.

'Very well. It's an eminently workable plan at this point. We will have to see what happens when we have a better idea of the landscape and disposition. The timing will have to be very tight to achieve what we're talking about.' He glanced across at Brutus. 'And some of this is still reliant on the mercy of the Gods. Brutus is right. Everyone should pay their proper respects and try to keep Jupiter happy for the near future.'

He straightened again.

'Very well. We will reconvene each morning and hammer out the dents in the scheme until we are convinced the time and situation are right. In the meantime, each of you needs to think on what your own forces can do to improve our chances and have scouts sent out to bring us accurate intelligence of the bay and the town. Dismissed.'

Fronto nodded to Caesar and joined the general exodus of officers.

Outside, the air was chilly, and there was a faint tang of salt, though the sky had cleared overnight, leaving wispy clouds on the horizon to both south and west; clouds which threatened less than the heavy-bellied ones that had hung over them for the past weeks. The day felt fresh and new.

He turned to Balbus as the man left the tent.

'You realise we've just volunteered for about the most dangerous part of the whole show?'

The older legate laughed.

'Nothing new there, Marcus. Care to join me for a bit of breakfast? We've a few things to think on.'

Fronto smiled.

'I'd like to, but I have a prior engagement. I'll call on you before lunchtime.'

Balbus nodded, slapped him on the shoulder and, turning, wandered back toward the camp of the Eighth. Fronto strode on toward the Tenth, smiling as he appreciated the dry crispness of the air. Was Fortuna favouring them at last?

His tent stood off to one side of the legion's headquarters and his prior engagement stood at ease beside the tent flap, idly examining the sky, while drumming his fingers on his thigh.

'Atenos? Thank you for coming.'

The huge Gaulish centurion turned his pale grey eyes on Fronto, and he saluted.

'Legate.'

Fronto wandered past him into the tent, gesturing for him to follow. As the big man stooped and entered the tent where the legate had not even ducked his head, Fronto wandered over to his cot and unclipped his cloak, sitting down to undo his boots.

'Please centurion, sit down.'

'That's disrespectful in the presence of a senior officer, legate.'

'My arse. Not when we're alone it isn't.'

The Gaul shrugged and dropped into the nearby chair, unfastening his chinstrap and removing his helmet.

'I expect you can guess why I've asked you over?'

Atenos nodded.

'I did, with respect, inform the legate that I was happy where I was.'

Fronto laughed and sat back.

'I'm sure it's all very comfortable working with a legion largely composed of Gauls. Very homely. But the thing is, not only do I agree with my primus pilus that you would be a serious asset to the Tenth, but I have been in consultation with the general and both he

167

and I are of the opinion that the division between the two largely Gallic legions and the rest has gone on too long.'

Atenos focused a shrewd look on the legate.

'You're planning a large shake-up, sir?'

'To an extent. There is a stigma attached to the Thirteenth and Fourteenth legions just because they were raised from Gauls. The thing is: we are trying to *build* something in this land, not to just wipe it out; a new Gallia Narbonensis in the north, if you will. If we have any hope of incorporating Gaul into Rome, we need to start getting both peoples used to one another. The Thirteenth and Fourteenth have become almost perfect model Roman legions in the last year. I rarely even hear your own language among them these days, since nearly everyone among them now has at least passable Latin. It's time to start mixing the blood in the legions.'

Atenos shrugged.

'It may not work. It may, in fact, cause resentment among the other legions.'

'Possibly, but it's not a given. Remember that most of the *Ninth* were raised in Spain. There are surprisingly few native Romans among the Ninth, and Balbus' legion are largely formed from the Gauls in Narbonensis. The future depends on the present, after all.'

The large Gaul nodded thoughtfully.

'If you are insistent, you will need to speak to Caesar, sir, since he is still nominally in charge of the Thirteenth.'

Fronto shook his head.

'No longer. Caesar has assigned the Thirteenth to Lucius Roscius. I'm not sure how brilliant an idea that is, given that the bulk of the Thirteenth has only been speaking Latin for a year and Roscius is from Illyricum with Greek as his first tongue. But... well we said it was time to start mixing the blood. Roscius won't deny me the transfer. He and a few of his friends are a little... frightened of me.'

Atenos leaned back in the seat.

'You do realise, legate, that if you assign me to train your men, I expect full and total control of the training regime. No interference from senior officers?'

The legate nodded with a smile. 'I'd expect nothing less. Velius used to say the same.'

He sighed and lay back on his bunk.

'Do the Gauls have any weather Gods that like slightly stale wine?'

Atenos frowned in incomprehension.

'Never mind' Fronto smiled. 'Jupiter will do.'

* * * * *

Fronto lay on the slope and brushed a few blades of grass with his fingertips, immensely grateful that the weather had held. Two weeks now of largely blue skies and soft breezes had dried out the land and lightened the mood of the entire army. Two weeks, moreover, that had seen intense activity throughout the camp in the planning of the upcoming strike, despite the enforced wait.

Scouts had been sent out immediately by both horse and ship following the meeting, and had roved for nine full days, before returning to produce a detailed and thorough plan of the area concerned. Fronto's concern that the two long promontories that almost sealed off the bay would be crowned with strongholds had been borne out.

Planning had then begun in earnest, and had concluded with the legions moving out two days later in individual fragmented groups, each on their own mission and with precise timing in mind. Brutus, along with his marine contingent, had left first, heading out to the open sea to practice before they were required for the third phase of the plan. Caesar and the bulk of four legions had left, heading inland to bring the second phase attack on Darioritum from the east as a surprise. Finally, Fronto and Balbus, with less than four hundred men between them, moved northeast up the coast, separating once they closed on their destination, Fronto waiting a full extra day to allow his peer the time to bring the other force down from the north.

Once more, Fronto glanced over his shoulder and down the gentle slope. Close behind him, two centuries from the Second Cohort crouched in the grass in the last embers of the fading light. Behind them, their cohort's artillery section loitered by the carts among the sparse trees. Next to him, the two centurions and two optios peered across the two hundred pace strip of land that led up to the walls of the fortress.

For a while as they had approached he had been filled with apprehension, worrying that he had underestimated the place with only two centuries at his command. The scouts had been spot on, though. The fort was only around two hundred and fifty paces across, built on a rise above the entrance to the bay, but with sloping land to each side rather than cliffs. The whole fortress could not hold more than a thousand men at most; likely less than half that.

Curtius, the optio to his right, rubbed his eyes and squinted again in the dim, fading light.

'There's hardly any movement. I make it perhaps three or four on the wall facing us.'

Fronto nodded.

'That was my estimate too. Assuming they have the same guard on each wall, there are only about a dozen men watching the defences. But then, I suppose, it's nightfall, and they're not expecting any trouble.' He turned to his left.

'Virius? What are your thoughts on the walls?'

'They're not bad, but quite low. I'm thinking that the whole place was designed more to watch over the channel than to defend against any land attack. Still don't know how we're going to do it sneakily, though.'

Fronto harrumphed quietly. His own opinion on the plan he kept staunchly to himself.

'It all depends on whether Tetricus was right and how good your men are. If Tetricus was wrong, then we're screwed when we get to the walls. If your legionaries aren't sneaky enough, then all hell could break loose any time before then. Alright. Do the men all know their assignments?'

Virius nodded, glancing over his shoulder.

'Forty men apiece, sir. Who are you going with?'

Fronto gazed out over the small fortress.

'I'm going with Curtius.' He leaned over toward the optio and waved a hand. 'No reflection on your ability. Yours is the most critical task, so I want to be there.'

Curtius nodded.

'Glad to have you, legate.'

Fronto returned the nod, his gaze lingering on the bearded optio for a moment. Curtius had distinguished himself two years ago at Bibracte as part of a death-defying mad charge against well-defended rocks, the only survivor of the four men who had made the attack. Despite being watched and appraised by his commanders following his actions, the man had been involved with dangerous lunacy regularly enough that it had taken well over a year before he was considered for a promotion. Tonight would be his first individual command and Fronto could not help but feel a little apprehensive.

'Alright. The artillery are well hidden, everyone knows what they've got to do, and it's almost dark. Time to start getting into position.'

The officers beside him saluted as best they could and then shuffled back down the slope. Fronto remained for a moment, studying the small fort. So much could go wrong tonight, beginning with crossing the intervening space to the walls. He briefly offered up a half-hearted prayer to both Nemesis and Fortuna and then shuffled back on his elbows until he was out of sight of the target.

Curtius beckoned to him from his section and the legate crawled down the slope to the forty-strong force. They hardly even looked Roman. Due to the nature of the mission, the legionaries had left their armour, helmets and shields in the carts with the artillery, now dressed only in tunic, breeches and dulled cloak with a belted sword.

'Alright. Remember: a crawl at most. You have to be virtually invisible from the walls. Stay close to scrub and rocks for cover and only move when you think they're not looking. It doesn't matter if we take an hour or more to get there, so long as we're not seen.'

There was a quiet murmur of understanding among the men.

'Good. The light's almost gone now. Let's get moving. When this is over, you can all have two days' leave to drink yourself into a stupor.'

Without waiting, he nodded to the optio and the group began to move slowly up the slope toward the crest. Fronto's heart thumped noisily in his chest as they reached the rise and slid gently over, slowly, like a tide of men. Making small hand gestures, he motioned for the men to separate and slow down.

The next moment was nervous enough to age Fronto several years as the men of the Second Cohort moved across the most open section of ground, far too tightly-packed, fast and obvious for his liking but, after that heart-stopping moment, they began to settle into a strange, broken rhythm.

Each man would wait until there was no movement close by, and would then shuffle slowly to the nearest piece of unoccupied cover. As soon as *he* was in place, someone else would move up to his unoccupied position and, gradually, the entire half-century moved forward at a barely noticeable speed.

Fronto grinned with relief as he realised it was possible. Other options had been quickly pushed aside, leaving this as the only feasible means of advance. Boats would be too obvious, and even swimming and then climbing the cliffs would draw too much attention. For all the openness of this approach, the defenders would be paying most of their attention to the water and the channel between the headlands, and much less to the remaining strip of land that connected them with the mainland.

With infinite slowness and care, the men of Curtius' unit crossed the space, descending to the lowest point, close to the beach, where the scrub petered out but left them with dunes and large jumbled rocks instead.

Fronto paused as he pushed his back up against one of the great boulders of granitelike stone. He ran his fingers across the hard surface and nodded. Seems like Tetricus knew what he was talking about. Casting his eyes across the spur of land, he could see the other groups of men, slowly trickling across the ground toward the walls in much the same fashion as this group.

They had crossed fully half the distance to the walls, by his reckoning, in just a little under a quarter of an hour, way ahead of his expectations. He glanced over the top of the rock and could just make out the faint shapes of the men on the wall in the darkness.

Once more, he was grateful that Fortuna had seen fit to give them high clouds that hardly moved in the still air, hanging helpfully in front of the moon and stars and hiding their light.

He realised that nobody nearby was moving and, taking a quick glance around the side of the boulder, dipped forward and crept across the sand and scrubby grass to the next low pile of rock. As he came to a halt and allowed himself to breathe once more, he watched one of the men behind steal forward into the place he had just vacated.

How was Balbus faring at the other side, he wondered?

The sound of a night bird drew his irritated attention for a moment before he realised that the noisy creature was, in fact, Curtius, trying to get his attention from a nearby boulder.

He gestured with a shrug and the optio pointed over the top of his stone shelter. Fronto turned and looked at the walls again. Two of the four figures he had been able to spot last time he looked had vanished and, as he watched, the other two converged on a spot close to the gate and gradually disappeared from view.

Fronto scratched his head. Had they left the walls for some reason? Had they seen something and were heading for the gate to come out and investigate? He winced and rubbed his scalp nervously. What to do?

A short distance away, Curtius flashed him a wide grin and, making a couple of expansive gestures to those behind them, ducked out from the boulder that covered him, and ran in clear view across twenty paces of open grass, ducking briefly behind a bush to make sure the wall was still empty before running on.

Fronto stared at him. What was the idiot doing? What would happen if the guards suddenly came back into view? Fronto ground his teeth, but his irritation at Curtius blossomed into full blown panic as the rest of the unit, having seen the optio's gesture, broke cover at a run and hurtled past the legate toward the fortress.

'Oh bloody hell!' Fronto grunted in a loud whisper and then, taking a deep breath, left the boulder and joined the running men.

Over the grass and sand he padded, willing the wall to remain empty as he neared the point where the men were gathering behind Curtius, not ten paces from the bottom of the defences. Fronto, snarling and frowning, ignored the helping hands that were thrust out to him from behind rocks and ran past the men until he ducked behind the low bush that sheltered the optio.

'You damn idiot!' he hissed. 'I nearly *died* when I saw you running. What possessed you to do that?'

Curtius shrugged with a faintly apologetic smile.

'Sorry, sir. Saw an opportunity and took it.'

'What would have happened if you'd been seen?'

Curtius grinned.

'Ah, but we weren't, sir. And now we're here.'

Fronto continued to grind his teeth as his glare bored into the junior officer, but he did not trust himself to say anything else without shouting.

'You and I are going to have *words* when this is over.'

'By all means, sir. Shall we have a look at the wall for now, though.'

Fronto's glare remained for a moment, and he pointed a warning finger at the optio. A quick glance upwards confirmed the footsteps he thought he'd heard a moment ago. Figures were reappearing on the wall. Must have changed the guard for the next watch. The unit was, indeed, ridiculously lucky that they had stopped running when they did. Fronto held his hand up, warning the others to stay still and, silently and slowly, ducked out from the bush, trying to avoid any noisy undergrowth.

It was only when his hands touched the chunks of rock that formed the face of the wall that he allowed his breath to escape. This was it.

Slowly, keeping close enough to the wall that he would be out of the defenders' line of sight, he ran his hands across the surface.

Tetricus was right, the clever little bastard. He would have to buy the tribune a whole cartload of drinks for this. The fort walls were constructed in much the same way as most Celtic defences. A frame of heavy timber beams formed the shape of the wall, faced with tightly fitted smooth stones and then filled with compacted earth. Very defensible. All very laudable. But *these* walls had been here for a very long time and, just as the tribune had predicted, decades, if not centuries, of salt water and wind had had a profound weathering effect on the sawn wooden ends of the beams as they punctuated the stone of the walls, while the hard, solid rock had hardly suffered a mark at their hands. The end result was that the periodic beam ends had shrunk back into the surface, creating ready-made hand holes in the otherwise unscalable walls. Nature, for once, seemed to be giving them a helping hand.

Fronto heaved a silent sigh of relief and turned to the men behind him, hidden in numerous places.

With a smile, he gestured with his thumb.

* * * * *

Fronto glanced once more with irritation at Curtius. The man seemed determined to do things his own way, regardless of the consequences. The legate had made it clear that the rest were to stay behind him, lower down, until he had reached the parapet and peered over and yet, as he pulled his face up to the edge, the optio was already level with him to his right and doing the same.

Again, he glanced past the man to see the other units further along the wall, slowly and quietly scaling the surface. Angrily, he waved an arm at Curtius, while clinging tightly to the parapet with his free hand. The optio, thankfully, saw the gesture and ducked back down. One of the defenders, wrapped tight in his woollen cloak, strode past perhaps five feet from where the legate clung.

Moments passed until finally he heard the distinctive nighttime call of the corn crake from down near the water; nothing unusual enough to attract the guards' attention, despite being replicated on this occasion with two notched sticks by one of the legionaries remaining at the beach on watch.

Fronto nodded. The call was short and singular and told him that all four units were in position along the walls.

Taking a deep breath, he nodded to the optio and hauled himself up onto the wall.

The guard had walked past him and almost reached Curtius' position. As quietly as he could, as he got his knees on the top of the wall, Fronto drew his gladius. A few paces away, the optio's hand shot out across the surface and grabbed the Gaul's ankle, yanking it forward. The guard gave a gasp and fell heavily backward. Fronto lunged forward to silence the man with his sword, but the fall had cracked the man's head hard and driven the consciousness from him before he could shout.

Along the wall, the other guards were disappearing with quiet gurgles and gasps. Fronto immediately dropped to a crouch and turned to examine the fort interior and the other walls, as the men of Curtius' unit began to arrive at the top. The only buildings in the Veneti fort were at the high, central point of the fort, just as they had found in all the coastal strongholds, and the only visible figures within were milling around in the central open space, around a small fire, largely hidden between the buildings.

There were more guards along the other walls, and they would likely be the big problem. Not the most important one, though...

Fronto's eyes were drawn once more to the central buildings. At the far side of those, a small artificial mound had been constructed, crowned by a wooden platform upon which stood a beacon of dried wood, rising like one of the great ancient obelisks of Aegyptus.

Now *that* was the important target. If that warning beacon sprang into life, the whole plan was for naught. Subtlety was the key...

The legate almost bit off his tongue in panic as a warning cry went up from a particularly alert guard along one of the other walls.

'Bugger it.'

Fronto stood and waved his arms madly.

'Go!'

Without waiting, he grabbed Curtius and stepped forward. The interior face of the wall was much lower than the exterior and was backed with a slightly-sloping earth rampart. Still clinging to the optio, he jumped from the wall, landing heavily and awkwardly on the turf, jarring his ankle and cursing. To add insult to injury, Curtius, next to him, landed lithe as a cat and grasped the legate's tunic to steady him.

'Thanks' Fronto said sourly as the first of the men behind him dropped from the wall to the turf. Around them, the camp burst into life as the occupants realised they were being attacked.

As planned, the first and second Roman groups split left and right and raced around the walls, securing all points of access and the main gate, dispatching the remaining wall guards and enclosing the whole complex before beginning to descend into the interior.

The third group formed up as they descended the stairs near the gate and began to move at a run to meet the first groups of defenders who were appearing between the houses, racing to meet the Roman attackers.

Fronto and Curtius, aware that their men were hot on their heels, however, moved off without pausing to form up, charging up the slope on a course to bypass the square and its surrounding houses, making directly for the beacon.

Fronto swore with every step as his sore ankle thudded to the floor, though he was damned if he was going to slow down and pander to it with the irritating figure of Curtius running alongside.

As they approached the level of the first buildings, six men burst out from a narrow alleyway, armed and shouting. Four turned to face the oncoming Romans, while the other two ran the other way, waving burning torches.

'Oh shit.'

The four Veneti warriors, two with strange decorative helmets, leapt forward into the fray, two at Fronto and two at Curtius. The legate lurched to a halt, raising his sword just in time to deflect the blow from a heavy Celtic blade. As he ducked back, looking for an opening, he glanced at Curtius, only to realise that the optio wasn't there.

The confusion did not have long to take hold as he was forced to parry yet another heavy blow. Three more men joined him from behind, two of them taking up the position where Curtius had been moments before.

Fronto growled as he ducked a vicious, scything blow and, grinning, stabbed the man in his shoulder where he had overextended

176

his attack. While the Gaul stumbled forward in shock, Fronto blinked as he saw Curtius over the man's shoulder, already way ahead of the fight and racing off into the darkness after the torchbearers. How in the name of a dozen Gods had he managed *that*?

Fronto readied himself for the next blow, but it never came. The man he had lightly wounded had suffered a horrendous blow at the hands of a legionary who had just appeared on the legate's left. The two Celts who remained standing were now hard pressed as over a dozen Romans lunged and stabbed at them, more arriving all the time.

Another seven Veneti appeared around the nearest building and made for the fray, bellowing harsh war cries. The legate grimaced and turned to the men around him, just as another Gaulish warrior collapsed in a heap alongside the dying legionary he had attacked.

Grabbing the nearest men, he yelled 'You two with me. Everyone else, get stuck in!'

He pointed at the approaching Veneti and the legionaries roared as they ran to meet the enemy. Leaving the fight behind and hoping that his men would be able to hold off what could very well be a superior force, Fronto and his two companions ran on into the darkness toward the looming deeper black of the signal beacon.

They rounded the corner of the last building just as the first orange flames licked the timbers at the base of the tower.

'Oh bollocks!'

Curtius was being held at bay by two warriors, swinging madly with their long blades, while another ducked in and out of the beacon with his flaming torch. Wherever he touched it to the dry kindling, orange flames burst into life.

'Get those bastards!' Fronto barked, and the three of them leapt forward to join Curtius. The sudden arrival of reinforcements quickly turned the tide of the scuffle and the two warriors, hard pressed, went down one after the other to sharp, efficient blows.

As soon as the men were no longer barring his way, Curtius leapt forward and clambered up the small mound. The remaining Veneti warrior turned to meet this new threat, waving his flaming torch defensively.

Fronto and the other two men started up the slope, but they were clearly too late. Orange fire was racing up the kindling that formed the heart of the beacon and already the heavier timbers were beginning to burn. There was nothing they could do, now.

Almost derisively, Curtius knocked the torch from the man's hands and drove his gladius deep into the man's chest, pinning him to one of the strong wooden beams that formed the corners of the obelisk-shaped beacon.

'Get back, man' Fronto yelled.

Curtius let go of the sword, leaving it on the pinned man, glanced at the legate once, a crazed grin on his face, and then stepped across the wooden platform. There was a loud bang and the central mass settled slightly, a small explosion of fire and shards of burning wood bursting out of the beacon, setting light to the fringe of Curtius' tunic. The man reeled back, the sudden intense heat blistering his face and arm.

Fronto watched in horror as the tunic caught fully, fire racing up the man's back as the optio stepped to the next corner.

As the next moments unfolded, Fronto watched one of the most astounding acts of individual stupidity he would ever witness, his jaw hanging open and his eyes drying out with the ever increasing heat this close to the beacon.

Curtius, his hair frazzled, reached around the beam at the corner and gripped it hard in a tight embrace, the extreme heat of the wood blistering and ruining his arms. The optio, afire and sizzling, wrenched at the beam with all his might and, after a moment's pause, there was a crack and a deep rumble.

The huge timber bole and the optio grasping it came away at the same time, falling back away from the beacon and tumbling down the slope. Fronto and his two companions stepped out of the way, still staring in astonishment as the entire beacon collapsed and rolled down the grassy artificial slope, the fire dissipating as the pyre disintegrated.

The legate blinked and leapt forward to the still form of Curtius on the grass. To his further amazement, as he reached sadly toward the prone, burning, figure, Curtius spun around onto his back and continued to roll for a moment until the flames on his tunic were out. As Fronto stared down at him, Curtius grinned through a blackened and blistered face, his white teeth a sharp contrast, and reached out.

'Mind helping me up, sir?'

Fronto stared and then burst out laughing as he reached down for the optio's hand. As the junior officer rose to his feet, shakily, smoke rising from his burned hair and clothes, Fronto turned to the other two.

'Check that everything's secure, then send for the artillery and make the signal to Balbus.'

He grinned.

'And find us a capsarius; preferably one who doesn't flinch at a hog roast!'

Chapter 10

(Quintilis: Darioritum, on the Armorican coast)

Tetricus sat in the cold pre-dawn gloom astride his horse looking uncomfortable. The other tribunes had ridden back along the line of the Tenth, making their final checks before moving off. Tetricus glanced over his shoulder. The front line of the First Cohort stood ready to march a few paces behind him; the primus pilus, next to the chief signifer, backed by the rest of the standard bearers, musicians and a few immunes with tasks of their own, the bulk of the men waiting patiently behind them all. The tribune waved a hand at the primus pilus in what he hoped was a good, commanding, beckoning motion. The centurion strode forward until he reached the mounted officer.

'*You* should be doing this.'

Carbo grinned at him.

'Your rank says otherwise, sir.'

Tetricus sighed and made a desperate gesture with his hands.

'Fronto always leaves the primus pilus in charge of the Tenth when he's absent. I'm pretty sure he doesn't trust tribunes, probably because they're all politicians-in-waiting. Priscus used to command the Tenth on a semiregular basis!'

That wide, infectious grin remained on the centurion's face.

'I'm not Priscus, sir. My job is to direct the lads when we're actually busy fighting, so I don't have time to look all posh and official. Besides, the legate trusts *you*, even if he doesn't trust the others.'

'And that's another thing' Tetricus grumbled unhappily. 'I'm the second most junior tribune, and yet I'm commanding the others. I'm going to be as popular as a turd in a bathhouse!'

Carbo gave him an expression of fake sympathy.

'Just mimic Fronto. Drink too much, argue with everyone, disobey some orders and then launch yourself into a potentially fatal situation. Everything will be fine...' the grin widened even further. 'If it's any consolation, you've already got his grumbling down to a tee.'

Somewhere way off to their right a buccina rang out with a call that was picked up instantly by the musicians of each legion. Tetricus started slightly in his saddle as the call blared out close behind. Traditionally the tribunes rode at the front of the marching column with the legate, but Fronto was somewhat unconventional and Tetricus usually travelled by choice with the artillerists and engineers at the rear of the column.

Carbo nodded and then saluted.

'Ready to move at your command, sir.'

Tetricus grunted again and settled unhappily into his saddle. The sound of racing hooves announced the return of the other five tribunes.

'Everything's ready, sir.'

Tetricus nodded, trying not to catch the eye of the senior tribune who had reported to him. He swallowed nervously, keeping his hands tight on the reins to prevent their shaking becoming too noticeable.

'Tenth Legion: advance!'

Slowly, he moved his horse into a walk. Behind him, the centurions bellowed their commands, the buccinas blaring out calls.

The Tenth Legion set off for battle and, keeping his gaze steadfastly ahead, trying not to look at the other five tribunes, Tetricus' mind raced ahead of them.

He was woefully unprepared for this. The tribunes were not meant to command the legion. Oh, in the old days, they did. These days, though, the big decisions were all made by the legate and the actual running of the legion, even in battle, was the province of the centurionate. The tribunes were expected to ponce around doing whatever menial chores the legate had for them.

By Tetricus' estimate, at least two thirds of the tribunes he had met across the whole army were a complete waste of time from a military point of view. Most of them were power-seeking members of the equites class from Rome who were desperately looking for a leg up in the political circles of Rome. The tribunate was a well-recognised step for that.

Tetricus, however, had taken his commission originally in the Seventh Legion not to climb the political ladder, but because even as a boy he had been fascinated by the great works of the army. At the age of five he had watched as the men of Strabo's legions had carried out emergency repairs to the aqueduct of his home city of Firmum Picenum after tremors had brought down an arch and effectively halved the city's water supply. Observation of three days of repair

181

work had instilled in him a life-long love of all things engineering, though reading accounts of the siege of Syracuse and the great military works of Archimedes had clinched his desire to serve in the legions.

And despite inauspicious beginnings in the Seventh, his great love, and talent, for designing ingenious and complex defensive and offensive systems had been given full reign since the army had first marched into Geneva two and a half years ago. He'd achieved all he ever really wanted from the legions: a certain level of autonomy and the opportunity to turn his mind to overcoming amazing challenges with his engineering skill. He'd certainly never pictured this: sitting nobly astride a horse at the head of several thousand men, leading an army into battle.

'Sit up straight, for Minerva's sake.'

Tetricus shot a glance in the direction of the hissed comment to see one of the other tribunes glaring at him. He opened his mouth to apologise and then realised how idiotic that would sound. Instead, he tried to stop wallowing in his own discomfort and to sit proud like a commander.

Slowly, interminably, the entire army moving at the lowest common speed, that of the ox carts, the legions of Julius Caesar began to cross the stretch of low ground toward the looming ramparts of Darioritum. The land here was decidedly flat, so the Veneti oppidum on the low rise by the water stood proud and impressive, though not as impressive as the walls, Tetricus suspected.

The general had decided that a show of force was needed. This whole attack was more about frightening the local tribes than the mere conquest of a city and to that end, all four legions, along with their cavalry and auxiliary support, backed by the wagon trains and the artillery that remained with them, would move together to bear down on the Gaulish city with standards raised and fanfares blaring.

The tribune squinted into the dim pre-dawn light, trying to pick out more detail on the oppidum and watched with relief as the first shaft of golden sunlight touched the tree tops high on the oppidum. The information they had on the oppidum itself was, to his mind, sadly lacking. The scouts had not come too close for fear of tipping the Veneti off about the coming attack and thus their knowledge of the defences came from long-distance and second-hand accounts.

Once again he wished that Fronto was here rather than he and again he wondered how Fronto and Balbus had fared during the night. This entire escapade would be for naught if the two legates had not managed to secure the bay entrance. If the Veneti still held the promontory fortresses, their companions in the city would wait until the Romans had expended a great deal of effort and time getting to them and would then simply board their ships and flee as they had so many times before in the past few months.

Slowly, still running through possibilities and alternatives in his mind, Tribune Tetricus led the Tenth Legion across the low ground toward the bulk of Darioritum and as the paces passed interminably by the sun rose behind them, adding to the impressive sight of the four legions walking out of the golden glow, and gradually illuminating the oppidum ahead.

Darioritum was an impressive sight.

The Veneti had countered the inadequacies of the territory by increasing the man-made defences of the city. In Tetricus' experience, most of the oppida the army had encountered across the whole of Gaul had taken advantage of a high site, bolstered by thick walls and occasionally a low ditch at the bottom.

Darioritum lacked great hills or rocky cliffs; there were no unassailable slopes. Three low hills surrounded the port at the head of the huge bay, and each was low and gentle. However, in response to nature's failure, a man that Tetricus would have loved to speak to had carried out defensive works on an impressive scale. The walls of Darioritum were unlike any he had ever seen.

The oppidum sat on the slopes of the northernmost of the three hills, its ramparts reaching down to the water's edge and rendering that approach impossible by the army. In place of the more common ditch, the architect of Darioritum's defences had traced the two small rivers that skirted the base of the hill to both east and west and had widened the channel to create a moat a hundred paces wide.

Even if an army had managed to find a way by boat across the bay to the port or across the river, which would clearly be within easy missile shot of any defender, the Veneti had settled for not one, but two walls. A low wall constructed of timber and earth, much like a Roman camp, rose from the banks of the rivers and the rear of the port, leaving no flat land on which to marshal an attacking force. Twenty paces behind those rose the true walls of the city, high and powerful, with towers taller than was usual, allowing the defenders an unrivalled view of what was happening below the smaller wall, should anyone manage to get that close.

183

The result, as Tetricus had surmised from the scant accounts of the scouts, was that the only conceivable route of assault was to climb that northern hill and approach the oppidum from that side. However, the planners of the city had accounted for this weak spot in the defences by continuing both huge walls over the rise and allowing the slope several hundred paces from the enceinte to fill with dense woodland. The occupants must enter and leave the oppidum by boat at the port.

Clever.

The only possible land approach was hampered by trees and undergrowth. An army could pass through the terrain, but only slowly and individually, marshalling as a force once they had reached open ground, which would be in direct sight of the missile-wielding defenders.

It was well thought-out.

Again, as they moved on toward the looming fortress, Tetricus' mind wheeled through ideas and concerns. This was why it was someone *else's* job to lead the army: he needed his mind free to think on the problems ahead.

They could cut down the forest. They certainly had the manpower to do so. But it would be a slow job. Such thick woodland, it would be the job of a full day or two just to clear it out enough to pass a legion through. Even then, the ground would be impassable to carts and the artillery. Any attack would be delayed for the minimum of a day and would be down purely to legionaries with no artillery support.

They could try diverting the river into a narrow channel and filling the wide ditch enough to cross. But then they would still be working under missile attack of the defenders, it would still take more than a day and, once again, the ground once they had reclaimed it from the water would be too soft for easy traversing and would be impossible for the wagons.

It was a problem.

'Tribune Tetricus?'

Reeling his mind back in, he turned in surprise to see an officer he did not recognise from the general staff, closing with him.

'Yes?'

'The general requests your presence.'

Tetricus nodded nervously and turned to the more senior tribune by his side.

'Carry on. I'll return as soon as I can.'

The man saluted, saying nothing, and Tetricus kicked his horse into action, following the officer back toward the command party.

Caesar, along with his senior officers, had ridden half a mile ahead of the slowly-moving army and they were standing beside their horses, staring out at the oppidum ahead. As the two riders bore down on them and slowed to a walk and then a stop, Caesar turned and nodded at them.

'Ah... Tetricus. Good. Join us.'

The tribune dismounted and led his horse by the reins to join the officers. He smiled as he recognised the figure of Appius Coruncanius Mamurra, the engineer from Formia. To his eternal satisfaction, the great engineer nodded at him as one professional to another.

'Mamurra tells me there is no quick and simple way into Darioritum. I brought him on board because he, like you, is a man who likes to find solutions to impossible problems. I refuse to believe there is a problem of defence that cannot be overcome by the pair of you. Find me my quick way in.'

Mamurra shrugged at Tetricus as though in apology.

'A full day is the quickest I can think of.'

The tribune nodded.

'A day either way; either to rechannel and reclaim the river, or to deforest and move in from the north. But either way we couldn't get the artillery close.'

The officer nodded thoughtfully.

'We could perhaps speed things up with the river if we could get men across who could pull down the first wall and use it to fill the ditch?'

'Yes, but it's still slow, and they'd be in direct line of any missiles from the walls. We'd lose a lot of men.' He shrugged. 'We could torch the woodland? It's brutal, but a lot faster than men with axes.'

Mamurra shook his head.

'The ground and foliage are drying out, but they'll still be very damp. If we burn it, it'll smoke and smoulder for days. Too slow.'

'Then we're back to axes and a full day.'

Caesar looked from one face to the other.

'The legions are catching up with us. Find me a solution.'

Mamurra frowned and rubbed his chin.

'Of course, we don't have to remove the whole woodland; just enough to get a column of men through. Once we can get a century or two at the front they can perhaps use wicker screens to cover the rest as they filter through into the open ground?'

Tetricus nodded.

'Then we should concentrate on the low edge near the river. The trees are sparser there, and the men would be in less danger from the walls as they got closer. I'd be happier if we could get vineae to the front to cover the men. Wicker screens are a bit feeble. But then we're back to being unable to move big, wheeled structures over the sawn stumps.'

'Oxen and ropes' Mamurra smiled.

'Better than axes.'

'And if they can tear the trees from the earth whole and with the roots intact, rather than just cutting them down, the ground can easily be levelled for the artillery carts.'

Caesar nodded.

'Good. Tetricus? Go back to the Tenth and bring them around to the north. We shall approach from that side.'

With a salute, the tribune shared a professional nod with Mamurra and then turned to ride back to the Tenth. It would still be a slow job but, with a little luck, they could be through the woods and able to begin the assault by the afternoon.

'Then we'll find out what other little tricks they have in store for us.'

He just hoped like hell that Fronto and Balbus had secured those forts.

* * * * *

Centurion Atenos, commander of the Second Cohort and chief training officer of the Tenth Legion, glanced around him, taking stock of the situation. The depleted cohort, some of his men being on detached duty with the legate, had joined the First Cohort at the head of the Roman advance. Legionaries and officers stretched away on both sides of him, filling the deforested ground from the water's edge along to the remaining tree line.

Behind, a detachment of engineers and legionaries moved around the denuded forest floor efficiently filling the holes left by the removed trees and levelling and packing the ground. Behind them, a dozen vineae trundled periodically forward as soon as the ground was readied for them, coming to a halt as they reached uneven earth once more.

Swinging his gaze back round to his left, he could see the river, wide and shallow at this point, washing away the debris cast from the dying forest by the multitude of workmen.

And finally back to the front.

Despite being the head of the army, the men of the Tenth were not the furthest forward at the moment. Ahead of them, soldiers of the engineering details strained, pushing the bellowing oxen as hard as they could until, with a horrendous tearing sound, another beech tree came loose, the huge root system snapping and creaking. As Atenos watched, the cart began to drag the tree toward the slope that dropped to the river so that the workmen could roll it down to the river with a quick push and watch it float out to the bay.

A call from ahead drew his attention again. Centurion Carbo, off to his left, took up the call. Only a few trees remained before the open space that lay between the woodland and the low outer wall of the oppidum. As carts lined up ready to remove the last boles and soldiers flattened out the ground behind them, the first two cohorts of the Tenth Legion moved forward, filtering past them and between the trees.

Atenos took a deep breath as his men stepped from the cover of the trees and into the open air once more.

'Shields!'

He was impressed by the speed and efficiency with which his new command put the order into action, the entire line raising and locking their shields and hunching over slightly as they advanced in order to present as small a target as possible to the enemy.

His call had been just in time, as the Veneti on the high walls let their first volley of arrows, stones and bullets go at that moment, the missiles rattling off shields and helmets or embedding themselves in wood with a 'thunk'. Here and there, Atenos could hear the squawk of a man who had been unlucky; still, the manoeuvre had been smooth and resulted in fewer casualties than he'd expected from the first volley. The Tenth's previous training officer had apparently done a good job.

A quick glance to either side, unimpeded by the cohort who were, to a man, at least a head shorter than he, told him that the entire line had moved into position, presenting a solid shield wall to the enemy from the water's edge across to the eaves of the remaining woodland. More missiles rattled off iron and bronze.

'Screens!' came the call from the primus pilus to his left.

Atenos waited tensely as huge wicker screens, rejected as the main defence of the Roman lines, but very useful as a temporary measure to shield the men working behind, were raised by the second and third line and then filtered through to the front. Within a few moments, the whole shield wall now stood behind a row of eight foot wicker screens that blocked a number of the incoming shots. The screen supports were jammed into place and then the second group of screens were brought forward, raised to form a higher level of the wall and held in place by straining legionaries.

The First and Second Cohorts were in place, forming the first line, guarding the workmen and protecting them from enemy attack while they cleared the passage.

Behind, the ox carts were already working on the last few trees. Atenos glanced across at Carbo as, behind him, a young oak was violently torn from the earth and dragged away. The eaves of the wood were disappearing. Even as he waited tensely, he could hear the creak and groan and then the crack and crash of more trees being removed. The intensity of missile shots increased as the Veneti realised that the Roman attackers had forged a clear passage through the woodland.

'Watch yourselves. Step back from the screens three paces.'

Carbo, off to his left, cast him a quizzical glance, but echoed the order to his own men. As the confused legionaries stepped back and lowered the top row of screens, one of the men close by cleared his throat.

'Sir?'

Atenos shrugged nonchalantly and fell into place just as the first fire arrow hit the wicker screens and burst into a fiery orange ball that sent tongues of flame licking across the face of the wicker defence.

'Clearly none of you have studied the tongue of your enemy this past two years. At least learn enough to understand what their commands mean!'

The legionary blinked.

'Yes, sir.'

Atenos stood silent and afforded a quick glance at the primus pilus. Carbo was nodding at him appreciatively. Behind, the last trees had gone and workmen were moving up, filling in the few remaining holes. As they neared the last victims of the ox carts, the attacks intensified yet again, and a few blows struck home, taking the labouring legionaries through thighs and torsos as they worked.

Carbo nodded to him and, simultaneously, the two lead centurions gave their cohorts the order to fall back and protect the workers in close order. With perfect timing, the shield wall retreated a dozen paces and then, directed by a few gestures from their officers, split off into groups to produce individual shield screens for the work gangs as they flattened the forest floor.

At extreme range fewer of the missiles reached their targets and the instances of wounding decreased as the defences were reconfigured. The men worked under the shelter of the Tenth's shields, and slowly the vineae, huge wheeled shelters, rumbled toward them. Beneath the protective roofs of the vehicles, the rest of the Tenth Legion moved toward the walls of Darioritum, the other legions preparing to move on after.

Atenos glanced around once more to make sure everything was in position and, raising his shield against the possibility of a lucky strike, marched across the uneven ground to where Carbo stood, directing the shield wall around a work party that had just completed the infill of another hole.

'Sir?'

Carbo looked up and nodded professionally.

'Centurion. Nice work back there with the fire arrows. I'd bet they were a bit disappointed at how little damage they did.'

Atenos ignored the compliment.

'Sir, when the rest pull forward this place is going to be seething with troops. I'd like permission to try something before it becomes impossible.'

Carbo frowned.

'Something dangerous?'

'I want to take the Second Cohort around the outside of the outer walls and try and get to the port. If the legates should fail and the fleet don't make it into the bay, we could do with trying to prevent the Veneti from boarding their ships the way they usually do. Even if the fleet *do* get here, it would be better for our marines if the enemy ships weren't packed to the rail with escaped warriors. Better to keep the numbers weighed in our favour.'

Carbo stood for only a moment before nodding.

189

'It's a good thought. Be bloody careful, though. Perhaps you should take a few more centuries from the First?'

Atenos shook his head.

'Space will be quite restrictive down there. There may be too many of us already, sir. If you're alright with that, I'll move the men out as soon as the workmen have finished.'

'Good luck.'

Saluting, Atenos strode back to his men, watching as the last workmen packed down the former forest floor to prepare the way for the rolling vineae and the bulk of Caesar's army that came with them.

The Second Cohort would miss out on the glorious assault and watching as the first Roman standard waved from the top of that high wall, but the enormous Gaul had served as a mercenary in some of the most hellish and deadly wars the world had to offer and he knew how much more satisfaction there was to be had by being an aged healthy veteran with a history of quiet successes than to be a crippled soldier after only half a campaign with a few proud medals to show for it.

Wars were won with the mind, not the heart.

Narrowing his eyes, he scanned the top of the high wall. Something was wrong; the missile shots had thinned out suddenly.

He took a quick look at the workmen and made a judgement call.

'It's flat enough for the vineae; get back and arm up for the assault. Men of the Second Cohort: rally on me!'

Gritting his teeth as the men charged toward him, he set his sights on the low wall that ran along the river bank toward the bay, just a narrow strip of sloping land.

'Time to move.'

* * * * *

Carbo watched as the Second Cohort with their hulking giant of a chief centurion moved at triple time across the open ground to the low wall and began to move along it, staying as close as possible to the structure itself and moving toward the bay. As the primus pilus watched, he realised just how dangerous the run truly was. Almost everywhere along the route the Second Cohort was open to attack from the high walls above and had to run with their shields overhead like a high speed testudo. Even as he watched, three men fell foul of

190

well placed shots and disappeared into the river and even as he turned away he saw two more topple.

Still, the First Cohort had its own troubles to look to. As the workmen had finished their tasks and fallen back to reequip and Atenos had taken his unit off along the river bank, Carbo and his men had moved back out of missile range to meet up with the advancing vineae. Space had been saved for the First Cohort beneath the cover of the vehicles and, as soon as they were in position, the buccina call had gone up, heralding the attack.

Now, the huge wheeled vehicles trundled toward the low walls, reaching the edge of the denuded woodland after a brief uncomfortable journey over the undulating ground. As soon as available space allowed the vineae, each sheltering half a cohort of men and either a huge tree trunk ram, carried by sweating legionaries, ladders or other siege gear, filtered out into a line three vehicles deep and four wide.

The arrows thudding into the dampened hide and timber roof were fewer than Carbo had expected, and while the lack of offensive activity should have been comforting, it wasn't. Too many times this summer they had broken the defences of a stronghold to find that the place was empty when they arrived.

Grinding his teeth, he mentally willed the offensive on, the legionaries around him heaving the huge wheeled edifice forward until it closed on the low wall. The vehicles behind moved up to form an armoured tunnel that stretched back toward the army waiting out of missile range. Once they were through the outer wall, the tunnel would provide safe cover as the legions closed on the walls and climbed.

The outer defences were, just as had appeared at a distance, almost identical to those that protected a temporary Roman camp. The construction was clearly recent: a response to the growing threat of Roman action, or in preparation for a planned uprising, and following lessons learned from Crassus the previous year.

Carbo smiled. At least in this kind of construction they knew what they were dealing with. The earth embankment was only four feet high with no outer ditch and the wheels and height of the vinea allowed the occupants to reach the point where they could directly attack the wall without first countering the problem of the bank.

Listening to the thuds and crunches of the missiles hitting the roof and side walls of the vehicle, the primus pilus barked out his orders and watched as the men filtered along the side, leaving room in the centre for the huge treetrunk ram to be brought up.

Manhandled by forty legionaries, the tree took a short while to build up the kind of swing needed to damage the defences. As the ram first connected with the palisade, there were shouts of pain and anger from the men, their arms almost dislocated by the jarring impact. The entire vehicle shuddered, and Carbo winced at the noise before peering through the cluttered interior, trying to examine the damage. He could not get a clear look before the second heavily-swung blow connected, and the whole place exploded in noise and shaking again.

The first blow had clearly had the desired effect, the second merely knocking the timbers of the broken palisade to the side. As the ram was drawn back through the shelter and discarded to the rear, the men at the front filled the gap and got to work tearing the timbers apart and pushing them away, opening a large gap, while others took their dolabra and began to work at the earth bank, shovelling it out of the way. The task was made surprisingly easy by such recent construction, since the turf sods that formed the mound were still solid and could be easily shifted.

Carbo watched with a growing sense of uneasiness as the men worked, rapidly clearing a wide enough space in the low wall to allow the whole vinea to pass through. Peering ahead, past the workmen, the primus pilus sized up their next move. The ground between the two walls was low grass, perhaps a hundred paces across. The grass showed the growth of the season, but was all too neat for Carbo's liking. Given the still decreasing quantity of missiles falling from the high walls, he was beginning to doubt vinea cover was even a necessity now.

He frowned and waved to his optio, who was busy directing the removal of the turf sods.

'Ovidius? Get back to the army and tell them that something's up. The defenders are abandoning the walls, and we have to move now. We're leaving the vineae at the first wall and moving forward at full speed. Get the army moving.'

The optio saluted and turned, pushing his way back through the men to make for the rest of the force. Carbo glanced out of the front aperture once more. Occasionally a stone or arrow would fall into the wide grassy plain that separated the walls, but it was hardly the concerted effort of a desperate group of defenders.

'Alright lads. We're going to move forward quickly. No towers this time. Got to be quick and bold, so we'll be raising ladders and using grapples. Once we're through the first rampart, go very carefully; we've seen them use lilia pits in the past few weeks and it's too nice and easy out there for my liking. If anyone slips into one and is wounded, we can't stop to help you out; you'll have to wait for the capsarii as they follow up after the assault.'

He waited as the various pieces of siege equipment were brought up from the rear of the vineae and then took a deep breath.

'Advance!'

Without waiting for the call to be taken up by other officers in the cohort, he began to move forward along with his men, clambering through the fallen rampart. As the legionaries of the First Cohort began to move across the intervening space at a run, watching the ground nervously and carrying grapples, ropes, and ladders, the primus pilus spared a moment to look to his right, where the other assault groups had broken through.

He squinted in surprise at the figure of tribune Tetricus, shield raised against the occasional projectile, running across toward him. Why wasn't the idiotic officer at the back where he was supposed to be? Carbo ground his teeth, weighing up the possibility of running on with his men and later claiming he had not seen the commander. Shaking his head in irritation, he turned his back on his assault and strode across to meet Tetricus.

'Tribune?'

The temporary commander of the Tenth Legion bore a worried expression.

'Carbo... something is very wrong here. The closer we get to them, the less resistance there is.'

'Yes, sir. I have a feeling they're pulling the same trick, but earlier than usual. Got to hope the legates managed to secure those forts or we might just have lost them for good.' In the privacy of his head, his thoughts flashed with sympathy to the sight of Atenos and his four centuries of men running under constant attack toward the rear end of the oppidum where the Veneti could take ship.

Tetricus sighed unhappily.

'As soon as we get confirmation from the first assault, get a message back to the army and tell them to send as many men as possible round between the walls to the far side. We have to try and catch them before they leave.'

Carbo nodded and glanced toward the walls where the first men of the Tenth were now raising ladders, the defending shots hardly noticeable any more. There were no casualties to pits so either the men of the Tenth had been ridiculously lucky, or the enemy were prepared to give away Darioritum and sure of their ability to flee the field of battle safely.

'Sir, Centurion Atenos already took the Second Cohort round the outside before we even got to the outer wall. He had the same idea, and I think he might be in considerable trouble.'

Tetricus' eyes widened.

'Jupiter's balls! The man could be knee deep in body parts by now!'

The tribune spun around, shaking slightly, and spotted the centurion that had led the assault group from the second breach.

'Niger? Forget the wall assault. Get your men together and take them between the walls and round to the port area as fast as you can.'

He turned back to Carbo and opened his mouth to say something but was interrupted by a voice from the walls. The two officers turned to look. The first ladder was already in position, and a brave legionary had reached the parapet to peer over. He was waving and pointing across the wall.

'Looks like they've already left.'

Tetricus shook his head in irritation.

'Let's hope the Second Cohort last until we get there.'

* * * * *

Atenos stared. The flow of missiles falling from the walls onto the four centuries of Romans skirting the edge of the outer defences had slowed almost to a stop as the column had approached the seaward end of the city, and now, as he peered around the stockade, he realised why. The defenders of Darioritum had not waited long under the threat of Roman victory before beginning the evacuation of the city.

Clearly the women, children and old folk had been moved out first while the warriors remained on the battlements creating the illusion of a fully-defended city. They must have started some time ago, given the empty supply carts that stood on the far side of the port area.

Atenos took in the situation at a glance.

194

The low outer wall's gate was open, and a steady flow of the Veneti made their way through it, hampered and slowed by the available space. The flat ground between the gate and the dock was narrow and full of milling people. Beyond, three wooden jetties strode out into the waters of the bay, lined with Veneti bound for the great oak ships.

Several of the vessels were already wallowing out in the water, groaning under the weight of civilians. By the looks of it, already most of the noncombatants were aboard, leaving only the cunning and tenacious Veneti warriors at the dock, where they had set guards to watch for Atenos' approach.

As the big Gaul came to the attention of the Veneti, a shout of alarm went up. The centurion ducked back around the wall to where the other three centurions had gathered to receive their orders.

'Alright' the big man said in a businesslike fashion. 'We're a bit outnumbered. Just over three hundred of us and thousands of them, but that means nothing. Remember Thermopylae?'

Two of the centurions grinned while the other looked dumbfounded.

'We need to stop them boarding any more people and try and contain the rest until the city is in the hands of the army.'

He pointed at the centurions of the Second and Fifth centuries.

'You two get the nastiest job. We're going to go in en masse and drive a wedge between the wall and the docks. As soon as we've done that, your centuries get to push any remaining warriors back through that gate into the fortress and then hold it against them until help arrives.'

As they nodded their understanding, he turned to the centurion of the fourth century.

'I'm going to take the first in the other direction and push the enemy back along the jetties. We're going to push them as far as the ships and, if things work out, we might even get on board and cause a bit of havoc. The job of the Fourth is, once we've pushed them clear, to demolish the landward end of the jetties and prevent any more boarding in case we're overcome. Then you turn round and help the others hold the gate. Everyone clear?'

The centurion of the fourth frowned, a harelip disfiguration making his expression peculiar.

'We'll be cutting off your exit, sir?'

195

'We can swim if need be, so just do it. And when we round that corner, no marching slowly forward in a traditional Roman line. Speed is of the essence. Run like Greek athletes and form up only when we reach them.'

The officers saluted and then ran back to their men to give the appropriate orders. Atenos waited until the men were in position and then raised his hand. Near him, the signifer of the First Cohort waved the standard and the three hundred men of the Tenth Legion raced around the corner at speed, bearing down like a wall of bellowing iron.

The Veneti stood firm, planting their feet ready to withstand the smash of the Roman line, their swords and axes ready, spears held high.

'Wedge!' barked the huge centurion as they closed and, to the surprise of the Veneti, within moments the jumbled line of running men, each at his own pace and with no sense of Roman order, reformed into a wedge, shields interlocked to create an armoured point. The manoeuvre was so swift and slick it was like watching water flowing.

The Veneti, still braced for the crash of two solid lines, were totally unable to withstand the sheer force of the wedge formation driving into the centre and, in a disorganised mass of screaming, desperate men, were driven apart into two groups: one by the dock and one by the gate.

Atenos, leading the charge and in prime position at the head of the wedge, ignored the sudden sharp pain of a lucky slash from a broadsword that trimmed the bronze edging from the top of his shield and left a long, thin gash on his shoulder. As soon as he realised that they had broken through the far side of the Veneti mass, he shouted the order and the centuries split and began to go about their appointed tasks.

Reforming, the First Cohort, formerly the left side of the wedge, turned and became a solid shield wall facing the Veneti dock. With shouts from Atenos, his optio, and century's signifer, the wall began to move forward, the legionaries in a line three deep putting all their strength into the action.

They were less than eight feet from the water's edge, and here the Veneti had taken the opportunity to cut out a proper dock side, so the gentle slope into the lake had become a sudden drop into cold water deeper than a man's height. Rather than trying to inflict damage and butcher the men before them, the First Cohort pushed at their shields, moving forward like a wall, gradually shoving the shouting warriors back toward the jetties.

Some of the enemy had foreseen what was about to happen and broke away from the fight, dodging back onto the wooden jetties to reform there. Others were less lucky and disappeared with shouts of dismay, plummeting into the cold water and effectively out of the fight as they swam variously for the Veneti ships or the nearest scalable bank.

Within moments the first century had reached the edge of the jetty, and with surprisingly few casualties, but then that was the advantage the legions had in cramped conditions: the traditional Gallic sword or spear required far more room to wield effectively than the enemy were being afforded in this desperate press of men.

As the space before them opened up, the remaining Veneti having retreated toward the ships, Atenos bellowed another command and the century split into three groups, each one numbering perhaps twenty men now, and moved as individual shield walls onto the wooden jetties.

The numbers here were easier, at perhaps two Gauls to each Roman, though the sudden acquisition of space now gave the defending Veneti enough room to wield their blades effectively.

Atenos grinned from the front rank of men as he eyed the biggest of the Veneti warriors; a big man by any comparison... except when compared to the centurion himself. The score of legionaries moved forward at a slow pace, presenting a column three men wide - as many as the space allowed.

Drawing a deep breath, the huge centurion growled something in the unintelligible language of the Gauls. The big Veneti warrior ahead blanched and shied away from the oncoming Romans, but the press of his fellows prevented him from escaping.

'What did you say to him, sir?' asked the legionary to his left curiously.

Atenos grinned. 'I told him we were going to eat them all.'

And then they were upon the enemy, and the killing began. Lunging with his gladius, Atenos felt his blade bite deep into flesh and the big Veneti warrior cried out in pain, raising his sword defiantly and bringing it down heavily in an overhead blow. The centurion raised his shield and blocked the blow, though the previous

197

damage that had shredded the bronze edging had weakened it and the broadsword cleaved down into the wood and leather, jamming deep into the central boss and just managing to draw blood from his arm behind.

'Bastard!'

Heaving the shield up and to his left, temporarily inconveniencing the legionary fighting by his side, Atenos pushed the man's heavy sword away from him and leaned forward, thrusting his blade out to the right to cripple another warrior who had turned toward him.

His left arm occupied with the shield and jammed sword up to his left, and his other hand gripping the blade, deeply embedded in another man's chest, Atenos gave up the hope of an organised attack and let go of both, lunging forward and head-butting the man, hard. His helmet struck the big warrior between the eyes, shattering his nose and cracking the skull. As the Gaul staggered back into the press of Veneti warriors, Atenos lurched forward again, bringing his face down into the curve of the man's neck just above the collarbone.

With a snarl, he bit down, severing arteries and snapping tendons as he pulled his head back and ripped a huge chunk of flesh from the crippled warrior. The Veneti man screamed and collapsed back to the floor.

From amid a face covered in blood and gristle, Atenos grinned at the warrior who suddenly became visible behind the falling body. As the man went pale, Atenos spat a sizeable chunk of meat at him and reached out to his right, ripping his blade back out of the dying warrior.

Next to him a legionary fell, to be replaced instantly by another from the second rank. The Veneti outnumbered them, but the first century had added to their arsenal the weapon of terror, and the rear ranks were already throwing themselves into the bay in desperation.

Some fifty paces behind them the Second and Fifth centuries had mirrored Atenos' initial manoeuvre, turning the outer face of the wedge and forming it easily into a heavy shield wall that began to heave the fleeing Veneti back toward the gate.

The low wall around the outer edge of Darioritum was formed after the Roman fashion, and the sole gate at the port end was no exception. The embankment, four feet high for most of its circumvallation, here rose to seven feet to allow room for a double heavy wooden gate, while the palisaded walkway marched up and across the top, giving the Veneti a defensible platform.

Simple mathematics told the men at the front of the Roman force that their mission was an impossible one. The number of Veneti already outside the gate equalled the Romans, without the many thousands behind the walls still trying to leave and the warriors who had climbed up to line the palisade and raised platform above the gate.

Valiantly, the centurions braced in the Roman line and began trying to heave the shield wall forward, pushing the warriors back toward the gate, but the sheer weight of the Gallic force pushing back out against them was at least equal, and the legionaries found they were having difficulty merely holding their ground.

Every few moments there would be a cry of pain or anguish as one of the Veneti warriors fell foul to a well placed or lucky sword blow from the heavy wall of iron. However, the cries of the wounded or dying Veneti were outnumbered heavily by Latin shouts of agony or consternation as the men of the two centuries fell to blows from the mass of warriors. The Veneti lining the palisade had found their range safely now and were throwing spears and releasing slingshot that fell constantly among the beleaguered Romans.

The shield wall buckled every second heartbeat as men collapsed and the legionary behind them stepped forward to take their place quickly before the momentary space became a full breach that the Gauls could push into.

The tussling back and forth between the two lines, one desperate to push through to freedom and the other frantically fighting to hold the line, gradually became more and more perilous as the moments passed, the ground beneath them becoming slick with blood and gore, men tripping and stumbling over the bodies of ally and enemy alike.

The centurion of the second century shook his head angrily. This was a disaster! A quick glance up and ahead confirmed his worst fears. The line was beginning to break in places and three of every four bodies he found beneath his feet as he was jostled back and forth in the press of men wore the tunic and mail of a Roman legionary.

They would not last another hundred heartbeats. By his estimate, a third of the men were already gone, and the number of Roman screams was on the increase as the odds gradually tipped further out of their favour.

Taking a deep breath, he roared the command for individual melee, recognising that the shield wall was doomed, and the men, understanding the reason for the call, abandoned all hope of holding the wall and fell, instead, to the precision butchery for which they were trained. They would not last too long, but at least this way they would take some of the bastards with them.

Centurion Cordius of the fourth century, a grey-haired veteran with a harelip and a face 'only a mother could love' as he was regularly told, glanced over his shoulder and watched with dismay as he realised that the line by the gate was failing fast.

His men were busy hacking with their swords or sawing with pugio daggers at the ropes that bound the jetty planks together. It was going to be a long job. They were not engineers and were ill-equipped for such a task. Again, his head snapped back to the working legionaries. The battle would be long over before they could take down even one jetty, though he could see the value in Atenos' decision. Likely the gate would fall shortly and, if the jetties were still accessible, the Veneti would flee along them, massacring the Romans in the way and clambering onto their ships.

He glanced over his shoulder just in time to see the shield wall by the gate buckle badly. They would never have time... unless...

Cordius grinned to himself, his harelip curling strangely.

'Stop work!'

The men looked up in surprise to see their centurion grinning and pointing to a small group of empty four-wheeled carts that stood off to one side up the gentle grassy slope, presumably having been used to load the ships with all the tribe's goods before they began to board themselves.

'Get the carts. We'll roll them down to the jetties. If you've cleared enough ropes, they might collapse them. If not, at least they'll block them nicely.'

The gate was lost. They all knew it. There were now more Roman bodies underfoot than desperately hacking at the Veneti, and those remaining men were falling with every heartbeat. The centurion of the Second century that had put out the call for melee sighed as he realised that Cordius and the fourth had joined them, having finished with the jetties. The arrival of the fourth century would merely slow down the inevitable. Would anyone remember what a good job his men had done here against unreasonable odds?

He clucked irritably as he lunged out and stabbed another enemy warrior, pausing then for a moment to wipe the blood from his eyes where it continued to stream and pool from the throbbing wound on his forehead where a powerful blow had sheared off his cheek piece and sent his helmet flying off to the ground somewhere.

Whatever the chief centurion had meant by 'Remember Thermopylae' had escaped him but, perhaps, if it was pertinent, it would at least lead to him being remembered. Angrily, he lashed out at another man with his shield boss and drew back his gladius, watching with a doomed resignation as three burly Veneti singled him out and closed on him in an arc.

Close to the actual gate post, a small knot of six Romans had managed to reach the rampart and formed a defensive half-circle on the sloping bank, their backs to the palisade. Lunging repeatedly in an effort to keep the Veneti mass back from them, the optio among them paused for a moment to glance over the heads of the press of enemy warriors, trying to weigh up the numbers.

'It's the lads!' he cried out suddenly and shook the man next to him by the shoulder. The legionary looked up in surprise and then grinned.

A moan of dismay flowed through the crowd of desperate Veneti as they saw the advancing lines of bronze and iron and red wool closing on them from both sides, filling the wide space between the high wall and the outer rampart and falling on the panicked rear of the fugitives.

Down in the press, the harelipped grin of Centurion Cordius turned to the centurion of the second whom he had rushed to support, relieved at the shouted news of reinforcements.

But the other centurion wasn't there. The headless body lay on the ground next to him, blood pooling around the medallions and torcs on his chest harness. Cordius sighed and looked back up just in time to see a Veneti warrior gripping the head by the hair, grinning at him with a raised sword.

A thousand Gauls could not have blocked Cordius' path as he bore down to take his revenge on the grinning warrior.

Atenos rolled his shoulders, allowing the mail shirt to settle into a more comfortable position. Glancing off to his left, he did a quick

201

mental calculation. There were perhaps thirty of his men left. They had lost more than half the century on the jetties, a fact that was equally testified to by the sight of his remaining men having to grip onto one another to prevent slipping on the bloody slick that covered the timber, and plunging into the cold bay.

Heavy casualties, but the number of Veneti dead on the decking or bobbing around in the water made him feel a little better about it. As they stood on the empty ends of the jetties, all they could do was to watch helplessly as the Veneti fleet moved slowly off into the bay, unfurling their sails in preparation to catch whatever wind there was and take flight to their next fortress.

Would Caesar be angry? Probably, but then Atenos had seen angry generals before as both mercenary and war captive. Strangely, he found himself more worried about disappointing his legate than angering one of the most powerful men in Rome. Interesting, given that he'd only served under Fronto for a few weeks and had only known him at all for a little over a month.

He looked over his shoulder and squinted at the defences back on land.

Centurion Cordius had done a good job with the resources he had: One jetty had collapsed entirely at the land end, leaving a twenty foot gap over the chilly water. Another was in fragments, a broken cart wedged among the piles that supported the broken walkway. Even the third, though intact, was largely blocked by two more broken carts. The six other vehicles jutting from the water's surface told of the effort required to do such damage.

The fighting around the gate had looked bad the last time he'd checked, the red of Roman lines seriously outnumbered by the multihued Veneti garb. Now, however, he could see the glinting lines of the other legions closing on the rear of the mass. Good. At least the day wasn't a total loss. Caesar would have his meaningful victory.

'Centurion!'

He turned to the legionary who had called him, standing at the edge of the jetty, crimson from head to foot with Gallic blood. The man was pointing, and Atenos followed his gesture, gazing out across the water until he broke into a wide grin.

The wide, square sails of Roman triremes and quinqueremes were clearly visible beyond the Veneti ships.

The fleet had arrived.

Chapter 11

(Quintilis: In the bay below Darioritum, on the Armorican coast)

Brutus glanced across at the trierarch of the *Aurora*.

'Think we can contain them all?'

The captain clearly registered the doubt in his voice and equally clearly shared it.

'Most of them, sir. All the ships near the port are still slow and wallowing. They've not got their sails full yet, and we can run circles round them so long as we can keep them from getting round us. There have got to be fifty or so ships out here already under full sail, though. Look: they're already pulling out to our left to pass us.'

Brutus nodded thoughtfully. He had not come all this way in good weather at last just to be bypassed again. The Veneti already under sail had the edge at the moment and would be round behind the Romans in moments.

'Then we'll have to split the fleet. Send out the signals. Have the first six squadrons surround the fleet at the port. They should be able to do that easily enough.'

The trierarch looked less than certain.

'Sixty ships against more than twice that number, sir?'

Brutus smiled.

'Ah, but they have them trapped. With the army at the port, it shouldn't take much to get a surrender from them. It's these other vermin I'm more concerned with.'

The trierarch cast his gaze soberly over the four dozen heavy Veneti ships making their way toward the other side of the immense bay. With the numerous small islands that spotted the huge expanse, it was of prime importance to keep the Veneti fleet in view, or they could quickly land any number of refugees on one of these isolated isles and tracking them down later would be near impossible.

Brutus frowned. It would take the fleet about an hour at full speed to reach the narrow entrance to the bay from Darioritum. Given the trierarch's estimate of the difference in speed between the two fleets, the enemy could be there almost quarter of an hour before the Romans, though that was based on estimates from a day with strong winds. The current occasional gusts would work against the

203

Veneti, especially loaded down with refugees as they were. A three-hundred count, then. That was enough to keep them in sight.

He nodded to himself and then turned back to the trierarch.

'And split the remaining four squadrons. I want them in a wide cordon as we chase down the fleeing ships. When they turn to deal with, us I want to be able to close the line like a net.'

The captain, his face still registering his lack of confidence in the plan, saluted and strode across to the naval signifer, standing near the long halyard that ran from the main sail along fully half the length of the hull. As Brutus watched, willing extra speed from his men, the trierarch relayed the commands and the signifer began selecting his crimson flags and running them up the line in view of the other ships.

Brutus heaved a sigh of relief when, almost instantly, the commanders of the other squadrons' flagships relayed the signals to their own vessels and within moments the entire fleet broke up into smaller groups to tend to their individual assignments.

Tensely, as the *Aurora* began to turn back toward the west, he watched the majority of the fleet bear down on the helpless vessels at the dockside and offered up a prayer to Neptune that his prediction would hold.

Many Gauls might have been tempted to fight to the death; to the last man. They had seen it happen time and again over the last few years. If the Veneti fell into that category, then the six squadrons would have trouble and might not even be able to hold them. The fact that the Veneti had fled every potential engagement with the Roman forces, however, suggested that they had their survival in mind at all times and, given the presence of four legions watching them from the shore and a determined fleet blockading them in, they would have to be insane to do anything other than surrender.

No. That part of the fleet was no longer an issue, Neptune willing.

It was the fifty or so ships already straining to pull ahead that were the problem.

They were trying to flee, and that would not happen. And when it *didn't* happen, they would have no choice but to turn on the Romans and try to fight their way clear.

Already the *Aurora* had come about, along with the remaining thirty five ships of these four squadrons, five having been lost to conditions out at sea over the past few months. Brutus watched with satisfaction as the pursuing flotilla spread out into a wide line, staggered to allow plenty of room for each vessel. Now that they were following the Veneti, racing in their wake, the oarsmen pulling with all their might, it was clear that heavy loads and lack of strong winds were hampering the enemy quite badly. Their lead on the Romans was fairly steady, occasionally widening and then shrinking as the wind gusted.

The young officer sighed and stood leaning back against the rail. The next three quarters of an hour would likely hold very much the same view, but with different scenery slipping past. In the intervening time, all he could realistically do was watch and perhaps eat something to keep his strength up. Taking a deep breath and nodding his satisfaction to the trierarch, he slid down the rail to sit on the deck, leaning into the corner. His weary frame sagged with relief.

It had been two days since he'd had a chance to shut his eyes properly. Yesterday had been filled with the tense journey up the coast. Then last night they had anchored offshore in the darkness and watched the headlands keenly for a signal from Fronto and Balbus. Oh, he'd had the opportunity for a rest then, but who could find easy sleep on the eve of such an important action and while waiting for news upon which everything hinged?

After Fronto's signal and then Balbus' in the early morning darkness, the fleet had approached and landed to convey supplies to the victorious Roman units and their engineers. He'd taken the opportunity for an hour's shut-eye then, but it had seemed ill-fitting for the commander of the fleet to lie abed on the flagship while his fleet worked throughout the night and morning to supply the forts.

Then, with the dawn light, the fleet had moved into the bay slowly, in a wide net, checking out each bay and cove on the many islands as they moved in toward their target. While Brutus had anticipated that the Veneti fleet would be docked in its entirety at Darioritum, it had been a necessary chore to scout the entire bay as they moved to make sure that no Veneti squadrons lay in wait to spring a trap from behind as they bore down on the city.

All in all, it had been a tiring two days with moments of sleep snatched where he could, out of sight of the men. He could not even *imagine* how the rowers kept up this tremendous pace, sleeping as they had been for only two hours at a time and in shifts. They must be exhausted.

He watched with admiration the crew working hard and the moments slipped past as he chewed on meat and bread and allowed the relief of a rest to wash through him.

Brutus realised to his embarrassment that he had actually fully drifted off as the trierarch shouted him for the second time.

'Yes?'

He clambered to his feet and glanced across to the man, who was pointing ahead. The young man rubbed his tired eyes. He could hardly blame himself for falling asleep in the circumstances, but he would have preferred not to do so in full view of the crew as they worked.

His gaze followed the trierarch's gesture past the rows of heaving oarsmen, across the massed ranks of the marines on the centre of the deck where they stood ready for action, and to the scene unfolding ahead of the ships.

He must have been asleep for some time and cursed the trierarch under his breath for leaving him to rest. They were rounding the last island, a long, narrow spit, and bearing down on the narrow entrance to the bay.

Ahead, the Veneti ships raced toward the gap.

Brutus straightened his tunic and shifted the cuirass that had slipped uncomfortably during his nap. Taking a deep breath, he strode to the rail where the trierarch stood.

'Have the hooks readied. We may only have one go at this, so it needs to work first time. If the wind picks up and they get an opening, we'll lose them.'

The trierarch nodded and bellowed out his commands as the officer watched the enemy intently. The first few Veneti ships were approaching the channel.

'*Now*, Fronto... *now!*' he grumbled to himself.

Why wasn't he...

But he was.

Brutus smiled as the first huge rock arced up from the stronghold on the promontory and fell into the water with a huge spray, halfway between the hulls of the two leading ships. Even at their current distance, Brutus could hear the shouts of panic and dismay.

'Any moment now' he muttered, his eyes flitting back and forth between the various ships.

Several more artillery shots left the ramparts of the two coastal forts. The first fell into deep water close to another vessel but the second and third hit home, one smashing through the hull of a ship, holing it instantly, the second shattering the deck boards of another and bouncing along the surface, wreaking havoc as it travelled.

The catapults having found their range, more and more heavy stones began to arc out from the promontories and fall among the Veneti fleet, while the ballistae began to loose, their huge bolts plunging in among the crews and passengers, killing indiscriminately.

Panic gripped the Veneti fleet and they veered as fast as they could, turning away from this deadly corridor. No vessel could make it though the narrow channel intact and they had quickly recognised that.

Brutus watched with satisfaction as the ships turned and tried to flee along the coast to the north, past Balbus' fortification, trying to find an exit other than through the narrow channel or past the Roman fleet.

The wind was beginning to pick up, just as Brutus had been nervously anticipating. Now was the time; now or never.

He signalled the trierarch and, as the orders were given and passed from ship to ship, the entire Roman force changed direction and moved in to cut off the Veneti's escape.

'Full speed! Bring us alongside them!'

A quick glance and he counted eleven vessels that were already disappearing beneath the waves at the entrance to the channel. Fronto and Balbus' artillery had done a fine job, but had now ceased the barrage, as the Veneti moved away, for fear of striking a Roman ship.

He watched, taking short, tense breaths, as the Roman ships bore down on an intercept course, while he willed the wind to stay down long enough.

Slowly, the *Aurora* edged close to a huge Veneti ship. This was the first time Brutus had been aboard a Roman vessel as it closed on one the Gaulish ships and he stared, a lump in his throat. The deck of the enemy ship seemed so much higher, close up. If he stood on the trierarch's shoulders, he could grip the rail, but not on his own. The timber used in the construction was weathered and seasoned oak, thick and dark and strong. The enormous mass of folk on deck was

207

an equally impressive and worrying sight. They would outnumber the Roman marines by about four to one.

In the last moments, Brutus had the heart-stopping fear that his hook-weapons would be too short.

The *Aurora* pulled alongside the fleeing Veneti vessel, the rowers shipping their oars at the last moment in order to allow the hulls to close safely.

'Hooks!' bellowed the captain.

All along the left hand side of the ship the ranks of rowers, having dropped their oars, grasped the weapons that had been stacked on the deck nearby and hoisted them up.

Brutus almost sagged with relief as he watched the hooks being raised. Thirty men along the rail lifted long, heavy poles with a sharpened hook affixed to the end, the base being held for stability by another rower.

Without waiting for a further command, the men began to hack at the halyards and rigging, and any rope they could reach with the long poles, even managing the occasional swipe at the sail itself. Here and there, as the surprised Veneti rushed to the edge to try and fight off this bizarre and unconventional attack, the hooks were used to gruesome effect on the sailors before their attention was turned to the next rope.

Brutus grinned as the main sail of the ship suddenly came away from its pinned position with a ripping noise and whipped around uselessly.

The effect on the Veneti ship was instant and far more profound than even Brutus had expected. Bereft of its propulsion, the huge ship slowed rapidly. The oarsmen on the free side of the *Aurora* were still rowing like mad, using the pressure between the two hulls to keep their course straight, and the change in speed of their target resulted in the Roman vessel shooting out ahead.

The oarsmen quickly stopped their work, but Brutus grinned and yelled down at them.

'Keep going. Bring us round their other side and we'll repeat the job there!'

His grin widened as he realised that the fleet were having similar successes all the way along, the Veneti ships being rendered helpless.

He turned to the trierarch.

'Ready the marines.'

* * * * *

Atenos narrowed his eyes. As soon as the Roman fleet had appeared around the headland in full view of the city of Darioritum, the Veneti ships had reacted in selfish panic. Those vessels that were already under sail and out on the water made a desperate run for the open sea cutting past the Romans dangerously close, perhaps a quarter of their fleet in all, but carrying many of the women and children who had already boarded.

The rest of them, wallowing in the port area and with no hope of achieving speed quickly enough to escape the Romans, desperately tried to set their sails. For a moment, the big centurion wondered what they were up to. As commander Brutus split his fleet and a number of triremes and quinqueremes raced off after the fleeing Veneti ships, the rest of the Roman vessels closed in on the port like a net.

Why were they setting their sails, then? They had no hope of running.

They could not be planning to fight?

And yet, as he watched, much of the remaining Veneti fleet prepared for action, while a few of the more sensible vessels made for the jetties and relative safety.

Atenos grinned as he watched the nearest heavy ship, its huge square sail still furled, using the low wind and the small sail at the bow to guide itself toward the smashed jetty upon which he stood.

Perhaps a third of the remaining Veneti had seen the futility of the situation and were now making for the docks or the bank nearby, the rest racing out to meet the Roman fleet. The legionary next to him cleared his throat.

'Do *we* accept their surrender, or send to the general to deal with it, sir?'

The huge Gallic centurion turned a wolfish grin on him.

'Neither. Form up!'

The legionary looked confused, but came to attention along with the other eight remaining men of Atenos' squad on the wooden boards. On the other jetties, the rest of his century heard the order and snapped to attention, wondering what they were doing.

The centurion watched the huge Veneti galley close on the jetty. The tall sides were at just the right height to board from the wooden walkway. It would be amusing then, watching the triremes trying to

209

disembark here onto a jetty some eight feet higher than their deck. He continued to gaze, stony faced, as the ship came alongside him.

To the rear of the port, the rest of the Roman force was busy dealing with the surrendering horde of warriors that had become trapped at the seaward end of the oppidum. Sooner or later they would have to clear the way to the jetties and repair the damage done to them. For now, though, the First Century of the Tenth Legion's First Cohort was alone on the wooden jetties.

The Veneti warriors on board had their hands raised in a gesture of surrender as the vessel bumped against the timber of the jetty and came to a stop. Several legionaries staggered with the impact, but regained their composure quickly and returned to attention.

Atenos turned his fearsome, blood-soaked face to the surrendering Veneti and barked out a number of commands in the guttural dialect of the Gauls. Warriors flinched and ran the plank out to the jetty, hurrying off the ship and past the Roman column to stand, dejected, on the wooden planks, awaiting the decision as to their fate and hoping, presumably, that their surrender would earn them clemency.

Atenos watched as the last of the hundred or so passengers disembarked and, as the crew made to follow, he held up his hand and shouted something else in Gaulish, causing them to return to their stations.

'Sir?'

Atenos turned to the small party of Romans.

'Get aboard!'

The legionaries, confused yet obedient, turned and rushed up the boarding plank to the deck of the huge Veneti ship. Atenos followed them up and turned his fierce gaze on the ship's captain.

'You speak Latin?'

The man's face gave him the answer to his question and he sighed before reeling off instructions in their native tongue. The man shook his head defiantly.

'Yes you damn well *will*.'

Striding over to the shaken captain, Atenos, a head taller than him and drenched in blood and gristle, grasped the man by the tunic and lifted him off the floor until they were face to face, before speaking to him slowly and deliberately, almost in a growl.

The captain looked terrified and quickly nodded. As soon as Atenos dropped him back to the floor, he turned and began shouting commands at the crew. The huge centurion returned to his men as, behind him, the crew began to get the ship moving once more.

'We're collecting the rest of the century and then we go out to help the fleet. At ease for now.'

As the men of the First century relaxed, Atenos stepped to the rail. It really was impressive watching the Veneti sailors at work. The ship was huge and heavy, powered only by the wind in the small front sail and yet they were already sliding through the water moments after the command was given.

He looked over at the captain and shouted another command before turning to look at the legionaries standing to attention on the other two jetties. Close by, other ships were making for the docks and this ship would be getting in the way.

'You men get ready.'

The big war galley slowed as it approached the end of the jetty and Atenos waited until he judged the timing to be right.

'Come aboard!'

The legionaries looked at one another in surprise. The ship was still moving, and there was a gap of several feet between the jetty and the deck. The first man who jumped landed badly, falling to his knees and grazing them on the deck. Atenos tutted at him and beckoned to the rest.

'Get aboard or you're swimming after us!'

The men ran in a small knot and leapt aboard, some landing well, others falling as they hit the deck. As soon as they were safely on the ship, the captain picked up the pace as he made for the next jetty. Behind them, another Veneti ship had already begun to dock at the jetty they had left, yet more vessels closing in behind.

The whole procedure was repeated at the third jetty, though with greater ease, since they knew what was coming. After another shouted command in Gaulish, the huge centurion turned to his men.

'Anyone here had experience of fighting as marines?'

There was a long, unbroken silence.

'Me neither, but I've seen it done. No shield walls or testudos. As soon as we get near the first enemy ship I want everyone near the rail. On my command you run and jump for the enemy deck. When you get there, you come up fighting and don't wait for orders or formations. Just kill anyone who isn't one of us. If you miss the jump, you'll fall between the hulls. I wouldn't recommend that, so jump carefully. Everyone clear?'

The legionaries roared their understanding and saluted.

Atenos turned to look ahead as they broke clear of the many vessels trying to reach the docks and into the open water, heading toward the fleets, where the conflict was already underway. The Veneti ships outnumbered the Roman fleet by almost two vessels to one, but the Roman crews had adopted a peculiar tactic: they were sailing around the beleaguered Veneti, safe in the knowledge that the lack of strong winds left the enemy slow to manoeuvre. What they were hoping to achieve with this peculiar activity was beyond him until he saw, with a grin, two huge ropes give way on the nearest enemy vessel, allowing the sail to flap loosely over to one side, where it fell to the deck, useless.

Roman sailors and marines were hacking with some kind of polearm at anything available and were crippling the enemy ships with surprising speed and efficiency. Rather than boarding them there and then, they were leaving them, helpless and immobile, while they moved onto the next. Once they had the whole Veneti fleet becalmed and unable to move, they could deal with them at their leisure.

Atenos laughed. He had, given the navy's record so far, presumed that the *Roman* fleet would be the ones desperately trying to outmanoeuvre the Veneti, but the situation seemed to have reversed this time. Commander Brutus had apparently identified a way to even the odds. Of course, there was still the issue of dealing with the aggravated, howling Veneti warriors on board the impotent vessels once they were stilled. The fight wasn't over yet.

Shouting another order in Gaulish, he pointed at the near vessel that had now been abandoned by the Roman fleet, the trireme moving on to cripple another ship. The captain shifted the steering oar and Atenos' heavy vessel swung toward the bestilled enemy.

The Veneti on board glanced at the healthy ship bearing toward them and cheered, yelling encouraging cries that turned only moments later into shouts of outrage and consternation as they realised that the warriors on board the new galley were the iron and crimson figures of Roman legionaries.

Atenos turned to the men beside him.

'What do you say, Porcius? Do we offer them terms?'

The legionary grinned up at his centurion.

'Be rude not to, sir?'

Atenos turned back to the captain, who was watching with deep regret as he steered his ship to deliver his tribe into the hands of their enemy. Stepping to the rail, the centurion bellowed an offer to the men on the helpless ship.

The answer was not immediate, as it took a moment for the Veneti warrior to drop his trousers and turn around. Atenos almost laughed at the audacity of the man, a warrior after his own heart, but that heart hardened and his face soured as he listened to the shouts and jeers and suggestions concerning possible animal stock in his lineage being issued defiantly from among the enemy.

'That would be a 'no' to surrender then, sir?'

The huge centurion closed his ears to the increasingly brutal insults and turned to his men.

'No quarter. They've been given the option to surrender and declined it, so I don't want to see you stop just because somebody waves their arms at you.'

There was an affirmative murmur among the men and Atenos turned back to the rail. The two ships were closing rapidly.

'Alright. To the rail. Prepare to board.'

The legionaries moved into position, twenty seven men, along with their officer, each professional and eager for the fight. Atenos nodded with satisfaction. It was men like this that made the Roman army the force that would eventually conquer the world, the sky, and possibly even the Gods themselves.

He watched as the gap narrowed, taking a deep breath. The Veneti warriors howled and bellowed, banging their swords on the rail, encouraging their enemy to make the first move. 'Well,' Atenos thought, 'let's not disappoint them.'

'Board!'

The two ships had closed to a distance of perhaps three or four feet when the first man jumped and was caught midflight by a Veneti spear thrust out in defence. The blow was far from fatal, catching him in the hip, but arrested his momentum and caused the man, screaming, to plummet into the cold water between the two ships. A second man joined him midjump as a swung sword blow scythed a jagged wound across his chest.

The rest of the men began to land on the enemy deck and come up fighting just as the ships finally met with a deep, resounding thump that mercifully drowned out the crack of bones and stifled screams of the two men caught between the grinding oak hulls.

213

Atenos leapt, not waiting for the last of his men to cross first.

Landing heavily, but allowing his knees and ankles to bend and take the strain, the huge centurion came up facing a group of Veneti warriors, his sword gripped in his right hand, the broken shield long-since discarded back on the jetty.

Three men leapt at him, shouting, and Atenos lashed out with his left fist, delivering a punch that would have floored an ox, the force of the blow knocking the leftmost man clean from his feet and sending him tumbling into the press of men behind. At the same time, his gladius parried the first lunge from another man, barely sidestepping an attack from the third in time. A legionary appeared to his right, trying to help push the enemy back from his beleaguered centurion, but was felled by a heavy blow from a man Atenos could not even see.

Sidestepping to his left, the centurion slashed out with his gladius, feeling it bite into flesh, though unable to identify whose in the mass of howling Veneti. The other man stabbed out with his spear, his blow restricted due to lack of room, but good enough to connect. Atenos grunted as the point of the spear dug into his chest close to his armpit, and ducked to the side before the man had the opportunity to drive the blow home, wincing instead as the blade came free, tearing out a chunk of flesh, which fell away amid the fragments of ruptured mail from his ruined shirt.

As he ducked down and grasped the fallen enemy's sword with his free hand, he heard a metallic clunk and realised that the blow had severed two of the leather straps on his harness, allowing the phalera he had won by the Selle River last year to roll away across the boards and disappear over the edge into the waters of the bay.

He growled angrily and stood, the long Celtic blade in his left hand too large to be wielded so by most men. He flexed his muscles, ignoring the pulsing pain in his armpit, and grinned through his crimson, streaked face at the man with the spear.

For a moment the man flinched, and then recovered himself, desperately gripping his spear and waving it defensively at the centurion.

Atenos rolled his shoulders and shouted something in Gaulish before leaping forward into the press of enemies, both swords slashing out as he attacked.

214

Behind him, legionary Porcius, back to back with a companion, fought off a howling warrior and realised a space had opened up before him. Glancing over at his centurion, he shook his head.

Last year, Porcius and four other men had caught one of the wretched Gallic recruits from the fledgling Thirteenth Legion in the latrines and had taken out their frustration on him, beating him half to death before they saw sense and fled. All because he was a Gaul and had not belonged in a Roman uniform. Hard to believe they had done that, given the Gaulish-born centurion before him now, carrying the pride of Rome into a screaming enemy with no thought for his own safety.

At that moment, Porcius would not have been the Veneti for all the gold in Rome. A fresh wave of shame for his past actions washed over him and he ground his teeth, turning to the man behind him.

'We're clear. Let's go help the centurion!'

* * * * *

Brutus pointed past the rigging.

'That one.'

The trierarch nodded and gestured to his men. The Roman fleet had worked systematically over the last quarter hour and more, shredding the sails and severing the cables on the Veneti ships and now, with most of the enemy floundering and waiting to be boarded under the watchful eye of a number of triremes and quinqueremes, the last eight Veneti ships were attempting to flee the engagement.

The *Aurora*, along with nine other Roman ships, bore down on the desperately fleeing Veneti, granted a higher speed by the lack of wind and determined to put an end finally to the attritive warfare of this tenacious coastal people.

What hope could they have of avoiding the inevitable at this point?

Brutus frowned as he squinted into the distance and slowly the reason for the Veneti flight became clear. What looked like the coastal undulations common along this region was, upon closer examination, the entrance to a river, wide at the mouth, but rapidly narrowing. The Gallic ships with their shallow draft and intimate knowledge of the area would know exactly where they could safely sail, while the Romans would be at a considerable disadvantage. The lack of wind would no longer be the deciding factor then.

215

They would simply have to stop the Veneti before they could reach the safety of the river. He realised as he stood, fuming at the situation, that the trierarch was watching him with concern.

'We need to stop them getting as far as that river, or we'll end up beached for certain.'

The trierarch nodded, though there was a smile on his face.

'I don't think that'll be a problem, sir.'

He turned, ignoring the look of confusion on the staff officer's face, and pointed to the celeusta at his goatskin drum, busy beating out a backbreaking rhythm for the oarsmen.

'Slow us right down.'

As Brutus watched in disbelief, the oarsmen settled into a relaxed mode, following the now-ponderous beat of the hammer, while the trierarch had the signal sent to the other ships to follow suit.

'What are you doing?'

The trierarch turned his grin on the commander.

'Listen, sir.'

Brutus cocked his head to the side and concentrated. He could hear the noises of the ship, the splashing of the waves, the distant shouts of the Veneti on their ships...

... and the onagers.

He grinned.

The artillery emplacements on the fort above, under the control of the Eighth legion, had begun to loose once more, gradually finding their range on the fleeing ships. The trierarch had slowed the Roman squadron to keep them clear of danger.

Brutus watched with relief as the range was quickly adjusted. Moments passed and then the first blow hit home. A massive boulder struck one of the central ships of the group, ripping through the ropes, wrecking the deck, smashing the mast and causing general devastation.

Shouts of alarm went up from the Veneti. The ships at the head of the group strained to try and get ahead, though there was little they could do, too reliant on a failing wind as they were.

The artillerists of the Eighth made their mark once more as the latest adjustments in range brought a group of five shots to the very head of the group of vessels. Two of the shots disappeared into the water harmlessly, overshooting slightly, while the other three hit the two lead vessels, all but crippling them immediately.

216

The Veneti fleet foundered and, with signals sent by the trierarch of the *Aurora*, their accompanying vessels spread out, each marking a target, leaving the flagship at the centre, following up on the rear of the fleeing vessels.

Chaos ensued among the Veneti.

After a further volley of deadly rocks had fallen among the lead vessels of the escaping flotilla, Balbus' men settled into a steady rate of attack that brought their missiles down ahead of the enemy bows, deterring them from proceeding into the river mouth.

Brutus grinned. He would have to buy Balbus and his men enough wine to float a trireme when this was over.

Three of the eight vessels were already beginning to disappear beneath the waves, the damage from the repeated artillery attack too much for them. Three others had come to a full stop, the artillery shots dangerously close ahead and realising that their fight was over.

The nearest two vessels, at the rear of the Veneti flotilla, however, seemed to have other ideas. Their steering oars moved, and the vessels began to turn, much more sharply than Brutus could have expected.

'I don't believe it. They're coming for us!'

The trierarch nodded.

'Your orders?'

Brutus shook his head. What could they do other than engage?

'Prepare the marines. As soon as we get close enough, have the men at the front and back use the hooks to do what they can while the marines board from amidships. Have the platforms raised for the marines so they can cross.'

The trierarch saluted and strode across the deck to his second in command, where he began to give out the orders.

Brutus once more watched the two approaching ships.

The quinquereme *Accipiter* and trireme *Excidium* came alongside for support, the remaining vessels concentrating on the surrendering or floundering ships.

'What are they hoping to do?' Brutus asked the trierarch, eying the enemy carefully. 'Two against three and we have better manoeuvrability. Our marines are trained legionaries. What can they possibly think to achieve?'

The trierarch frowned.

217

'Not sure, sir. But whatever it is, they mean business. They've trimmed their sails just right. There's not a lot of wind, but what there is, they're using to the maximum. That man's a good sailor.'

'They're coming surprisingly fast.'

The trierarch continued to watch, and a frown fell across his face. Brutus glanced across at him.

'What?'

'They seem to have no sense of self preservation. A sensible captain would be turning to concentrate on the *Excidium* first. Take the smaller ship down and then concentrate on the others. Or at least split off and send one ship around each flank: one against the *Excidium* and the other on the *Accipiter*. But they're both running central, straight for us. They'll be surrounded by the other ships, and then they're doomed.'

Brutus watched the ships bearing down on them. The trierarch was right. In a few moments those two vessels would slide neatly into the gaps between the three Roman ships.

'A symbolic victory!'

'Sir?' The trierarch furrowed his brow.

Brutus shook his head in disbelief.

'They're only doing what the general did. Caesar went for their capital. It was a grand gesture of Roman power; a symbolic victory to break the spirit of the tribes. The Veneti have lost the war, and they know it, but they've identified the flagship of the fleet. Two against one. A symbolic victory. They don't care about the *Accipiter* or the *Excidium* at all, and they don't expect to survive.'

The trierarch nodded.

'Full speed! We need to outmanoeuvre them!'

But his calls were too late, and Brutus could see that already. The Veneti war galleys closed on the three Roman vessels. The trierarch of the *Excidium* was prepared and the oarsmen withdraw their oars, leaving a bare side to the approaching enemy. The Accipiter followed suit, but too slow, some of the complex five banks of oars failing to withdraw in time.

The *Aurora*, however, was still under orders to make full speed and the row upon row of oars remained in the water, pushing the vessel forward. The two Veneti vessels barged into the gaps between the Roman ships, smashing whatever oars remained protruding from the hull as they slid tightly into place.

The enemy captains were every bit the sailors that the trierarch had imagined. Their timing had been perfect. Rather than *racing* into the gaps, as they approached, their sails were loosened and luffed heavily, failing to catch the wind and slowing the ships rapidly. By the time the two hulls drew alongside the *Aurora* they were almost at a stop.

Sailors aboard the two high hulls threw out ropes and grapples, grabbing the Roman ship and pinning themselves to it, bring the three vessels to a virtual halt and dragging the hulls together. The *Accipiter* and the *Excidium* were unprepared for the manoeuvre and shot on forward, passing their targets and trying to pull to a stop urgently.

The oarsmen of the *Aurora*, already aware of the situation before the orders began to ring out, grasped swords, shattered oars, or whatever makeshift weapons they could find and rose from their seats to deal with the coming onslaught. The centurion in charge of the marines barked out an order and his men split into two units that stepped toward the rail at either side.

And suddenly the world was filled with deadly activity.

Not bothering waiting to lower boarding planks, knowing that their attack was virtual suicide, and they would not be sailing home, the Veneti leapt from the higher decks of their ships and down to the timber surface of the Roman flagship as soon as the vessels were close enough. The number of people that had been on board the enemy vessels was astounding, the ships having picked up as many refugees from the city as they could manage, and Brutus watched with fascinated horror as waves of Veneti poured over the edge of their vessels onto the *Aurora*'s deck, like violent, screaming waterfalls.

The staff officer stood close to the steering oars and the trierarch, watching the attack with a glassy stare. The enemy that leapt from the two ships were not what he had been expecting. There were traditional Celtic warriors among them, certainly, but this attack was something different; something sad and horrifying. The vast majority of the boarding enemy were women, children and old men, wielding whatever weapons they could find aboard their vessel, down to even sharpened sticks.

These were no Gallic army, but the desperate refugees of Darioritum, and yet they launched themselves into a violent attack that would end with them all dead, just in a last effort to destroy the Roman flagship and ruin the pride of Caesar's fleet.

Madness.

And yet it looked very much as though they might succeed. The *Aurora*'s accompanying vessels were even now reversing their oars and moving slowly back to the fight but, even when they arrived alongside the enemy vessels, they would not be in a position to help the flagship until they had first secured the two Veneti vessels, the former being trapped and squeezed between them.

The Roman crew were largely well-trained and well-armed, particularly the marines, a detachment drawn from the Ninth, but experience and equipment was only of so much use against odds of at least five men to one, which was Brutus' estimate as he watched.

The last of the Veneti leapt down into the fray, their own vessels now abandoned to fate. The commander watched in amazement as the melee seethed across the deck ahead. The sheer number of people aboard the Aurora was making it impossible to see how things were going. There were so many bodies heaving back and forth that hardly any deck space was visible. And the fighting was spreading.

Spreading his way.

Brutus blinked. The far end was already secured, with little or no activity around the ship's bow. Yet there had been but a moment ago. And now the fighting was getting dangerously close.

The young officer shook his head in realisation as he drew the sword from the expensive, decorative scabbard at his waist. Not only were the Veneti targeting the Roman flagship for a symbolic victory, they were well aware of where the ship's commanders would be and what a Roman officer looked like.

The fighting was getting ever closer, and the bow was now empty simply because the Veneti were trying to reach Brutus and the trierarch. A *really* symbolic action if they could defiantly present their conquerors with the head of the fleet's commander.

Close by, the trierarch drew a blade and stepped toward him, the celeusta joining them. A group of four marines broke from the fighting and ran toward them, forming up in front as a small shield wall.

Brutus closed his eyes for a moment and offered up a silent prayer to Juno. For all the expensive training he had, he'd very little experience in actually using his sword in combat. Staff officers rarely found themselves in life or death situations. People like Fronto and

Balbus, who were just as at home in personal combat as they were on a horse giving out orders, were a rarity even in the modern army. Brutus was a strategist, not a gladiator.

Opening his eyes once again in response to a loud, guttural cry, he saw the first of the Veneti burst through the mass toward them. The action was still moving this way and the Roman forces were clearly still horribly outnumbered, a thin line of armed oarsmen fighting madly to hold the Veneti away from the stern.

The first man who broke out had been quickly and efficiently put down by one of the marines from the Ninth and Brutus looked down at the spindly figure of the old man. Ridiculous. The Gaul must have been a sixty year old civilian, and he had attacked Roman legionaries with a belaying pin!

There was little time for more than a passing glance, though, as three more men burst out of the press. This time, two were civilians, but the third was a warrior, armoured in mail and wielding both a heavy axe and a stolen Roman gladius.

The three attacked the marine shield wall and Brutus watched in horror as the big warrior felled one of the marines instantly with a double blow. Another Roman disappeared to the deck beneath two young Veneti lads who combined their attack to butcher the screaming legionary with their daggers. Quickly, the remaining two marines reacted to the situation and once more got things under control. The legionaries dealt with the warrior and then leaned down and swiftly dispatched the two young men, though not quickly enough to save their compatriot, who lay on the deck in a spreading crimson pool, stabbed a dozen times and staring lifelessly at the sky.

Brutus rolled his shoulders. Was this to be their fate? Lying untended on a deck, staring at the Gods and testament to the rebellious nature of the Gauls?

Four more of the Veneti lunged through and, as they did, the remaining cordon of Roman sailors that had been keeping the fight away from the officers broke, the whole screaming melee flooding toward them.

Brutus steadied himself. The Veneti were now coming in force. The five men, two legionaries and three naval officers, retreated to the heavy rear rail of the ship, the last refuge. Among the bellowing Gauls running toward them were occasional Roman sailors or legionaries, hacking madly at the men, women and children around

221

them, largely ignored by their victims who, in a lust driven by desperation, fixed their sights on the officers.

The trierarch watched the oncoming flood of Veneti and turned to his commander.

'Get overboard, sir.'

'What?' Brutus stared at him.

'We're dead men now. Even if the other crews are on their way, they'll never be in time. You need to go overboard *now*.'

Brutus shook his head. He may not be prepared for, or any real use in, a fight to the death, but he was damned if a Roman fleet commander was going to be seen fleeing the scene. Better to die honourably than to run away.

'Just pay attention to them, not me.'

The trierarch held the officer in his gaze for a long moment. He'd always assumed that he would die aboard a ship, and at least they had won the war, even if they lost this particular battle. The rest of the squadron would take their revenge on these bastards, but they could not be allowed to take the head of the commander first.

Brutus set himself in the stance he'd seen Fronto take, preparing for the clash.

He was totally unprepared when the trierarch smashed a sword pommel into his bared head, driving the consciousness from him instantly. Morpheus enfolded him in his arms and together they sunk into blackness.

The trierarch halted the officer's fall and gestured to the celeusta. The rowing officer nodded, dropping his sword and grabbing Brutus, hauling him easily up. Turning his back on the attacking Gauls, he heaved the officer over the rail and watched as the young man plummeted heavily into the water, the cuirass pulling him instantly beneath the waves.

Moments later, the celeusta hit the water, his buoyancy guaranteed by his lack of armour, and he kicked down into the cold deep until his hands touched the cold steel of the officer's chest plate. Looping his arms beneath Brutus' shoulders, he kicked for the surface.

As he broke into open air, gasping, he wrestled with difficulty with the man's shoulder and side straps until the cuirass came away and disappeared into the deep. A small rivulet of blood bloomed on the officer's head where he had been struck by the trierarch.

222

The celeusta looked back up toward the deck above. The sounds of violent melee were clearly audible, but *his* fight was over for now. His job was to get the commander to safety.

Turning his back on the Aurora as its last Roman occupant fell to a scything blow, the celeusta secured his grip on Brutus and began to swim for the shore.

Chapter 12

(Quintilis: Below the headlands at the entrance to the bay of Darioritum)

White light…
Painful white light…
The taste of bile and salt…
The roaring of unbearable noise…
A smiling face.

Brutus shook his head and stared.
'Is this really the time and the place to be going for a swim?'
Fronto grinned.
'Whurr?'
The capsarius who was tending to the cut on his head tutted and pushed him back against the hard surface below. Brutus closed his eyes and tried to think back and organise his thoughts. Everything swam around rather unpleasantly when he closed his eyes.
'Whurr…'
Fronto's grin took on a note of comprehension.
'We're on the deck of the *Excidium*; on our way to shore.'
Brutus continued to shake his head in semi-confusion.
'Wha? Can' think.'
The face of the Tenth's legate took on a slightly more sombre look.
'No survivors, I'm afraid. Other than you and the man who dragged you to the *Excidium*, that is. Good man there… suspect he'll be in line for a bonus, eh?'
'No survivors?'
'Not one. The Veneti were pretty ruthless with the crew of the Aurora. They were still sawing the bodies to pieces when the two relief crews arrived. I haven't asked, but I somehow doubt there were any survivors on *their* side, either. I gather the captains of the *Excidium* and the *Accipiter* took the attack and the death of their colleague sort of personally.'
Brutus shook his head again and winced.
'But they were women and children, Marcus.'
Fronto allowed a certain unconcern to show on his face.

'They were an enemy who showed you no mercy. I won't mourn them, and neither will you.'

Brutus sat up slowly with the aid of the capsarius, who nodded in satisfaction.

'Nothing a rest won't sort out now, sir, but go slow til you find your strength.'

As the man hurried off to tend to other casualties, Fronto reached down and helped the bedraggled officer slowly to his feet. Brutus wobbled uncertainly and grasped the rail for support. For the first time, he took stock of their surroundings.

'Where are we now?'

'At the north side of the channel. Once the captain here found you and dealt with the remaining Veneti, he came across to pick me up. Now we're on our way to collect Balbus and then he's ferrying the three of us back to Darioritum to Caesar. I'm assuming that things are settled there.'

Brutus nodded uncertainly.

'They *should* be. We left enough ships to deal with the rest of their fleet and it looked as though Caesar's forces had control of the city. Oooh...'

For a moment he wobbled forward, sagging against the rail.

'I feel rather unwell.'

Fronto grinned.

'I feel like that on board most ships. But at least it's nice and calm here, and in an hour we'll be back among the lads, and I can find Cita and requisition enough wine to half-drown you again.'

Brutus gave him a weak smile.

'Then it's over. The Veneti are quashed.'

'Hopefully. Strangely, though, I've been hating this place since we returned, with all the wet and the wind and the storms. Now that it's settled and becoming quite nice, I'm getting used to it again. We're about to dock... hold tight.'

The trireme pulled slowly up to the small jetty that marched out into the bay below the fort. A small group of armoured men with red cloaks stood in a knot at the far end. Fronto watched with interest as the *Excidium* came to a stop and ropes were thrown ashore and then tied.

The small group began to move slowly down the jetty, and Fronto's face tightened. Something was wrong. A lump in his throat, he focused on the small knot of men as they strode toward the

225

trireme. He did not know the centurions and optios of the Eighth that Balbus had taken with him, let alone the legionaries, but he could see the figure of the ageing legate in the centre.

Fronto closed his eyes and threw a prayer out.

Balbus did not look good.

The legate was being helped along the jetty and, though fully armoured and on his feet after a fashion, he was paler than many corpses Fronto had seen. Paying no further heed to Brutus or the crew of the ship, Fronto leapt over the rail to the jetty and ran along the boards to the men.

Balbus smiled weakly at him.

'Hell.' Fronto's voice was like lead.

The older legate's face had a faintly blue tint and Fronto shook his head desperately.

'Stop, stop, stop!' he barked at the men.

Balbus sighed, and Fronto noted how he winced and shuddered when he did so.

'Oh shit. Show me your hands!'

The legate of the Eighth, confused, but too weak and pained to argue, held out a hand, the other still being grasped for support. Fronto looked down at the pale blue hand. The finger nails were bulging and wide, to the point of being unsightly. The legate of the Tenth grasped Balbus and gently took the strain, brushing the soldiers aside as he gained sole support of his friend.

Pausing long enough to give the older legate a breather, though that breath was shallow and came in gasps, he took his arm across his shoulder and began to help him slowly along the jetty, waving the other soldiers away.

Balbus smiled at him again and opened his mouth to speak, but the effort was too much and he sighed.

Fronto grimaced and took a deep breath.

'Get those ropes in and prepare to sail as soon as we're aboard. I want to get back to the army faster than Mercury himself.'

The trierarch of the *Excidium* took one look at the legate and his burden and nodded, barking out orders. As the two men closed on the rail, Brutus, now largely recovered from his bleariness, reached out and helped the older legate aboard.

As they planted their feet on the deck, the hammering of a fast rhythm began, and the oars began to dip. Brutus helped Fronto support the legate of the Eighth across to a free rowing bench and

226

lowered him to it. As Fronto held him steady, the young staff officer grabbed a barrel and moved it closer to serve as a backrest.

'Is he...' Brutus tried to find a way to be circumspect in front of Balbus but, failing, gave up. 'Is he dying?'

Fronto gave him a sharp glance.

'Not as long as I'm here, he damn well isn't! But I want to get him to a proper medicus as soon as possible.'

Brutus frowned as he examined the ailing man.

'I'm not sure, but I think he's slowly getting his colour back.'

'Good. But that might not be the end of it.'

Brutus turned his frown on the legate of the Tenth.

'Don't tell me you know medicine, Fronto?'

'Hardly. But I recognise this. Happened to my dad three times in a year and the third one took him from us for good.'

He ground his teeth and glared at Balbus before smashing his fist so hard on the bench he left a crack.

'I should have damn well seen it coming. I should have spotted it!'

Brutus shrugged.

'You couldn't have.'

'Yes I bloody could. Three times he's complained recently of heartburn. That's how it starts. It'll come to you as no surprise that my father was a lover of the vine. We thought nothing of his increased indigestion and heartburn, but then this started to happen: the collapsing; the blue skin and the fat fingers.'

'But he's clearly recovering, Marcus. Look: his colour is returning rapidly and his breathing's steadying.'

Fronto shook his head angrily.

'Yes, but this will have weakened him for good. Once it starts, it sets off a decline.'

He turned and grasped Balbus by the shoulders, pushing him a little more upright, and stared into the older man's face.

'You mad old bastard. You *knew* something was wrong. You *knew* you weren't well, and you volunteer to go personally invading a fort at night? Are you crazy?'

Balbus blinked and shook his head gently. The blue had faded. He was pale as could be, but better than before. With a sad smile, he opened his mouth and took a deep breath.

'Marcus? Couldn't let you have *all* the fun.'

'You mad old bastard. Don't you *dare* do this to me. I lost Velius last year and Longinus the year before. I'm not losing anyone this year. Gaul's had its last taste of my friends.'

Balbus chuckled quietly and wearily.

'I'm not dead, Marcus. Far from it… just overexerted myself a little.'

Fronto continued to stare in saddened anger at him.

'Rest. Stop speaking and rest. The medicus will sort you out.'

Balbus nodded and sank gratefully back to lean against the barrel. Fronto shot a meaningful look at two sailors who stood nearby furling ropes and gestured to the older legate. The men nodded and, dropping the ropes, leaned down to take hold of the weakened officer, supporting him as he sagged into a relieved doze.

Fronto marched angrily across the deck to the far rail and smashed his fist on the wood once again, wincing at the pain. Brutus followed him over and placed his hand gingerly on the legate's shoulder.

'He might be alright yet, Fronto? Just because it happened to your father more than once, doesn't mean it will to Balbus.'

Fronto shook his head.

'It will. Might be years before it happens again, but it will. And each time it'll weaken him until he just can't fight it anymore. After my father I… consulted several physicians. Balbus might be around for years yet, but not with *us*.'

'Sorry?'

'It's the end of his military career. Can't continue to command the Eighth. He'll have to go back to Massilia for Corvinia to look after. She'll be beside herself when she finds out.'

Brutus sighed and turned to lean on the railing, gazing out to sea.

'I can't imagine the staff without his input. You know the younger officers and tribunes call him 'granddad'? Not as an insult, mind you. He's probably the most popular officer in the army. More so than *you*!'

Fronto snorted derisively.

'I'm not popular. I piss too many people off.'

Brutus laughed.

'I think you might be surprised. That's one of the *reasons* you're popular.'

Fronto fell into a sad silence and stared down at the water.

'I hope this is it. Hope this is the end of Gallic revolts. Time to turn this place into a province and go home. I think I might ask Caesar to relieve me and then I can go with Balbus. Someone needs to take him home, and it should be someone Corvinia knows.'

Brutus shook his head.

'If there's anything left to do, you know Caesar won't let you go, especially if he's already losing the legate of the Eighth.'

Fronto ignored the comment, staring into the churning water, his mind refusing to let him rest. Balbus could not have looked different from Lucius Falerius Fronto, a tall man with speckled black and grey hair and a wide face with a permanent five-o'clock shadow, and yet whenever Fronto thought of the older legate now, he could not help but draw a disturbing number of parallels between the two.

Balbus had been the first friendly and sympathetic person he'd met after leaving Cremona with the Tenth more than two years ago. He'd grown close to the man in that time and realised that Balbus was, in fact, the only man in Caesar's army that he trusted implicitly and automatically deferred to the opinion of.

The conquest of Gaul was exerting a high price indeed.

He stared out across the bay toward where he presumed Darioritum to be and willed the trireme on as fast as he could.

* * * * *

Fronto paced and fretted.

'For Juno's sake, sit down! You're giving me a headache.'

Brutus pointed meaningfully at the bench next to him and raised an eyebrow at Fronto.

'Can't relax until I hear the medicus' opinion.'

'I know, but he's not going to work any faster just because you're wearing a rut in the turf.'

He watched as Fronto kicked at a tuft of grass in irritation and tried to identify a way to turn the legate's mind to a different subject.

'I expected you to explode at Caesar. At least an argument.'

Fronto stopped pacing and glared at him.

'He's the general. It's his game, so let him choose his rules.'

Brutus was beginning to worry. Fronto being argumentative and out of sorts was *normal* Fronto. Fronto being acquiescent and submissive was a disturbing sight. They had arrived at Caesar's hastily-erected headquarters tent less than an hour ago. The oppidum

229

was being systematically cleared and searched by the Eleventh and Thirteenth legions prior to becoming a temporary encampment, but in the meantime, Caesar had needed somewhere to debrief with his officers and the temporary camp prefect had responded by providing a tent near the docks.

As soon as they had landed on the jetty, Balbus had been taken off his hands by one of the capsarii that was working nearby and escorted to another hastily-raised surgical tent where the chief medicus could check him over. Fronto had refused to attend Caesar and had gone with Balbus, only to find that the medicus would not admit him. Angrily, he had raged impotently for a few moments and then rejoined the officers at the general's tent.

There had been surprisingly few casualties at Darioritum, given the scale of the operation, and Caesar had been in an uncharacteristically good mood, offering a great deal of praise to most of those involved, and particularly to Fronto, Brutus and the absent Balbus. Fronto had all but ignored the compliment, staring glassily into a dark corner, his mind elsewhere.

The news of Caesar's designs for the Veneti had met with varied responses. The execution of the leaders was to be expected, given the fact that they had risen in revolt against Rome after having accepted terms only the year before. Examples had to be made, and every officer knew the value of that, but the decision to ship the rest of the tribe: men, women and children indiscriminately, off to Rome to the slave markets had been more of a surprise.

Given the current objective of Romanising the Gauls, depopulating an entire region was perhaps working against their goal. The idea had been popular in some circles, though. The profit from the mass slave sales would be passed down from the general to the officers and men of the army. A legionary with a cash bonus was a happy legionary, regardless of the source of the money. Brutus had been less enthralled with the decision and had prepared for a huge outburst from Fronto. Indeed, he had not been alone. Most knowing eyes turned to the commander of the Tenth at the news, but Fronto nodded blankly, staring into the shadows.

The entire meeting had taken less than half an hour, and then Brutus had accompanied the worried legate as he had left the command tent, striding across the grass while officers and men went about their assorted business, rank upon rank of Veneti captives being roped and penned ready for their long journey to permanent servitude. On the high walls of the oppidum, close to the main gate, the leaders of the Veneti were being crucified on 'T' shaped posts, where they would remain until exposure or carrion feeders took their last breath from them, or until Caesar relented and decided to grant them a quick death by the sword.

And now, for the last quarter of an hour, they had stayed outside the tent of the chief medicus on Caesar's staff, Brutus sitting in a gloom of his own while Fronto paced and grumbled.

'Fronto!'

The pair of them looked up at the call. Crispus, the young legate of the Eleventh, was making his way toward them alongside an officer Fronto did not recognise. The worried legate waved a hand half-heartedly in greeting.

'How's he doing?' Crispus asked as they reached the bench, his voice full of concern.

'How the bloody hell would *we* know?' Fronto barked irritably. Crispus drew back in surprise, his companion's face registering the same expression.

'Sorry' Brutus apologised for him. 'The medicus won't let him in.'

Fronto glared at them.

'Look,' Crispus said quietly, 'I know that you're vexed. As soon as you have seen the medicus, we are going to take you into the city and find a purveyor of alcohol where we can let you drown that sorrow.'

Fronto shook his head silently, still pacing.

'It wasn't an offer, Fronto. It was a statement.'

Fronto rounded on him, a finger raised, and opened his mouth, just as the tent flap opened. The four men attending outside looked up apprehensively.

'Legate Balbus is resting.'

'Out of the way.'

As Fronto tried to push the medicus aside, the man stood firm in the doorway until the other three officers pulled the struggling legate back into the open. Fronto rounded on the unknown officer, a pale, thin, serious looking fellow with straight black hair.

'*These* two can get away with that.' He raised his hand threateningly. '*You* I don't know, and you'd better be on first name terms with the Styx boatman if you ever touch me again.'

Crispus hauled Fronto around.

231

'This is Lucius Roscius, your fellow legate from the Thirteenth. Roscius, don't mind Fronto, he's just a little upset right now.'

Fronto turned a withering glare on them and then swung back to the medicus, who was standing rigid and blocking the doorway.

'Let me in.'

'No, legate Fronto. Your friend is resting and may well already be asleep. I have administered a mixture of henbane and opium to induce extended rest. If he is strong enough, I will allow you to visit tomorrow morning. He will not be disturbed or moved now until tonight when he can be carefully transferred to a safe, hygienic, building in the oppidum.'

Fronto glared at the medicus, and Brutus frowned.

'So what is your diagnosis?'

'I have let his blood in appropriate quantities and slowed the flow with mandragora. The symptoms I have had described to me are consistent with a condition Galen noted, and the physical evidence supports that diagnosis. If there are no complications of which I am unaware, legate Balbus can prevent further attacks of this kind with a careful regimen of diet, light exercise and a calm environment that is not too wet and earthy, since his black bile is, I fear, in excess. There should also be periodic bloodletting to help restore the balance of the humors and bring the black bile back down.'

Fronto shook his head angrily.

'He doesn't need cutting. They did that to my dad, and it made no difference.'

The medicus glared at him.

'Do not presume, legate, to lecture me on medicine. I know nothing of your father's progression, but I am entirely confident in my diagnosis. You may visit tomorrow morning.'

Without a further word, he turned and retreated into the tent. Fronto lunged for the doorway, but Brutus stepped into the way.

'Come and have a drink. You need it, whether you want it or not.'

Grasping the shoulder of the grumbling legate, Brutus turned him away from the tent. Almost as though a spell were broken when he lost sight of the leather door flap, Fronto took a deep breath and gripped and released his hands a couple of times.

'Yes. Wine. Or possibly even Gaulish beer. Preferably by the cask, in either case.'

232

As the four men strode toward the oppidum's gate, Fronto turned to the pale young man in the burnished breastplate to his left.

'Sorry. Rude of me. Not your fault. I guess we met in Rome?'

Roscius smiled, an odd sight on his grave, alabaster face.

'I had the honour of accompanying Caesar to your home on the Aventine, yes, legate, though we had no opportunity to speak then.'

Fronto nodded.

'Good thing really. I don't think I was a very courteous host that day. But then, I *was* piss wet through.'

Roscius smiled again.

'I believe you merely corrected bad manners among your guests. No gentleman could find fault with that.'

Fronto gave a weak smile, his first in hours.

'I think I like you, Roscius.'

'High praise indeed' the man said, his face straight, but a twinkle in his eye.

Fronto laughed as the four officers approached the gate of Darioritum.

Balbus had been one of his best friends these past few years, but it was occasionally driven home into his gloomy consciousness that there were more people he relied on in this army than the legate of the Eighth. A small collection of good friends always seemed to be on hand whenever he needed them.

The oppidum was eerie. The entire population of Darioritum had been rounded up, along with the other Veneti refugees, and placed in guarded stockades nearby. The town itself stood hollow and empty, like Carthage after Scipio was done with it. The only signs of life were the occasional contubernium of legionaries, performing a secondary sweep of the buildings, and the occasional moans of the crucified leaders on the wall.

The gate remained intact, the huge portal standing open; a testament to how easily the Roman force had stormed the oppidum.

'I'm not sure I like the 'Carthage' solution. When we occupy a Gallic oppidum, there's usually local merchants and innkeepers still there to serve us afterwards. That's how it goes: we beat them, but then we invite them to become part of our empire and we pay them for their services appropriately. It's all good... but when they're systematically extinguished, it feels wrong.'

Crispus nodded sagely.

'It is an old-fashioned response. And brutal, I admit. However, in terms of inn keeping, I fear I have frequented enough establishments these days to have a strong grasp of what is required. Let us find a tavern, and *I* shall serve the drinks.'

Fronto smiled at him.

'You, Crispus, are a constant source of support to a weary old soldier.'

'Sir?' a strong voice called out from behind.

The four men turned together to see Atenos, chief centurion of the Second Cohort in the Tenth Legion, striding after them.

'Centurion?'

'Legate, I have a message for you.'

Fronto nodded 'Go on then?'

The huge Gallic centurion held out his hand. A neat scroll tube lay in it.

'Oh, a *written* message. Alright.'

As he grasped it, he frowned.

'This has come from Priscus in Rome. He doesn't let other people handle these?'

Atenos shrugged.

'I wasn't about to let the courier disturb you now, legate. I may have made him soil his breeches before he agreed to hand it over, though.'

Fronto stared.

'Anyway, Atenos... I've been hearing stories about your performance since we parted. What the hell did you think you were doing?'

The big Gaul shrugged.

'Training, sir.'

With a salute, he turned and strode off. Fronto shook his head.

'That man is going to either make or break the Tenth. I'm not sure which, but I'm certainly glad he's on *our* side.'

A chorus of chuckles greeted the comment, and the officers ambled on through the main street until they spotted, not far along, a tavern sign hanging over a low, oaken building.

'That'll do.'

As they made their way into the murky interior, Crispus trotted lightly over to the bar area and began to look up and down behind it.

'They've got some fairly potent looking brews here; the smell is curling my nose hair. There's some wine here, though. Looks like its

234

come all the way from Gallia Narbonensis. Could be just the thing to relax you, Marcus.'

As Fronto wandered across to the table by the window and sank into a chair, Brutus gathered other seating from around the bar where it had been overturned, and Roscius, an intrigued frown on his pale brow, walked across to the bar to help Crispus.

'You actually drink the local brews?'

'Indeed, yes. Try them... you might be surprised. I've grown quite accustomed to them. When we returned to Rome in the winter, I had to pay an emperor's ransom to import beer from Vesontio. Imagine that: importing Gallic goods to the capital.'

As the two men laughed and went along the kegs, Fronto undid the scroll case and unrolled the letter.

Marcus.

I do not know where to begin. Things are beginning to fall apart in Rome. I would be careful how you pass this on, but the elder Cicero has been before the senate a few times, attacking Caesar's various bill and achievements. Not sure why or what he hopes to achieve, but he is definitely stirring up trouble for the general.

Clodius appears to have stopped visiting Pompey's house. I suspect we have been seen observing them, since the two never meet now, but I have seen Philopater speaking to some of Pompey's men from time to time, so there is still something going on.

A number of people who gave evidence for Caelius in the trial have come to a nasty end in the last week. It appears that Philopater has been a busy man. Three known allies turned up on the banks of the Tiber following a swim while attached to marble busts of the general, so I think we can read a message into that, and two more died when their houses mysteriously burned to the ground.

But I'm afraid I have saved the worst for last.

Your mother was attacked at the market yesterday. I was not present. She was out shopping with Posco when, according to witnesses, they were jumped by four men and dragged into an alleyway. Do not worry unduly. I had a medicus visit the house straight away as soon as they returned. Your mother was beaten, but not seriously wounded. She is more shaken and frightened than in actual pain. Posco fared worse, as he tried to fight them off.

I have no hope of discovering the identity of the men who attacked them, since there was no sign of them when I got to the site of the attack, but there is one ray of light. A beggar saw what happened. The four attackers took them into the alley and, moments later, another man entered too. The beggar said he looked like he might be a retired soldier, but whoever he was, it looks like he saved the pair of them as, moments later, they returned to the street, running for home, and shortly after, he reappeared and left the scene. The enterprising beggar followed the old soldier and gave me an address for a paltry sum of money.

I go today to try and track this man down and find out whether he is involved or merely a brave passer-by. Either way, I have spent considerable amounts of your money hiring more men and have put a permanent large guard on your mother and Faleria, and all the house and servants.

I will write again as soon as I know more. I have received nothing from you yet since my last letter, but then I assume your courier is still on route to me. I hope the campaign out there finishes soon, as we really could do with you being back here.

Hoping Fortuna continues to watch over you.

Gnaeus.

* * * * *

'The answer is no.'

Fronto ripped his hands away from the table in disgust and whirled away from the general, grinding his teeth. He took a deep breath, willing himself calm, and then turned back.

'But we're done here, and the legions are staying. You don't need me.'

'Fronto, whether we're done here or not remains to be seen. The battle only concluded today, for the love of Venus!'

The general sighed and cradled his hands on the flat, wooden surface, fixing Fronto with a sympathetic look.

'I *know* you want to go home. I *understand* that, Marcus. I want to, as well. And I'm aware that Balbus is going to have to be sent back to Massilia and that you'll want to go with him, but the timing is simply not auspicious for such acts.'

236

Fronto shook his head.

'Then what are we waiting for? Tell me that!'

'We have to give it at least a week here to make sure that we have all of the Veneti and that no more centres of resistance are going to spring up. We need to contact the Osismii along the coast and make sure that they know the situation and are willing to take their oaths and acquiesce to the power of Rome. We have to wait on word from Crassus, Labienus and Sabinus to make sure their actions have also been a success. I am simply not willing to leave the job unfinished and march back to Rome without being certain that Gaul is completely pacified.'

Fronto growled.

'This benighted bloody country is *never* going to be pacified. Crispus has this lovely analogy of a lumpy sleeping pallet that describes the whole damn situation in disgusting detail. And anyway, Sabinus and Labienus are capable of doing all this for you, and Crassus will probably have executed half the population of the south west by now, so you could go to Rome if you really wanted.'

A sly look crossed his face.

'Remember the letter I showed you? Cicero's causing you trouble. You need to get home too and deal with that.'

Caesar's eyes hardened.

'Marcus, you are *not* changing my mind; you are merely beginning to aggravate me. We will remain at Darioritum until we receive word from the other armies…'

Fronto started to speak, but Caesar raised his voice and shouted over the top.

'AND IF WE ARE REQUIRED TO CARRY OUT FURTHER ACTIONS WE WILL DO THAT TOO!'

He fell silent under the glare of the Tenth's legate and sighed again.

'Look, Marcus, I am not unsympathetic, but you are a soldier. You know how this has to be done, and if you were *thinking* like a soldier right now, it would be *you* saying these things and not me. You are angry, tired, worried and saddened by both Balbus and your family's plight. However, your place is with me and with the Tenth until the campaign is at an end for the year.'

Fronto opened his mouth again, but Caesar held up his finger.

'You can be of no help to Balbus right now. In fact, your presence and involvement is more likely to cause him further discomfort than to relax him. As soon as my personal medicus says he can travel, I will send Balbus home with the best physicians we have to offer, a small group of helpers and an escort of veterans from Ingenuus' guard. Likely the Eighth will want to send an escort too. And then, when the time comes and we are done in Gaul, you and I shall both visit Balbus and his lovely wife on our journey back.'

Fronto grumbled, but kept his mouth shut.

'Your sister and mother are in the best hands available, Fronto, as you well know. Priscus is not going to let anything happen to them. Your mother has suffered, I know, but now Priscus will be looking after her and making sure it doesn't happen again.'

Again, Fronto grumbled, but said nothing.

'Marcus, we have to be sure *here* first. Logical. Methodical. Certain. Go and find your close friends, drink yourself into a comfortable stupor, get some good solid sleep, visit Balbus in the morning, and then we'll talk again. I can't spare you until the campaign's over and you know that, but in the morning you'll be rested and thinking straight.'

The general smiled slyly.

'How often do I actually advocate your binges, Marcus? Look on this as an opportunity, as I will not expect you at the staff meeting in the morning.'

Fronto sagged. The problem was that the general was correct in everything he said. His presence would only make Balbus try harder and strain himself, when he should be lying back and relaxing. Priscus would have taken the attack on his mother rather personally and would tear Rome to pieces to stop it happening again. And most of all, if the army did not complete the job here in Gaul, they would end up coming back again later in the year, or early in the next, to put down yet another rebellious tribe.

It galled him, but he could not fault the reasoning. Of course, he did not *feel* very reasonable, right now.

'I'll do just that. Try not to be too surprised if I'm not here tomorrow, though.'

It was a stupid and petty thing to say, and he knew it. His gaze refused to rise to meet that of Caesar. The general smiled as though he saw plainly through the childishness.

'Drink, relax and sleep, Marcus. Tomorrow is a new day.'

Fronto glared up at him, but nodded despondently and then turned and scuffed his feet angrily on the way out of the tent.

By now, all the Veneti prisoners had been processed and were safely locked away in guarded stockades. The commotion had died down considerably, the Roman fleet moored in the bay, and much of the army organising themselves ready to move into the oppidum, leaving large vexillations of troops outside in camps. Fronto marched past them, ignoring the activity as he made his way back to the gate with its grisly decoration and the street beyond with the tavern sign that marked the location of his friends.

As he rounded the gate entrance and entered the main thoroughfare, his gaze fell on four men making their way down the centre of the road toward him, and he frowned.

The two men in the centre were staggering, supported by legionaries at their shoulders. They appeared to be Gauls, dirty and unkempt; perhaps refugees who had hidden in a pig pen or a...

He blinked as he realised that the brown, stained and torn tunics that the men wore beneath the fresh woollen cloaks about their shoulders had once been the crimson tunics of Romans. The two men were Romans. His eyes refocused. They were Romans, but they had beards and long hair. Dirty and disfigured.

No... not disfigured, but walking with limps and cradling weakened or broken arms.

'Who's that?'

The legionaries, startled by the sudden attention from a legate, almost jumped to a salute, remembering at the last moment to hold on to the men they escorted. One of the hairy, unkempt figures looked up in surprise.

'Fronto?'

The legate frowned.

'Who the hell *are* you?'

The man opened his mouth and grinned, three missing teeth making a conspicuous hole in his smile.

'Quintus Velanius.'

'Velanius?'

He knew the name, but could not place it.

'Oh come on, Fronto. We played dice often enough last year? Senior tribune of the Eleventh.'

Fronto's eyes widened.

'Velanius? I thought you were dead. *Everyone* thought you were dead. It's been months!'

239

The legate came to a halt as the groups met and he looked the tribune and his companion up and down. They had clearly been brutalised and tortured, but nothing that would not mend. He could not believe it.

'Stop shaking your head, Fronto. You look like there's something wrong with you.'

'But how?'

'We were kept in a cellar; a virtual dungeon. It's like the tullianum. We've been shouting for hours, since we heard the Veneti leave, but these lads only just found us.'

Fronto grinned, feeling a little of the weight of anger and sadness fall away.

'You need a shave.'

The tribune next to Velanius, whose name escaped Fronto, laughed.

'Not just shave, but scrape months of crud from the skin. I feel like I've been living in a latrine... a *cramped* latrine.'

'And then' Fronto added, 'after you've had a bath, you need to report to the general, get yourself debriefed as quickly as possible, and then get back here and make for that building over there, with the hanging sign.'

Velanius shook his head, smiling.

'You never change, Fronto. We'll join you tomorrow, perhaps. Today, we need to recuperate and sleep.'

Fronto shrugged.

'Suit yourself, but my purse only stays open for so long.'

'Yes, until you've lost it all at dice.'

'Sod off' he said, grinning madly.

The officers continued to smile at one another for a while, and then Velanius sighed.

'Come on. We need to go. See you later, Fronto.'

The legate nodded, smiling, as the two men limped off with their escort. He watched them until they passed through the gate and out of sight, and then turned and crossed the street, entering the tavern. To his surprise, no one else had yet joined the other three occupants.

'Fronto. How'd it go?'

As he entered, he strode across to the seat he'd left around an hour ago as he'd finished reading Priscus' letter, and sank gratefully into it. As he exhaled slowly, Crispus placed a mug in front of him. Fronto eyed it and then looked up at this friend, an eyebrow raised.

240

'No wine?'

'Drink that. It will do you good. I've tested three or four now, and I think I can safely say that this is the one you need tonight.'

Reaching forward, he sniffed the mug and recoiled before grasping it and tentatively taking a sip.

'Juno's arse... that tastes like... well, I suppose it tastes like Juno's arse, probably.'

'Get it down you.'

Opposite, Brutus, grasping a cup of wine that Fronto eyed enviously, sat back.

'I assume that Caesar said no?'

Fronto nodded.

'Not really a surprise. We knew he would. What did he say about Balbus? Is he sending him back straight away?'

'Soon as the medicus agrees to it.'

'Has he decided on what to do with the Eighth?'

Fronto frowned.

'You have the sound of a man angling for a legate's position?'

Brutus shrugged.

'Little need for more naval activity. I don't want to jump into Balbus' boots while they're still warm but... well, yes. I can see myself in the position. Can't you?'

Fronto shook his head.

'Probably not. Maybe, but probably not. The general had already lined up Cicero for the next available legate position. Not sure whether he'll still go through with it, given that Cicero's brother's busy calling him names in front of the senate, but there you go.'

Crispus retrieved his own drink, and Roscius of the Thirteenth used a foot to push a chair out for him. Crispus nodded and sat.

'So the situation in Rome is not troublesome enough to encourage Caesar back there yet? Not even the disturbing possibility that Pompey and Cicero are now in league together against him; possibly even with Clodius?'

Fronto shook his head and eyed the mug of dark, frothy liquid suspiciously.

'There's no real evidence of that. It's just conjecture. Problem is: I *like* Pompey. Always did. If Caesar had *half* of Pompey's honour; his way with *people*, he could rule the world.'

He smiled.

'Mind you, if Pompey had half of Caesar's *guts*, so could he.'

Crispus nodded.

'Between *them*, Crassus and Clodius, the future of Rome is beginning to look distinctly oligarchic.'

Fronto frowned in incomprehension, and Roscius smiled.

'Run by a few powerful men. Like multiple kings' he said quietly.

Fronto sighed.

'There was me being desperate to get home, but the more you lot talk about it, the gladder I am that I'm out here.'

Brutus smiled and took a sip of wine.

'On the bright side, Marcus, we've some time to breathe, rest and recover. Nothing else is likely to happen until we have word from the other armies.'

Fronto leaned back in his seat and, closing his eyes tight, threw down the entire mug of insipid ale in three huge gulps, before belching loudly and slamming the mug on the table.

'Resting it is, then. Now take this shit away and find me something in a nice red.'

Interim - Late Quintilis: Rome

Gnaeus Vinicius Priscus slumped against the cold marble and winced. He'd been kidding himself all winter and spring that by the end of the year he would be as strong on his feet as ever he was, but this last day of ducking into doorways and stomping around the streets of the city had made it abundantly clear that he would never be *that* Priscus again. His lame leg was strong enough to support him and walk for a while though after an hour every step became a dull, painful ache. The limp slowed him down and, after a day on his feet, he was beginning to worry that, if he fell over, he might never get up again.

But the day was almost over. The sun had already sunk behind the Esquiline Gate away behind him and night was beginning to draw in.

He'd been curious this morning when he first shadowed the address the beggar had given him. The apartment block in which the mysterious man had been renting a room was what could charitably be called 'humble', and Priscus had loitered across the passageway at dawn, wrapped in a plain woollen cloak, waiting for the man to show his face.

And when he did, Priscus had frowned and watched the man intently, trying not to register his surprise. He knew him from *somewhere*. Perhaps he was a veteran of the Tenth, or someone he'd met among the other legions over the past couple of years. He could not place the face precisely, but the man was hauntingly familiar, with his light and athletic frame and chiselled, suntanned features.

For a while, he had worried that his limp and slight deformity would make his pursuit obvious. He had not realised until he paid attention to the people in the streets around him, however, just how many lame or crippled folk littered the streets of the great city in the lower class areas, and his prey remained unaware of the former centurion following his every move.

It was humbling to think on how many of these lame people all around had also served in the legions until that wound crippled them and took away their livelihood. It struck home how privileged he was to be allowed to continue to serve in such a condition.

And so he had blended with the poor folk of Rome as he followed his quarry throughout the day, and the man had busied himself with what Priscus considered to be the most dull and mundane routine possible. The absolute high point of excitement had been a visit to the baths and a bite of lunch, breaking up the monotony of shopping, washing clothes, reading the notices of the acta diurna in the forum, a couple of visits to temples and an hour or two spent poring through records in the tabularium. Priscus had tried, but had not managed to get close enough to see what records the man had examined. All in all, a frustrating day for the lame spy.

He had been about to give up on the whole affair and pass off the situation and the saving of lady Faleria, Fronto's mother, as pure good chance. As a last nod toward thoroughness, he had followed the man, clearly a former soldier, back toward his rooms as the sun began to sink, only to watch him walk straight past the building and to the market stall along the street, where he stopped to purchase a spray of colourful and sweet smelling flowers.

Intrigued now, he had followed the man once more as he made his way east to the edge of the city and then out through the Esquiline Gate, past the suburban spread beyond, and out along the great Via Labicana, lined with its tombs, monuments and mausolea.

He had been forced to fall back a little once they had left the press of city folk and made their way along the sparsely populated road.

Finally, but a moment ago, the man had stopped and, producing a key, ducked furtively to the roadside and unlocked the gate of a tall, circular mausoleum.

Priscus watched with interest as he leaned against the marble, rubbing his hip and thigh and wincing with the pain. When this was over, he would have to travel half the width of the city to get back to the Falerius household. He would need a soak and a drink when he got back.

Grumbling, he watched the silent bulk of the circular tomb. The light continued to fade, and he had to pull sharply back into the shadows as the man reappeared and, locking the gate, turned back toward the city and strode off with a weary, heavy gait.

Priscus dithered, unsure whether to follow the man back to town or investigate the mausoleum, but the pause allowed his curiosity to get the better of him and he spared one last glance at the retreating figure of his quarry before lumbering quietly across the road and to the solid iron gate of the tomb.

Inset into a smooth marble façade, the gate was fastened with a sturdy lock, the interior obscured by a second curved wall that formed a passage around the edge of the mausoleum and circled a central chamber. Priscus could see a small oil lamp on the shelf opposite, and the heady, mixed aroma of sweet flowers and burning oil proclaimed that the lamp had been used recently. A striking flint stood on the shelf next to it.

Was it sacrilegious? Would he be pursued throughout the rest of his life by the lemures if he did what he was thinking of doing? He smiled. Fronto was getting all superstitious and worrying about ghosts and demons, but the Vinicii were made of more practical stuff.

Still smiling, he reached into his tunic and withdrew a steel spike around a handwidth long. He may be from a respectable family himself, but there were skills one learned that came from lower-born influences. The smile sliding into a wide grin, he began to work at the lock with the spike, his tongue protruding from the side of his mouth until, after a short pause, there was a click and the lock fell open.

Much better this way. A rock would have been quicker, but it would have been impossible to conceal the fact that someone unauthorised had been here.

Taking a quick glance around the area, he satisfied himself that he was alone in the near dark. Taking a deep breath, he swung the gate open, grateful that it did not grind or squeak.

Lighting the oil lamp was quick and easy, since it had only very recently been extinguished and Priscus raised it above his head so as not to blind his night vision with the flickering flame. The encircling corridor stretched off for a couple of paces ahead but, as he shuffled down it, the arch into the central enclosure was close by.

Taking a deep breath, the possibility that someone could be lurking in the dark only now occurring to him, Priscus ducked swiftly through the arch and stood, his jaw agape as he took in the sight of the central chamber.

As with most high-born family mausolea of this fashion, the walls were dotted with alcoves, each of which held a cinerary urn for a member of the family. Between them, often below the urns, small inscriptions of high quality named the deceased, though none were large enough to be visible in the flickering lamplight from the doorway.

It was not these that had caused Priscus' jaw to drop.

A large slab or table stood in the centre of the chamber and upon it lay the body of a woman. Priscus almost dropped the lamp as he stared at the peaceful form of the lady Clodia, coins on her eyes for the journey, her arms folded across her chest and topped with fresh flowers, the body wrapped from feet to sternum in expensive white Egyptian linen.

Priscus stumbled forward, his mind reeling. Clodia had been missing for months, though clearly, from the lack of decay, she had only died some time in the last day or two. His heart racing, he crossed to her and looked at the body in a low panic. Her throat bore a thin purple line. Strangled with something narrow; possibly a leather thong. He shuddered. Clodia was, there was no denying it, a wicked and troublesome woman, and she had likely deserved this; earned it a hundred times over. And yet it was with a strange sadness that Priscus stood over the sleeping woman, her perfect face finally peaceful in death.

His hip gave way again and he staggered, fumbling with the lamp and almost dropping it. Wincing, he fell back against the wall, his heart leaping as two of the funeral urns wobbled distressingly for a moment. He grasped the base of an alcove and steadied himself as, for the first time, his eyes fell upon one of the inscriptions.

Q Aelius Paetus Numidius

Priscus' mind swam. He stared and then, shaking his head, pulled himself across to one of the other alcoves.

T Paetus Corvus

More.
Every alcove another Paetus.
Priscus stood blinking in the presence of the innumerable dead, heaving in deep breaths. Fronto was going to *love* his next letter!

PART TWO: ROMA INVICTA

Chapter 13

(Iunius: 5 miles from the north coast of Gaul, several weeks prior to Caesar's victory over the Veneti at the battle of Darioritum.)

'It's an actual city, then?'

Galba shrugged.

'Crociatonum? By Roman terms, hardly. But it's certainly bigger and more... civic, than the oppida and villages we've been coming across. All evidence points to it being the centre of the Unelli's tribal lands, and it's crawling with thousands of people.'

Sabinus nodded thoughtfully, tapping his finger on his lip as his horse danced impatiently.

'The Unelli do seem to be at the centre of this grouping. The question is how to approach the situation.'

The three legates, each sat ahorse beside the commander, frowned to a man.

'If what we've been hearing is true, there could be a massive army lurking there; more even than the thousands the scouts reported. I'd have to counsel caution' Galba said quietly.

Rufus nodded.

'At least until the scouts return and give us more detailed information. Perhaps we can set up a temporary camp here.'

Sabinus glanced up at Plancus, who wore a thoughtful look.

'Has anyone given thought to why the Unelli would be gathering an army?' the man asked quietly.

'Because the Veneti have stirred up this entire corner of Gaul' Sabinus said flatly.

'Not true,' the legate of the Fourteenth said, frowning. 'Crassus' reports stated that the leaders of the Unelli and the Lexovii, at least, were very much pro-Roman late last year. Of all the tribes he dealt with up here, the Unelli chieftains actually supported him and even lent him troops. Why then would they revolt now?'

Sabinus sat silent, staring at the legate. Plancus had a point. The man had built such a bad reputation in the first year or two of the campaign that the rest of the officer corps had reached the point where they were automatically ignoring his opinions, in much the same fashion as the legions were treating Plancus' heavily-Gallic Fourteenth.

'Interesting,' he nodded finally. 'Certainly the Lexovii have sent their warriors here; numerous scouts have confirmed that. Although we cannot be sure the same is true of the Curiosolitae, the same seems likely to be the case. But then that raises a second question: if they've gathered a large army here, why is it just sitting in their city and not marching south to help their countrymen fight off Caesar?'

The four men exchanged doubtful glances. This entire action was an unknown quantity and, while Sabinus had the might of three Roman legions at his beck and call, the reduced and largely untrained Twelfth, the unpopular Fourteenth, and the understrength Ninth constituted less than two full legions between them in terms of proper numbers. If all three of these tribes had sent their strength to this place, then estimates were that the Roman force would be facing odds of at least three to one, if not more.

'Sir!'

The officers turned to the cavalry trooper who was trotting up the hill toward them.

'What is it, soldier?'

'One of the scout parties is returning, general.'

Sabinus smiled.

'Good. Some useful information, hopefully.'

The trooper frowned.

'Sir, I don't think they're alone. There is a small party of native riders following them.'

'Chasing them?'

Rufus squinted into the distance.

'I don't think so. They seem to be riding casually. I think we're about to have visitors, sir.'

Sabinus nodded and looked around him before turning to the buccina player.

'Have the legions fall in and put the call out for the tribunes to join us.'

As the horn blared out, he smiled at the officers around him. 'I know the men are tired, but we need to make an impression here. We need to present a solid core of hardened officers.'

Turning to Plancus, he pursed his lips.

'Do you have any senior officers in the Fourteenth who are still predominantly Gaulish?'

Plancus nodded, his face sour.

'*Most* of my officers are still braid-haired Gauls, general. Only half of them understand me at all.'

Sabinus chuckled.

'I'd like one of the most senior to join us. It could be very useful having someone who speaks their tongue up here.'

Plancus saluted and wheeled his horse, riding the hundred paces or so to the head of the Fourteenth Legion, which was busy coming to full attention at the buccina call. As Sabinus and his officers watched the approaching parties, Plancus quickly returned, a centurion jogging along beside him. The general glanced down at the man, who stopped running and, without even a laboured breath, saluted and dropped into a formal posture.

'Centurion? I am given to understand you speak the dialect?'

'Better than Latin, sir.'

'Good.' He pointed at the approaching riders. 'I would like you to listen carefully. So long as one of them speaks Latin, you shouldn't need to be involved unless you hear something that makes interruption necessary. I would just like a trained ear on them.'

He smiled.

'Of course, if they don't speak Latin at all, I may require a little translation.'

The centurion saluted again, and Sabinus nodded with satisfaction. The man was clearly Gallic, from his stature and colouring and, while his flaxen hair had been trimmed down to fit well with a Roman helm, the bushy, drooping moustache clearly marked his origins.

Sabinus made a gesture to the approaching scouts, and they rode off to one side to join the small cavalry detachment on the flank of the army.

The officers sat at the crest of the hill, tribunes from three legions forming up behind them, as they looked down the long slope toward the distant, messy sprawl of Crociatonum and the small party of almost a dozen riders approaching from that direction.

The general gave a last look round to his legions and the officers gathered behind him in their burnished glory. If anything spoke of the sheer power of Rome, it was this. Good. There was little else he could do until they knew what they were up against. He watched, alongside his silent officers, as the riders slowed to a halt and gathered in a small knot opposite them.

Sabinus had seen enough of these tribes over the last few years to immediately pick out the important characters. Rather than this being a deputation of chieftains from the various tribes, this was a strange and different gathering.

The man who took the centre and was clearly the leader of the party was a warrior of, at most, middling status. He bore the torcs and armour of a wealthy warrior, but not the jewels and decoration they had come to expect in chieftains and kings. The men around him were equally warriors rather than purely nobles, armed for brutality and not for parley. The grey, brooding presence of a black-haired and bearded druid at the rear of the group gave further weight to this being anything but a peaceful party. Where were the chieftains and leaders?

Sabinus hid his bafflement, keeping his expression carefully neutral.

'I am speaking to the king of the Unelli, perhaps?'

The man on the lead horse folded his muscular, etched arms and his moustache twitched.

'You are Roman general, Caesar?'

Sabinus smiled mirthlessly.

'I am *a* Roman general, yes. Quintus Titurius Sabinus, commander of the Ninth, Twelfth and Fourteenth Legions. And you are?'

'I Viridovix. Leader of free Gaul.'

Sabinus drew a deep breath.

'A bold statement. The Unelli and their neighbours have been allies of Rome this past year. Yet now we are led to understand that you gather an army?'

Muttering in low voices among the Gauls increased at the question and, as Sabinus shot a sidelong glance to the centurion from the Fourteenth to make sure he was paying attention, Viridovix turned his glare on the chattering men behind him, silencing them with a look. Sabinus nodded to himself. Whoever this man was, he had absolute authority here.

'Unelli chieftains weak... they grovel to southern apes. Warriors of Gaul not grovel, so we execute weak chieftains and form alliance as free Gaul.'

Sabinus nodded again.

'I see. You have pulled off a coup among your tribe. I hope for your sake that you can satisfy your people better than those who

250

preceded you. A rise to power in such a fashion often acts as a spur for others to try the same. Your position could be more delicate than you imagine.'

Viridovix put his head on one side, and the druid pushed forward through the crowd, leaning close enough to interpret for his leader. Sabinus was impressed at the deference the druid seemed to pay to this warrior. In two years of campaigning he had never seen a druid pay that sort of respect to any man.

Viridovix laughed.

'I not have time to mess words with general. I give this chance: go now. Run to Rome and hide behind big walls. You stay here, free Gauls will tear off heads and use as beer mug.'

Sabinus nodded.

'And I offer *you* one last ultimatum: disband this army, send the warriors back to their tribes, and this can end peacefully. I give my word that, should you offer no arms against us, we will continue to treat you as the allies you were.'

The Gaul sneered.

'One day. You gone when sun next up and you live.'

Without waiting for an answer, the powerful warrior wheeled his horse, followed by his companions, and rode back toward the city.

As soon as the figures were out of sight, Sabinus sagged.

'Looks like we're in for a fair old fight, my friends.'

Galba nodded.

'Looks like my winter at Octodurus all over again. If they've overthrown their own leaders, they're unlikely to stop just because of threats and cajoling.'

'Indeed. But the problem is that, for all my ultimatum, the outcome of any action here is hardly a fore drawn conclusion. At best we're one man against three, but it could be a lot higher than that.'

Plancus cleared his throat.

'I despise even suggesting this, general, but might it not be a better idea to actually take him up on his offer and withdraw until we can field a larger, stronger army?'

Sabinus shook his head.

'The longer we leave this, the worse it could get. Remember the Belgae? We left them too long, and they managed to gather half the northern world against us. We need to stop them now before their numbers double.'

Galba nodded with feeling.

251

'If word gets out that this 'free Gaul' has run off an army of three legions, we could see an uprising of the whole Gaulish people. The general's right: we need to deal with it now.'

Sabinus realised that the centurion was standing at attention and almost vibrating with the need to interrupt.

'What did you hear?'

'Sir... they have no intention of giving us until tomorrow morning. They will come at night, once the sun has fallen.'

Sabinus sagged again.

'Oh hell. Anything else?'

'Yes sir. The army massed in Crociatonum is not just Unelli and Lexovii. There are many of the Curiosolitae and others: refugees, bandits, rebels and warriors of allied tribes that are unhappy at Rome.'

'Six to one?' hazarded Galba as he addressed his commander. Sabinus shrugged.

'Probably. It gets worse.'

'Much worse, general.'

Sabinus raised an eyebrow at the centurion. 'Go on?'

'I heard mention of the Durotriges.'

'Durotriges?' Sabinus frowned. 'Not heard of them.'

The centurion nodded.

'They are from across the water in Britannia, sir. Not sure what was said about them, because Viridovix silenced the man at that point.'

Sabinus nodded unhappily.

'I hope, for the sake of Mars, that we're not facing an invasion of British Celts in addition. This could be a disaster.'

He turned back to the centurion.

'Thank you for your help, centurion. I am most grateful. You had best return to your unit.'

As the centurion saluted and strode off, Sabinus sighed and looked around at the three legates.

'We cannot run, but besieging an oppidum that holds such vast numbers could be considered tantamount to throwing ourselves on our swords. Anyone have any better idea than simply fortifying and praying very hard?'

The three men sat silent and glum until Rufus spread his hands and shrugged.

'There's no better plan, general. We might be able to come up with something but, given the fact that in five or six hours we could be under attack by half a million Gauls, we should get fortifying as fast as we can.'

Sabinus nodded.

'At least we have good high ground here, with a nasty approach to all sides. If we're going to be trapped rats, we couldn't pick a better trap.'

He took a deep breath.

'Alright... break out the trenching tools. Let's get ourselves dug in.'

* * * * *

Volusenus, senior tribune of the Twelfth, leaned across and muttered something to his legate, who nodded sagely and turned his serious, dark features on Sabinus.

'We are in very grave danger of repeating the disaster with which our year began in Octodurus.'

He tried to ignore the noise going on outside, but it was difficult. The three legions had constructed a large camp with all the standard defences during the afternoon following Viridovix's ultimatum, but had barely had time even for that, let alone any extra measures, before the first attack came.

Since then the Gaulish assaults had come at regular intervals, three pushes a day for the last three days, each different from the last, as the enemy tested the Roman defences and capabilities. Each attack was carefully planned and slowly executed, a necessity given the long and steep slope atop which the Roman fort stood, between which they would retreat to the comfort and safety of the oppidum. While Sabinus had been unwilling to make any foray outside the defences, the Gauls were equally disinclined to commit a large force to the wholesale slaughter of a charge up the steep hill, across the ditches, and against the defended walls of the fort.

However, they never tired of finding inventive new ways to put the legions to the test, wearing them down and picking off as many as they could without fully committing.

Even now, the morning attack had been under way for half an hour, enemy archers lurking among the trees at the bottom of the northern slope keeping up a steady volley that forced the defenders to remain low behind the parapet. Lacking strong auxiliary missile support, Sabinus' force was unable to return shots, and tried to keep themselves as safe as possible from the deadly shafts, only appearing above the wall when the occasional small forays of brave Gaulish warriors made their way up the slope to the defences to attempt to pull the palisade down.

It was, in short, a war of attrition.

Galba raised his voice to be heard more clearly above the commotion outside.

'We've got to do something. The Gauls are trying to provoke us into making a mass sortie, and these nit-picking scuffles are hardly huge and noteworthy, but we can't go on this way forever. Baculus estimates that we're taking down three of them for each man of ours that falls, but there are perhaps seven or eight times as many of them to begin with. You don't have to be a mathematician to work that problem out to its unpleasant conclusion.'

Sabinus nodded.

'I'm just grateful that we happened upon such a damn good position for the camp when we first arrived. If we were on low ground, they'd probably have wiped us out by now. It's at least bought us the time to work out our next move.'

Volusenus cleared his throat.

'This may not be a very popular idea, general, but I think we need to give serious consideration to the possibility of using one of the lulls to withdraw. It was irritating having to do that at Octodurus, but if we hadn't there would no longer *be* a Twelfth Legion.'

Sabinus shook his head.

'We can't run, tribune, no matter how sensible it might be. Caesar gave us specific orders: we're to stop the tribes here from joining up with the Veneti. Even if the only way we have to keep them occupied is to let them chop bits off us, we have to stay and do that. No, we need a better solution, I'm afraid.'

Standing in the doorway, arms folded, and a grim expression on his face, Plancus, legate of the Fourteenth, grunted.

'We should be launching the attack the barbarians keep asking for; meet them on the field like a real Roman army. Seven to one is nothing when a shield wall is involved.'

Sabinus glared at the man.

'Not a stroke of genius, man. We have little support of auxiliaries, artillery or cavalry, a lot of half-trained soldiers and a serious deficit in numbers. I think you underestimate the enemy.' He sighed. 'But there is some validity to the fact that we need to change our approach and make our strengths work for us. While the enemy's provision status is unknown, ours is somewhat limited.'

The officers in the room fell into a thoughtful silence for a moment.

'What we *really* need to do' Rufus said, scratching his chin, 'is to somehow goad the enemy into making a full scale assault on this place. Do to them what they're trying to do to us.'

Sabinus frowned.

'It's a nice idea, but the question is: how would we get them to commit to such a ridiculously suicidal act? They've been unwilling to commit to a large scale attack for three days because they know how costly it would be. That's why they're trying to get *us* to come out and meet *them*.'

Again, the officers fell into a silence that only served to emphasise the need for a solution, as the sounds of combat ringing on the distant west rampart intruded upon the meeting.

Slowly, Sabinus began to smile.

'You have an idea?'

The commander turned his smile on the speaker, and it widened.

'What could provoke the enemy into launching such a dangerously reckless attack?'

Galba shrugged.

'Either desperation in the face of likely defeat, or the certainty of victory. Sadly, neither is true of Viridovix's Gauls.'

'At the moment, yes. But what if we could plant the seed of one of those notions among them?'

Galba tapped his lip.

'How are you proposing to do that, general?'

'Plancus?'

'Sir?'

'Do me a favour and send for that centurion of yours that helped us with their leaders.'

The Fourteenth's legate, frowning with a lack of understanding, saluted and ducked out of the tent door, issuing quick orders to one of the guards outside before returning.

Galba was shaking his head as the legate dipped back in.

'It would give us the edge, but *however* you go about tricking them into attacking us, as soon as they realise they've made a mistake, they'll just retreat back to Crociatonum and this whole attritive nightmare will start up again. Without keeping them committed, matters won't change much.'

Sabinus grinned at him and pointed at Plancus as the man returned.

'That's where *he* was right. We can't cower behind the walls, because they'll run away again, yet equally we can't go out and meet them in battle, since they'll walk all over us with sheer numbers. But… if we *can* get them to charge us, they'll be exhausted when they reach the top of this long slope, and trapped against our defences. Then we can send the best, freshest men out and carry out the good old-fashioned Roman battle that Plancus is angling for, all the time keeping wearing away at them from the top of the walls.'

Galba frowned and drummed his fingers on his knee.

'It has merit, sir. We'd need to give them more than just a reason to attack us, though. If you want a mad, exhausting charge, they have to believe that time is of the essence. Not an easy thing to achieve. If you can, though, we could use a day or so to perhaps set up some surprises for them. We picked up some very inventive ideas from the tribes in the Alpine passes last winter.'

Sabinus nodded, smiling.

'Anything that helps give us that little bit more edge. I have some ideas but, until Plancus' man gets here, let's concentrate on how we deal with them once they're here.'

The commander, along with his legates and tribunes, fell into an involved discussion, bandying ideas back and forth and picking apart every angle, and the tent buzzed with animated conversation a short while later when there was a polite knock on the tent frame by the door.

'Come!'

The figure of the centurion who had accompanied them at the parley appeared in the doorway, standing respectfully to attention.

'Come on in, man, and stand at ease.'

'Yes general. How can I be of service?'

Sabinus smiled at the man.

'I would like you to perform a rather *special* duty; a sort of recruitment officer.'

The centurion frowned, but remained silent. Sabinus laughed.

'What's your name, centurion?'

'Cantorix, general.'

'Well, Cantorix, I would like you to go back to the Fourteenth and pick out as many soldiers of a certain nature as you can find.'

'Sir?'

'I want you to put together a vexillation of men for a special mission, and I have three criteria for selection. Firstly, they need to look as Gallic as possible; no Roman style haircuts or clean shaven faces. Secondly, they need to be the most bloodthirsty, powerful bastards the Fourteenth has to offer. And thirdly, I don't want anyone too virtuous and fair. Select the sort of men you wouldn't play dice against; the sort of men you wouldn't leave alone in your tent or let follow you down a dark alley. You get my drift?'

Cantorix nodded, uncertainly.

'May I ask what will be required of them, general?'

Sabinus smiled.

'Indeed you may, though I would prefer this information were not disseminated among the men yet, so keep your peace until you've organised the men and spoken with us again.'

He leaned forward.

'We're going to infiltrate Viridovix's army with our own. You heard the other day that their army is accepting all the waifs and strays from all over Armorica, including rebels, bandits and any Roman haters? Well it's time for you and your men to *become* rebels and bandits. You need to join them in the guise of Veneti refugees. You'll tell them that Caesar has defeated the Veneti and is on his way north. In fact, you'll tell him that we appear to be preparing to leave. It needs to sound desperate enough that they'll want to deal with us as a matter of urgency.'

Galba smiled.

'They'll assume the two armies are about to join up. Yes... that would frighten them as a possibility: the three legions they face now suddenly becoming seven.'

'Indeed,' Sabinus nodded, 'and it should be enough impetus to make them launch an attack. They'll believe that they have to obliterate us before we get a chance to move out and join up with Caesar.'

Cantorix wore a faintly uncertain look.

'Problem, centurion?'

'Not as such, general, but this is a lot to ask of men who have been treated like an inferior unit from the outset and continually assigned to menial tasks. Morale has never been high in the

257

Fourteenth, because they know the other legions look down on them. I'm not saying they wouldn't do it, sir. Of course not, but I feel duty bound to my men to report the situation as it stands.'

Sabinus' eye flickered irritably.

'I wasn't aware that the situation was that bad.'

'With respect sir, *nobody* is aware, because nobody ever asks.'

The general let out a low grumble, the twitch still evident. He was barely controlling his temper, and the centurion bit his tongue as he waited. 'Then we have a problem. The Fourteenth are the only legion that can do it. Perhaps we can apply a little incentive?'

'Sir?'

'For the morale of your men, I offer phalerae to every survivor who takes a part, along with a crown to pin to the legion's standards. If such is not enough of an incentive, there are other, more 'disciplinary' methods, if you follow me. I understand the plight of the Fourteenth and the stigma that has become attached to them, but I cannot allow the attitude of the men to dictate our strategy. The legions serve Rome, not the other way around.'

Cantorix pursed his lips.

'Yes sir. I meant in no way to imply that the men were rebellious or anything, sir, and a little recognition does buy a great deal of morale, sir.'

Sabinus leaned back in his chair and nodded.

'Go select your men Cantorix; as many as you can find. It's time to teach the 'free Gauls' the cost of liberty.'

* * * * *

Cantorix, centurion in command of the Third century in the Third cohort of the Fourteenth Legion, wrinkled his nose in disgust. The grand Roman officers in this army still thought of the Gauls as a single people with a common culture and identity, a laughable idea to Cantorix, who had been raised as one of the Segusiavi, far from here, near the borders of Roman territory. The Segusiavi had traded with Rome for as long as the tribe could remember; many spoke Latin and some even Greek, and wine - not beer - was the beverage of choice among the more wealthy.

How far removed could he be from these coastal 'barbaroi' who lived in relative squalor, many still running into battle naked to prove their vitality and resisting the inevitable march of progress. Yet the

Roman-born officers saw them all the same, assuming that these men, enlisted into the Roman army a little over a year ago, but from a very civilised culture and already largely 'Roman' in their outlook, would find it a simple job to assume the guise of the northern Veneti warriors.

He ground his teeth, wondering whether to try and affect a local accent. The idea would likely be a disaster. He would stand more chance of sounding like a native Greek than a native of Armorica.

Beside him, Idocus, a flaxen-braided optio from the Fifth cohort, held out a pair of trousers and stared at them as though they might bite him.

'Do these Unelli not understand the principle of washing clothes?'

He sniffed the material and recoiled. Cantorix gave him a lopsided smile.

'Be fair; a man died in them a few hours ago. He probably soiled himself.'

'Thanks' the optio replied drily. 'I wish we had time to take them to a river and give them a good scrub. I'm worried I might catch something. These trousers smell like a sick dog with an arse infection.'

'Just stop complaining and put the damn things on.'

The other thirteen men were busy climbing into their new clothes, mostly with looks of disgust and one even holding his nose. Cantorix shook his head. Thousands of men to choose from, and the general had clearly expected him to produce a large force. The fact was, though, that over the last year, most of the men of the Fourteenth had adopted the Roman style so thoroughly that very few legionaries retained enough of a Gallic look to even attempt this. These fifteen were the only ones with the appropriate physical and mental qualities that the centurion believed could even faintly pass as natives.

They had waited until the last attack by the Unelli and their allies, not long before sundown, and, once the enemy had returned to their town, the squad of soldiers had had their pick of disguises and armament from among the hundred or so enemies killed in the latest engagement close to the wall.

Cantorix straightened and held the torc up to his neck for a moment, but then decided against it. They had to look nondescript;

no good wearing or carrying anything that could easily be identified as belonging to a fallen warrior of the Unelli.

Rolling his shoulders, he allowed the clothing to settle and watched Idocus trying to tie the trousers around his waist while touching as little material as possible with his hands.

'Will you stop buggering around?'

The optio looked at him with distaste.

'I have to *eat* with these hands. I may never feel clean again.'

Cantorix stepped across to the doorway of the tent and turned to his men.

'Alright. Let's get moving. Come on.'

The other fourteen soldiers finished their dressing and gathered the swords, axes and spears before filing out into the early evening gloom.

'Right. Simple route. Out of the back gate of the camp, down the hill and a quarter of a mile out into the woods, then we swing out wide and come at Crociatonum from the west. Once we leave the gate, I don't want to hear a word spoken in Latin and remember to *concentrate* on your conversation. Don't even *think* Roman, or it'll still show through. And no discipline or attention. Try not to look like legionaries. Got it?'

The men nodded, variously grinning and grimacing. They were, as the general had requested, the sort of men who, if they were not in the army, would be robbing and murdering for profit. He watched them with interest as they filed past into the evening air. On the bright side, they really *looked* like thieves and vagabonds, and they *smelled* like refugees who had been travelling for days without a change of clothes. Possibly they could pull this off after all.

Once they were all outside, the centurion nodded with apparent satisfaction, concealing his shaky nerves.

'Right. Let's go. Remember everything we agreed.'

As they strode across the grass of the camp, Cantorix noted the watching faces of the many legionaries who stood beside their tents. Many held a look of vague, unintentional contempt. Others, though, nodded respectfully, fully aware of what these ragged men were about to attempt.

The rear gate of the camp opened as they approached, without the need for orders, and the legionaries on guard saluted as they passed. Cantorix peered into the gloom as he broke into a jog, the light from the torches and braziers in the camp fading behind him.

He was impressed, as they reached the bottom of the slope and made for the eaves of the nearby woodland, at the singular lack of noise the men around him made. They moved like cats in the night, hardly a twig cracking when they passed among the boles of the trees. After a few moments the silence became oppressive and the centurion cleared his throat, speaking in his native Gallic tongue.

'Alright. I think we've probably come far enough south. Let's cut west and make our way round. Feel free to talk, but only in low voices. We're supposed to be refugees and bandits, after all, not thieves. But remember to watch what you're saying.'

He took a deep breath. 'And don't try to put on any kind of accent. It'll just end up sounding stupid and obvious. We'll just have to hope that they don't know the Veneti accent that well. We're more than a hundred miles from their lands, so that wouldn't surprise me.'

One of the men grinned at him.

'Are you doin' all the talkin', or are we all goin' to chatter?'

Cantorix nodded back at the man.

'You all need to talk; we spoke about that before. We're not supposed to be soldiers, so act just like you would expect fleeing Veneti warriors to. Just leave the initial explanation of matters to me. Feel free to chip in with bits and pieces, but don't get too creative.'

The man grinned.

'Oh I know. Art of any scam's keepin' it simple as possible. So's not to trip yerself up.'

The centurion smiled. 'Precisely. So *everyone* should talk.'

''cept Villu, 'course.'

Cantorix glared at the man's poor taste in jokes, and glanced across at the aforementioned man, who was grinning wide and displaying the messy hole where his tongue should be, result of some unknown incident many years ago.

'Come on.'

Listening to the general conversation as they moved speedily through the woodland, the centurion began finally to relax a little. He had to admit that, to his own untrained ear at least, they sounded every bit the band of Gallic brigands. But then, truth be told, when you took away the mail and the tunic, that was very much what they were.

No surprise really that they were treated the way they were by the other legions. He resolved to try, once this was over, to get these

261

men to mingle more with the other legions. Closing the cultural rift would require effort on both sides, after all.

He was still pondering on what could be done for the Fourteenth when they reached the edge of the woodland and gazed out across the open grass to the walls of Crociatonum, the fort they had so recently left rising from the crest of the impressive hill off to the right.

'Alright. Let's run. Try to look relieved.'

Breaking into a fast pace as they left the trees, the fifteen men sped across the open land, keeping low and moving like a pack of wolves on the hunt. They were perhaps four hundred paces from the walls when the shout went up from within.

Warily, mindful of the possibility of missiles being hurled at them before any opportunity was given to explain themselves, the unit slowed and raised their arms, indicating the fact that their hands were empty of weapons. They continued to walk like that toward the town's solid gate until, perhaps ten paces out and without the need for an order, the unit came to a stop.

Cantorix, listening carefully, could just make out the noise of urgent discussion behind the gate. Screwing his eyes shut momentarily, he took a deep breath.

'For Belenus' sake, let us in. There's thousands of Romans a cat's fart away!'

He could not stop himself flinching, but managed to stay steady and not drop to the ground in case of missile attack. Straightening, he threw an angry glare in the direction of the optio who was stifling a small laugh.

'Who are you?' called a voice from an unseen figure above the gate.

'I'm Cantorix of the Veneti!'

There was another muffled exchange and finally a figure appeared above the gate, tall and powerful, wearing bronze helm and a chain mail shirt, a heavy blade in his hand.

'You bring us a message?'

Good; a chance. 'A message? Shit, *yes*, I bring you a message. Let us in and get ready for the sky to fall.'

'Explain yourself, stranger.'

'The Roman, Caesar is about a day behind us with enough men to trample a forest.'

262

Cantorix was pleased to note a sudden, yet more urgent murmur behind the gate.

Off to his right, one of the men bellowed 'Bloody Romans everywhere. How come you haven't flattened that lot on the hill?'

The leader dipped down behind the parapet for a moment, and then reappeared from a discussion with his compatriots.

'The Veneti have fallen to Caesar?'

'I'm not bloody proud of it, but yes' Cantorix snapped. 'Now will you let us *in*? There was a lot of activity in that fort when we came past, and I don't want to be standing in the open playing with myself when they decide to come and stand on my throat.'

He had to force himself not to smile as the urgent voices muttered again, a little louder and with a note of panic. The leader tilted his head to one side; a sign of worry, perhaps?

'Activity? What activity?' he asked.

'A lot of men moving around late at night and clanking stuff. Sounds a lot like the army of bastards we've had nipping our heels all the way. You wouldn't believe how fast those bastards can move when they want to!'

'And you said Caesar is a day away?'

'Yes, now let us *in*!'

'Where are the rest of the survivors?'

'How the hell should *I* know? Some left by ship and headed for the Osismii. Others fled into the woods to hide. It was chaos. The Romans enslaved most of the survivors. A few of us got out ahead of them to bring warning to the other tribes. We've been running for four days.'

The armoured leader stood silent for a moment.

'Think very carefully, stranger… when you saw the activity at the Roman camp, was it concentrated at the rear gate?'

Cantorix smiled to himself. The man was hooked now. Time to haul him in.

'I think so. What would you say, Idocus?'

'Yeah… off t'the other side, defnitly!'

There was another pregnant pause as Cantorix held his breath and finally, after an age of nerves had passed, the gates of Crociatonum crept slowly open.

Chapter 14

(Iunius: Sabinus' camp, near Crociatonum.)

'I'd say that Cantorix and his men pulled it off, then?'

Sabinus glanced at legate Galba of the Twelfth beside him and then turned his gaze back on the approaching mass and smiled.

'I would say so, yes. How far would you say that is?'

'About a mile I'd say, sir.'

Sabinus' smile widened.

'About a mile. Up a gradually steepening hill. And running.'

Galba nodded.

'And apparently carrying piles of kindling.'

'That'll be the bulk to help fill in the ditches so they can get to us quicker. Sensible idea under most circumstances, but I'm not sure that if I were their leader I would have sent them running up a steep slope carrying them.'

The legate sighed.

'I wish you'd let me use the fire arrows and set fire to them while they're running. It'd scare the hell out of them.'

'No. They must think we're leaving and not prepared for this. You warn them while they're still a mile off, and we'll lose the small chance we have. Besides, we only have a few archers and precious little ammunition, so we can't waste it. Stick to the plan.'

They returned to looking down the long slope, soldiers and officers of three legions stretched out along the ramparts to either side of them, mostly crouched out of sight, the occasional man standing at the wall, giving the impression of a badly defended palisade. The Unelli would expect the bulk of the Roman force to be at the rear gates, preparing to march.

The Gaulish force, enormous and chaotic, came on at a surprising speed, given the gradient of the approach. The front runners among them carried huge bundles of faggots and wood, those behind ready with their swords and spears, and all ran swift as the wind, desperate to overcome these invading foreigners before they had the chance to join with an even larger army.

The Romans stood silent behind their wall, watching.

'Now?'

'I think so. For the sake of realism.'

Galba turned and shouted along the wall.

'Raise the alarm!'

Buccinas blared and, in a carefully organised manoeuvre, other soldiers appeared at the wall, standing from where they crouched, creating the illusion that the warning of attack had gone up, and men were being rushed to a hurried defence.

'I hope this works' Galba grumbled darkly. 'One hopeless last stand in defence of a fort is enough in a single year.'

Sabinus nodded.

'It'll work. So long as the timing's right.'

Silently they continued to watch, faked commotion all around them, and the confederation of northern tribes, along with their allied refugees, bandits and vagabonds ran ever upwards, bellowing their defiance, their anger and their determination to rid Armorica of the Roman presence. Sabinus' gaze strayed to the ground before them, and he noted carefully the location of the marker. All along the hillside, these markers stood in a line, crimson against the green; small enough to be unnoticed by the attacking mass and just large enough for the men of the legions to locate when concentrating.

Fixing his eyes on the red mark, he nodded with relief as the front ranks of Gauls raced past it, hurrying up the hill. He risked a quick glance up to the faces of the approaching warriors and was gratified to see the heaving, laboured breaths the enemy were now taking as they approached the Roman position, their faces red and sweating with exertion.

For a moment he worried that he had lost the marked position as his eyes wandered back and forth, but it took only a moment to pick it up from the terrain, without being able to see the crimson mark beneath the stomping boots of the Celts. Almost ready... the Gauls were perhaps two hundred paces from the outer ditch.

He watched, tense, as the Gaulish throng passed over the spot he had kept in mind and, finally, squinting, he saw the bright red mark emerge once again between the heads of the charging Gauls, at the back of the mob.

Turning to Galba, he noted relief in the face of the legate.

'First stage: loose!'

At the shout, a dozen archers, part of the small complement of auxiliaries accompanying them, rose above the parapet, the tips of their arrows already flaming, aimed and released in a smooth action before retreating below the palisade once more.

The fiery missiles arced out over the heads of the Gallic army, now so exhausted and obsessed that they hardly paid any heed to the act until the arrows came down behind them, several striking the hillside along the line of crimson markers and only a few going astray.

The swathe of ground where they struck, amid the deep, dry grass, held small pockets of pitch that had been carefully distributed the previous night, small enough to go unnoticed by the Gallic army as they ran past and across them, some inevitably coating the bottom of running boots, but most remaining in place.

In several locations across the slope, pockets of pitch caught, the fire spreading into the dry grass, quickly igniting the next and, within moments, a curtain of flame extended across the hill behind the Gauls, effectively sealing off their retreat.

Largely due to the sheer size of the attacking army and its lack of organisation, most of the enemy failed even to notice the move, the few at the back who did going unheard by the rest. A veritable sea of bodies rushed up toward the ramparts and their encircling ditches. Sabinus watched, his breath held, as the front lines cast their burdens of sticks and brush into the ditches.

'Second stage!'

In a fluid move, a dozen legionaries along the length of the wall reached out and grasped the burning torches that had been used to ignite the arrows and climbed up to the parapet. As they emerged above, the huge Gallic army was already pouring across the filled ditches. Each legionary took careful aim, identifying a spot where a gap opened up and casting their torches almost in unison.

The flaming missiles dropped among the Gauls who were too consumed by a combination of exhaustion and desperate blood lust to pay too much attention to a small number of falling weapons. The flaming torches landed among the dry brush infill beneath their feet, and it took only moments for the fire to catch, wood and dried undergrowth spitting into orange life and spreading the fire rapidly. Within moments a swathe in the midst of the huge army was consumed by the roaring inferno, a small number of men trapped between the burning ditches and the rampart.

'Third and Fourth stage! Sally!'

At the command, the crouched legionaries rose up along the wall and began to cast their first pilum down into the ranks of yelling Gauls. In places along the ramparts, pockets of the less exhausted enemy managed to reach the palisade, climbing the slope and thrusting upward with spears or delivering heavy, scything overhead blows with their swords.

The number of men who had reached the wall in any state to commit to action was small, however, and the legionary defenders had little trouble holding them back, pushing them away from the palisade and stabbing at them with their second pila where they could. The massive bulk of the enemy were still contained between the ditches that now roared with deadly fire, and the wall of burning pitch and grass behind them, the narrow causeway across the ditches that led to the north gate filled with howling Gauls trying to reach the Roman palisade without falling into the raging inferno to either side.

Sabinus offered up thanks to the Gods once again that the rain had held off for so many days. What they would have done if this morning had brought a downpour, he could not imagine, but things would likely be looking a great deal bleaker.

The flanks of the Gaulish force were already attempting to separate from the trapped mass, moving around the slope, trying to escape the burning traps afore and aft, and make their way into clear land around the other sides of the hill. At a call from the buccina, however, the east and west gates of the camp opened and the slow, deliberate stomping feet of thousands of legionaries issued forth.

The Twelfth remained at the wall and throughout the rest of the camp, dealing with those men who managed to find their way as far as the walls without burning, while the Ninth and Fourteenth exited the gate and moved in formation, shield walls solid and strong, around the edge of the defences and toward the Gauls as they spilled out from the flaming trap.

'Advance!' called centurions around the hillside, and the wall of armoured men rumbled slowly into the mass of fleeing Gauls, coming to a halt as further commands were issued. The Ninth and Fourteenth now contained the enemy in a space between them and the walls of flame, holding their shield walls as an impenetrable barrier and hacking and stabbing at those who came close enough.

The effect of the trap was impressive, and Sabinus smiled from his position atop the defences. The combination of exhaustion, frustration, and terrified surprise, had turned the mood of the enemy in moments from vicious lust to desperate panic. Far from the unprepared Romans, busy trying to decamp and move off, that the

Gauls had expected, they had, instead, run straight into a deadly mix of steel and fire.

'Surrender and mercy will be *considered*!' bellowed Sabinus, his words deliberately ambiguous. He was well aware of the danger that would be inherent in accepting a surrender and leaving an intact army behind them with only the word of their leaders for assurance.

Calls went up from among the mass and for a strange moment, the fighting stopped, everything falling silent and still, bar the roaring of the flames.

Sabinus readied himself. He would offer harsh terms for their surrender, but it had to be still within the realm of acceptability. He had them now, but if they really wished, there were still enough of them that they could break through the trap at an awful cost and crush the defenders. Terms had to be preferable to the losses they would incur if they continued.

A loud voice called something out in the local language, and Sabinus watched in astonishment as the speaker, a nobleman judging by his dress and equipment, threw down his sword in a gesture of surrender, only to have his head removed by a sudden, scything blow from the man beside him. The act of defiance did something to the crowd, and Sabinus could only stare in disbelief as the Gallic army flowed like a sea crashing against the rocks, those flanks that had been contained by the legions pulling back in.

The warriors at the rear, contained by the burning pitch and holding themselves desperately back from the roaring flames, were suddenly pushed, screaming, into the inferno by their comrades, the fire rapidly extinguishing with the sheer weight of men being thrown into the flames.

As he stared in horror, he saw the rear flaming wall of the trap put out by the sizzling, melting fat of a human carpet, and the mass of 'free Gauls' running back down the hill toward the distant gates of their city, trampling their dead and dying comrades as they fled.

He turned his sickened gaze away to Galba.

'I cannot decide whether that was a stunningly brave act of tribal preservation, or an atrocious act of barbarism.'

Galba nodded soberly.

'We have to deal with them now, sir, while they're tired and on the run. If we give them a chance to catch their breath and reform, we're in trouble.'

'Indeed. Can't let them fortify against us. Have the general advance sounded. Let's chase them down.'

* * * * *

Cantorix sighed and turned to look over the parapet once more. It had taken the rebellious tribes a matter of only a few hours to argue among themselves as to what to do about the Roman threat, to reach the conclusion that they had to be dealt with before they could leave and join Caesar's army, and then to put their plan into action. Cantorix and his companions were untrustworthy foreigners to them and had spent that time safely locked in a dark, oppressive room deep in the oppidum, two men guarding the door.

When, just after first light, the leaders had finally assembled their men at the gate of Crociatonum and goaded them into a killing frenzy, the presence of the foreigners seemed to have been entirely forgotten, or at least ignored, the guards joining the attack and leaving the fifteen 'Veneti' refugees locked in their prison and unattended.

Given the background and dubious skills of some of these men, it had come as no surprise to Cantorix that someone had the lock undone and the door open within moments of the army leaving, the sound of bellowing violence dying away as the enormous force charged away up the hill.

Briefly the centurion had considered calling the unit to order and going to join the fight, but the sheer lunacy of the notion soon imposed itself as he recalled the throng of thousands of angry warriors and weighed it against the relative size of his small force. At least the enemy had not seen fit to drag the strangers along with them, as it would have been hard for his men to identify themselves before the general and his legions skewered them.

Instead, he had made his way to the gate and climbed to the walkway above where he would observe the action as best he could. Though they must be two miles away at the Roman defences, he could safely assume that the battle proper had started by now.

As he appeared over the parapet, he noted spots of flickering yellow flame appear in the haze, punctuating the rear of the distant Gallic force, a grey homogenous mass at this distance.

The other legionaries, whom he had allowed to go about their business, had begun to enter the various buildings around them,

269

looting anything they could carry. Cantorix turned his gaze from the distant battle and glanced back down along the main thoroughfare toward the house where they had so recently been kept. One of the legionaries left a doorway, staggering under the weight of his spoils and almost bumped into a companion, similarly burdened.

It would have been comic under other circumstances. The centurion, however, was too tense to smile. Each time he saw a figure within the walls of the oppidum, he had to frown for a moment, worrying whether it was truly one of his men, dressed Gallic style, or a stray local who had been left behind. The oppidum seemed, though, to have completely emptied, as the rebel army moved on their hated enemy. At least it appeared that the rebel Gauls had moved their women and children somewhere else and used this 'city' as a staging post for war, else the houses would still be packed with nervous noncombatant Gauls.

'Sir?'

He blinked and concentrated his gaze in the direction of the voice. One of the men was waving from a house a few doors down from their erstwhile cell.

Cantorix squinted.

The man was carrying a different burden to those of his mates; a body, draped across his arms and hanging limp, at least one limb mangled and beyond use, the horrible wounding evident even from up here. The figure was decked in a drab tunic that had once been red.

The centurion shook his head sadly. The officers had charged them to be on the lookout for a tribune from the Ninth by the name of Gallus that had been sent to these tribes months ago.

'Get him on a cart or a pallet. We'll have to take him back to the officers when it's all over. How long has he been dead?'

The man shrugged, a difficult manoeuvre under the weight of the body.

'Not long. Maybe a few days. He was messed up badly first, though.'

Again, the centurion shook his head. The barbarians had kept him alive all this time, torturing and beating him, keeping him in case he became of use, but the arrival of general Sabinus and his army had diminished the need for hostages and Gallus had become superfluous.

'Get him…'

His voice tailed off as his eyes had strayed casually back to the view over the parapet and widened. The centurion choked and scrambled to his feet.

'Drop everything! Legionaries of the Fourteenth, form on me!'

Without waiting for an answer, he leapt down the stairs that descended the wall's inner face three at a time, dropping the last seven or eight feet, his knees bent against the impact.

He was gratified that, despite the unsavoury nature of his unit, the past year of service had drilled the necessity of discipline into the men and, without question, the legionaries had dropped their plunder and hurried to the open space before the gate.

'What is it, Centurion? We was only lootin' the enemy. The general encourages that!'

Cantorix waved the comment aside as he stood, rubbing his jarred knee.

'Get that gate closed.'

'Sir?'

'The Unelli are on the way back! Get the sodding gate closed or you're going to be knee deep in your own blood.'

As he shouted, the centurion was already scanning the area, picking out anything they might use to brace the huge wooden portal. Fortunately, the Unelli seemed to be somewhat lacking in keeping their streets tidy, and various broken timbers, long beams, shutters, and ramshackle animal pens littered the settlement.

As the legionaries rushed past him to close the gate, he grabbed one of them by the shoulder and gestured to him and three others.

'You four go get some beams and timber; biggest and strongest you can find and carry them back to the gate. We've not got long before that lot get here.'

As the men ran off about their task, Cantorix turned to see the other ten men busy heaving the heavy gates closed, their shoulders to the timber, grunting and groaning as they pushed. Nodding with tense satisfaction, he strode across to them.

'Alright. You men: get those bars across and locked down. Idocus and Dannos: get running round the walls in both directions. I didn't see any other gates, and I doubt there's much, but we can't ignore the possibility there's another way in. Be quick, cause we'll need you.'

The two men ran like hares along the inner face of the oppidum's defences, searching for posterns or other main exits, and Cantorix took a deep breath. There was maybe a count of two hundred left he thought as he made himself breathe calmly. The remaining eight men had easily manoeuvred two heavy oak bars across the gate and into their cradles, bars designed to protect the Unelli against the Romans... an irony not lost on the centurion.

'Alright. Two of you get up on that parapet. I want to know when they pass the quarter mile and around two hundred paces.'

As the force split once more, Cantorix nodded and rubbed his temples.

'Four more of you gather any stones, or anything heavy or pointed you could drop on the enemy, and fill some of these abandoned baskets. Get them up on the wall. You've got a count of two hundred to shift as much ammunition as you can.'

As they ran off, the remaining four legionaries turned to him.

'Good' he said, rubbing his hands. 'Now go find anything heavy and strong you can use to help brace the gates.'

Pinching the bridge of his nose and rubbing his tired eyes, he wished he'd felt relaxed enough during the previous night to have slept in their prison, like some of the more conscience-free of his companions. Exhaustion was no good in a soldier, but in a commander during a battle it was potentially catastrophic and therefore unforgivable. He turned to see the four men he'd sent off first approaching with a long, heavy oak beam, struggling under the weight.

'Good. Let's get it into position.'

He hurried over to help the men and between the five of them, they manoeuvred the beam into position.

'It ain't gonna hold against a push, sir.'

Cantorix nodded and pointed at the floor, drawing a line in the dust with the toe of his boot.

'Dig a pit over a foot deep there and when you've done, slide the beam across and jam it into the hole. That's about as braced as we can get. I'd like to see anyone short of *Hercules* shift *that*.'

As the four men lowered the end of the beam to the dust and began to dig the pit with their heavy, Gallic, knives, Cantorix turned to see the others carrying various beams and poles.

'Follow this example. Let's have that gate harder to move than thc walls either side.'

A voice above called something and the centurion looked up, holding his hands out, palms up while he shrugged.

272

'Quarter mile or less' the soldier shouted again.

'Shit.'

He fretted again, rubbing his face as the legionaries hauled rocks and chunks of timber up to the wall top, dug small pits and sunk great beams into them. Time was hardly on their side.

'Can you see what's happened up at the camp?'

There was a brief pause and then the legionary shouted again.

'Looks like the enemy are panicked. Our lads are chasing them down, but slower. I think the three legions are all on the way behind them, but one bunch is way off at the back.'

'Probably ours' muttered Cantorix. 'Alright. Get ready. We'll have to hold this gate for just a little while. After that the enemy'll be in enough trouble with the rest of the lads pounding on them without worrying about us.'

He shook his head.

'Right. Everyone in position. Four men on the walls with the rocks. Rest of us hold the gate steady.'

He looked up.

'Shout if you're in trouble.'

Without listening further, Cantorix ran forward to the gate. Constructed of heavy oak, the timber was almost entirely flush fitting, with precious few cracks and openings.

'Don't lean into the gate yet, 'cause you'll just exhaust yourself, but be prepared. If you see a bracing beam giving way a little, get on it and reinforce it; hold it down. If you hear a shout from the lads above, get up there and help. Otherwise, keep your eye on any holes in the timber. If you can jab a blade through it and do some damage, get it done. No throwing yourself into anything. This is about holding on long enough for the rest of the army to do their job.'

'Brace yourself' one of the men above bellowed.

'Here they come.'

The sound of the panicked Gaulish army desperately trying to retreat to the safety of their suddenly inaccessible oppidum was immense, a roar and babble of shouts, mixed with the thumping of feet, the crash of metal and wood and screams from the few unlucky enough to fall and be trampled.

Cantorix closed his eyes and offered up a quick prayer to Mars, Fortuna, Minerva... and to Belenus and Nodens too, just in case.

The initial blow as the mass of the enemy threw themselves against the gate was as impressive as any forceful charge the centurion had seen. Despite the heavy timber of the construction and the two cross beams in their cradles, both gates shifted inwards by more than a foot, the bracing beams creaking and jumping in their earthen sockets.

'Bloody hell!' shouted one of the men in front of him and Cantorix could not find a better expletive at that moment.

He threw his gaze around to take in the top walkway that had actually shaken under the blow, the dust and dirt that had fallen, dislodged from above, and the fact that the very walls had given a tiny amount to either side of the gate, earth slipping out and pouring to the ground from the timber-framed, soil-packed fortification.

'Swords' he bellowed, and the men under his command began to jab their blades through any hole they could find in sharp, swift blows, so as not to allow the weapons to become jammed.

The centurion leaned back and scratched his head as the second huge blow came, the gates shaking and releasing yet more dirt. With a loud retort, a thin crack appeared across one of the huge cross beams. Impressive. He'd seen similar results with a battering ram, but with shoulders and muscle alone? They *must* be desperate.

'Crap, I hope the legions hurry up.'

Pounding feet behind him made him turn. Dannos came to a halt, dropping his hands to his knees and breathing in deep gasps, Idocus close behind him.

'Two small posterns, sir. Both at the other side. Got 'em locked, barred and piled up wi' whatever shit we could get 'us hands on.'

Cantorix sighed.

'Let's just hope they don't get that far then. Draw a sword and fall in.'

As the optio and the legionary rushed over to join the men at the gate, Cantorix pinched his nose again and gritted his teeth.

A hundred-count was all they would need, but hundred-count might just be pushing it against that lot.

A third blow widened the crack on the beam and knocked one of the defending legionaries from his feet.

* * * * *

Galba frowned as he looked ahead.

'Baculus? They're starting to spread along the walls. Those lads from the Fourteenth must have barred the gate.'

274

The primus pilus, a short distance to his right and moving at triple time, nodded.

'Got to keep them contained, sir.'

'Agreed.'

Ahead of them, the Ninth and Fourteenth legions nipped at the heels of the fleeing enemy, not allowing them the opportunity to pause and reform. In a moment they would have them pinned against the walls of Crociatonum and trapped. As soon as they formed a solid shield wall the enemy were done for, but there was still the possibility that a large number of the Gauls would escape along the walls first.

'Baculus: take the First through Fifth cohorts and break right to cut them off. Fast as you can.'

As the veteran officer saluted and began bellowing orders, moving off with half the legion to contain the fleeing Gauls on the far side, Galba gestured to the centurions and signifers behind him and peeled off to the left, picking up the already tortuous pace they had maintained down the hill. He could only *imagine* how the Gauls must feel. He himself was at the peak of his physical condition these days, yet the muscles in his legs strained and complained and his lungs burned from the activity at the fort and the long run down the hill after the fleeing Gauls. The enemy, on the other hand, had run *up* the hill, carrying bundles of wood, before even that.

Indeed, the Gauls' state of near exhaustion was evident in the numerous bodies of those who had collapsed on their return journey, unable to go on. The two front legions, the Ninth and Fourteenth, had run on past the collapsed enemies, rear ranks pausing only to drive a blade through them before running on to catch up.

He risked taking his eyes off the ground ahead and looked around to the officers behind him.

'Spread the men out. Let's come at them like a gate, swinging down and right and closing the exit for them.'

The men barked their confirmations and the legate turned back just in time to spot the rabbit hole and shift his pace to jump across it. There was something simple and powerful about a headlong charge into battle. Fronto had tried to explain it to him once but, for one reason or another, the Twelfth seemed generally to end up in a position where they were bracing themselves to take the force of an enemy attack. Now, the fresh wind battering his face, the turf springing under his feet and the men of his command roaring behind and around him, he began to see Fronto's point.

The moments passed as they charged down the rapidly levelling slope and by the time they reached the flat ground that stretched out before the walls of Crociatonum, the desperate and fatigued Gauls had reached the defences and were spilling out along it and milling around.

Their panic expressed itself in many ways as the Gauls found themselves trapped. A number of them fled along the walls, though the men of the Twelfth were already swinging down on an intercept course to cut them off. Others began desperately to climb the wall, though to no avail. Despite its rough surface, no man among the Gaulish army had the strength remaining to make such an arduous climb. Still, others tried to push their way through their compatriots in an effort to get to the oppidum's gate, unaware that it remained fast against them. The rest either turned, wearily, raising their weapons with hopeless expressions, staring death in the steel-armoured face, or dropped their weapons, drooping and giving up entirely.

A quick glance to left and right confirmed that the edges of the Twelfth had reached the wall and joined the flank of the Fourteenth, effectively sealing the enemy in. At calls from the centurions, needing no prompting from their commander, the whole legion settled into powerful shield walls, closing on the hopeless enemy.

Somewhere off to his right, several blasts issued from the instrument of the cornicen on the general's staff. Along the line, the soldiers that were already involved in fighting stepped back, disengaging. The field fell strangely silent as the melee paused.

'Warriors of the Unelli and their allies!'

Galba smiled to himself. The voice was that of Sabinus, every bit as powerful and commanding as a Roman general *should* sound.

'Hear my terms. They are neither flexible nor negotiable.'

There was a low murmur among the enemy.

'Your tribes took an oath of allegiance to Rome and you have broken that allegiance. That makes you not only enemies, but criminals and traitors in the eyes of all civilised men. I am a man inclined toward mercy, but this situation tests my patience.'

Galba smiled to himself. Sabinus was starting to sound distinctly like Caesar.

'The leaders of this insurrection, including Viridovix and the top hundred noblemen of your tribes will submit to Roman justice and suffer the appropriate punishments for what they have done. I am willing to accept that blame can be largely apportioned among the instigators and, for that reason, should you deliver those hundred and one men before me, here and now, I will allow the tribes to dissipate and return to their lands peaceably, once they have renewed their oaths to Rome.'

Galba noted the murmur once more increase as the truth of the situation imposed itself on the rebel Gauls. A few paces in front of the Twelfth's legate, a tall warrior, with a grey, braided beard, decorative bronze helm, and torc around his neck, bellowed something defiantly, raising his sword in the air as if to rouse his men against the general.

Galba watched with interest as three of the low-born warriors around him grasped his wrists, threw an arm around his neck and dragged him to the ground, out of sight, where his grisly end was audible only as sounds akin to those that issue from a butcher's shop. The Gaulish rebels had had enough, and their leaders' failure would be punished even without Sabinus' call.

Here and there among the crowd, noblemen who had led the insurrection, or who were merely unlucky enough to be among Sabinus' top hundred men, were grabbed and held by their own warriors before being pushed roughly out to the front of the mass, their weapons jerked from their hands as they fell to their knees.

Galba tried to see through the crowd, or across the narrow gap that lay between the two disengaged armies, but Sabinus was out of sight somewhere to the right.

'Good' the general called. 'Keep them coming, and send me Viridovix so that we can conclude our business.'

An oppressive silence fell over the assembled armies.

'*Where* is Viridovix?'

* * * * *

Galba entered the tent of the general, his cloak flapping in the gentle breeze, Cantorix of the Fourteenth at his heel. The other officers were already assembled, and Sabinus looked up, his face dark.

'Well?'

277

Galba shrugged.

'Complete search, sir. Those of us who met him, centurion Cantorix particularly, and several of the more cooperative locals. We went through the enemy to the last man. Viridovix is simply not among them. Whether he slipped away as the army fled down the hill, or perhaps left even before the attack, we can't say.'

Sabinus slapped his palm on the table.

'That man was at the very *centre* of this rebellion. I want him found, gutted and displayed to every man, woman and child in Armorica, Galba.'

'I understand that, sir, and we have already made it clear to the tribes that any man reported to be harbouring the criminal will bring upon him a dreadful sentence. There will be nowhere in Armorica he can find comfort when word gets out.'

Sabinus glared at him and then fell silent and slumped into the chair.

'Alright. Are you suggesting that I allow the tribes to leave peacefully anyway? Viridovix was the central part of my terms.'

Galba shrugged.

'With respect, sir, if the man had been there today, they'd have handed him to you in pieces if necessary. In fact, I suspect the fact that he fled from their side before they failed has lost him his last friends among the Unelli. I fear it would be unjust to severely prosecute the tribes for the cowardice of their leader.'

'Agreed' Sabinus sighed. 'We need peace and we need them to go back to farming and sending us grain. Very well, we'll go ahead with the terms, but I want an active hunt for that treacherous bastard. I want him to run like a boar, knowing there are a thousand spears stalking through every forest looking for him.'

Galba nodded and stepped to one side, a move calculated to put Cantorix in the fore, lit by the afternoon sun shining in through the tent doorway.

Sabinus gave a weak smile.

'Cantorix? Good. Some good comes out of even the most irritating situations. Your men all survived?'

The centurion saluted, nodding.

'To a man, sir. They're survivors, my lot, sir.' He grinned. 'Like cockroaches, sir.'

Sabinus laughed and gestured to the legate standing to one side.

'These men did your legion credit this past day, Plancus. They performed like the best of veterans, as did, I might add, the rest of the Fourteenth. Commendations, awards and preferential shares of the spoils will be forthcoming as soon as the matter of taking slaves, performing executions and dispersing the tribes is complete.'

He glanced past Cantorix.

'The Ninth and Twelfth also acquitted themselves well, particularly given the reduced nature of both legions at this time. Rest assured that mention of that will be made to Caesar when we return.'

He leaned back.

'And that brings me to the question of how we proceed from here. The tribal alliance here is broken, but we need to be sure it stays broken.'

He reached forward to the map of Armorica spread out on the table before him.

'The oppidum of Crociatonum has been used by the rebels as a military fortress, stripped of its civil population. The legions will settle here as a garrison for the foreseeable future, at least until Caesar orders their movement or withdrawal. While based here, I want regular vexillations of three cohorts in size sent out to look for Viridovix, to gather supplies and information concerning the tribes that have just retaken their oaths, and to make sure that a strong Roman presence is continually felt in the area in order to put the notion of further rebellion far from their minds.'

He leaned back again.

'Our small cavalry detachment, along with a couple of the tribunes in command, will ride for Caesar's army to inform him of the completion of our mission here and will return with any news from the campaign against the Veneti. In the meantime, we will see to our dead, including the recovered body of tribune Gallus, and process the Gauls. Are there any questions?'

Silence filled the tent, and Sabinus gave a weary smile.

'Then let's get things tidied up. It has been a *very* long day.' He eyed Cantorix. 'Even longer for some of us. Time to rest and recover, eh centurion?'

279

Chapter 15

(Iunius: Inland Aquitania, two months prior to Caesar's victory over the Veneti at the battle of Darioritum)

Gaius Pinarius Rusca, senior tribune of the Seventh Legion, shuffled in his saddle.

'What are we waiting for, sir?'

Crassus shot him an irritable glance; the man asked too many questions. Still, while Rusca was as military-minded as a bag of brassica, a fresh-faced political 'would be' from Rome, he would likely be gone within the year and, after all, being surrounded by such idiots did one's *own* image no harm.

'Reinforcements, tribune.'

'Sir?'

Crassus sighed.

'We are a single legion, as you may have noted, Rusca, not a force of three or four such as those being led in the north.'

Galronus of the Remi, leader of the strong auxiliary cavalry force accompanying the Seventh Legion, rolled his eyes, his own irritation barely contained behind clenched teeth. Throughout the three week march south into Aquitanian lands, the legate of the Seventh, a man Fronto had told him to be careful of, had persisted with the attitude that the Seventh Legion were effectively a noble and veteran force, moving alone through hostile territory, while the numerous detachments of Gallic cavalry were little more than a hindrance that blocked an otherwise impressive view.

Rusca looked taken aback.

'Of course, sir. But one legion was enough for you to crush the north west.'

Oh good. Stupid *and* sycophantic.

'Rusca, the Armorican tribes were relatively civilised Gauls in small groups, with their own internecine wars to attend to. Conquering them was like laying down the law to a group of squabbling children by comparison with *this*.'

At least Galronus could agree with him on that point.

'Aquitania constitutes fully a third of Gaulish territory, Rusca. We are not talking about a few squabbling tribes here, but what amounts to an entire nation. There may be many tribes in Aquitania, but there are a few very powerful ones at the top of the heap who maintain power in the region. If we wish to control Aquitania, we must first seek to control those tribes.'

He squinted into the distance and gave a small half-smile.

'Don't forget, Rusca, that very clever and powerful men have fallen foul of this place over the last century and more. Praeconinus and his army died here. Manilius barely escaped back to Narbonensis with his life. We will find no allies here and no friendly supplies. Make no mistake: in Aquitania, the Seventh Legion is utterly alone.'

Again, Galronus ground his teeth as he glanced over his shoulder at the assembled mass of thousands of Gallic cavalry, but his attention was drawn back to the legate as the man laughed.

'So we must be prepared. And like all good commanders, I prepared as much as possible before we even left Vindunum. I sent a few requests and messages ahead with some trusted couriers. See how my preparations begin to pay off?'

He pointed to the saddle further down the valley, the few flitting clouds casting patchy shadows along the ridge. As Galronus and the tribune watched, men began to pour over the rise in their direction.

Galronus frowned.

'With respect, legate, may I ask how you managed to arrange such a large force of reinforcements?'

Crassus shrugged.

'I have a not-inconsiderable supply of money and influence. Add to that the authority of Caesar and you'd be surprised how easy it is to raise an army. I can only imagine how the decurions of Tolosa, Narbo and Carcaso must have panicked and fallen over one another to provide my troops and supplies in time.'

Galronus narrowed his eyes.

'The general authorised extra troops, sir?'

Crassus turned an angry look on him.

'Beware the pit trap of insolence, commander. *I* authorised them in the general's name. Such authority is implied in my command. The general would rather we cost him a little inconvenience and succeeded in our task than we lost him an entire legion in the wilds of Aquitania; of that I'm certain.'

Galronus turned his astonished gaze back to the army pouring over the crest and down the valley toward them.

'There are thousands of them!'

'Somewhere in the region of three thousand, if my requests have all been met; mostly archers and spear men, along with a good supply train of grain and other goods.'

Crassus smiled smugly as he watched the army pouring toward them to almost double the size of his force.

'Let's move on and pick up our new allies. They are, after all, solid Roman stock of Narbonensis who have had a long journey to join us.'

Galronus glared at the legate as he turned his back, wheeled his horse and threw up an arm to signal the army forward. 'Solid Roman stock' indeed... the men of Narbo were almost as Gallic as the Remi; *had* been less than a century ago.

As the legion and its auxiliary support moved off, the senior officers moving ahead with Crassus, Galronus walked his horse out to the side, deliberately detaching from the column.

He was surprised when, a moment later, one of the five remaining tribunes of the Seventh trotted out to join him. As the army marched on, Galronus looked the man up and down.

He had seen the tribune, as he had seen them all during the journey, usually with their heads up the legate's backside. This one, one of the juniors, was surprisingly elderly to be filling such a post. From what Galronus understood, the tribunate was almost exclusively filled with young politicians climbing their ladder to success, alongside just a few clever veterans who stayed in the position in the hope of securing the command of a legion when the previous legate moved on.

This man, however, would be perhaps fifty years old or more. His hair was peppered black and white, his face lined and displaying a weariness that had little to do with physical exertion. The officer gave him a sad smile and pulled alongside.

'Can I help you, tribune?'

The man glanced ahead, but the command party had picked up the pace to meet the new troops and was clearly out of audible distance, even if they had been listening.

'Watch yourself carefully, commander.'

Galronus frowned.

'I already was, tribune.'

'*More* carefully. Young Crassus has taken a very personal dislike to you and you may find yourself in a great deal of danger unless you tread lightly.'

Galronus sighed.

'I am used to dealing with prejudice, tribune. The officers of Caesar's army mostly see me as an barbarian warrior given too much authority for my own good.'

'Not like Crassus. He despises your cavalry and even their commander, Varus. He would never move against Varus, for the man is of noble Roman blood, but you...?'

The Remi commander nodded sadly.

'Do you know, tribune, that I spent the winter in Rome? I had only a loose command of Latin before my time there, and much the same even when I first arrived. And yet, in the city itself, no one treated me as anything other than another face in the street. No prejudice. The distrust of the Gallic peoples seems to be the province of the military alone.'

The tribune chuckled.

'Give them a little room there. They've spent the last two years *fighting* Gauls, so there's bound to be a certain uneasiness. Things will change in time, but not until the army stops campaigning here. In the meantime, mark my words and watch your back. I will do what I can to help, but I will not, you understand, defy the legate for you.'

Galronus nodded.

'I would not expect it. I am surprised to find a tribune in the Seventh who would lower himself enough to speak to an auxiliary commander, let alone one of your... experience.'

The man laughed.

'"Age', you mean. Yes, I'm no young hopeful, I'm aware.'

He held out a hand.

'Publius Tertullus. I have the esteemed honour of being young master Crassus' uncle, through marriage.'

Galronus raised his brow.

'And you serve as a tribune?'

Tertullus laughed.

'I am not the most popular man of my line. I fear the lad's father keeps me close to look after him.'

The Remi officer smiled and took the proffered hand.

'It is good to know that someone of apparently good honest sense has a commanding role in this campaign. This role is not one of my choosing. I would have been back among my own people serving under Labienus if commander Varus had been willing to take this command instead.'

Again, the older tribune gave a light laugh.

'I must return to the others. I may be required when we meet up with these new reinforcements. Remember my words, though, Galronus of the Remi.'

The cavalry officer smiled and nodded.

He *would* remember.

* * * * *

The army had been travelling through the lands of the Sotiates for a day now, and Galronus had begun to feel distinctly tense, jumping at each unexpected sound. The officers in their accustomed position in the vanguard seemed to be treating the whole expedition as some sort of jaunt through the country, laughing and joking, pausing the army's march to take a meal on a hill with a particularly splendid view and riding out on small forays to hunt as the army travelled.

The Remi commander had met a number of men like this in his winter sojourn in Rome with Fronto, men more interested in themselves than their assigned task. Men who were heading for a fall.

The scenery here *was* stunning, though, he had to admit. As a man from the largely low and flat lands of the Remi, Galronus had little experience of terrain like this. Aquitania seemed to consist largely of deep valleys and gorges, thick woodland and high waterfalls, separated by high rock formations and bald moorlands. The landscape reminded him of the folds and dips in a cloak cast uncaringly to the floor.

Also, since leaving Vindunum and separating from Caesar's army, the weather had been improving the further south they travelled, leading to blue skies and warm sun among the Aquitanian hills, the buzz and hum of bees and the twitter of birds a constant companion.

But no amount of breathtaking scenery or stunning weather could shake the mood from the cavalry commander.

Three days into what was considered to be Aquitania and no sign of anything but a few small hamlets and lonely woodcutters' huts. One full day into the lands of the Sotiates, the largest tribe of this

284

land, and nothing to show for it but a tanned face and the smell of summer flowers.

Galronus had approached the legate and suggested a number of measures, almost all of which had been ignored out of hand.

Crassus did not deem these woodcutters worth interrogating, though Galronus had seen the look in their eyes as they had watched the legion pass. They *knew* something and each gaze he met set his nerves a notch higher. The legate refused to reorganise the army's marching order so as to be less predictable; the Seventh were apparently invincible in Crassus' eyes. Even the suggestion that they change their route and make for some of the smaller tribes first to gain more of an idea of what they were facing fell on deaf ears. Finally the two men had agreed on roving scouts provided by the Gallic auxiliary cavalry, but even that seemed but a tiny measure to the Remi commander.

A noise cleared the cobwebs from his head.

He was relieved, as usual, to hear the double blast on the Gallic horn that announced the return of the scouts. To his left, the hillside sloped away sharply, becoming a gradient far too steep for horses as it plunged down to a narrow river valley. Ahead, a more gentle and civilised slope led down the valley side, their route to the river they would be following to its confluence.

The scouts appeared to the right flank of the column, where the hillside continued to rise to a lush, grassy moor, punctuated by white rocks that created unusual and fascinating formations on the crest.

From among those white rocks the riders returned, scattered rather than in formation, and at a casual pace. The two blasts on the horn indicated that they were rejoining the column to report, and that the land hereabouts was still clear.

Despite the news, Galronus' heart still pounded; something was going to happen. He could feel it in his bones and in his blood... something was up. He turned to the cavalry officers trotting along behind him at the head of their units.

'Be prepared.'

The men, mostly Gallic auxiliaries themselves, a number of them from the Remi tribe, looked at one another in confused concern. While they had no reason to suspect trouble, they knew, to a man, how much they could trust and rely on their commander.

Quiet commands were passed out among the cavalry and Galronus picked up a little speed on his mount, riding ahead to the van.

Tertullus sat at the rear of the tribunes and smiled at the Remi commander as he approached.

'Good morning, Galronus. You have news?'

Crassus turned and cast a look of supreme disinterest at the horseman.

'Something is happening' Galronus said in a matter-of-fact voice. 'I don't know what it is, but there is something in the air. The legion should stand to, legate.'

Crassus sniffed and turned away again.

'Take your superstitious mutterings back to the cavalry, Gaul.'

Galronus ground his teeth again and, narrowing his eyes, made a suggestive motion to Tertullus before turning and riding back to his men, each of whom now had a firm grip on his spear, shield strapped on ready for combat.

The scouts were now trotting down the hillside toward the column and Galronus began to become angry with himself. A sense of foreboding was no use without a direction for it. The scouts had given the all clear to the right, and the landscape was visible in all other directions. Unless the legends of old were true and the sky was about to fall, there was no evidence of trouble. The scouts would…

He frowned.

The scouts had been circling in units of a dozen men, three out at all times, covering the landscape ahead and all around them. How the three units had met up to their right and…

'Sound the alarm!' he bellowed.

Men all around him stared.

'They're not our scouts! Sound the damn alarm!'

As chaos broke out around him, Galronus kicked his horse to life and rode ahead. Sure enough, there were more and more riders pouring over the crest of the hill. A hundred or more men already, and the numbers were thickening all the time. And here the legion and their support were trapped, the hill from which the enemy poured rising to their right, a steep drop to their left, which no man with a sense of self preservation would attempt with anything other than critical, slow care.

The enemy had learned their call code, which means they had already captured and interrogated the scouts and had waited until the Roman force was at its most vulnerable.

By the time Galronus reached the vanguard, the fighting had already begun. The tribunes and their legate were busy bellowing desperate commands, the cornicens and signifers relaying the orders as the legion tried to reorganise from a line six men abreast, into a solid shield wall facing the enemy. By sheer chance, either happy or unhappy depending on the viewer, the bulk of the cavalry were travelling on the army's left flank and were now cut off from the enemy by the beleaguered legion, trapped between the Seventh and the steep drop to the valley below.

'Legate: pull the legion back to the brink of the precipice, and I'll have my cavalry ride out to the rear out of the way.'

'What?'

Crassus sounded incredulous.

'The enemy riders will have to be very careful on horseback close to that drop. Your men can arrest their fall quickly if they go over the edge, but a mounted warrior has no such chance.'

Crassus glared at him.

'I will not take the brunt of a battle against an enemy that used your own cavalry to surprise us while you take your men and slink off somewhere safe!'

Galronus blinked, and the legate snarled at him.

'Now get your men round behind them and fight as though you were Romans.'

The Gaulish officer stared in disbelief at his commander. Had *Varus* been the man here and now, he would likely have defied the legate, but Varus had the benefit of being both a senior commander, appointed by Caesar, and a Roman nobleman who theoretically outranked Crassus. Galronus had no such advantage and was well aware of his tenuous grip on command. Should he push Crassus too far, the man would simply remove him from his position and place one of the tribunes in control of the auxiliary cavalry.

'Very well, sir.' With an exaggerated salute, he turned and rode back to his men who, already and without the need for such an order, had begun to move back toward the rear of the column.

'Come on. Let's get out there and flank them before they do too much damage.'

The units of Gallic horsemen kicked their steeds into a stronger pace and raced along the side of the legion, who were holding the line well and paying no heed to their own cavalry detachment behind them.

As he rode, Galronus frowned. Something was still not right. There must be a thousand or more enemy riders over there; probably *two* thousand. But that was nowhere near enough to take on an army this size. What did the Sotiates think they were doing?

The legion, now facing the enemy and the rocky hillside behind, formed a shield wall, supported by five further lines of men. The Sotiates, in traditional fashion, had ridden in sharply, cast a first spear into the lines, and then wheeled away before they met the shield wall. That initial volley had caused a reasonable amount of damage but, in the grand scheme of the army, had hardly made a difference, many of the spears being knocked aside with shields or falling short.

Since then the enemy had taken to riding forth in small groups, racing along the line of solid steel, jabbing down with their remaining spears in an overhand manner and then wrenching it back before riding away to rest as another group came forth. The same was happening all along the line. Here and there a spear blow would strike muscle and bone and a legionary would collapse, screaming, back among his fellows, but the vast majority of blows were caught and turned aside with the heavy legionary shields.

What could the Sotiates hope to gain from this? Sooner or later the legionary commanders would tire of watching this attritive warfare and would order an advance. Then it would all be over for these horsemen.

Galronus had reached the far end of the column now, where the newly-raised auxiliary spear bearers and archers brought up the rear, protecting the artillery, the baggage train and the supply wagons. To the cavalry commander's secret delight, these auxiliary units under their own commanders seemed to be faring a great deal better than Crassus' formidable legion. The spear men formed a veritable hedge of long, sharpened points, inaccessible to horses, while the archers behind kept up a steady volley that fell among any of the enemy that dared get close enough. The rear of the column was safe and the enemy were already moving toward the front, keeping a safe distance from this deadly combination of spear and arrow.

At least the supplies were protected.

As he watched, the first few units of his cavalry appeared at the other side, riding wide to flank the enemy and trap them against the column.

Galronus smiled and nodded to himself. *Now* things would change.

A moment later, he himself, along with his first unit, rounded the supply wagons and began to race toward the fray, picking up speed tremendously now that they were safely away from the precipice.

Galronus settled into his saddle, hauling the shield from his back onto his arm, and gripping his own spear tight as his knees guided the beast left and right.

The Sotiates were already pulling toward the front of the column, out of the reach of the archers and their deadly rain. The auxiliary cavalry came in at a wide arc from the slope above the fracas, driving for the flank of the enemy, where they met with shouts and the ringing sound of sword blows pounding shields or the metallic shriek of spear points sliding along bronze helmets or iron blades.

The legionaries close by, where the two cavalry forces had met, simply stood ready and stayed out of the way unless one of the Sotiates made a lunge for them. For a moment, Galronus wondered why they were not pressing home the attack, and then realised that, once the two forces were enjoined in combat, no legionary could tell the difference between the enemy horsemen and their own Gallic cavalry and were staying safely out of the situation for fear of causing allied casualties.

Gritting his teeth, the commander spotted a gap in the fighting and drove his horse down the slope toward a man in a mail vest with a splintered shield and a spear whose tip ran with crimson.

'Taranis, my arm is your thunderbolt!'

With a quick glance skyward, Galronus raised the spear above his shoulder and charged.

The moments that followed went by in a blur of confusion. Suddenly there was bucking, screaming, a jolting sensation, and he was free of the saddle, thundering through the air.

A lucky blow from one of the enemy horsemen had taken his steed in the neck, just above the shoulder and in shock and pain the horse had stumbled to a halt before rearing. The sudden stop, however, had dislodged the commander from his saddle mid-charge.

His mind whirling, the action around him a smudged mess, Galronus reacted the only way he could. To fall to the floor here, amid a cavalry battle, was to be trampled to death for certain. As his horse reared and collapsed behind him, Galronus let go of both spear and shield and grabbed for the first thing he could reach.

The enemy warrior gasped in surprise. He'd barely noticed the Roman horsemen as he turned to attack and had instantly pushed him from his thoughts as the man's horse was stuck with a passing spear, but it appeared that the man was *far* from done.

Galronus clung desperately to the horse's bridle with his left hand, gripping the saddle horn with his right as his legs dangled, his feet brushing the ground and bouncing painfully along.

In an urgent reaction, the Sotiate warrior brought his shield arm down, the edge of the heavy wood smashing into Galronus' shoulder in an attempt to dislodge him. The man was trying to manoeuvre his spear over the top so that he could jab down at the burden that clung to his horse's flank.

Gritting his teeth, ignoring the searing pain in his shoulder and the turf tugging at his feet, the Remi commander tightened his grip on the bridle, letting go with his right hand and swinging loose, bringing up his legs so that he hung by one hand from the horse's neck, knees bent and facing the man whose spear was slowly passing over the top in an arc.

In a fluid move, he drew the broad bladed Roman dagger from his belt and hooked it beneath the strap that passed from the saddle around the horse's girth. Two sharp tugs was all the sharpened blade needed, and the leather snapped with the tremendous strain put on it from above.

The rider, his spear ready to plunge down at his unwanted passenger, squawked in shock as he plummeted from the side of the horse, knees still gripping the suddenly detached saddle.

Galronus watched as the man fell away, disappearing with a shriek beneath the hooves of two other struggling horses.

Changing his grip on the bridle, the commander vaulted up and onto the bare back of the horse, grasping the reins. The priority now was to removing himself from danger. With no saddle, he would find it difficult to manoeuvre without being unhorsed and, with only a dagger to hand, he was of precious little use in the current melee.

Wheeling the beast, he rode for the clear ground to the rear, turning once he was safely free of the fight.

The battle was all but over. Trapped between the steel wall of the Seventh Legion and the vicious and well-trained auxiliary cavalry, the Sotiates had lost many of their men and had already pulled away toward the front of the column.

Even as he watched, the last few struggles ended as the enemy warriors fell or retreated, the entire remaining force disengaging and racing along the Roman lines, down the gentle slope into the valley.

The Remi officer heaved a sigh of relief and reached up to his tender shoulder. The chain armour had been torn apart by the blow as though it were merely old wool. The tunic beneath was torn and blood soaked the material. At least nothing appeared to have been broken, but for the next few days any movement of the arm would bring exquisite agony.

Wincing, he withdrew his hand and trotted forward, watching the fleeing enemy. His officers looked at him expectantly, and he shook his head, smiling at the looks of disappointment from those men whose blood was already up.

Riding on past, he reached the vanguard to find the officers in deep discussion.

'And that's where their chief settlement should be?'

A tribune nodded.

'We believe it lies where this river meets the main water of Aquitania, legate.'

'Then we will bring our forces to bear on them before they can prepare.'

He noted Galronus and barely gave a glance to the state of the man and his new steed.

'Good. Have your cavalry form up and chase down those horsemen. I don't want them to reach their city and give warning of our imminent arrival. Make sure you get rid of them all, though.'

Galronus blinked.

'Legate, that is foolhardy at best. We should be moving slowly and carefully, given what just happened, not splitting the force up and riding into unknown territory.'

Crassus sneered at him.

'*Coward*! It was *your* cavalry and *your* scouts that gave them this chance. My legion took it away from them again. Now get out there and put down that cavalry.'

Galronus shook his head.

'Impossible, sir. They know the terrain and have a considerable start on us. We'll never stop them all. Besides, they likely had a reserve of scouts watching that are already busy reporting to their leaders. Whatever we do now, they will already be prepared.'

Crassus issued a low growl.

'If you will not lead your men down there, I will select someone who *will*.'

The Remi officer smiled.

'Good luck, then.'

Ignoring the crimson face and the spluttering of the legate, Galronus wheeled his horse and rode back along the line to the cavalry.

* * * * *

Tribune Tertullus sighed.

'I warned you.'

Galronus nodded gently and drew a sharp breath as the capsarius put the final stitch in his shoulder wound.

'It is *his* loss now. He can remove me from command, but under the terms of our agreement with Caesar, he can do nothing more to me without the general's authorisation. I'm quite safe. Safer than ever now, in fact, since I'm not down there on a lunatic errand.'

Tertullus turned and glanced down the slope.

The cavalry had been placed under the command of one of the other junior tribunes and had ridden off ahead to chase down the Sotiates on Crassus' order. The legion, however, was moving at triple time, close behind them.

Back here, among the baggage train among the few wounded, Galronus and Tertullus sat on a gently-bouncing wagon as it descended the slope, bringing up the rear of the Roman column. It was a rather impressive vantage point, allowing them an unrivalled view of the entire column stretching out ahead and the valley beyond with its steep slopes.

'Still,' the tribune said, scratching his greying scalp, 'it might have been better if you'd stayed with your men. With Sextius commanding them, they're probably more of a danger to each other than the enemy.'

Galronus grinned.

'You're assuming they'll do as he says. Most of those men and their commanders are as loyal to me and to Varus as the legions are to Caesar. They are well aware of what my refusal means and they will not put themselves in unnecessary danger. Your Sextius might find he has bitten off a little more than he can chew trying to command a large force of Gauls.'

The tribune laughed and leaned back.

'I hope you're right. From what I hear of Aquitania, we're likely to need every man we have before this is over.'

'Hardly,' Galronus said with a sly smile. 'Your man Crassus tells me he could charge the very gates of the underworld with his precious Seventh.'

'Ha.'

The two men fell silent as the truth of the situation continued to nag at them both.

Down ahead, something was happening. A blast from a buccina rang out, to be picked up quickly by others.

'What was that?'

Galronus squinted off into the distance. A mass of dark shapes were issuing from the trees and copses to either side of the valley.

'Ambush' the commander said flatly. 'I was *expecting* something like this.'

The tribune frowned and looked at the activity in the distance.

'The cavalry are separate from the legion, out ahead.'

Galronus nodded.

'My officers were expecting it too. As soon as they saw the enemy, they'll have pulled ahead to somewhere they can marshal their forces.'

Tertullus shook his head.

'There are a hell of a lot of them. The legion could be in trouble.'

Again, Galronus shrugged.

'Not my concern anymore. I'm just a passenger now.'

The tribune narrowed his eyes at the Remi commander.

'You don't believe that any more than I do. We need to do something.'

Galronus squared his shoulders, wincing at the pain in the fresh wound. The capsarius, who had moved on to the next man, turned an angry glare on him.

'If you undo all my work, when I restitch it I'll sew a coin inside. Sit still.'

Once again the two men turned their gaze to the activity ahead. The valley was narrow and with steep sides. The auxiliary cavalry had formed up ahead, creating a barrier that prevented the remaining enemy horsemen from rejoining their fellow tribesmen, but remained largely removed from the action.

It was hard to credit how well the trap had been laid, really. The number of Sotiates pouring down the slopes onto the Roman forces was more than a match, the enemy outnumbering the legion by perhaps two to one. How they had managed to secrete such a large force in such a small area without being spotted earlier was truly marvellous.

The legion had organised into squares against the enemy coming at them from all sides.

'At least he's had the sense to form them defensively' Galronus nodded. 'I'd have half expected him to charge them.'

Tertullus shook his head.

'I know that the lad has faults, and plenty of them, and that he has little regard for you and your men, but I think that perhaps you do him a disservice tactically.'

Galronus turned a surprised look on him.

'Don't forget,' the tribune said 'he pacified the north west with one legion. His methods are a little brutal, but don't confuse aggression with stupidity. He's fairly shrewd in terms of actual tactics.'

The Remi commander looked distinctly unconvinced.

'What can we do to help them?' the tribune nudged.

'He's underusing the forces he has.'

'What?'

Galronus shrugged and winced again, sucking in air through his teeth.

'It's a common failing I've seen in Roman commanders. No disrespect, but most Roman officers concentrate all their energy on the legions, to the exclusion of all others. See how, once the cavalry are out ahead, he appears to have forgotten they exist. While the legion is manoeuvring into the most protective formation possible, what is he doing with the spearmen and archers?'

Tertullus shrugged. The three thousand or so spearmen and archers had taken position part way up the slope, creating a wall of bristling points that could hold most forces from reaching the support column.

'They're protecting the baggage. That's a common role for them, and I, for one, am happy they're doing so, since we're sat in one such cart.'

Galronus frowned.

'Why *are* you here? *I'm* wounded and removed from command, but *you're* a tribune. Your place is down there.'

Tertullus sighed.

'The legate likes to keep me out of danger if possible. His mother would be furious with him if anything happened to me.'

Galronus laughed.

'You Romans have such a strange set of values.'

He pointed down the slope.

'What I was trying to bring to your attention is that fully a third of the legate's forces are standing still on the slope and waiting for the enemy to make for the wagons. The Sotiates might not have any intention of doing so, since they're too busy slaughtering legionaries by the cartload. Wasteful.'

'So what's your alternative?'

Galronus grinned and stood, wobbling slightly.

'I may be a passenger now, but you're still a senior commander. Let's take control of the auxiliaries and provide a little support.'

Tertullus smiled and clambered down from the cart.

'So what do we do?'

'You take the archers, and I'll take the spear men. Imagine what damage a thousand arrows could do falling from the top of the valley side?'

The tribune's smile widened.

'We might be able to thin them out quite well. And the spears?'

'Spears are no use up there, but there are a lot of loose rocks on these hillsides. Imagine the damage a heavy rock could do rolling down that hillside and into a mass of warriors.'

Tertullus laughed.

'I see what you mean about not thinking exclusively.'

Reaching up, he grasped Galronus and helped him down from the cart.

'Come on. Let's go and save my nephew's backside.'

Chapter 16

(Iunius: Inland Aquitania, territory of the Sotiates.)

Gaius Pinarius Rusca licked his lips, his eyes darting back and forth in panic. What in the name of all the Gods was he doing here? The closest he'd ever come to fighting was a tussle with a peer who stole his seat at the games when he was a teenager.

Eight months ago he had been sitting in his cosy little triclinium contemplating his future with the delectable Laevinia and now, standing on this springy turf with his legs shaking uncontrollably and a dangerous slackening around his bladder, he could not believe how excited he'd been to have had his posting to the legions approved.

His father had served under the elder Crassus years ago and had managed to secure him the most prestigious tribunate within the Seventh beneath the young legate, since when Rusca had spent the past months in Vindunum lording it over the others and turning his ability with numbers and attention to detail to the disposition of units and supply problems.

A distant bellow of rage brought his attention rudely back to the current situation.

'Hold the line!' he shouted, noting the way his voice cracked in fear and hoping that no one else had.

The legate had sent the cavalry on chasing the Sotiates and had marched the legions as fast as they could move in formation down the hill behind.

They had descended, eager to bring Roman vengeance to these skirmishing horsemen and Rusca had watched from his forward position as the pursuing auxiliary cavalry engaged the enemy once again, only to be completely cut off from the rest of the army as untold thousands of screaming, bloodthirsty barbarians, some wearing wild animal pelts around their shoulders, had poured seemingly out of the very ground to either side of them.

Rusca's world had fallen apart. He was a natural mathematician; a studious and quiet young man hoping to achieve at least a minor public appointment back in the city on the strength of his military experience. What he was truly not, he thought, as the embarrassing warm trickle began, was a soldier.

296

Crassus himself had been close by and Rusca had been surprised at how the man dealt with the situation. The legate was no older than he and had only served the legions for a couple of years and yet he took control of the disaster like those Cretan bull leapers grabbed their acrobatic steeds and pulled the legion together; like a veteran commander.

On the legate's orders, the legion had split into individual cohorts, each forming a defensive square in the face of the charging enemy. Suddenly, and without time to even attempt mental preparation, the inexperienced senior tribune had found himself in nominal command of the Second Cohort as they braced for the clash, though in truth, the cohort's senior centurion was already shouting the appropriate commands, most of the troops largely unaware of even the presence of the tribune.

The square consisted of shield walls thirty men across and four deep, with the tribune, the cornicens and the capsarii in the central space.

The Sotiates, wrapped in their pelts, furs, leathers and occasional mail shirts poured down the slope like a shabby sea, crashing against the rocks of the Second Cohort with a spray of blood, spittle and sweat and Rusca felt a fresh wave of panic as the shield walls on two sides gave a little under the onslaught, bowing inwards toward the noncombatants in the centre. The scent of urine brought a burning shame to the tribune's cheeks, though he was sure no one would notice in the general stink of sweat that threatened to make him gag.

How could there be so many barbarians in all the world? Already the shield walls were under attack by a vast force, and yet all he could see from his central vantage point were yet more and more enemy warriors charging, screaming into the fray.

'Hold the line!' he bellowed again, aware of how pointless it was as a command. As if the men were about to part and let the sea of Gauls into their midst.

A commotion drew his attention to the north face of the formation, where a particularly violent assault was taking place, the enemy literally throwing themselves in a blind rage on top of the shield wall, breaking the square. As he watched, a huge barbarian with a broad bladed axe appeared, the weapon held high above his head, as he stood on the back of a fallen comrade, one foot held firm on a discarded Roman shield, and brought the vicious weapon down in a massive swing.

297

Something bounced off Rusca's cheek guard and rattled around the helmet's bronze rim, and his sight went black.

In an urgent and terrified panic, Rusca raised his free hand, his sword arm hanging pointlessly at his side, and wiped desperately at his suddenly blind eyes. What had happened?

His vision returned as he wiped the excess blood from his eyes and he gagged, realising that the axe blow had sent half the legionary's head flying through the air in pieces. Stepping back, pale and shaking, Rusca leaned forward and vomited copiously, fresh waves of horror assailing him as shards of bone and fractured teeth fell out of his helmet where they had become lodged following the blow.

How he remained standing at that point, white, terrified and sick, he would never know, but the young tribune's world changed in that moment.

He stared down at the fragments of the unknown legionary on the floor below him and spat the remains of the bile away. Reaching up with a shaking arm, he unlaced his helmet and let it fall, blood-soaked and dented, to the ground with the rest of the detritus.

Blinking away more of the sweat and blood, he reached down for the crimson linen scarf around his neck, studied it until he found a relatively dry and clean section, and wiped his face, noting with surprise the sheer quantity of blood that was still there.

He looked around him, his terror having metamorphosised into something different; something beyond mere fear. Rusca was going to die today and now that he knew it, he felt curiously prepared. The legionary who had succumbed to the axe blow had died so instantaneously he could not possibly have felt the pain for longer than a heartbeat.

The cohort was collapsing around him.

What had begun as five hundred men had perhaps halved already, and two areas of the shield wall were precariously thin.

As he watched, contemplating what he could do to help, there was a second violent clash in that same spot, huge powerful warriors leaping onto and across the shield wall with apparent unconcern for their own life. Suddenly, like the bursting of a dam, the shield wall gave, and three wild, growling men burst through.

The centurion, somewhere off to Rusca's left, called his orders and the breach was quickly sealed, men pushing from either side until they connected and formed a solid front once again. At a second order, the few free capsarii in the centre, ready to tend to any wounded men who were passed back inside from the line, grasped their swords and stepped forward to intercept the three Gauls who were making straight for the man in the burnished cuirass, clearly the senior officer.

It took Rusca a moment to realise that they were rushing to protect him, and he felt a fresh wave of shame rise on his cheeks. There were men he had met this past half year, men who occupied the same position as he in other legions, who would think nothing of charging, barehanded, into the enemy at this point. Yet here *he* was being nothing but a burden to the men under his command.

For a moment, the fatalism that had clouded his thoughts these last moments threatened to drive him into action. It would be nice to go to the Elysian fields knowing that he had made one heroic stand with his men and fought like a soldier.

Unfortunately his knees did not see things the same way and refused to carry him forward, instead trembling uncontrollably and threatening to make him collapse to the ground.

Four capsarii leapt in front of him, one slipping on the mess of blood, bone and vomit and crashing to the ground, causing a fresh wave of guilt and shame to batter the tribune. The other three ran at the intruders, gladius in one hand and dagger in the other, their shields already discarded to allow for medical duties.

Rusca watched, shuddering, as the men fought, stabbing, slashing and hacking at the barbarians, who returned the favour, their own swords and axes swinging and slicing. The tribune could not pick out the detail in the flurry of action, his knees barely holding him upright, and the moment he realised that the capsarii had failed, his trembling legs finally gave way, bringing him to a kneeling position, as though penitent. Shuddering, he collapsed to all fours in the filth.

The capsarii had dispatched two of the Sotiate warriors, but the third seemed to be entirely unharmed as he stabbed down almost casually, ending the life of the man who had been attacking him, and then strode purposefully across toward the tribune.

The soldier who had slipped in the mess before the tribune was already picking himself up, sword in hand, ready to stand and defend his commander to the last.

'Get back!'

The capsarius jumped in shock as Rusca put a hand on his shoulder and pulled him backward, sliding him to the rear and away from the approaching warrior.

His father had been a soldier; ten times the soldier he could ever hope to be, and had imparted a great deal of military expertise around the dinner table over the years, particularly when his uncles had been visiting. In this moment, at the end of his life, Rusca could clearly remember one such pearl of wisdom: 'in battle, anything goes'. There is no right or wrong way. The *noble* warrior faced his enemy and stared him in the eye as they fought; the *noble* warrior would allow an opponent mercy if he sought it; the *noble* warrior looked after his equipment and followed his training to the letter. All good and *noble*, but the *victorious* warrior did the unexpected, kicked, bit, head-butted and dodged away. He did whatever he could to *be* the victorious warrior.

The great hulking barbarian stepped toward him, grinning and raising his long blade in two hands, ready to bring it down in an overhand blow that would drive it clean through the tribune and at least a foot of the earth beneath him.

Already sickened at the fact that he was on his hands and knees in his own vomit and the blood of several men, Rusca took a deep breath and threw himself flat on his front in the mess, swinging his sword arm out with all his strength as he did so.

The gladius was traditionally used for stabbing, its point vicious and its blade well made for repeated thrusts and withdrawals. The legions were trained to use them this way for efficiency and the high probability of mortal wounding with each blow, but it was not unknown, according to his father, for the blade to be used to slice, as in the horrible Macedonian conflicts a hundred years ago where tales of severed limbs had abounded.

The blow was powerful, driven by fear, desperation and a curious cold determination that had formed like ice from the tears of his panic. As the Gaul's sword reached its apex, prepared for its deadly descent into the tribune's back, Rusca's gladius swept out and bit into his leg just above the ankle, the force carrying the blow deep enough to snap the bone.

The warrior gave a bloodcurdling cry as his leg slipped sideways, separating from the foot above the ankle, the severed shin dropping to the turf.

The man collapsed, screaming in agony, his attack entirely forgotten.

Rusca blinked in frightened amazement as the man's sword, relinquished in mid-air, plunged point first into the earth less than a foot from the tribune's grimy hand. Shuddering, he pushed himself back into a kneeling position and stared at his slick, crimson sword.

Suddenly an arm was beneath his shoulder, helping him to stand. His legs seemed to have regained some of their strength, and he pushed himself upright without too much difficulty, turning to stare in confusion at the capsarius who had helped him. The man was saying something.

'What?'

'I said thanks for that, sir.'

The man laughed.

'Actually, what I really said, sir, was *'bloody hell!'*'

Rusca continued to stare at him blankly. The man shrugged.

'Never seen an officer fight like that, sir. Hell, I've rarely seen *anyone* fight like that!'

Rusca gave a croaky laugh.

'Better to be a living thug than a dead hero, eh?'

The capsarius nodded, grinning, as he stepped past the tribune and sank his blade into the writhing form of the one-footed Gaul, dispatching him with ease.

The tribune wiped the sweat and grime from his eyes and frowned into the fray.

'Can't see what's happening. Can you? I appear to have all manner of shit in my eyes.'

The capsarius laughed and squinted as he turned and took in the scene around him.

'I think we're down to about half numbers, but a lot of those will be walking wounded; salvageable, if we can get out of here.'

Rusca raised an eyebrow.

'I wasn't really seeking a medical opinion, man, more a tactical one.'

''Course, sir. Think they're thinning out. Looks like we've got the edge.'

The pair turned and stared as the scene up and down the valley became apparent. Ahead, the Sotiates were retreating, running as fast as they could down the valley, while Crassus and the First Cohort reorganised to follow them. The enemy horse had fled already, and

301

Galronus' cavalry had turned and were harrying the fleeing Gauls. Further back along the line, among the other cohorts, the Gauls were already beginning to disengage.

'Why are they running?' Rusca wondered aloud.

''Cause of the auxilia, sir. Look!'

The tribune raised his eyes and scanned the top of the valley side, where his companion was pointing. Units of auxiliary archers were pouring arrows down into the rear ranks of the enemy, while others, probably the spear men, were heaving at the loose rocks, setting them rolling down the steep incline and into the mass of Sotiates.

'Ha. Their ambush has been ambushed.'

The capsarius wore a look of concern as he turned back.

'What's the matter?'

'You're very pale, sir. It's hard to see beneath all the blood, but you're white as a Vestal's dress. Are you wounded?'

Rusca grinned.

'Far from it.'

He turned and scanned the men until he spotted the senior centurion.

'Looks like they're breaking, centurion. Soon as they do, get formed up and follow, joining up with the First Cohort.'

The centurion saluted, and Rusca turned back to the capsarius.

'You and I, however, are going to wait until the enemy are cleared back and then head to the supply carts where I can get water for a wash, and some clean clothes.'

The capsarius grinned.

'Up to you sir, but if I were you I'd stay just like that. The very sight of you would loosen their bowels!'

* * * * *

The chief oppidum of the Sotiates had been a surprise to all. After an initial chase, it had become clear that, with its accompanying auxilia and baggage train, there was little hope of catching the fleeing Gauls before they reached their settlement and so Crassus had called an immediate halt to the fruitless chase and had changed tactics entirely.

Scouts sent ahead confirmed that over the next ten miles the land gradually lowered and flattened until it became a huge plain that extended all the way to the distant shore. The oppidum was constructed on only a very low hill, that being all that was available, and surrounded by low walls that, in quality and size, fell short of the impressive defences they had seen in other parts of Gaul.

Clearly the Sotiates had placed all their faith in the ambush in the valley, knowing that once the Roman forces reached the plain their defensive capabilities were drastically reduced.

Crassus had greeted the news from the scouts with a smile, reforming the Seventh Legion and its auxilia and taking two days in the last of the forested hills before descending to the plain. While this delay would have given the Sotiates the time to recover from their heavy losses and panicked retreat, it would not be long enough for them to effect heavier defences or gather great reinforcements, yet would allow the Roman force the time to perform the onerous post-battle tasks: the tending of the wounded and the funerals of the dead and raising of a mound.

More importantly it had given the engineers of the legion plenty of time to strip areas of woodland and use the timber to construct a number of siege machines in preparation for the coming assault. From his position outside the army's current command chain, Galronus had watched the engineers with interest. His duties with the cavalry had rarely allowed him time to observe the feats of the engineers in progress and the work was fascinating to watch. Clearly these men had worked together so many times that there was hardly any need for commands or directions, the soldiers going about their tasks with ordered precision, as though performing some sort of complicated dance.

By the time they had set off on the march again yesterday morning, the huge train of carts that followed the army had acquired mobile shelters that the engineers called vineae, two tall towers and a number of great screens that could protect troops.

The additional heavy engines had slowed the pace of the army a little and consequently the unnamed oppidum had only finally come into view this morning as the army continued along the line of the river down across the plains.

Tribune Tertullus had been lauded for their actions in the valley, with no mention being made of Galronus' part. The lack of recognition had hardly bothered the Remi horseman, but the absence of the friendly tribune, as the man had been called to ride with the van once more, left a hole that had filled with tedium.

Even now, while the legions stood in shining ranks on the plain below the walls of the oppidum, awaiting the order to advance, the siege engines in place and ready to be launched forth, Galronus sat apart from the action, lounging on a flat, warm rock in the sunshine as he watched the glorious Roman parade before him.

Somewhere among the mass musicians issued calls and the army split and began to carry out carefully prepared manoeuvres, some trundling the siege towers forward, others sheltering in the vineae as they rolled toward the walls, the artillery details manning the onager and ballistae, firing off their initial aiming shots to find the range. The huge screens moved forward, protection for the auxiliary archers. It was so ordered it could have been a latrunculi board with two players shifting their markers.

Galronus shook his head and smiled. Fronto's fault, that. A year ago he'd been Remi to the core, unaware of the very existence of the game. Now here he was after a winter in the great city under the dour legate's influence, and the first metaphor that came to mind was a Roman game. Briefly he wondered how his friend was doing, far away to the north, dealing with the rebellious Veneti, and found with surprise that he was suffering feelings that he would be hard put to call anything other than homesickness for Rome. *That* was a surprise.

And yet, as he watched the first volleys issue from the attackers and from the walls of the settlement, he could see the future of the world mapped out among the cohorts and centuries before him.

Before Caesar came to the lands of the Belgae, the Remi tribe had weighed their options and made the decision to support the forces of the general. Had they not, they may now be like the Aduatuci: nothing more than a name on a map, gradually fading into obscurity. Rome was coming to the whole world and embracing its arrival was the only sensible option. Aquitania would fall soon enough.

Distant cries of dismay drew his attention, and he used his hand to shade his eyes and passed his gaze across the forces below the walls. Something was happening by one of the two huge siege towers. The structure was leaning at a precarious angle, and it was with a smile that Galronus realised that two of the huge wheels had sunk into the ground. As he watched the legionaries desperately trying to right the huge construction, he almost laughed aloud when the tower swayed dangerously and then finally, ponderously, toppled forward and disappeared from view.

He frowned as he tried to focus on the distant spot, trying to work out what had happened and let out another bark of laughter as he realised that the structure had sunk into a tunnel, then tipped forward and vanished into the subterranean passage in its entirety.

The advance faltered for a moment as decisions were made. Galronus grinned and reached down for his sack of watered wine, purloined from the baggage train last night, and yet another indication of the influence Fronto had had on him this past year.

On the plain below, the bright silver and crimson figures of the tribunes marched around between the other officers, relaying Crassus' commands. Galronus tried for a moment to identify them: the ageing Tertullus who had become a friend and ally so easily, and Rusca, who had arrived at the baggage train two days ago covered in gore, smelling of unearthly filth, and had spoken to him for the first time, lightly and with a gentle humour. The distance was too great, though, and one shining officer looked very much like another from this position.

It was curious. From here, with no command of his own and no direct influence on events, watching the army of Crassus at their work felt like those lazy days in early spring when he'd risen blearily from his bed in Fronto's house and gone to watch the morning races in the circus. Momentarily he considered whether it would be in bad taste to find one of the medics or support staff that remained back from the battle and lay a few wagers.

Almost certainly they would think him callous, or an idiot. But then the betting of coin on games was a habit to which Rome had introduced him and not a natural pastime for the Belgae.

Taking another swig from the wine, he lay back on the rock and dozed, half listening to the battle going on below and before him. Some decision had clearly been made about how to avoid a repeat of the tower incident and the legions were marching again, accompanied by the groan and clonk of the huge timber constructions and the constant distant whisper of arrows and other projectiles flying back and forth.

In a way, he was glad to be so far out of it that the battle appeared little more than a game, unable to hear the cries of the wounded and dying and smell the sick odours of war.

A series of shouts and a crash announced another setback and Galronus pushed himself upright once again and opened his eyes. Another tunnel had been discovered, this time by one of the heavy, trundling vineae that had sagged to one side, its wheels sinking into the ground. With a great deal of effort, the legionaries managed to heave it back up to the flat and push it off to one side, avoiding the likely line of the passage.

By now the screens were in place and the units of auxiliary archers close enough to strafe the parapet of the low walls, quickly clearing them of defenders.

The Remi officer was about to close his eyes and sink back down to the rock when there was a tremendous roar. Pushing himself fully upright, he shaded his eyes once more and watched as a postern gate opened off to the far left and a mass of screaming Sotiate warriors issued forth, pouring toward the archers and their screen. Galronus nodded to himself as he watched events unfold.

The archers were apparently undefended, simply auxiliaries hiding behind screens; easy pickings for the enemy and too far from the nearest legionary cohort for the regular troops to intervene in time. The Sotiates had seen their only opportunity to try and even the field a little, but Crassus had planned ahead, likely for this very event, else why would he not have concentrated on the postern gate.

As half a thousand warriors poured forth, the nearest cohort of the Seventh changed its tack instantly, picking up speed and moving at triple time across the front of the archers, beneath the walls.

The bellowing, desperate Sotiate warriors threw themselves at the undefended archers, only to discover that the screen had concealed more than just the auxiliary bowmen. The spearmen who had filtered among them suddenly raised and braced their spears, using the weapons to create a barrier of deadly points protecting the archers, who continued to rain death on the oppidum's walls.

The enemy realised their error too late, pulling back from lunging at the deadly spear wall and turning to flee to their gate, only to find that the speedy cohort had cut them off from their own walls. Suddenly trapped between the Narbonese spear men and the soldiers of the Seventh, busy settling into a shield wall, the despondent warriors threw down their weapons.

The Sotiates in the oppidum cut their losses and shut the gate on their friends.

'You are a Gaul. What do you think they will do?'

Galronus spun round in surprise to find Crassus standing behind him, burnished cuirass dazzling in the sunlight, crimson cloak waving in the light breeze.

306

'I am Remi, from half a world away, not one of them.'

Crassus shrugged, dismissing the comment as irrelevant.

'Well' Galronus mused, frowning at this unwarranted and unusual attention from the legate. 'There is nothing they can do. They must surrender.'

Crassus nodded.

'I believe so. The question is whether we accept the surrender. We must continue on after this, deeper into Aquitania, to the very foothills of the Pyrenees, and it is never wise to leave a live enemy behind one. Even if I were inclined to mercy, the option of extermination is not a ridiculous one.'

Galronus narrowed his eyes and looked the man up and down. There was something in Crassus' voice that he'd not noticed before. The legate appeared to be trying to talk himself into something.

'And *are* you?'

'Am I what?'

'Are you inclined to mercy?'

Crassus gestured to the landscape around them with a sweep of his hand.

'I am considering it, certainly. I brought down the Roman heel on the throat of Armorica last year, and it seems to have had the opposite effect to that for which I had hoped. Instead of squeezing the resistance from them, I seem to have squeezed a mass of Gauls into a hardened resistance. We can scarce afford a similar situation developing in Aquitania. Whatever we do here must be a permanent end if we are to label Gaul conquered.'

Galronus nodded.

'One way or the other, you mean. Pax Romana with the peoples of Aquitania, or a region totally empty save the graves of uncounted tribes.'

The legate gave a curious smile.

'You dislike and distrust me, Gaul. I can see it in your eyes.'

Galronus opened his mouth, but Crassus waved his unspoken words aside.

'Do not deny it, and rest assured that I dislike you also, though I find, curiously, that I do not *distrust* you. So tell me truthfully what you believe I should do with the Sotiates?'

Galronus pondered again, scratching his neck. He reached for his wine sack and offered it up to Crassus, who made a face.

'*Hardly.*'

307

Shrugging, the Remi officer took a deep swig and leaned back.

'You should accept their surrender in good faith. Offer acceptable terms; even terms favourable to them if you wish to have them watch your back as you move on. But remember too that the sort of leader who will lure you into an ambush is the sort of man to watch even when there is peace.'

Crassus nodded.

'Your thoughts are sensible, Gaul, and I tend to agree.'

Galronus took a deep breath.

'Forgive me, legate, but you didn't come and find me just to ask my opinion on something you had already thought through yourself.'

Crassus nodded.

'I find myself in the uncomfortable position of requesting that you retake command of the cavalry.'

Galronus smiled knowingly.

'They react somewhat 'inefficiently' to your tribunes' orders?'

The legate glared at him.

'They are Gauls. They are used to serving under a Gaulish commander. I fear you have a grip on your men that no Roman could break.'

Galronus laughed.

'It's called trust and respect, legate.'

Crassus nodded, his face expressionless.

'Very well' Galronus said, standing and stretching slowly. 'I will have to insist that the disposition of the cavalry becomes my responsibility alone, though. You have seen now how shared authority works out.'

Crassus nodded again.

'Agreed. Return to your men, then, commander, and prepare them. We may need to contain attempts to flee, and we will certainly require numerous scout patrols in the coming hours and days.'

As the Remi officer rolled his shoulders, he grinned and pointed out toward the oppidum.

'And you, I suspect, will be busy too, legate. If I'm not mistaken, that looks like their leaders riding out to parley with you.'

* * * * *

Galronus patted the neck of his steed and stroked her mane as he watched the procedure. The surrender had been civilised and swift, the half dozen top men of the Sotiates riding out to meet the Roman officers and requesting terms. Crassus had, as he had intimated he would to Galronus, offered almost unprecedented good terms, ordering the Gauls to deliver up their arms for disposal, take the oath of allegiance to Rome and forbidding them to take up arms except in the defence of Rome or against mutual enemies. In return, no repercussions would be felt by the Sotiates for their resistance, no hostages taken and no slavery or looting. That last had been particularly surprising, given Crassus' reputation and the disfavour such an edict would bring on him from his men.

Rusca, the senior tribune, had been placed in charge of processing the surrendering Gauls, collecting their arms and administering the oath. The man seemed to have a knack for organisation and the whole affair was ordered and efficient, the population leaving the oppidum by the main gate, passing before Rusca and his guard, giving their names and professions and surrendering their weapons before moving off to assemble in ordered rows on the plain below the walls, where they would later take the oath before being free to return to their homes.

Galronus sighed. Perhaps the young legate's thirst for bloodshed had finally been slaked, and he was settling into the role of the praetor in a traditional Roman fashion. Still, it would be a long time before the Remi chieftain would be comfortable giving Crassus the benefit of the doubt.

The auxiliary cavalry sat ahorse in large units, keeping a watchful eye on events and upon the assembling unarmed Gauls. He felt some sympathy for them as he glanced up and down the rows, the pride still evident in their eyes, unbroken. Pride was hard to come by in Gaul these days.

A call drew his attention, and he turned to see two of his men escorting one of the more important Sotiate warriors toward him. The man was still dressed for battle, his chain shirt a deep grey, the golden torc slung around his neck above it drawing the attention. Though disarmed, the man had retained his armour and the trappings of his rank, sitting astride a horse several hands taller than Galronus' own.

The man nodded in familiar salute, his long, white-blond hair dropping across his face and hiding the bushy moustache and the steel grey eyes.

'Sir, this man asked to speak to you.'

Galronus smiled at the trooper and then nodded to the Gaulish leader.

'Thank you soldier. You can leave us.'

The troopers trotted off, leaving the two horsemen alone in the summer haze.

'You were once a Gaul.'

Galronus laughed and slipped with ease into his own language, a much different dialect, but close enough to converse easily.

'How incredibly closed-minded of you. I am *still* a Gaul.'

'You look like a Roman now. Where is your beard? Where is your torc? You wear the uniform of Rome, and you talk like them. Even speaking *our* language, you have *their* accent.'

Galronus shrugged.

'All things change, my friend. I shave and wear their armour, but my friend who leads their Tenth Legion rarely shaves and wears a Belgic torc over his Roman trappings. The tribes could never unite to become one Gaul, and so instead we shall become one *Roman* Gaul.'

The leader shook his head sadly.

'It may well be as you say, but I will continue to mourn the passing of our freedom.'

'Come,' Galronus prompted, 'you did not request to see me to discuss our cultural differences.'

The man straightened in his saddle.

'You are right, of course... I come to bring you a warning. If I am to take an oath of allegiance I would have a clear conscience and not have broken the oath while still uttering it.'

The Remi officer narrowed his eyes.

'You know of some treachery?'

'Six men lead the Sotiates into war. If you look at the horsemen from where I just came, you will see that only five of us have left the city.'

Galronus' frown deepened.

'One of you intends to bar the town to us again? He would have to be mad.'

'The Sotiates have offered you their surrender, but Adcantuannus and his 'soldurii' have refused to accept the terms and lurk inside the town. I offer you this information in the name of your commander's generous terms.'

The cavalry officer stared past him at the town.

'What are these 'soldurii'?'

'They are Adcantuannus' personal war band: thirty score of warriors loyal to *him* rather than to the tribe. Since Adcantuannus has refused the terms, then so have the soldurii.'

Galronus sighed.

'These men are aware that they endanger the terms granted everyone else by continuing to resist?'

The man nodded wearily.

'They will likely run to join the coalition.'

The Remi officer's head snapped round sharply.

'The *what*?'

'The Vocates and the Tarusates' army. You have not heard of this?'

Galronus straightened again, his blood pumping fast.

'*Army*?'

The man smiled now, a smug smile that worried Galronus.

'The Vocates and their neighbours have been sending for allies since your legion first crossed the Charanta river. They have sent their warriors and leaders to mass an army in the mountains, where the Spanish tribes will join them.'

Galronus blinked.

'The *Spanish* tribes?'

The man laughed.

'It would appear we will not have to hold to our oath for too long.'

Galronus' gaze passed swiftly across the field until he spied Crassus, standing with the other tribunes and a couple of centurions by his hastily-erected command tent, deep in conversation.

'Go over there and relay this to the legate. He may be very generous.'

The man shrugged.

'I tell you this, not for my own gain, but because it is right to do so and because your knowing your own doom will not change it.'

Galronus glared at him.

'Just go and tell everything to the commander.'

For a moment, he watched the man ride off, and then wheeled his horse and trotted across to two large gatherings of cavalry, sitting ahorse as they monitored the passage of the tribesfolk. As he reined in, he gestured to two of the officers.

311

'You, gather fully half the cavalry and have them split and posted around all the other entrances to the oppidum. Be prepared for anyone trying to leave and stop them any way you have to.'

The officer saluted and rode off, and Galronus turned to the other man.

'I want you to take a detachment of five hundred men. Have half of them dismount. We're going into the city. Meet me at the main gate when you have the men.'

The officer saluted and rode across to his juniors, and Galronus sighed. Nothing was ever easy. Sparing a brief glance for the command tent and the Sotiate noble riding toward it, he wheeled once again and rode swiftly across the open space before the gathering tribe. The tribune was deeply involved in his bureaucracy, lines of gleaming legionaries overseeing the disarming process.

'Tribune?' he called as he reined in again and dismounted.

'Commander?'

Rusca gestured to the line to halt and lowered his wax tablet and stylus.

'I have a favour to ask.'

'Go on?'

'I need some heavy troops used to fighting on foot. Could I requisition two of your centuries and their officers? We may be looking at trouble in the town.'

The man frowned and tapped his lip with the stylus.

'It's most irregular. Requests like that should go through the chain of command and come down to me from the legate.'

Galronus nodded.

'I appreciate that, but the matter is of some urgency.'

Rusca glanced past him at the dismounted cavalry, their mounted comrades riding alongside them as they descended on the gate.

'If it's serious, take the Second and Fourth centuries. Their centurions are over by the gate.'

Galronus nodded and gave a half-hearted salute, handing his horse's reins to a legionary and striding across to the centurions.

'You two have been assigned to me for a short time.'

The centurions shared a surprised glance and saluted as the cavalry began to arrive.

'Alright' the officer addressed his mixed force. 'We have a rogue leader somewhere in the oppidum, likely trying to break out and make for the mountains. He has a fanatically loyal guard of some six

312

hundred men. If we can get them to surrender without a fight, all to the good, but whatever happens, they don't leave the settlement except under our guard. We're going inside, and each time we pass a side street, I want mixed parties of legionaries, horsemen and dismounted cavalry to clear the area. You know your ground tactics better than I, but six hundred men should not be hard to find. They can hardly hide in a house.'

The centurions saluted and turned to the cornicen and signifers nearby, calling out their orders.

Galronus gazed through the gate at the broad street beyond. At least this place was small.

* * * * *

The oppidum was even smaller inside than Galronus had expected, the streets forming roughly concentric circles around a central square, with major thoroughfares crossing them and leading from the centre toward the gates, curving and bending as necessary to make their way around structures that had been present before the road system was formed.

It was unusual in Gaulish settlements, but Galronus had seen similar forms before. At some time in the recent decades, fire must have ravaged the oppidum and the town had been rebuilt with more spacious streets in an almost Roman style, allowing for the buildings that had survived the catastrophe to remain.

Whether that was the cause of the layout or not, Galronus was thankful of it. Sweeping the streets of the town with his troops had been made considerably easier by the simple shape they took. Here and there they had come across groups of tribesmen who were making for the main gate to comply with the legate's terms, though already most of the population had left.

It had taken less than half an hour to sweep most of the settlement clear, and now, as the entire scattered force began to join up once again, closing in on the remaining section of town, Galronus was beginning to wonder whether he had been the victim of a strange trick.

His doubts were assuaged, however, as the cavalryman at the front of his small force was suddenly plucked from his saddle and thrown with a shriek against the squat, timber wall of the house behind him.

Before the cry of alarm went up, more arrows struck, peppering the mixed force. Half a dozen men had fallen before the legionaries filtered through the mass to the front, raising their heavy shields and forming a barrier to the deadly hail.

Galronus ran forward, waving a signal to the cavalry officer ahead. While the mounted troops were good for searching the streets and chasing down survivors, they would be of precious little use in harsh fighting at street level. Responding instantly to his orders, the officer called to his men, and they raced on past the side street from which the arrows had issued before dismounting and hurriedly finding something to which to tie their reins so they could fall in on foot and join the fight.

Arrows continued to pound the shields of the legionaries as Galronus appeared between the dismounted cavalry and peered round the corner.

The street was seething with men. The Remi commander's sharp eyes picked out the four important facets of the enemy force in moments. The near side was formed of perhaps a hundred men with spears and bows, defending the rear of Adcantuannus' soldurii. Far ahead, he could see another smaller group of perhaps fifty or so men making for the postern gate at the end of the road, a plausible route to escape the city. The leader himself was clearly distinguishable, gleaming in bronze and gold, toward the far end of the street with half a dozen burly men around him. The last group that made up the force were the bulk of the 'soldurii' gathered at the centre, close by their leader and ready to fight or flee depending upon the circumstances.

Galronus frowned.

This street was a side street that shouldn't lead to a gate. He'd been round the periphery of the oppidum earlier and marked the location of all the gates with his forces. *This* gate shouldn't exist, damn it.

Gritting his teeth, he turned to one of the legionaries, crouching behind his large shield in the third row.

'Give me that!'

The soldier relinquished his shield unhappily and shuffled closer to the man beside him, and Galronus mimicked the stance of a defending legionary, hunkering down behind his shield as he squeezed his way through the crowd and out to the front.

314

As he reached open space, he risked glancing over the rim and immediately ducked back as two arrows thudded into the wood and leather.

'Adcantuannus!'

There was a pause during which the only sound was the occasional thud of arrows against shields and then slowly the firing stopped. Galronus risked another look. The archers stood ready with their arrows nocked, tensing.

'What is it, Roman?'

With a smile, Galronus switched to his native tongue.

'There is nowhere to go, Adcantuannus. The cavalry has you penned in outside. I have more than twice your number here...' a lie, though the man could not know, 'and your countrymen are being treated with honour and care. Stop this madness while you can.'

The warrior with the gleaming bronze helm appeared above the crowd, standing high on something unseen. He stood silent for a long moment as, not far behind him, the advance group of warriors had unbarred the gate and were heaving it open.

Adcantuannus turned, gesturing expansively with his outstretched arm. Galronus could not see too much detail but would be willing to bet that the man was grinning.

'See, Roman, how we have a secret exit, unseen from without. Your troops will not be on us before we melt into the landscape and disappear. You will see us again, though, soon enough.'

Galronus smiled.

'I fear you are mistaken, my chief.'

As the gate swung open, a roar erupted outside. The Remi officer could not see past the occupants of the street, but that battle cry from the unseen force beyond the gate was all too familiar to the man who had taught it to the auxilia. Somehow, though *he'd* not seen the gate on their earlier foray, *someone* had.

The roar died away, but not the noise, as the cavalry's voices were replaced by the ground-shaking thunder of their hooves. Galronus almost chuckled as he could see, at the far end of the street, the warriors desperately forcing the gate shut once again, panicked urgency gripping them.

Adcantuannus turned back to him.

'We will still take the head of every man here before we fall.'

Galronus ground his teeth. What was it with these lunatics? There was everything to be said for pride, bravery and honour, but to

315

throw oneself away in the face in hopeless odds was far more suicidal than brave.

Taking a deep breath, he dropped the shield.

He could almost hear the strain of the bows as the archers fought their own instincts to loose.

'Adcantuannus? Don't be wasteful and short sighted. If Rome is destined to take Aquitania, then the sacrifice of your soldurii will do little to prevent it, other than leaving your wives alone, and your children fatherless. If this gathering of warriors in the mountains is destined to stop us, then they can do it without you and the soldurii will still be here when we are gone.'

He sighed.

'Use your head, man!'

There was a thickness to the atmosphere that one could almost cut with a sword.

'There can be no going back for us now. We have denied your terms and your commander will not be lenient. The name of Crassus, the hammer of Armorica, is known to us.'

Galronus took a relieved breath. The tone of the man had shifted barely perceptibly from defiance to defeat. A Roman would not have been able to pick up on it, but a native speaker could spot it in the language, and if they felt defeated, he had them.

With a smile, he looked back down at the shield he had discarded and threw his sword down to join it.

'I give you my word as both a commander in the army of Rome under the praetor Julius Caesar, and as Galronus, a chieftain of the Remi tribe in the lands of the Belgae. I will speak to the legate on your behalf, and I promise to secure you the same terms as your brethren who you have spurned, if you will halt this violence and join the other townsfolk in their disarming.'

Adcantuannus paused again, and Galronus could still hear the strain of the bow strings.

'You are of the Belgae? It is said the Belgae surpass all the northern peoples in battle?'

'We do' Galronus said in a matter-of-fact voice. 'Now give me your word and I won't have to tear your men limb from limb with my bare hands!'

The enemy chief barked out a genuine laugh.

'Very well. You secure those terms for us, and we will march out and take your oath. If the Belgae can live with the shame, then I suppose *we* can.'

The creaking stopped as the arrows were removed and the bows lowered. Galronus sighed again.

'Thank you Adcantuannus.'

Turning his back and sauntering away in a deliberate show of trust, the Remi officer collected the fallen sword and shield and returned to his men, passing the shield to its owner.

'Thank you sir. Thought you was a goner for a moment.'

Galronus smiled.

'Me too, soldier. Me too. I must find the man who located that gate outside and buy him a shipload of wine!'

The centurion close by smiled at him.

'I suppose that's it for now then, sir. We'll be making camp and securing the land for a few days before we move on?'

Galronus shook his head and clapped a hand on the man's shoulder, causing the harness full of phalerae to jingle and clink against the mail beneath.

'Hardly, centurion. We are now in a race against possibly the entire population of Hispania. I suspect the preparations to march are already underway.'

He glanced past the disarming rebels in the street, on past the low town wall and to the distant, hazy, blue-grey peaks of the mountains that separated the Celts of Gaul from their brothers in Spain.

'Mountains full of howling defiance await us yet.'

317

Chapter 17

(Quintilis: The foothills of the Pyrenees.)

Crassus strode through the tent's doorway, brushing the leather flap aside without taking his eyes from the fortification ahead.

'Well, commander? What have the scouts found?'

The army had arrived at the foothills of the mighty mountain range that separated the tribes of Spain and Gaul two days ago, following rumours and reports of the massing of tribes gathered from scattered farmers by the scouts. Then, yesterday afternoon, as the Seventh and their support entered the lowest channels of the passes into the peaks, they had made a disquieting discovery.

The confederation of tribes, or at least a part of it, had constructed a camp on a high ridge that stood above a fork in the valleys and commanded a powerful position. This in itself was hardly a surprise, but the form of the camp and its defenders was startlingly familiar.

Now, as Galronus stood before the legate, his eyes turned to follow the man's gaze, falling on the fortifications opposite. The tribes had constructed a camp of a perfectly Roman form, with ramparts, ditches, gatehouses and towers and even from this distance the two men could see the rows of ordered tents within, gathered around a central headquarters area. They might as well have been looking at their own camp.

Galronus drew a deep breath.

'It's very much as you feared, legate. Their fort is well constructed on a perfect Roman model and sizeable enough to hold at least twice our number. As yet it seems to be half empty, so presumably they're still expecting many more reinforcements from across the mountains, but my scouts have spotted nothing so far. I've set them keeping watch on every pass and valley for eight miles, so we'll have plenty of warning before they arrive.'

'And what of the fort's defences? Anything I can use?'

The Remi commander shrugged.

'The rampart and palisade are perfectly Roman, so you know exactly what to expect. I would guess that any leader who has adopted your ways that far probably doesn't stop at the walls. The camp seems to be laid out in Roman fashion and I heard calls being issued by a great horn. The only slight advantage we can identify is the southern side. The camp is surrounded by a triple ditch on all the other approaches, but only by one half-cut ditch on the south, due to the nature of the rocky ground there. Problem is that the approach to the south is a narrow spur with a frightening drop at either side; what Fronto calls a 'killing ground'.'

Crassus nodded.

'They have very much adopted our ways. I have heard of this before in the northern reaches of Spain. The tribes there fought in the great war under Sertorius almost twenty years ago. They hailed him the 'new Hannibal' if you can believe it. Sertorius spent years in Spain teaching their tribes and leaders how to be more Roman. Now look how it turned out.'

Galronus took another deep breath. Being the bearer of bad tidings was never a good thing, and Crassus hardly held him in high regard as it was.

'There's worse news.'

The legate squared his shoulders and spoke without taking his eyes from the fortified position on the opposite spur.

'Go on.'

'They are sending forays out down into the valley. The supplies we brought with us up here are all we're likely to get. Groups of enemies are scattered all over the countryside below, effectively sealing off the passes. No new supplies will reach us unless we send a sizeable escort for them.'

Crassus nodded.

'Which, of course, we cannot do without weakening ourselves too much here. We should have brought months' worth of supplies, but haste was of the essence, sadly.'

He turned to the tribunes, standing silent nearby.

'What is the situation with our supplies?'

'We have food supplies for a week. More if we stretch and ration it, but we risk weakening the men. Water is not an issue as there are streams and springs in the area.'

Crassus shook his head.

'Unless those springs are in sight of our current position, disregard them. If the enemy are setting small ambush groups up in the valleys below, be sure they are also sealing off any free supplies. If they haven't found a way to poison the water against us, they will be watching it, ready to take us on. No. We rely on what we brought or what we can see from here.'

Galronus nodded thoughtfully. Tertullus had told him that Crassus, for all his faults, was no fool tactically, and the ageing tribune appeared to be absolutely right. Galronus would be willing to bet that any source of food or drink within reach had already been dealt with.

'Scouts have given a clear report of several passes a few miles to the east. Perhaps we can reroute the supply wagons to come to our position by a circuitous route? We could besiege them then and slowly force them to capitulate.'

Crassus nodded.

'It's worth a try... the supplies, I mean. Have riders dispatched with the appropriate orders and have small units posted to keep a clear view on the route. But the supplies will be seriously delayed and may have trouble with the terrain, so we cannot rely on them.'

He clapped his hands together in the misty mountain air.

'No. No sieges. We have to move quickly and decisively. You may be able to give us half a day's warning of approaching reinforcements, but we cannot be sure that the enemy do not have other, more secret, ways across the mountains. They know this land far better than any of us, and I can't risk waking one morning to find they outnumber us ten to one.'

He turned to the tribunes.

'What say you?'

The men glanced at one another nervously until Tertullus shrugged.

'We didn't come this far to sit on our hands and watch the whole of Spain arrive across the mountains. Let's go over there and give them a lesson in how a *real* Roman army works.'

There was a murmur of assent from the others and Crassus nodded again.

'Seems like there's only one clear course of action. Have the senior centurions gather for a briefing. We move at dawn tomorrow.'

* * * * *

Galronus walked his horse slowly forward at the head of a detachment of auxiliary cavalry on the army's left wing and glanced across the lines of advancing troops appreciatively. The organisation

320

of the army seemed nonsensical unless one had listened to the legate explain it.

Shunning the traditional formations, Crassus had placed his auxiliary spearmen and archers at the very centre of his force, the position usually reserved for the heavy infantry, with three cohorts of the Seventh flanking them on each side, the cavalry split into four groups at the two edges and following on behind and the remaining four cohorts guarding the Roman camp on the spur opposite.

Presenting such a weak centre had stirred discontent among the veteran centurions, who considered it their job to hold the prime position, but the subtlety of the plan soon quietened them.

The auxiliaries were a lure. Since the enemy knew Roman tactics well, they would expect a standard Roman advance and would be prepared to deal with it. This would perhaps throw them a little off guard, but would hopefully also lead them to believe their opposition to be tactically incompetent. After all, what general in his right mind fields his weakest troops in the centre?

The Remi officer clenched his teeth. They were getting too close. The speed of the Roman march perhaps had not given the enemy enough time to draw the appropriate conclusions.

Surely such a formation would be too tempting for the enemy to pass up?

And as soon as they poured forth from the gate, even should they do so as a Roman style shield wall, and engaged the auxiliary spearmen, the centre would begin an orderly fall back, keeping a line of spears to their pursuers, as the two wings of legionaries would swing round and turn inward, flanking the enemy, effectively boxing them in until they were trapped and slaughtered. The cavalry, at this point, could create a cordon around the periphery to prevent any escapes and try to gain and hold the fort's gate.

It was an ingenious move; a manoeuvre subtle and cunning in its formation.

But something was wrong. The lure had not worked.

By now the enemy should be rushing from the gate, or at least forming up. No horn blasts sounded, and no warriors appeared. The Roman forces were now no more than a quarter of a mile from the enemy fortifications, which stood proud on the crest of the long slope. They were not coming.

Grinding his teeth, Galronus wheeled his horse and raced off past his men to the rear of the advancing Seventh Legion and toward the commanders who rode behind, shining silver and crimson in the early morning sun.

His thoughts must have been shared by the legate and his tribunes since, just as he rounded the rear and made for the officers, the cornicen blew the call for the legion to halt. As the entire advancing force stopped in perfect unison, Galronus trotted up to the command group.

'Clever fellow' the legate was saying to the tribunes.

'Clever, sir?'

'He's not been fooled by the weak formation. This leader we face knows exactly what he's doing. He's going to sit inside his fortifications and wait until he has enough men to squash us like a fly.'

Rusca frowned.

'Then what do we do, sir?'

'Quite simple. We attack. What other choice do we have?'

The legate turned to the cornicen, noting Galronus' presence for the first time with a flick of his eyes.

'Send out the calls' he addressed the man. 'I want the auxiliaries withdrawn to the rear, and the Seventh to form up in standard battle formation.'

Dismissing the musician, he turned to Galronus.

'Can't see much use for the cavalry in a direct assault. I suggest that you just keep your men back and send them anywhere you think they might be useful as the opportunity arises.'

Galronus shifted in his saddle. For his entire force to be so summarily dismissed was irritating, but there really was no way he could think of to fault the legate's reasoning. He would just have to make sure that a situation that he could use arose.

As he waved to his own standard bearers with their dragon-headed banners and Celtic horns, ready to give them their orders, Crassus watched the auxilia pull back and reassemble to the rear, the legion shifting to present a solid shield wall.

Horns were blown across the hillside, and the cavalry pulled back in their four groups to a distance from which to observe events. Galronus watched them and then frowned in surprise as Crassus rode forward, approaching the rear lines of the legion, an enterprising optio giving hasty commands and having a passageway opened for the legate.

322

Crassus nodded at the man and rode between the ranks of the Seventh until he reached the front, where he turned his horse and looked down at the men.

'Our Aquitanian and Spanish friends appear to be a little nervous?'

A ripple of laughter spread out across the crowd.

'How do we reward their resistance?'

A deep, raspy voice from somewhere amid the ranks called out 'death?'

Crassus pointed in the man's direction.

'Death is a *start*, but even heroes die. *You and I* will die some day. How do we reward these cowards trembling behind their fake Roman walls for closing their gates to the Seventh?'

A lighter voice muttered something and one of the centurions on the front rank raised his vine staff over his head.

'Obliteration, gutting, burning, dismantling and salting the land, sir!'

Crassus laughed.

'I fear you missed the looting from your list, but good man nonetheless!'

This time the laughter raced around the army in a roar.

'So do we go back and prepare for a siege, men?'

The negative murmur was clear indication of the feeling of the troops. Galronus smiled to himself. This was a Caesarean speech if ever he'd heard one. Fronto rarely made speeches of this kind; his men were so tightly bound to him they would follow him into Tarterus if he asked. Caesar, however, relied on his oratory to goad his men and stiffen their resolve, like the public speakers Galronus had heard urging the crowds in Rome. Remarkably, it seemed to work and, more remarkably yet, the young legate seemed to be turning into a shadow of the general himself. The mood was suddenly tingling and electric, like the air between a crash of thunder and the flash of the lightning.

'Or do we march on and flatten that camp and every last living thing in it?' the legate bellowed.

A roar arose from the crowd, and Crassus allowed his horse to rear up and paw at the air a couple of times heroically before settling back down as silence returned.

'Good men. Let's go and show them a taste of true Roman power!'

As he turned and rode his horse back through the narrow passageway to the rear, the Seventh Legion cheered, and men reached up to try and touch the passing legate's boot or harness for luck. Galronus had had to force himself not to cheer along.

Really there was so little to cheer about, he thought as he set his gaze on the strong defences awaiting them at the top of the slope.

* * * * *

Crassus hauled on his reins and turned his horse to get a better view of what was happening along the left flank.

The approach was brutal, and he knew it. The men knew it as well, but they were professionals and had marched forward with the pride of Rome glowing in their eyes to take the fortress. A particularly astute soldier at the front had called a warning as they approached the causeway leading to the gate, noticing the tell-tale depressions that spoke of lilia pits waiting to cripple anyone who dared take the easy approach.

The first task was to cross the ditches, three of them in all, cut to the perfect angle to inconvenience infantry. The First Cohort of the legion had managed, with some difficulty, and no small number of casualties, to cross the first ditch and had formed a solid shield wall between the first and second, under the constant barrage of defensive missiles. As soon as they were in position, however, the auxiliary archers had rushed across and dropped down behind them before rising to send their own repeated volleys at the walls, pinning down the defenders.

It irked Crassus immensely to watch his glorious Seventh reduced to the status of a gigantic shield, while the auxilia did the bulk of the work right now, the archers crippling the enemy defences and the spearmen bringing forth bundles of foliage and sods of earth to infill the ditch, enabling the remaining five cohorts to cross.

But then, the auxilia were there to use and he was sure his veterans would be happier playing shield wall than carrying the turf.

As he watched, tensely, a new wave of defenders appeared all along the fort wall, armed with heavy darts, rocks, slings and bows. The resulting sudden intense enemy attack punctured holes all along the shield wall, forcing reinforcement legionaries to run across the partially filled ditch to take their place, less than half of whom made it across alive.

324

The plan was solid, though. In a few hours the ditches would be no obstacle. Of course, there were bound to be lilia below the walls too if they were following the Sertorian model, and the defences themselves would be difficult enough to take, but the whole thing could be over by nightfall, depending on what these clever little barbarians had prepared within the camp itself. He would be prepared to bet there were a few nasty surprised in store when they got that close.

He ground his teeth as the fresh wave of defenders was pushed back down behind their defences again by concentrated attack from the auxiliary archers. The problem was that in the time it took to get his men into that fortification, he may only have half his army left.

The alternative, of course, was to march the legion blindly across the ditch with no further delay and try to take them in a straight assault, since there was no chance of getting siege engines up that slope in a hurry. That would be a greater gamble still, though. This way, the battle was drawn out over a longer period, extending the time to which his men were subject to enemy attack, but at least they were in a good defensive position. If he charged them and opened them up to the full strength of enemy attack as they tried to cross the ditches...

It didn't even bear thinking about.

He *couldn't* lose this battle, and he couldn't lose the whole action. His father had spoken at length in his last letter of the likelihood of attaining a gubernatorial posting next year, which would mean that he himself would likely be recalled to Rome at the end of this season and, if that was the case, he needed victory beneath his belt to assure him of a good position in the city when his father left.

In all, this meant that not only did he have to destroy the benighted Aquitanian alliance, but he would have to do it with such force, pomp and show and with enough of a surviving force to drive the idea of resistance and rebellion from the minds of all. The Gaulish cavalryman had been right to counsel mercy down on the plains, but this was different. This had to be a statement.

Noting with satisfaction that the first ditch was now fully traversable with little difficulty and that the cornicen was sending out the orders to advance the shield wall and archers to the next intervallum, he turned and frowned.

325

He had not spared a thought for the cavalry for the past half hour and had seen little of them, skirting the edge of the field as they were. And yet, as he scanned the periphery, past the lines of legionaries waiting for the order to advance, there was Galronus, cresting the hill from the west with a small party of riders at his back. The man was in a hurry.

Patting his restless, prancing steed calmingly on the neck, Crassus watched as the cavalry officer bore down on him, and hauled on the reins as he closed.

'I assume you've kept yourself busy patrolling the periphery?'

Galronus grinned.

'Something like that. I think I have some good news for you.'

Crassus nodded soberly. Good news would be welcome about now.

'The southern approach?' Galronus smiled, pointing at the fort. 'I told you about the pitiful ditch there? Well it would appear that they've stripped the bulk of the defence from that wall to bolster this one. Clearly they're aware that the legion is concentrating here.'

Crassus nodded again, his eyes narrowing.

'Stripped by how much?'

Galronus grinned.

'Give me a drunken circus crowd and I could probably get in there.'

The legate bit his lip.

'I cannot withdraw from here, or they will become wise to the situation and even up their defences again. But then *you* cannot take that approach with purely cavalry.'

Galronus nodded, pointing across the valley.

'But...'

'Yes, the four cohorts in reserve.'

Crassus squared his shoulders and turned to spy the small group of tribunes gathered nearby with the signifers and cornicen.

'Rusca? Ride back to the camp with this man.'

As the tribune rode over to join them, his head cocked to one side quizzically, Crassus gestured to the pair of them.

'A joint force of cavalry detachment and four cohorts, led by the two of you.' He pointed at Galronus. 'Your men know the area now. Lead them round by a distant route; the most hidden you can find. I don't care how you do it, but get those men to the southern approach

326

without being seen. We will continue to prosecute the main fight here and draw their attention as much as possible.'

He took a deep breath.

'Be as fast as you can, but do not sacrifice secrecy for speed, or all is for naught. You know what to do when you get there?'

Rusca looked vaguely uncomfortable, but Galronus nodded.

'Get inside the walls and cause mayhem!'

'Mayhem, indeed. Good. Juno watch over you both. Now go.'

He watched the two men ride off, the small group of riders at their heels, and took a deep breath.

'Juno watch over us all!'

* * * * *

Rusca peered around the bole of the tree and squinted into the distance.

'So how are we going to do this?'

Galronus shrugged.

'I'm a cavalry man, tribune. Siege is not my forte.'

Rusca nodded and, turning, waved the senior centurion forward.

'Sir?'

'I want your thoughts on how we assail that place.'

The centurion frowned.

'Direct and fast, sir. Not much in the way of a ditch to stop us, so we can be at the walls at a run in a few moments. There's not many defenders, so we need to get control before they can draw reinforcements to the wall.'

Galronus pursed his lips.

'Will you go *over* the wall or *through* it?'

'Both have merits' the man shrugged. 'To bring sections of the palisade down is a slower job and would delay the assault, but we'd be inside en masse a lot quicker. Scaling the walls would give us speed and surprise, but it would be a while before we had any kind of force inside.'

He smiled and spread his hands.

'What *I'd* do, sir, is both at once.'

'Both?'

'Yessir. There's a lot of powerful horses here that can't do anything until they can get inside. The First Cohort attacks, climbs the walls, cuts the palisade binding and secures ropes, then passes them to the cavalry. The horses can probably pull that palisade clean out of the ground one stake at a time. As soon as there are a few small holes, the other three cohorts come in, take the rest apart quickly and then get inside. Soon as we're in and there's a sizeable hole, the cavalry can do their bit too, sir.'

Rusca frowned.

'Where do you think we might find ropes at such short notice?'

'Brought them with us, sir, along with a lot of other trenching tools, caltrops and more. Never know what you might need, sir.'

Galronus grinned at the tribune.

'The plan has merit. Shall we?'

The tribune swallowed nervously.

'I suppose. Whatever we do, we need to do it fast.'

The Remi commander nodded at the centurion.

'Get the men moving. I'll marshal a group of cavalry to haul the ropes for you.'

As the two men ran off toward their respective units, Gaius Pinarius Rusca sighed and ran his eyes once more across the wall top. He was acutely aware that he was entirely unsuited to this job. A few weeks ago, Crassus would have pondered deeply before assigning him to anything more deadly than stocktaking in the supply wagons, but then his reputation seemed to have blossomed after that incident with the ambush. For some reason just because he'd fought with the desperation of a cornered beast and ended the day covered head to foot in gore, the men had cheered him, and the officers assumed that he was some sort of crazed killer contained in a small bureaucratic frame.

He was not.

Yet now he was nominally in charge of the most important assault in the battle and the responsibility was immense. Oh, clearly Galronus and the centurion knew what they were doing, but his was the accountability.

He shrank back behind the tree trunk, peering at the defences a few hundred paces away. Already, he felt that worrying loosening in his bladder area again.

'You alright, sir? You've gone really pale.'

Rusca almost shouted out in shock and turned, his heart racing, to discover that a legionary had taken position by the tree next to him, others moving up all through the woodland, the cavalry gathering in a clear area not far back where they were hidden from the fort by the woodland.

He felt like a child, out of his depth and on the verge of panic. Before he could stop himself, he found his mouth was busy, working independently of his brain and blabbing his worst fears to this ordinary soldier. In horror, he clamped his mouth shut and tried to think of a way to downplay what he had just admitted, but the legionary shrugged.

'It's natural to be scared a bit, sir. Only a complete nutcase would feel *no* fear. Trick is to go piss your heart out in the woods first. Start every battle with an empty bladder and an empty bowel, sir. Me? I'd piss myself soon as I got within arrow reach otherwise!'

Rusca stared at the man.

'Sorry sir. Didn't meant to speak out of turn.'

Slowly, a smile spread across the tribune's face.

'Which bit of the palisade are we aiming for then, soldier?'

The legionary pointed at a stretch where a slight hump in the ground caused the palisade to rise and fall.

'Good' Rusca smiled. 'Should be easier to get to the stakes. Think I'll pop off and relieve myself before we go.'

The legionary grinned.

As Rusca trotted off through the advancing ranks of men until he found a convenient spot, he chewed on his cheek. It *was* right to be nervous. Of *course* it was... so long as the fear did not stop you, it did not control you, and the only answer was to tackle it face on.

Sighing with relief, he fastened his breeches again and made his way back through the ranks of men to the front, where it took a few moments to locate his original position and the man who had spoken to him. The lump in the palisade, however, guided him true.

As he fell into place behind the tree, he became aware that the centurion off to his right was waving an arm. Rusca was still waiting for the cornu to blare out the call in response when the men sprang from their hiding places and ran out into the open. Of course! The element of surprise was paramount. Why would they use musicians?

Biting his lip, he ducked out from the bole of the tree and drew his sword. Stretching out his legs ready to run, he became aware that the centurion was shaking his head. Yes, an officer should be dignified. No running.

Close to the centurion, Rusca strode out into the open ground with a purposeful gait. Ahead, the legionaries of the First Cohort were running for the wall, eerily quiet, roughly one man in every twenty carrying a rope.

The whole situation was so strange. The minimal number of defenders on this side had been so unprepared to witness any action and had spent the past hour or more staring at nothing, becoming bored beyond endurance, that they took far too long to react to the sudden rush of silent men. Moreover, the whole assault was so quiet that the overriding sound was that of Crassus' assault on the far side of the large camp.

The running legionaries were almost at the contemptible excuse for a ditch by the time the cry went up from the scant defenders on the wall. Rusca ground his teeth as he marched along behind the assault, next to the centurion. Time was now very much of the essence. Once that cry had gone up it was a race to see whether the four cohorts could break in and consolidate their position before the defenders sent reinforcements to the wall.

The tribune strode forward, his heart racing, as the men of the First Cohort ahead reached the earth embankment below the palisade and threw themselves against the timbers, scrambling for holds and pushing one another up, climbing precariously with one hand and a sword in the other, or with both hands and a pugio clamped between their teeth.

By the time Rusca reached the ditch, fighting was already occurring at the wall top, men falling with pained cries back down to the turf outside. The number of men on the walls appeared to have grown, but only a little; presumably a number of warriors had been standing by to support them in case of just such an event: enough to make the assault harder, but not enough to change the course of the battle, certainly.

He altered his stride to jump across the pitiful little ditch. Around the other three sides of the fort, the ground on the slope was turf with deep earth beneath, or grit that could easily be carved and dug. Here, the rocky bones of the spur neared the surface and had made the digging of the ditch near impossible, resulting in a channel hacked through the rock with great difficulty, a mere two feet wide and two feet deep. Barely enough to slow a running man.

A cry ahead drew his attention. One of the men had managed to achieve the wall walk and was busy fighting off warriors on both sides while his companions climbed up behind him. His task was hopeless, fighting on two sides and with no shield, and he

330

disappeared with a shriek as a barbarian raised a huge spear in two hands and then brought it down behind the palisade, ending the legionary's life out of view of the tribune.

The man's achievement had been enough, though. His valiant fight had allowed time for two more men to reach the top, and the spear man was quickly dealt with, the legionaries pushing the defenders back along the wall as more and more of the cohort arrived. Slowly and painstakingly, the wall was coming under Roman control and, as he watched, the men at the base of the palisade threw ropes up to the top where they were caught and secured.

Rusca had not even been aware that the cavalry had joined them until four horsemen raced past him, leaping the ditch with ridiculous ease and slowing at the wall. The tribune, now approaching the rampart, watched as the ropes were secured to the horses and the cavalrymen slowly walked their horses forward, each line threaded round the saddles and straps of two beasts.

A cry from above announced that something had happened on the wall, but Rusca was now too close to see clearly and his first warning that the defenders had gained the upper hand was when half a legionary plummeted to the ground next to him, his spine severed above the pelvis and the lower portion remaining somewhere above. He stared in horror as another man fell, screaming, a rent so deep through his shoulder and into his chest that his arm flapped about unpleasantly as he landed.

He stepped back, fighting the bile back down in his throat and tore his gaze away from the men and to the horses, who had reached the strain limit of the ropes and were pulling with all their might, their riders urging them on, ropes groaning and creaking with the tremendous force. Rusca took a deep breath and offered up a quick prayer to Minerva, hastily promising to raise a new altar as soon as he was somewhere he could do it reasonably.

Whether it was Minerva listening or pure chance, the tribune almost lost control of his bowels as the palisade suddenly gave way a few feet from him. The whole defence had been constructed Roman fashion, with the palisade backed by a huge earth embankment that formed the walk at the top and which would give great support to the timber when pounded by siege weapons but was of precious little use when the walls were pulled outwards.

The sudden force as they gave way, the bindings at the top having been cut by the legionaries in their initial attack, was so powerful that four of the great timbers were literally torn from the ground. The one directly attached to the horses hurtled into the air like some gargantuan pilum, crashing to the earth with tremendous force some twenty paces away. The other three, still initially bound near the base, but wrenched from the earth with the fourth, exploded and smashed to the ground all around, one whooshing dangerously close to the ear of the devoutly praying tribune.

Rusca stared as the great log that had almost taken off his head rolled slowly into the ditch where it came to rest at an odd angle, pointing accusingly at him.

He was still watching, stunned, when the cornu sounded and the remaining three cohorts ran screaming from the eaves of the wood toward the ramparts. The earthen embankment behind the shattered wall had crumbled, being only a recent construction, and was now a mere mound that stood between the tribune's forces and the interior of the enemy camp.

The centurion, about whom he had almost entirely forgotten, but who remained close by, nodded in his direction.

'Would you like the honour, sir?'

Rusca wondered what the man meant for a moment, then realised and, swallowing nervously, nodded and strode forward toward the breach.

As he reached the shattered section of wall, he heard the explosive sound of the timber being wrenched free in two other locations along the defences, the distant thunder of hooves that announced the cavalry were on the way, and the roar of the three other cohorts rapidly closing the distance behind him.

Readying his sword arm, the tribune stepped up onto the slippery, smashed earth bank and clambered up into the gap. His heart almost failed him as he crested the top. A virtual sea of enemy warriors swarmed toward the attackers between him and the fort's interior buildings. His knuckles whitened as he tightened his grip on the sword.

So many men. How could they ever hope…

Beside him, the centurion clambered onto the bank and grinned.

'Now we've got the whore dogs on the run, eh sir?'

Rusca turned to stare at the centurion but, as he did so, two barbarians that had been running along the interior of the earth bank bellowed and ran at them.

The tribune raised his blade as the first man launched at him and managed to turn the initial blow aside, more by luck then skill. He prepared himself for the lethal blow as the second man lunged, but the centurion was already there, smashing the sword aside and leaping at him, shouting curses.

Rusca drew back. The barbarian lunged again, a blow that the tribune narrowly dodged. Panic began to set in as he took two more steps back. Any moment he would be at the loose soil where the palisade had been and then he was in trouble… unless he could make it work for him. Fight dirty. Always fight dirty.

Watching nervously as the barbarian ducked left and right, his eyes darting around, Rusca felt back with a foot and encountered only empty air. He'd been *that* close already.

Preparing himself, he watched the man. It was all about which way he went. He'd been on his right foot for both attacks so far, so Rusca needed to go left.

The man attacked with lightning speed, the long, leaf-bladed Spanish sword, so similar to a gladius in many ways, lashing out toward him. The tribune was prepared, however. As soon as the man put the weight on that foot and pushed, Rusca was already dodging to his left. Grasping the warrior by the shoulder, he used the man's weight to throw him forward and past. The Celt cried out in surprise, his balance suddenly upset, as he plunged on and down the shattered bank. Rusca regained his own footing and shot his gaze around him. What had looked so hopeless mere moments before now held a strong grain of hope.

Galronus' cavalry were pouring in through a hole in the rampart further along, and the four cohorts of legionaries were now almost all at the defences and beginning to push inside, the First forcing a bridgehead in the very heart of the enemy camp. One of the advancing legionaries paused as he climbed the bank to thrust his blade through the back of Rusca's fallen adversary and curiously the tribune felt cheated and a little disappointed.

The wall was theirs and, given the calls that he recognised from a cornicen far away, Crassus' force knew it and were pushing with renewed vigour.

It would all be over soon.

Gritting his teeth and silently thanking both Minerva for her assistance and the unnamed legionary for his advice, Rusca stepped down the embankment and put every ounce of his strength into the kick that he delivered with feeling into the dead Gaul's bared crotch.

* * * * *

Rusca and his senior centurion straightened, their helmets beneath their arms, as they strode across the centre of the enemy camp toward the legate. The battle had ended only a quarter of an hour after the south wall fell, the situation becoming increasingly hopeless for the enemy with every passing moment.

Once the Roman force was inside, forming up into shield walls and squares, the fort had effectively fallen and many of the enemy had clambered over their own defences, fleeing down the slopes and into the woodland, leaving their comrades behind and running for their lives. Those who remained and surrendered had been surprisingly few in number.

Crassus stood in the central space before the enemy commander's tent, his standard bearers, cornicen and the other tribunes behind him, various senior centurions about and legionaries lining the square. Before him and under guard, perhaps two dozen richly attired and adorned Celts knelt, their heads bowed. Roman spears hovered close to their necks.

The legate looked up and gave Rusca a rare and uncharacteristic smile.

'Ah, tribune. My congratulations and thanks for a very successful action. Is the cavalry commander not present?'

Rusca smiled back at him.

'Galronus has gone for a while. I doubt he'll return before nightfall. He and his men went off to hunt down the fleeing enemy. Whether he intends to return with them in chains, or just 'chastise' them, I'm not sure.'

Crassus nodded in satisfaction.

'He is to be commended.'

The legate turned his attention back to the cowering men before him.

'Who is your leader?'

There was a pregnant pause and finally one of the kneeling figures spoke in a deep, cracked voice.

'I am Beltas of the Cantabri. I lead this camp.'

Crassus shook his head.

'You *led* this camp. I am impressed with the scale of your adoption of our ways, though I am somewhat dismayed to find you using them against us, particularly in the defence of another people.'

The man remained silent.

'Good. At least you know when not to talk. Not all the Cantabri crossed the mountains to fight us?'

'No, general.'

Crassus nodded.

'Good. I do not want to be remembered as the man who destroyed an *entire* people. You realise that I am not afforded a great deal of room for mercy?'

Silence again.

'You must die, Beltas; you and your followers. I cannot have the peoples of Aquitania and Spain believing they can rebel as much as they like without punishment. You have forced my hand to this, but you can rest comfortably in the knowledge that I will carry no campaign against your people across the mountains. *You* will suffer for what you have done, but your wives and children will live on safe in their homes, so long as they stay there.'

The legate turned to the tribunes behind him.

'Round up every survivor you can find from the area, marshal them here in the fort and then split them into tribal groupings. There are at least a dozen different peoples involved here, some Aquitanian and others Spanish. Take them in those groups and crucify them in all the high places so that they can be seen from afar.'

A moan of dismay rose from several of the kneeling men.

'Make sure that any Spanish tribesmen are raised on their posts in the passes that lead down from the mountains to greet any reinforcements that may be tempted to continue on against us.'

He turned to walk away, but stopped, tapping his lip as though with an afterthought.

'But I *shall* still show the little mercy that I can. Should any man request mercy, you may cut and break them to speed their death. Moreover, any survivor you find that you feel should be too young or too old to take up arms, send them home and tell them to stay there and grow crops.'

As the legate strode away, Rusca wandered across to him.

'Mercy? Is it wise?'

Crassus shrugged.

'With the will of the Gods, this will be our last battle in Gaul, and I have no wish to provoke any further rebellion. Hopefully this will have broken resistance but not prompted the surviving tribes to continue the troubles. We will wait three days to see if any other force turns up and then I shall send to Caesar my compliments and the message that Aquitania is ours. I don't think we will see any trouble in those three days.'

Rusca nodded.

'But we stay here as garrison for now, sir? To be sure?'

The legate nodded.

'For now. At least until Caesar clears my return to Rome. Summer passes rapidly, tribune, and I have no desire to winter with the troops another year.'

Rusca nodded his heartfelt agreement. The more he thought about Rome and its pleasant diversions, the more he yearned for it. Perhaps they would all return soon, if the general had managed to suppress the Veneti.

Chapter 18

(Sextilis: Darioritum, Caesar's camp on the Armorican coast.)

Fronto drummed his fingers irritably on the tent frame, half hoping that the noise would distract the general inside enough to open up. The courier had been inside for a while now, while Fronto paced back and forth, grumbling, under the watchful eyes of Brutus, Roscius and Crispus. Sighing, he rapped angrily on the wood and then began to pace once more.

'You'll wear a rut in the turf, then we'll all trip over it on our way out.'

Fronto threw a dark look at Brutus and continued to stomp in the springy grass.

'Well we're clearly not going home, anyway.'

'What makes you think that?'

Fronto pointed at the tent door in an exaggerated gesture.

'Don't you think that if everything was tidy and neat and dealt with, the general would have bounded out of there like a spring lamb, all smiles and so on? No. Something's happened.'

Brutus frowned. The messages of Sabinus' success on the north coast of Armorica and then the remarkable news that Crassus had tamed Aquitania had come in swift succession, a cause for celebration throughout the army, both officers and men alike. It did appear that finally the general's claim to have conquered Gaul could actually be said to be accurate. The northwest was settled, the south west cowed, the centre and southeast largely allied with the general...

Which left the northeast; the territory of the Belgae and the Germanic tribes, under the watch of Titus Labienus and his small force. The past two weeks had seen the celebratory atmosphere fade once more as the army settled into an uneasy wait for news from the northeast. And this morning, just as Fronto had finished bathing away his bad head and dressed in clean gear, Labienus' riders had finally arrived and made straight for the general's tent.

Crispus shook his head dismissively.

'Don't read anything into it yet, Marcus. Only the Gods and the entrails of goats know the future. You've just been on edge ever since Priscus' last letter.'

337

Again, Fronto stopped pacing to throw an irritated look at one of his friends, and there was a muted warning in that gaze.

'Oh come on, Fronto. You've been so edgy since then, your friends have been walking on egg shells. Your patience seems to have all but vanished. Why won't you tell anyone what was in the letter.'

'Aulus, you of all people should know when you need to keep that nose out of things. It's personal, alright?'

Brutus shook his head.

' It's not just the letter... I think he's been like this ever since Balbus left.'

Fronto drew a deep breath. His face was beginning to colour.

'Why don't you lot piss off and stop trying to analyse my mood? I just want to get home and...' he threw his arms up in the air 'I just want to go *home*, right?'

The others fell silent, unwilling to provoke the older legate again. Fronto had been quick to anger for the last fortnight. He had been involved in three brawls and had blackened the eye of one of the staff officers who'd had the unfortunate luck to remark on men of Balbus' age being allowed to remain in command while in Fronto's earshot.

'I just want to go home' Fronto repeated as though to himself, his gaze falling to the floor.

He'd been unaware of the general's presence until Caesar's smooth voice spoke nearby.

'Not quite yet, I'm afraid, Fronto.'

He looked up sharply to see the general standing in the tent's doorway. The man moved with such silence and grace when he wanted to and had made no noise as he lifted the tent flap aside.

'Come in' he addressed the officers.

Fronto was first through the flap and, while the other three walked across and hovered by chairs until the general returned to his desk, the legate of the Tenth simply sank straight into a chair. The general gave him a sharp look, but then seated himself and gestured to the rest to do the same. A cavalry trooper, still dirty and fully equipped from his ride, stood to attention to the side of the table.

'I expect you're all eager to know the situation?'

'We're not going home. That means someone else needs a kicking' Fronto said flatly.

338

Again, Caesar's sharp gaze passed across the legate. Brutus frowned. Could it be that even the general was treading carefully around him?

'There will be a little delay in our campaign's conclusion, yes. Labienus has done some sterling work among the Belgae. It appears that Nemetocenna is becoming something of a cultural centre, where the locals are beginning to learn a more civilised tongue and to appreciate the benefits of heated floors, fresh water supplies, and the security afforded by Rome. He believes he has the trust of the local tribes now to the extent that he feels a caretaker garrison will soon be entirely unnecessary.'

The general leaned back.

'He has a number of men due their retirement and has requested that they and any others among our own legions who are amenable be granted funds and lands around the Belgae. He believes that mixing our veterans in the local environment will help lead them toward becoming more Roman.'

Fronto let out a low rumble.

'What was that?'

The legate looked up, his head still lowered so that his eyes shone white, and slightly pink, in the dim tent interior.

'I said: why the hell are we not going home then?'

Caesar's eyes flashed again momentarily and then he forced a smile, clearly covering his irritation.

'Not all of the north eastern tribes are settling with Labienus' view of the future. Two tribes...' Caesar unrolled the scroll on the table and scanned down it once more 'the Morini and the Menapii, are causing trouble.'

Brutus frowned.

'They're coastal tribes if I remember my geography correctly? On the north coast, opposite Britannia, yes? Is the fleet to be mobilised?'

Fronto shook his head.

'Screw the fleet. Labienus has a cohort of legionaries, loads of auxiliary units and enough cavalry to flatten a small country. Why can't *he* deal with them? Is he too busy teaching Belgic children to read and massaging the feet of their women?'

The general glared at him again.

'Try to act like a commander in the army of Rome, Fronto, and not a petulant child. The bulk of Labienus' forces are spread out all

339

along the Rhine, making sure that the German tribes don't decide to cross and get involved. To withdraw them to deal with two rebellious tribes would be to put the entire Belgic region in danger of German raids or even invasion. The tribes across the Rhine have not forgotten the chastisement at Vesontio two years ago.'

He sighed and stood.

'I am allowing the remainder of the day to put the army in order. They have languished here a full month now, but it is time to gather their equipment, to take down the tents and prepare to move. In the morning we march for the coast, collect Sabinus and his forces, and then turn east. I will not return to Rome while any of Gaul is still refusing us. Gaul must be settled before we leave.'

* * * * *

The vanguard reined in on a low hillock, the army stretching out along the plain behind them. Caesar narrowed his eyes at the forests ahead as the senior officers walked their horses forward to join him.

The journey had been long and tedious since Darioritum, despite the camaraderie of the reunion with Sabinus and the tales he had to tell of his Gaulish warriors and their infiltration of the enemy. Sextilis with its welcome glorious sunshine and armour-heating temperatures had given way to September with its earlier nights that drew in with a chill, particularly this close to the roiling northern sea. Often the officers would awake in the morning to find that the night had brought with it a sprinkling of rain that left the morning grass damp.

The change in the season, following such a brief summer, affected the mood of every last man, and there was little joy to be found among the seven legions of Caesar's army.

The knowledge that they were travelling to put down yet another insurrection by the ever rebellious Gallic tribes also frayed at the edges of Roman nerves across the whole range of rank and file. The officers had initially fallen in line with Caesar's hope for a brief punitive push before turning south, but the past four days in the territory of the Morini had forced a change of plan.

Like the Veneti before, who had abandoned all their settlements and retreated to their coastal fortresses, the Morini and the Menapii had taken all the goods they could transport, left their oppida and

340

villages, and disappeared into the deep woodland that stretched from the lands of the Belgae to the marshy delta of the Rhine.

The tribes had been short sighted in only one regard. Had they not left tracks, they could have disappeared without trace and the army of Rome might have searched the northern lands for a year without pinning down any number of the enemy to fight. But the Menapii particularly had been unwilling to leave anything behind for the Romans that they might save, and the wreckage done to the landscape by the traversing of thousands of feet and heavily laden carts spoke clearly not only of the directions that the tribes had taken, but also of how recently they had done so.

And now, here at what felt like the end of the world on an afternoon when the weather was threatening to turn inclement, the officers came to a halt with their general on the low rise, watching the tracks in the dirt before them that disappeared into the eaves of the forest in four different places.

'Do we split the legions and send them in, Caesar?'

The general turned to look at Sabinus and shook his head.

'No; it would be suicidally reckless to string out the army in the depths of the forest with the enemy already ensconced. It would be all too easy for them to decimate the legions that way. We need to meet them on open ground, which means forcing them out of there.'

Fronto frowned and gestured expansively at the forest's edge.

'Easy enough to say, but there's a hundred miles of woodland there. They could survive there almost indefinitely, especially with all their goods they've taken in. We could send in scouts?'

Again the general shook his head.

'These are *their* woods; they know them well. Our scouts would likely never return.'

'So what do we do?'

'Firstly we make camp, and we make well-defended camp at that.'

He turned and cast his gaze left and right along the tree line.

'Sabinus and Crispus? Take the Eleventh to the northwest and make camp within sight of the sea, close to the woodland; that's about fifteen miles. As you travel, have signal stations set along the route. Rufus? You head east for twenty miles and do the same. Galba? You follow them and go a further twenty. We will create a cordon around these woods and keep them trapped and penned in while we work. Sooner or later they will have to show themselves.'

Fronto grumbled.

'We could be here for a year doing that. And what happens when they just move further and further east and then leave the woodlands and pass round the end of your cordon?'

The general smiled.

'Always so negative and pessimistic, Fronto. The lands to the east of that line are already being patrolled by Labienus' cavalry and auxiliaries. The chances of the enemy fleeing the forests there are ridiculously small. And as for a timescale, I don't think you need to worry too much. I have no intention of just sitting by and waiting for them to become bored enough to seek us out.'

He spread his arms to take in the whole forest before him.

'There is nowhere they can take ship across the sea, the Rhine delta is too dangerous to cross, and we hold the south. Once we're encamped, and the cordon is up, we will begin the task of deforestation. Some of the timber will be used to further fortify our positions around the woodland. As for the rest: I'm certain that Labienus could use the timber to build his 'new Rome' among the Belgae, and the rest will fetch a small profit back in Cisalpine Gaul. Let us see how long the Morini and the Menapii can last as the forest disappears around them.'

'Months' Fronto grumbled under his breath as he looked at the gloomy, looming eaves of the woodland.

* * * * *

Fronto mopped his brow and contemplated replacing the helmet on his head, but shrugged and let it hang by his side instead.

'Carbo?'

The primus pilus of the Tenth turned at hearing his name and saluted before striding over, his vine staff jammed beneath his arm.

'Sir?'

'I know this is going to sound petty, Carbo, but I was rather hoping the tents would go up first before you started chopping the forest down?'

The centurion smiled, the sweat running from beneath the brow of his helmet and trickling down his cheek to his chin. Thunder was coming; probably before nightfall, and the lack of air was almost unbearable.

'Camp prefect gave us all orders, legate, supported by the general. Caesar wants the palisade, mound and ditch up before anything else.'

Fronto rolled his eyes.

'I notice that doesn't apply to *him*. *His* tent is up and furnished already.'

'If you don't mind me saying, sir' Carbo grinned, 'it isn't seemly for a senior officer to be parading round like that in front of the men. If you're not going to wear your armour, you should be all togate and patrician.'

Fronto stared at him.

'It's as sweaty as a Numidian's boot here. I'm having enough trouble breathing in this armpit of a country without slapping on layers of leather and steel too. I don't know how you can stand it under all that equipment.'

'Practice, sir. Well…' he winked knowingly 'practice and a lack of underwear, anyway.'

'There are some things, Carbo, that you really don't need to share with me. Are you sure you can't spare just four men to help me get the command tent up. I could find a nice convincing military reason if you like.'

The centurion laughed.

'If you don't tell the general, sir, I'll spare the men.'

He turned to the group of four legionaries who were busy a few feet away, hacking away at the bole of an oak with their axes. He had opened his mouth to speak, but the smile slid from his face.

'To arms!' he bellowed, and, as the men turned to look at him, three arrows thudded into the timber, a fourth passing straight through a legionary's neck and continuing merrily on its path as the surprised man grasped his throat with both hands, his eyes wide.

Fronto stared.

'Oh shit, shit, shit.'

Around them legionaries across the edge of the woods scrambled back to grab their weapons, helmets and shields that lay in bundles nearby. Here and there a screech announced that another arrow had found its target.

Carbo turned back to Fronto.

'Back to the camp, sir.'

'Sod off.'

The centurion glared at him.

'You're unarmoured, a clear target, and being stupid, legate. Get back to camp.'

Fronto ignored the man and dived to the ground where a legionary had left his shield lying with his helmet, sword and other gear on it. Picking up the sword, he tipped the rest from the shield and slid his arm into the straps before jamming his helmet firmly back on his head.

'Sir' Carbo said again, his voice admonishing.

'Rally to me!' Fronto called.

As the men of the Tenth, along with a few stray workers from the Eighth and the Fourteenth, ran toward the officer's call, Carbo glared at him and then collected his own shield.

Figures had appeared among the trees.

'What the hell does he think he's doing?'

Fronto turned to see Atenos, the Tenth's new training centurion, stomping across the grass toward him.

Carbo shrugged.

'He seems to think he's invincible even without armour.'

'Form up!' the huge Gaulish centurion bellowed as he fell in to the other side of Fronto, his shoulder at the same height as the legate's scalp. Soldiers began to form a line around them, raising their shields protectively as arrows continued to whistle out of the woodland.

'Here they come' Fronto pointed.

Among the trees, the figures were clearer, more pronounced, as they neared the edge. The arrows stopped coming, and suddenly warriors were pouring out of the forest, brandishing a variety of weapons and screaming guttural war cries as they bore down on the Romans, many of whom were still unarmoured, gathering their weapons or running to fall in.

'What's going on?' Fronto barked as he was suddenly squeezed between the two centurions until he found himself pushed out past them and standing behind the defensive line.

'Stay back, sir.'

Fronto glared angrily at the men in front of him. He began to form a diatribe in his mind along the lines of how Priscus and Velius would never have dared to do such a thing, but realised with a strange fondness that this was *exactly* the sort of thing his old friends would have done. The more things changed, the more they stayed the same. But just like those former veterans, these two had underestimated how headstrong their commander was.

Ducking to the side, avoiding the enormous looming bulk of Atenos, he gazed over Carbo's shoulder. The enemy were almost on them. Legionaries were now falling in to either side of him, nodding respectfully as they took up their position in the second line. Fronto looked past them. Other soldiers had been less prepared or just less fortunate, and disappeared with a scream under the blows of axes and swords before they could reach their gear.

The legate concentrated for a moment, cocking his head and lifting the cheekpiece of his helmet. His fears were confirmed by the distant shouts and buccina calls: this was no small localised attack. The Menapii and their allies had waited just out of sight in the woods until their Roman pursuers had become complacent enough to drop their defensive line and go about the work of constructing the camp.

The surprise had paid off. Roman bodies littered the edge of the wood just within sight of Fronto, around the area the Tenth and Fourteenth worked. This could have been a disaster, but for the fact that the men were disciplined, trained, and prepared for just this sort of circumstance. This very tactic had almost obliterated the Twelfth last year, and these days no work party went about their business without their weapons and armour close to hand.

The enemy rushed on, warriors approaching the rapidly-forming shield wall and slowing to a more cautious pace. Elsewhere the situation was different, the Celts swarming over small pockets of Romans fleeing the trees. Here, though, the centurions were forming a solid defence quickly and efficiently.

As the enemy came on, running through the bracken and high grass, their fur-clad or naked torsos rippling, their muscular arms hefting axes, swords and spears, a man sprang onto a large rock, directly opposite them. His bushy beard and flaxen braids were peppered and tangled with bones and feathers, his arms wrapped in gold bangles, a grey, stained robe hanging limp in the warm, damp air. He bellowed something unintelligible and raised a staff, surmounted by a huge bird's skull, waving it in encouragement.

'Druid' said Atenos flatly.

'That's a bloody *druid*?' Fronto stared. 'I thought they were all quiet and grim. That bugger looks like a cannibal madman!'

Atenos crouched for a moment and stood once more as the druid spat out curses and yelled something in a shrill voice, pointing at the officers with his bird-staff.

'Same to you' yelled Atenos and cast the large stone he had collected from the ground with a tremendous force and a surprising accuracy. The boulder caught the druid full in the face with a very unpleasant noise, hurling him from the rock and back into the unseen undergrowth behind. The staff arced up through the air and disappeared into the grass.

Carbo grinned at his subordinate.

'You do a lot for Gallo-Roman relations, you know.'

'He was pissing me off.'

Fronto smiled as the two men continued to banter while the enemy finally reached the line and threw themselves at the shield wall. A sword was thrust toward them and Carbo casually turned it aside before flicking his blade back and driving it forward into the man's bared chest.

Beside him, Atenos leaned back as a swung axe whistled past his nose before the big man leaned forward again, putting all his not-inconsiderable weight behind his shield and punching the bronzed boss into the man's face, shattering bones.

The two men continued to hack, parry, stab and duck, occasionally sparing a moment to sling a snappy and sarcastic comment at each other. Fronto smiled as he backed out of the line, unnoticed by the two centurions. The legionaries shuffled to fill the gap.

Stretching, he tightened his grip on the gladius. Scanning left and right, he watched the fighting carefully.

To the right, sections of the Eighth legion had managed to create a solid shield wall, just like Carbo's, and were bringing up the rest of their men to plug the gap where the worst of the fighting was going on and join up with the Tenth. The situation was very much under control there.

To the left, however, a group of soldiers from the Tenth and the Fourteenth were forming a small core defence, but were clearly beleaguered and outnumbered.

Fronto glanced over his shoulder to see a soldier, clutching an arm that ran with a river of crimson, jogging back toward the future site of the camp to find a capsarius.

'You!'

The soldier turned and tried to salute, but his arm was unresponsive.

'Sir?'

'Sorry, lad. Go see the physician, but find the reserves of the Tenth and the Eighth back there and tell them to stop digging and get down here.'

The soldier nodded, his teeth clenched against the pain, and ran on.

Fronto turned and took a deep breath. Carbo and Atenos and their growing force were beginning slowly to advance, pushing the desperately fighting Celts back toward the trees.

The combined units of the Tenth and Fourteenth were formed into some sort of mess of a war band, rather than a solid shield wall. Hefting the sword and feeling a faint twang in his arm, the occasional reminder as to how close he'd come to losing it last year, he turned and ran off down the gentle slope toward the mess.

'Who's in command here?'

The group, resembling a Belgic war band more than a Roman force, was fighting off enemies en masse and, miraculously, given the lack of defensive formation, seemed to be holding their own.

There was no answer, but the constant grunting and crashing and battering noises as the legate stood at the relatively peaceful rear side of the group.

'I said: who's in command here?'

'*You* are' a voice bellowed from the centre.

'Good. You're about to be flanked. On my command, draw back three steps, keeping your shields to the enemy, and form a solid line.'

There was no response but the ongoing sounds of battle.

'Now!' he bellowed, and was gratified to hear a lessening of noise from the front as the soldiers disengaged.

'Now form second, third and fourth ranks.'

Pushing his way in among the men, he heaved his way through the bodies until he was only a few men from the front line, once more under severe pressure by the enemy warriors. Reaching out, he tapped a man on the shoulder.

'You're the corner. Everyone to the right of you, swing back and form a side wall of shields.' Another man got a tap. 'You're the other corner. That's it. Now form into a square and seal off the rear with another shield wall.'

347

He watched as best he could from amid the centre of the mass, wishing he had Atenos' height advantage. The man must have the clearest view of what was going on around him in a fight. It appeared that the shapeless mob of men had, without having to bare its underbelly to the enemy, managed to reform into a good, defensive square.

He grinned as he hefted his sword again and shifted his grip on his shield.

Better still, he was involved in it, with no irritating underlings that knew him to force him back to dull safety. He leaned closer to the men in the second and first line in front of him.

'Are you lads going to be all good and deferential to a senior officer and make room for me? I've got an itch I need to scratch.'

* * * * *

Fronto gave a crazed grin as he lunged forward past the rim of his shield, plunging his sword into the mass of attacking barbarians and connecting with something soft and unseen. A squawk from somewhere among the pile of hairy, bellowing men announced his success. He withdrew the blade and shifted the shield slightly just in time to deflect the point of a spear, thrust from one of the warriors behind the front row.

It wasn't that he had come to *enjoy* the killing, or at least he hoped not. It was a mix of two things: partially it was the sheer simplicity of an 'us against them' situation that took all the thought, complication and grey areas out of life and presented him with a very straightforward path and goal. But then there was also the incredibly cathartic release of pent up stress and anger.

The past months had brought so much pressure to bear on Fronto that he was almost weighed down to ground level. He had not realised just how tense he'd been until these poor bastards had run out of the woods and directly into his path.

The situation in Rome was becoming worse all the time, with his family living in terror and having to be escorted to the market to buy food for fear that they might be attacked by the thugs of Clodius. Priscus was there, looking after them, but that was *Fronto's* job, not his.

And then Priscus' last letter had come, and Fronto had almost torn himself to pieces, unable to decide how he felt about the knowledge that Paetus was alive, possibly a traitor to the army, certainly for some reason playing guardian spirit for Fronto's family and friends, murdering noblewomen and likely with plans to deal harshly with Clodius and/or Caesar. He'd not shared that knowledge with anyone, least of all Caesar. If he were abiding by his loyalty to his patron, he should be telling the general about this potential danger, but for some reason he could not bring himself to do so.

And Priscus not being here still felt wrong, same as Velius. Carbo was an admirable man in the job, and clearly Atenos had fallen into place like the piece of a puzzle. They both fitted the Tenth seamlessly, and the legion had moved on from the loss of their two senior centurions without issue, but not having Priscus around was like losing a limb. He'd known the man so long it was like losing family.

But of everything that had happened, and something that came as a surprise to Fronto, it was the strange hole left by the absence of Quintus Balbus, former legate of the Eighth, that most affected him. By now the ageing officer would be sitting on the veranda of his villa at Massilia, sipping wine and watching the sparkle of the waves on the Mare Nostrum, but the gap he left was surprisingly large. The Eighth were currently without a legate, under Balventius' able control.

Three years he'd known Balbus; only three years, but it felt like a lifetime. The man had become something of a father-figure in a peculiar way. He had looked after Fronto and reined him in when necessary, preventing the worst of his potential outbursts and joining him in revels and excitement when appropriate. He had been a central character in Fronto's military life for those three years and...

It had come as something of a shock to Fronto to realise that he was now the oldest serving legate or senior officer in Caesar's command. He still thought of himself as a young man... hell, only recently passed his fortieth year, so he was hardly a shrivelled old prune, but to be the second oldest officer in Gaul after the general himself was a sudden worry.

Perhaps the most pressing thing that continued to weigh him down was that, despite everything, he could have coped with all of these problems and issues if he only had the opportunity, but the general could not let him go until the Gauls were finally settled. And they just would not *stay* settled.

What *was* it with these people? It wasn't that they were stupid or backward; Galronus and Atenos were Gaulish and they were among the most impressive and intelligent men Fronto knew. He'd met leaders, warriors, innkeepers and more in their three years in Gaul, and they were intelligent, quiet, productive people. Why then could they not just accept that Rome was here to stay, reap the benefits of it and settle? Why the annual explosion of revolts and rebellions?

He gritted his teeth angrily and stabbed out at the man before him.

The enemy had thinned out while he had been lost deep in his own thoughts, stabbing and parrying automatically without the need to concentrate too hard. The warrior before him was fighting desperately, the look of violent triumph that had been evident at the start of the attack gone and replaced by a look of panicked failure.

Fronto allowed his eyes to flick up and past the man. The Gauls were fleeing back into the woods all along the line.

The man in front of him lurched backward, Fronto's latest blow cutting a jagged rent along his ribs. Somewhere behind Fronto, a centurion yelled out 'Melee!' and the line broke, soldiers bellowing and racing off after the fleeing Gauls, trying to kill or capture as many as possible before they melted into the trees and were gone.

The man before Fronto, his eyes wide and fearful, threw his arms up, allowing his sword to fall to the ground. He jabbered something unintelligible, but Fronto snarled.

'Why can't you lot just bloody accept it?'

The Gaul frowned in incomprehension and Fronto threw down his sword, the blade landing point first and jamming into the turf. Without taking his eyes from the Gaul, the legate let his shield fall away and unfastened his helmet strap, pushing the brim so that it toppled to the ground and rolled away.

'Independent Gaul is gone... don't you understand?'

The Gaul shook his head and emphasised his surrender with his hands.

'It's *no good* just giving up and surrendering yourself, though, is it?'

The Gaul stared, unable to follow the words of this mad Roman.

Fronto cracked the knuckles of his right hand.

'Because when you *do* surrender, we smile and help you rebuild. We send you engineers and grain and we trade and buy your goods, but then as soon as the legion moves on, you just up and revolt and kill hostages and kill each other and shout for the Germans to come over and help you. But there *is* no helping you because you just don't *want to be helped!*'

Snarling again, Fronto threw a punch at the man's face so hard that he felt his little finger break as it connected with the jaw. The man hurtled backward and crashed to the ground, desperately trying to scramble away, but Fronto was already stamping toward him, rubbing his hand, his face red and angry.

'Everything is falling apart here, and at home but I don't have time to try and hold it together or pick up the pieces because you lot can't just keep yourselves civilised and out of trouble for half a bloody hour!'

The man pulled himself up to an almost seated position, blood trickling from the corner of his mouth and Fronto roared, a noise filled with rage, impotence and frustration. His second blow caught the man on the cheek and sent him sprawling on his side.

'I could be going home to help my family, or to check on Balbus and see if he's even still alive. I could be finding Paetus and trying to console him for what they did to him! I could be doing any bloody thing but stamping around Gaul continually putting out the little fires of rebellion!'

The Gaul had the good sense to stay down, cowering, and Fronto drew back his leg for a brutal kick to the man's side, but suddenly found that hands were wrapping themselves around his arms and gently hauling him back. His head spun from side to side, but all he could see of the two men that were restraining him was the red tunic of legionaries.

'Let go of me or I'll personally tear out your liver!'

A voice by his ear spoke calmly and quietly.

'Let the man go, lad. He's surrendered and beaten. You keep kicking him, and you're dishonouring that uniform.'

Fronto blinked.

'Lad'?

It took him a moment to remember that he was dressed only in his nondescript crimson tunic and breeches, with no armour or emblem that could possibly denote his rank and, moreover, he was surrounded mostly by men of the Fourteenth who had little call to recognise him.

He shook his head.

Dishonour the uniform? The very thought of that stopped him in his tracks, and he went limp.

The men beside him loosened their grip on his arms as a third legionary helped the fallen enemy to his feet, accepting his surrender. Fronto turned to the men slowly.

'I'm not really sure what just happened.'

He looked up into the faces of two soldiers. Both were clearly of Gallic stock, their hair still braided and moustaches and beards still adorning their faces. Fronto was suddenly acutely aware that his recent outburst had been largely anti-Gallic and likely right in front of these men. The taller man wore the crest and harness of a centurion.

'You snapped' the centurion said. 'Happens to the best of us. Pressure gets too much, and you snap. But the important thing is to not snap in the middle of a battle. You could have got yourself carved up badly there.'

The smaller man grinned.

'Fights like a friggin' weasel on heat tho', dun't 'e.'

Fronto smiled.

'I've had plenty of experience... er...'

'Cantorix' said the centurion and gestured to his companion with a turned thumb. 'Centurion of the Third cohort's Third century. And this is Dannos. He's part weasel himself, though for Gods' sake don't let him tell you which part, 'cause that's a conversation you just don't want to have!'

Fronto laughed and stretched.

'You're not one of mine' the centurion said, looking him up and down. 'One of the Tenth? You must be due your honesta missio, yes? Ready for retirement.'

Fronto blinked. That was a question he just did not know how to answer. Instead he sighed.

'Yup. From the Tenth. Saw you were in the shit, so I joined in.'

Cantorix smiled.

'Shame. I could use you in the Fourteenth. You'd best run along. Sounds like your legion's putting out the call.'

Fronto laughed.

'I suspect they'll wait for me.'

'No man's *that* useful. Run along, lad.'

Fronto threw a full salute to the centurion and, turning professionally on his heel, jogged back across the grass. All along the forest's edge the action had ended, the battle clearly over. The survivors had fled into the forest, and the legions were calling their men to muster. All around him, small pockets of two or three legionaries wearily dragged their feet back to their units.

Not Fronto.

For some reason he felt almost impossibly good. There was a spring in his step that he just could not subdue, and he couldn't stop smiling. He might have to look up centurion Cantorix of the Fourteenth and buy him a drink some time soon. *That* would shake the bugger, when he turned up at the centurion's tent in full dress! He grinned and, casting his eyes around, spotted Carbo and Atenos following a detachment of the Tenth back toward the camping site.

The two men glanced at him and shared unheard words as he jogged across to them. Carbo raised an eyebrow.

'I see our legate managed to slip away from us and get himself covered in blood somehow.'

Atenos nodded.

'I expect he was helping an injured man, Carbo. He would never have deliberately launched himself unarmoured into a fight, 'specially after you warning him not to. After all, that'd be stupid. No, I'm sure there's some sensible explanation.'

He turned back to the legate.

'May we ask where you've been, sir?'

Fronto grinned at them.

'Therapy.'

353

Chapter 19

(Septembris: Caesar's camp, in Menapii territory.)

Fronto rapped quickly on the frame next to the tent's door and, lifting the flap aside, strode in without ceremony. The general looked up from his desk, where he was making marks on a number of wax tablets.

'Ah, Fronto… good.'

'You called' the legate said and, strolling across to the table, indicated the seat with a question on his face.

'Yes. By all means, sit.'

Fronto sank into the seat and shuffled until he was comfortable. Caesar was looking him up and down with interest.

'Something wrong, general?'

'Not at all. In fact, Brutus was right: you actually appear almost *content*. It is very disconcerting, particularly after weeks of moping and stomping around.'

Fronto laughed.

'We are almost at the end, Caesar, I think.'

The general nodded, quietly, his face giving nothing away.

'I hope you're right. I really do hope you are right. I need to return to Rome as much as you do, Marcus, and I need a settled Gaul before I do.'

Fronto shrugged.

'It's been a week without more than the occasional gnat bite from these tribes. They've retreated so deep in the forests it's pretty clear they have no wish to fight us. Perhaps it's time we tried to bring things to a conclusion? Perhaps force the issue so that they might accept terms?'

Caesar nodded.

'I had been considering the possibility. Slaves and an example made are good things, but at this point expediency may call for a temperate response to the situation. The deforestation seems to be proceeding apace. I can barely see as far as the tree line now.'

'Yes, we've taken the forest back well over a mile now. But to keep doing so will take so long it'll be winter before we leave here. We need to do something now to try and bring things to a satisfactory end.'

Caesar frowned. There was a sparkle in Fronto's eyes that he recognised.

'What are you planning, Marcus? I know that look: you have an idea.'

'I was talking to the scouts on the way over here. The latest searches along the forest paths have become a little more revealing.'

'Go on...'

'Yesterday they found a clearing only a half mile from the current forest edge. It had clearly held wagons in large numbers until recently.'

The general nodded.

'I debriefed them myself, yes.'

Fronto smiled.

'The tracks that led from the clearing deeper into the woods were fresh; a day or two old at the most.'

'And...'

'And that means that the enemy's supplies, their entire wagon train, is closer to us than it really should be. It can't be far inside the forest. I suspect that, while the tribes can easily move deeper and deeper into the woods, they have left the area where their trails and tracks are and moved into inhospitable terrain. They'll be having to hack and clear a path for their wagons as they move, and it'll be slowing the whole process down. Their wagon train is exposed, general.'

Caesar cracked a slow smile.

'And with no supplies, their resistance would soon falter.'

Fronto grinned in return.

'I see you get my point.'

The general steepled his fingers and sat back.

'I presume this sudden enthusiasm is by way of you volunteering?'

The legate shrugged.

'Can't really send more than a small vexillation in there. Marching a whole legion into the forest would be asking for trouble and they'd have difficulty manoeuvring. A smaller unit of, say, two or three centuries would have the size and flexibility to work within the woods.'

The general nodded and spread his hands on the table before him.

'Three of your centuries will be enough? With a few scouts who know the paths, of course?'

'Actually, I was thinking of taking two of mine and one from the Fourteenth if Plancus is amenable. They're Gauls themselves and might be useful.'

Caesar nodded.

'Whatever you think best. Plancus will give you the troops. If he is reluctant, feel free to drop my name in the conversation.'

Fronto nodded and stood slowly, pausing with a faint look of surprise.

'I just realised that I never even asked why you called for me in the first place?'

'Nothing that cannot wait, Marcus.'

Fronto grinned and straightened.

'Then if you'll excuse me, general, I'll just run out and end the war...'

Still smiling, the legate strode out of the tent and stopped there. Four of Ingenuus' cavalry guard stood to attention around the tent, and three soldiers, clerks by the look of it, stood waiting to see the general, tablets and scrolls in their arms. With a chuckle, he leaned across to the nearest, pulled the documents from the surprised man's hands and dropped them on the pile of the man in front.

'There. Now you're free. Do me a favour and run to the camp of the Fourteenth. There's a centurion there by the name of...' He stopped and frowned for a moment as he dredged through his memory. 'Cantorix, I believe. Tell him that Legate Fronto of the Tenth has requested that he and his century attend in full kit at his earliest convenience. Then find the scouts that came back this morning and send them too.'

The clerk looked confused and a little worried for a moment.

'Run along now. Your figures can wait.'

As the man saluted and ran off in the direction of Plancus' camp, Fronto strode on, whistling, toward his own men. Making his way along the main thoroughfare between the tents and past the larger quarters of the tribunes, he spotted the primus pilus waving his vine staff at two legionaries.

'Carbo?'

The ruddy-faced centurion turned and saluted.

'Have two centuries fall in. We're going for a jaunt in the woods.'

The primus pilus gave him a broad grin.

'Nice day for a stroll.'

Turning, he bellowed a command at the two legionaries and, paying them no further attention, strode off into the camp to find his men.

Fronto wandered across to his own tent and ducked inside. Scanning quickly around the interior, he found his helmet, baldric and cuirass and, collecting them, went to sit on his bunk and start strapping things on. Early on in his command, Priscus had tried to persuade him to take a body slave to help with these things, as was the custom with senior officers, but it just felt a little soft having a person dress you. How could a man be expected to hold his head high and command a legion when he could not even dress himself?

It was therefore a minor irritation when he realised that he'd fastened the wrong buckle on his cuirass while thinking and been left with a spare strap.

By the time he had adjusted it and slung the baldric across his shoulder, fastened the ribbon around his middle and tucked the liner into his helmet before jamming it unceremoniously on, he could hear the general hubbub of men assembling on the open ground outside. Standing, he straightened, flexed his knuckles, and strode outside.

Carbo and a centurion he knew by sight, a big man with a flattened nose, stood to attention with their men lined up behind them parade-style.

Fronto nodded in satisfaction and cast his eyes back up toward the centre of the enormous camp, where he could see other legionaries jogging in formation toward them. No one in the ranks spoke as they awaited the arrival of the Fourteenth, who reached the parade ground area and fell into place next to the others. Fronto glanced at them out of the corner of his eye and could see the centurion smiling in realisation.

'Good morning, men.'

A roar answered him from the three centuries.

'I've a little job for you all. We're going to take a wander in woods, with the help of the scouts who went out this morning, and we're going to lay first eyes, then hands, on the enemy supply wagons. By lunchtime I want those wagons back here and being distributed into the army's stores. Think you can do that?'

Another roar.

357

'Good. Stand at ease for a few moments until the scouts arrive. Get to know one another, since you'll be working quite closely over the next few hours.'

He grinned.

'Officers to me, please.'

Carbo and the broken-nosed centurion strode out front, closely followed by the officer of the Fourteenth, who was shaking his head, smiling.

'You two? I'd like you to meet Cantorix of the Fourteenth. I have it on good authority his century are good men, and I thought the presence of a staunchly Gallic unit might be advantageous this morning.'

Cantorix grinned.

'You could have *told* me you were an officer, sir. I'd have given you due deference.'

Carbo glanced across at him.

'A less officer-like officer you never will meet, Cantorix. If he turns up among your lot again, would you be kind enough to send him somewhere safe at the back?'

Cantorix laughed out loud.

'I suspect it's not that easy!'

'True.' The primus pilus turned back to his commander. 'I suppose there's no point in trying to persuade you that we can do this without you and that a senior officer shouldn't be putting himself in such a frankly stupid position?'

Fronto shook his head.

'My plan... my unit. Besides, there's something else I might want to do, and that would require someone with staff authority.'

Cantorix shuffled and shrugged his shoulders so that his mail shirt slipped into a more comfortable position.

'Legate Plancus is going to throw a major fit when he hears we've been seconded without his say so, sir.'

Fronto brushed that aside.

'Caesar agreed, so Plancus can go piss up a pilum or argue it with the general.'

The braided Gaulish centurion smiled.

'Fair enough, sir. How are you planning to do this?'

'First step is to head to the previous site of their wagons, then to move on to the current location. We'll split the scouts into three groups, one with each century. Cantorix? You and yours will take the main forest path that the wagons took at a nice slow stroll. Feel free to let your entire century talk in their native tongue. I know the officers usually discourage such a thing, but I'm hoping to try and talk these tribes down from their pedestal and convince them that without supplies to keep them going, they're better off joining us, and you could go a long way to helping with that.'

He smiled.

'That, of course, means that I'll be going with you. The other two centuries will make their way as fast as they can by circuitous routes, guided by the scouts, until they can come at the clearing from other directions. That way, if we have to do this the hard way, we'll have a solid advantage. Hopefully, you'll get there moving fast before we do at our leisurely pace and be in position before we arrive. When you get there, spread out ready for trouble, but stay back and hidden.'

The other two centurions nodded.

'And then, sir?'

'*Then* we become heavily reliant on the scouts. I would like to try and repeat the procedure on the current position of the wagons, but that might be more troublesome, depending on what trails the scouts can find and where they lead. Be aware at all times of your bearings, as one century getting horribly lost in those woods with an antagonistic bunch of the enemy wandering around could be a somewhat fatal experience.'

He took a deep breath.

'If all goes well and the three centuries converge on the wagons, we'll overcome whatever resistance there is and then two centuries can form a line and hold them off if necessary while the third leads the wagons back out of the forest. All clear?'

The three men nodded.

'Good, then you'd best fall back in. The scouts are coming.'

* * * * *

Fronto and Cantorix jogged forward along the trail as quietly as they possibly could; surprisingly so, really, given the mail shirt and phalera harness the centurion was wearing. The scout waved them to the side of the track and the two officers moved quickly off the road and onto the grass verge, beneath the branches, as they approached the point where the Gaulish scout was peering around a bend in the track.

Fronto appeared behind the man and leaned out to look. The clearing was large, perhaps a hundred and fifty or even two hundred feet in diameter, and packed with everything the tribe on the run might need. The wagons, which numbered in the dozens, were arrayed in half of the clearing, carefully manoeuvred and parked between the remaining stumps where the tribe had cut the trees down to widen the clearing and also to form the fence that sealed off the remaining half of the clearing and which held cattle, goats and pigs in tight confines.

Fronto ducked back, irritation plastered across his face. Cantorix shrugged and then peered out himself. Nodding, he pulled his head back in to the side. There were a few ordinary folk of the tribes, going about feeding the animals and gathering items from the wagons.

That wasn't what was annoying the legate, though.

The wagons had been carefully arranged to fit between the stumps and it must have taken hours to get them in that position. Freeing them and taking them back along the trail to the Roman camp would be near impossible in anything less than half a day.

For some reason, Fronto had expected them to be on the run, prepared to flee at all times, the beasts still hooked up to the vehicles and in a position for a quick escape. He had not planned on them having set up a semipermanent store.

He slumped and shrugged.

Cantorix frowned and made strange arcane dances with his fingers, miming something incomprehensible. Fronto stared at him and shrugged again. The centurion sighed and repeated the gestures, slowly and elaborately, waggling his eyebrows meaningfully. Fronto sighed.

'I don't know what you're saying' he whispered through gritted teeth.

'Kill the cattle, burn the wagons' the man hissed back at him quietly.

Fronto frowned. It was a thought that had occurred to him before now. Shame to waste it all, but the primary goal of the whole escapade was to cut off the supplies of the rebels. The smoke from the wagons would alert the whole lot, of course. And then, with it having been dry for days there was always the possibility of the woods catching fire. Could it be worth it?

He shook his head. No. His reason for this was more than merely depriving them of goods. It was goading them into accepting terms and surrendering.

He shook his head again, this time directly at Cantorix.

'No. We go ahead and take them all. If it takes all day, we'll still do it. Let's just hope the others got here too.'

The Gaulish centurion gave him a helpless look, but nodded, and Fronto nudged the scout and pointed back along the track. The three men wandered back to the seventy men standing in formation on the trail a couple of hundred paces away. Fronto looked them up and down.

'Well, centurion, that's an end to the sneaking. Can't sneak a whole century up there, Besides, we need the others to hear that we've arrived.'

Cantorix nodded and gestured to his optio.

'Idocus? You get the animal job. When we get to the clearing, the left side is a huge animal pen, separated into three parts. Send three men to the pigs and three to the goats. Get them roped together and start leading them back to camp. Take another twenty men and start moving the oxen out two at a time onto the track. While you're doing that, I'll take another twenty, and we'll start moving the carts out to hook them up to the animals. Soon as they're done we can start moving them off, with one driver per cart.'

He turned to Fronto.

'That leaves only about twenty five men to defend us while we work. Will that be enough, sir?'

Fronto shrugged. 'It'll have to be. Hopefully, the other centuries have made it round through the woods and are waiting for us. I'll take the carts, you lead the defence. If the Tenth arrive to help, send more men back to help us with the carts and animals. Alright?'

Cantorix nodded.

'I'm sending Dannos and Villu to help you. Villu used to be a thief and cattle rustler, I believe, so he should be quite useful, but he also had his tongue cut out, so don't expect much conversation.'

Fronto rolled his eyes.

'Let's go and hope Fortuna's watching over us.'

Taking a deep breath, he raised his arm and let it fall, and the century of men began to tramp forward in perfect unison. Fronto smiled to himself. Despite recent outbursts he would rather forget, he was surprised to find, as he thought about it, how many Gauls in whose company he had spent the past year and upon whom he had come to rely. Perhaps what the army was doing wasn't merely an impediment to getting home, but was purposeful and worthwhile on a higher level.

The alarm went up in the clearing before the century even came within sight. There was a certain advantage to the alarm, in a way, since the noncombatant folk of the tribe would have time to stop milking goats and flee before they became involved in a brawl.

The century of Gallic legionaries rounded the slight bend in the track and the forest opened up ahead. Somewhere in the distance, beneath the canopy of the woods, a deep horn blow sounded.

The century marched out of the trail, four abreast, into the open and shouted commands went up. A column of men led by the optio picked up the pace to treble time and ran off to the left, toward the animal pens.

Another call from the centurion led a second group to peel off to the right. Fronto veered away with them, watching the centurion run straight ahead with his men, doubling their speed as they made their way through the middle of the clearing toward the group of tribal warriors who had been on watch and who were now hurriedly arming themselves and taking up a defensive stance.

The ground in the clearing was uneven and, though cleared of undergrowth, still plagued by hidden rocks and the gnarled, bulging roots of the cleared trees. The sounds of commotion in the near distance, muffled by the trees, spoke volumes about the sudden activity of the tribes. Their camp must be close, given the proximity of the noise, clearly caused by the tribes rallying their warriors to run and defend the supplies.

Fronto and his men reached the nearest wagon and the legate scrambled up onto the tree stump next to it, just high enough to afford him a view over the carts. Behind him, men started hauling the cart back, grunting and groaning with the exertion as they pulled the vehicle back into the open toward the track. As it passed slowly by, Fronto lifted the rainproof cover and nodded in appreciation at the many sacks of wheat that were stored beneath; enough grain for an entire tribe for at least a week.

He was busy mentally congratulating himself for the speed and efficiency with which they had shifted the first cart and was beginning to believe that he had overestimated the work and that the whole job would be over quicker than he had initially thought when his face fell. A quick glance across the clearing, taking in the number of carts and how some of them were wedged in narrow spaces swept that thought aside. Yes, they had moved the first vehicle easily, but then it was in the easiest position to begin with.

As the cart cleared the tree stumps and more of the men ran in to approach the second cart, it became clear that already this one would be trouble, wedged sideways. He frowned and scanned the tops. They would have to move two other carts into the edge of the wood just to free up the space to move this one along. The whole thing was like some child's wooden puzzle.

A crash across the clearing, followed by the grating and jarring sounds of steel on steel announced that Cantorix and his men had engaged the guards. The amount of shouting in guttural tongues, however, clearly showed that reinforcements were on the way from the camp deeper in the woods. Briefly, Fronto wondered whether it might have been a better idea just to attack their camp, but he quickly brushed the idea aside as potentially suicidal. Three centuries could probably hold the clearing against the enemy and shift the goods, but that was fighting a purely defensive action with no expectation of victory. A full attack would be a whole different matter.

He gradually became aware, as his men moved the next cart, that there were more metallic sounds, coming from a different direction. For a moment he held his breath, tensely, but the sound was a familiar one: that of a century of men in mail, their weapons and shields out and ready. He craned to see over the carts.

One of the other centuries from the Tenth was pouring into the clearing from the eaves of the woods past the carts. Fronto grinned. He could not tell which century it was from here, but he could see the centurion's crest at the front as it disappeared among the carts, leading the men into the fight.

Good. He had been starting to worry whether the others would get here. If all had gone according to plan, they would have been here already, ready to come in as pincers and close the trap. Clearly that had not happened, since only one century had arrived at all and *they* were late.

Still, better now than later when they were all dead.

Gesturing to the men to keep working on the carts, Fronto clambered up from the stump and onto the nearest wagon. Standing high, he took in the scene. As ordered, men were roping the animals together ready to lead them back along the track, while a pair of oxen were being brought forward to lead the first cart away. The irritating and befuddling puzzle of which carts to move to free the others was gradually being unravelled by three particular legionaries from the Fourteenth, who were arguing and pointing, the one called Villu making strange angry noises with his tongueless mouth as he jabbed his finger at another legionary's chest. In the distance, at the far end of the clearing, Cantorix was struggling with his two dozen men to hold the wide track that led back toward the enemy encampment. Already he was facing odds of three to one, though the century from the Tenth were closing for support.

Fronto nodded in satisfaction and was about to drop back down from the wagon when he saw the enemy reserves beginning to arrive. Between the trees and along the track, Gauls were flooding toward the clearing. His plan for a quick attack, in and out with the wagons, was looking extremely foolish now. As he watched, the flood of reinforcements poured into the fight, meeting the fresh steel and muscle of the Tenth's century as they came up from the wagons. The struggle was becoming bitter and hard-fought.

There had to be something he could do to tip the situation? Something that would stop the madness or at least speed up their capturing of the goods. If the Gauls...

His attention was drawn to the other side of the clearing as a pig screamed. Fronto frowned as he tried to see what had happened, but as he surveyed the animal pens, his vision refocused on the arrows falling among them. The Gauls were shooting into the clearing indiscriminately, careless of whether they killed animals or men!

Fronto shook his head in disbelief. Were these people so blinded and stupid that they would kill the animals needlessly rather than let them fall into enemy hands? The policy of deprivation that had plagued the early days of the campaign?

As he raged mentally over the stupidity of it all, he realised that more arrows were issuing from beneath the boundary of the wood and the archers hidden therein. These, though, flashed orange and flickering through the air, soaked in pitch and burning bright. He stared in disbelief as the first successful shot hit a wagon of grain and flour nearby, sending flames racing out across the material and sacking.

The danger had not occurred to him until he realised that the missile blow that punctured the sack had also sent a cloud of white dust into the air, which, catching the flame from the arrow, exploded with a powerful flash that seared his face and left him with purple and green blotches obscuring his vision.

Fronto staggered back and collapsed onto the wagon as more fire arrows fell among the supplies.

'The idiots!' he bellowed to nobody in particular as he struggled upright, rubbing his eyes to try and clear the blotchy colours.

'The stupid, mindless idiots. Destroy anything rather than let it become Roman. Idiocy!'

He became aware that the men working on the carts had stopped to look up at him in surprise.

'Leave that. Keep the carts safe and try to put the fires out. Piss on them if you have to.'

Shaking his head and blinking, Fronto jumped to the next cart, a low grumble beginning in his throat. From wagon to wagon he hopped, the grumble growing into an angry growl and threatening to become a roar as he picked up pace, moving across the clearing toward the fight, ignoring the deadly flaming shafts that whipped past him.

The fighting was becoming more deadly and vicious as the reinforcements from both sides turned it from a skirmish into more of a small battle. Screams and clanks filled the air as Fronto jumped from a cart to a wagon and, reaching the edge of the affray, threw his arms up.

'Disengage!' he bellowed.

The command was such a surprise that it took a while for the legionaries to obey and pull back. The Gauls seemed as astonished as the Romans and hovered for a moment, uncertain as to what was expected of them. Even the arrow storm faltered and slowed to a stop.

A Gallic warrior, bare-chested and with a large, heavy sword held in his two hands, raised it and stepped forward.

Fronto pointed at him.

'That means you too!'

The Gaul glanced up at him in confusion.

'I know *some* of you understand me, if not all. Now disengage. Stop this stupidity at once!'

365

The Gauls stared, and low conversation broke out in confused tones. Fronto became aware that Cantorix and Carbo were both looking up at him expectantly.

'This is quite enough. Lower your weapons, all of you.'

Here and there, warriors allowed the tips of their swords to descend to the turf.

'Right. I knew some of you understood. Who's in charge there?'

There was a good deal more conversation and argument and finally a warrior with a mail shirt and a spear, a torc around his throat, standing somewhere in the centre, looked up at Fronto as a circle opened around him.

'You? Good. I don't care whether you're a king, a chief, a druid or whatever. This fight is ridiculous, as is this whole rebellion. You spent over a year living quite happily alongside the Roman forces at Nemetocenna, less than fifty miles from here. I expect you traded with them? It's very likely that soldiers from the garrison there have been helping construct important structures on the borders of your lands: aqueducts? Drainage channels?'

He paused and realised that all conversation had stopped as they listened.

'And now you revolt, like sheep following the other tribes of the north. The Veneti have a problem with the commander in their region and discontent spreads out like ripples in a pond until over here on the opposite side of Gaul, you throw off the imagined yoke of a non-existent oppression and rise up in pointless anger.'

He gestured in irritation at the armed men from both forces before him.

'We came to settle things, and in your first attack you lost so many men that you've done nothing but run around in the forest picking at us and jabbing at us like an irritating mosquito. You cannot win this, as I'm sure you are all now very well aware. All you are doing now is putting off the inevitable end of this uprising, and with every day you drag it out, you make a conclusion favourable to yourselves less and less likely.'

He pointed back along the track.

'The general can be a merciful man if he is given the room to be so, but often he is pushed to the edge and has no choice but to punish. Don't make him punish you just because you were foolish enough to rise up for something that wasn't your cause to begin with. I came here today to take away your supplies and try to force a quick end to this, but that is clearly not the way it must be done. I see that, with boundless stupidity, you would rather starve yourself to death than make peace, so I must force the issue a different way.'

'Here is what will happen now. I state this for a *fact* since, though you will initially argue, in time you will see that there is no other logical choice. The soldiers present with me will return to our camp. We will leave your supplies here and do no further damage.'

He glared at the leader.

'In return for us leaving you your food and your lives, you will pack up and return to your lands and your farms, live like sensible and peaceful people, raise your children, grow your crops and go back to trading with general Labienus and his garrison at Nemetocenna, for which he will continue to protect you from Germans crossing the great river and standing on your neck like they used to.'

He fell silent and folded his arms.

An uneasy quiet descended, broken only by the lowing of the cattle and the twittering of birds. No one moved. Fronto sighed and waved his arms in a dismissing motion.

'Go home!'

He dropped from the wagon to the rear of the legionaries and shrugged as Carbo frowned at him.

'Get the men formed up and take them back to the camp. Hopefully the other century will turn up some time soon. If they appear at the enemy camp and attack, we could be in the shit, so we'd best send the rest of the scouts out to find them. In the meantime, I fear I have to go and explain a few things to the general.'

The centurion laughed.

'I'm not sure what he'll say about this, sir.'

'Neither am I, Carbo. Neither am I.'

* * * * *

'He did what?'

Brutus stared over the rim of his goblet, choking.

Carbo grinned.

'He told them to go home. It was like watching a parent telling off their boisterous children.'

Brutus shook his head.

367

'He never ceases to amaze me.'

'What amazed *me* was the way they actually listened to him and did what he said. I swear that as I looked across at them, even big hairy bastards with an axe that could split a tree down the middle managed to look uncomfortable and embarrassed. It was a sight to behold.'

Brutus laughed and sat back, taking another swig of his wine. Across the tent, Crispus smiled as he poured himself a drink.

'People think Fronto is simple and straightforward, but the longer I know him, the more I come to realise that you just cannot predict what he will do next. He is *not* a simple man.'

'It was just funny. I had trouble not laughing, but that would have sent them the wrong message.'

Brutus nodded.

'Might have detracted from the message a little.'

The centurion was about to reply when the tent flap was thrown back, and the Tenth's legate strode in and collapsed onto his cot, immediately beginning to unlace his boots.

'Drink?' Crispus prompted.

Fronto stopped his work for a moment and looked up.

'An amphora full if you have it.'

As he took off the first boot and rubbed his foot, Crispus poured him a drink and, leaning over, placed it on the chest next to the cot. Brutus frowned.

'What did he say, then? You've been hours.'

'He took some convincing at first, but he was surprisingly open to the possibilities. He's as eager to finish this and go home as most of us, and I think he's almost at the point where he'd pay a lot of good money just to keep this land calm. We'll be staying here for the next week or so, pending the next move of the Morini and Menapii. If they show up in peace at the edge of the forest anywhere along the line, Caesar's given the order that they should be allowed to pass and return to their lands. The scouts report that they've located the other century of men, about three miles north of where they should have been. I'd have a go at them, but to be honest I'm just too tired and relieved that it seems to be over.'

He let his second boot drop and gave that foot a quick rub before reaching for the goblet, draining it in one large mouthful and pushing it back meaningfully toward Crispus.

'So we should be going home in a week or two then?'

Fronto nodded.

'If all is well, we should, yes. I can't see these lot causing any more trouble. We've battered them a bit and hopefully made them see the futility of it all. When we head south, we'll have to stop in at Nemetocenna and make sure Labienus is aware of the situation, so that he can keep an eye on them, but the man is a born diplomat. The Belgae are rapidly becoming allies largely because of the way he's treating them.'

Brutus nodded.

'And then we head back to Rome. Not the legions, though. Where will they go?'

Fronto finished undoing his cuirass and let it fall unceremoniously to the floor with a clank.

'They'll be posted somewhere in the north. Probably not around here though, or it would work against our potential peaceful relations. Maybe back toward Armorica, or toward the Rhine.'

Brutus smiled and leaned back.

'And then we go south to Italia and the warmth of home.'

Fronto turned a wicked grin on him.

'Not you, I fear. You still have a fleet to attend to. Caesar was talking about them, wondering whether to leave them anchored in the west, or bring them up to the north coast, or even take them back to the Mare Nostrum. You could have the fun of leading them through the Pillars of Hercules!'

Brutus glared at him.

'That's not funny.'

'Not meant to be. But it is.'

He ignored the dark look on the man's face and reached for his refilled goblet.

'I, on the other hand, probably along with the general and any senior officers returning to Rome by land, will head for Massilia and check in on Balbus. I can't wait to see the old sod again and make sure he's alright.'

Carbo shook his head sadly.

'It's been a very long time since I saw Rome.'

'You must be due leave?' Fronto frowned. 'I could always arrange it for you? Your second can keep the legion in order while you're away.'

The primus pilus laughed.

369

'It would be nice, but not right now. When the campaign's definitely over, and the legions are pulled south, I'll take the time. For now I need to stay with the Tenth.'

Fronto smiled.

'Ever the professional.'

'*One* of us has to be!' Carbo grinned.

Crispus leaned back and sighed.

'Do you think that's it? Is Gaul finally pacified?'

'For now' Fronto replied with a shrug. 'We can just hope it stays this way. Rome could do with these people, you know? I've watched the Thirteenth and Fourteenth legions, with all their Gaulish legionaries, and Galronus' cavalry, and they bring a certain something to the army that it was lacking. I don't know what you'd call it? Inventiveness? Freshness? Spirit? I don't know, but whatever it is, we needed it.'

Brutus nodded and raised his cup.

'To Gaul and Rome... to *Roman Gaul.*'

Chapter 20

(Octobris: the hills above Massilia.)

Fronto reined in and took a deep breath, half in relief and half in nervous anticipation. He almost jumped in the saddle as the general's hand fell gently on his shoulder.

'You go on first, Fronto. I doubt it would be conducive to good health to have the entire sweaty, travel-worn officer corps follow you in. We will stay here and break our fast until you are ready for company.'

Fronto looked around into the general's serious, sympathetic gaze and nodded quietly. He wasn't at all sure about this, now. It had been months since Balbus had left the army and been taken south, pale and gaunt.

After Fronto's escapade in the Belgic forests, the northeast had settled remarkably swiftly. From the rumours he had heard that next week in camp, the Menapii and Morini had returned to their lands in triumph, considering their resistance a success and claiming to have held off the might of Rome, yet they had notably resumed their peaceful life and trade with the garrison at Nemetocenna while conveniently forgetting about the large Roman army camped in the centre of their territory. Caesar had been irritated by the locals' attitude, but had been relieved enough that the last resistance in Gaul had finally settled that he had overlooked the situation and allowed them to claim their petty victory, while he prepared to end the season's campaign.

Early the next week, the army had been sent along the coast to winter there under the steady and stable command of Sabinus, while many of the senior officers prepared to travel back to Rome or to their estates in Cisalpine Gaul, Illyricum or Italia.

The two week journey across the length of Gaul had been swift and purposeful, every member of the group itching to return to their homes, supported by Caesar's cavalry guard under Aulus Ingenuus, while the baggage train trundled along many days behind under heavy guard. All the way, Fronto had been almost twitching with the need to see his old friend and confirm for himself that everything was truly alright and yet now, as he sat ahorse on the hill above Balbus' rural villa, the churning waters of the Mare Nostrum and the hectic bustle of Massilia below and beyond, he finally had pause to worry.

Had Balbus even made it back here? There had been no word; the ageing legate would not have sent couriers to Caesar anyway, given the likelihood the entire army would have moved on long before then. What if he had reached this place and then the final boatman had come for him before Fronto arrived? If he was in fine health, would he even be pleased to see Fronto?

The legate shifted uneasily in his saddle and became aware that the gathered officers of Caesar's army, particularly the longer-serving ones, were watching him intently.

'Best go, then' he said, his voice cracking slightly, and he kicked his horse into life and walked Bucephalus slowly down toward the villa.

The outbuildings were quiet, the orchards heavy and laden with unharvested fruit, the grass long and wild, causing a nervous lump to appear in Fronto's throat as he rode past them and toward the main house. It would have been easiest to approach through the orchard at the rear of the house, but certain proprieties had to be maintained.

The front of the villa was exactly as Fronto remembered from their brief stop on the way to Gaul. The roses that had been lovingly grown and carefully trained grew up the white walls, reaching toward the red tiled roof and providing just the right splash of colour to make the place look truly homely. No group waited at the gate to speak to him this time.

Fronto took a deep breath as he rode to the front gate and dismounted slowly and nervously. There was no movement in the doorway or the few external windows as he tied the reins to the post and walked quietly down the path.

The door stood firmly shut and again Fronto hesitated as he reached it. Biting the inside of his cheek, he reached out finally and gave three sharp raps on the wood. There was silence and his heart rose into his mouth as he stood in the sweet smelling garden watching for any movement out of the corner of his eye.

He actually jumped a little when there was a heavy metallic click and the door swung inwards. A house slave, thin and tall and likely as old as his master looked Fronto up and down and gave a curt bow. The legate faltered again. The man bore such a serious expression.

'Marcus Falerius Fronto to see your master' he finally said and hoped he'd managed to keep the rising worry out of his voice.

The man gave him a sad look and then stepped to one side.

'If you would care to follow me, sir, I shall lead you to the summer triclinium. The sunlight this time of year brings the room to life.'

Again, the legate faltered as he followed the slave into the house.

'Master Fronto?'

He stopped, his brow raised in surprise as he turned to look down the corridor to the peristyle garden and its covered walkway. Balbina, the household's youngest daughter, had stopped as she appeared in the corridor from a side room and was staring at him, the glass of water in her hand suddenly forgotten.

Fronto smiled, and the slave came to a halt as he waited patiently. The sight of the young lady was a welcome one; a sign that something of ordinary life went on in the house.

'Balbina?'

'Oh, master Fronto. We wondered whether you would ever come?'

Again, the legate's heart skipped a beat. Was there something hidden in that?

'You did?'

'Yes. Father has been getting more irritable as the season wore on. He was sure you would be here before the summer's end.'

A massive weight suddenly left Fronto's chest, and he felt himself relax almost to the point of collapse.

'Everything was so quiet... I thought...' he shook his head. 'Where *is* your father?'

The girl wandered across to him, and he crouched to meet her smiling countenance.

'He is in the store room. The merchant in Ostia has sent him the wrong wine and he is busy checking each amphora, just in case.'

Fronto laughed.

'Obviously I had more effect on him that I realised. Can you take me to him?'

The slave cleared his throat.

'Pardon, my lady, but I thought to escort legate Fronto to the *summer triclinium* before I fetched your father?'

Fronto narrowed his eyes at the stressed words, but spun back to Balbina as she replied with a smile 'Ah, yes the summer triclinium. A perfect idea. Keep him company Caro, while I fetch father.'

Fronto straightened, his frown still deep as the young lady danced off down the corridor whence she had come. Turning his suspicious frown on the slave, he nodded.

'Lead on, then, Caro.'

What the slave had said about the summer triclinium had been an understatement. The arcade of windows that looked out into the central garden gave a stunning view of the apple, orange and lemon trees outside in their varying stages of ripeness, but the real effect was that caused by the golden sun lighting the red tiles of the veranda opposite and its columns of yellow African marble and the reflected glow this brought to the room.

It was a beautiful sight, and yet Fronto found his attention drawn more to the figure lounging on one of the couches by a low table laden with fruit.

'Lucilia?'

The knowing looks on the faces of slave and young girl alike suddenly fell into place as Balbus' older daughter looked up, her eyelashes fluttering masterfully, her fingers teasing the bunch of grapes. Fronto suddenly felt warm and extremely uncomfortable.

'Thank you Caro. I shall entertain our guest until father returns.'

Fronto's mind ran through a number of reasons to protest, but failed to find his voice before the slave had bowed and retreated from the room.

'The Gaulish air seems to suit you, Marcus. You appear in fine health. Ruddy, even.'

Fronto silently cursed the colour rising in his face.

'You look... nice, Lucilia. How are you enjoying country life?'

She laughed, and the sound sent a tingle up Fronto's spine. He collapsed heavily onto one of the couches.

'I tire of fruit and fields, to be honest' she said, her face slightly lowered in such a careful way as to accentuate her piercing blue eyes with their kohl-blackened lining. Fronto swallowed.

'Yes... well, I'm a city man myself. Pavement and... and so on' he finished weakly. He was finding it extremely hard not to focus on her low neckline with the way the golden glow from the window seemed to focus there.

Lucilia laughed again.

'Father will be very pleased to see you. I'm sure he's rushing through the villa as we speak at a breakneck speed somewhat detrimental to his health.'

Fronto looked up, tearing his eyes from her chest as he gratefully found a subject to concentrate on.

'How *is* your father's health? I have worried all season.'

Lucilia smiled warmly.

'He appears to have taken what happened on duty as a warning. He has slowed his pace of life a great deal, though not' she added drily 'his love of the vine. I fear that comes from his association with his colleagues.'

Fronto smiled.

'Wine never did anyone real harm.'

'Perhaps.' She sighed. 'No, father is actually in as good a health as I have seen him in years. He plans great works for the villa, but truly few of them are started as he seems to prefer to walk in the orchards and to pop down to the town to visit the markets.'

'Good,' Fronto said with a relieved sigh. 'And your mother?'

'Mother is good. She will be busy finalising everything now that she knows you're here.'

Once more, Fronto's brow fell into his customary frown, but before he could say anything, there was a shout from the corridor.

'Marcus? By all the Gods it was about *time* you showed up.'

Fronto stood as Balbus appeared, clad in his tunic and breeches and nothing more. He looked so out of place without the addition of sword and cuirass it took a moment to adjust. Balbus had thinned down considerably in the few months, though not unhealthily so. He appeared more lithe and muscular than he had when he had carried the extra meat required in the field.

'You look so much better than I feared, my friend.'

'It's been months, Marcus. I've had time to recuperate. What kept you?'

Fronto rolled his eyes.

'Gaul, as usual, kept its claws in us until winter was threatening. Finally, I think we can say we have the whole damned place under control. Most of the officer corps is waiting on the hill above to come and check on you, but they deferred to me first.'

He felt something brush his wrist and shuddered involuntarily, turning to see that Lucilia had stood and crossed the room to his side.

'I must go and make sure that mother is being thorough. I will see you later, Marcus.'

He stuttered an affirmative noise as she raised herself on her toes and kissed his cheek before sweeping from the room as though she were floating.

'You've gone red' Balbus said with a smile.

'Lucilia's changed. She's quite... forward.'

Again the older man laughed.

'She knows what she's doing. She is the shadow of her mother at that age.'

Fronto nodded and turned, his brow furrowing again.

'What was she saying about her mother finalising things? It sounded like you were expecting me for something.'

Balbus gestured to a seat and clapped his hands. Before they had fully relaxed onto the couches, Caro had reappeared with a tray, two goblets and a jar of wine.

'This would be your 'wrong' wine?'

Balbus smiled.

'Happily just mislabelled. I would hate to have had to send it back, given the costs of transporting anything back to Latium.'

The two men sipped, and Fronto pursed his lips.

'You neatly avoided my question.'

'I would have preferred to have broached the matter later, at my own leisure.'

'And once I was up to the eyeballs in soothing wine?' Fronto relied astutely.

Balbus smiled.

'I have a favour to ask of you.'

'Go on...'

'Lucilia is to go to Rome. I am contemplating a match between her and a young man of the Caecilii, but I will not confirm anything until she has had the chance to approve or disapprove. I will not match her against her will.'

Fronto nodded, relieved for some unknown reason, by the news.

'Good family, the Caecilii. She could do well. Why with me, though? Would she not be better travelling with you?'

Balbus shrugged.

'The medicus has warned me against strenuous travel for some time yet, and you know the crossing from Massilia in the autumn and winter months. No, I must stay here until the winter is past, but Lucilia must go to Rome.'

Fronto nodded.

'I would be remiss in my duty to a friend if I refused, Quintus. Where will she be staying? With the Caecilii?'

'Hardly, Marcus. It would be rather unseemly, at least until a match is agreed, to land her upon their doorstep. I was hoping...' he smiled weakly. 'Well your sister might take her under her wing and...'

Fronto blinked.

'Gods, you want to turn her into another Faleria? Are you mad? Rome trembles at the presence of just one!'

Balbus smiled uncomfortably.

'I was dreading asking you. I have a cousin who can look after her, of course.'

Fronto sat silently, his teeth grinding.

'No. Of *course* she must stay with Faleria.' He smiled wearily. '*I*, however, may have to descend on your cousin with a third woman adding to the matriarchy that is my house.'

Balbus laughed.

'I have missed your companionship, Marcus. Will you have time to stay for a few days? Corvinia has everything packed and prepared, of course. She has had for months, in case you flew past in a hurry once again.'

Fronto grinned.

'I am in something of a hurry to get home, for certain, but a few days would hardly cost me the world. Of course, at least for a few hours you are going to have to play host to the general's staff who are waiting on the hill, no doubt impatiently, to descend on you. There are friends among them, though: Crispus and Varus among others. It may be that Galronus will also arrive shortly. We had word that he and Crassus and a few others passed through Narbo several days ago to meet up with us before we take ship.'

Balbus smiled and leaned back with his goblet.

'Then we had best spend a private half hour in happy contemplation of the vine before we send out to them, eh? I'm sure you have much to tell me.'

Fronto leaned back, reached for the goblet on the table before him and sagged into the chair as the tension of months flooded out along with the easy conversation.

* * * * *

377

The party of officers had gathered on the roadway in front of the villa. Fronto frowned as he stepped out of the doorway. Caesar and several of the officers who had no connection to Balbus had made their excuses and left politely the day after they had first arrived, not wishing to put any pressure on the family to accommodate so many guests. The rest had respectfully left the villa then and found temporary lodgings in Massilia until Fronto was ready to sail.

He had expected Crispus, Brutus and Varus, and had hoped to see Galronus, since the officers from the Seventh had apparently arrived in Massilia late the previous evening, but the other four were more of a surprise. Roscius, the quiet and thoughtful legate of the Thirteenth, had separated from the other Illyrian officers who would be taking a different ship, and his presence was unexpected. More surprising was that of Crassus and two of his tribunes that Fronto did not know and particularly the fact that one of these tribunes stood in pleasant conversation with Galronus and the two were laughing. There would be time to ask questions on the voyage, of course.

Turning his back on the men, he stepped to one side to allow Lucilia room to pass, Caro, the house's head slave walking patiently behind her with both arms straining under the weight of her travelling gear. Fronto shook his head in mock disbelief and smiled as he saw the almost hidden look in Caro's eye.

As he turned back to the door, the three remaining family members filled the portal. Balbina stepped forward, and Fronto crouched to hug her.

'Will you come back soon?'

The legate grinned.

'I will be here in December, at the latest. I try to be away from home during the Saturnalia, as my sister tends to become a little disapproving of my behaviour during the festival, and Galronus tells me that the following day they have a huge festival to a horse goddess called Epona in Gaul.'

Balbus nodded.

'In Massilia they have a full day of horse races and feasting.'

'Yes, I suspect that's what Galronus has in mind.'

He stood once more, and Corvinia reached out and embraced him.

'It has been good to see you again, Marcus. We shall have rooms prepared for you and your friends from the Ides of December onwards, but do not be reticent. Come early if you wish it. Please pass on my regards to your family.'

Fronto smiled as they separated.

'Should you have the chance to visit Rome next year, do call in. My mother would be more than happy to meet you, I'm sure.'

He turned to Balbus.

'Another farewell, eh Quintus?'

The older man smiled.

'A temporary one. Two months and I'll see you again. Corvinia might even let me join you and Galronus at the circuit.'

'I doubt it' she replied with a sly smile.

Fronto grinned at him.

'It feels like I've only been here a few moments. I would stay on, but there are things that need my attention at home. You understand?'

Balbus nodded.

'Go help Priscus look after your family. Tell him I asked after him.'

'I will.'

The small group spent a moment in silence before Fronto took a deep breath and picked up his bag of freshly laundered clothes.

'Right. Off to jolly old sea we go.'

With a smile, he turned his back to the villa and strode out to the waiting party. He was amused to see the reactions Lucilia was causing. Crassus was openly admiring her, Varus had a strange smirk on his face as though he were weighing her up in some way, and Crispus was looking almost anywhere but directly at her.

'Very well gentlemen, and lady of course. Shall we depart?'

Caro bowed respectfully.

'Just throw those on the cart, Caro. You don't need to lug them all the way to the docks.'

The slave looked across at Lucilia hopefully, and she smiled at him.

'Go and look after father.'

Caro carefully stacked and wedged the luggage in the cart and then delicately helped the young lady up into it before bowing and returning to the villa.

Watching the family in the doorway, waving their goodbyes, Fronto smiled a last smile at them and clambered up onto Bucephalus and trotted off after the party that had already begun to descend the gravelled path down toward the bustling metropolis below.

Falling in at the back, he stretched and leaned back, exposing his face to the late autumn sunlight before glancing once more with some trepidation at the rocking boats in the harbour and the churning surface of the Mare Nostrum.

'She's going to cause you trouble.'

He blinked and turned to see the grinning face of Varus, riding along next to him. It took him a moment to realise that the man was speaking of Lucilia and not the sea herself.

'She's going to meet a suitor in Rome. If anything, I'm just a chaperone.'

Varus laughed.

'I think you could be in for a surprise there, my friend. I saw those looks of hers. Keep your drawstring tight and your bedroom door locked.'

Fronto glared at him.

'That's *Balbus'* daughter you're talking about, Varus.'

'My point precisely' the man replied with a grin.

Fronto turned back to face the party ahead. Lucilia rode almost regally, her travelling cloak having already fallen slightly to reveal pale, creamy shoulders. He swallowed hard and flashed a nervous look across at Varus, who merely grinned and nodded.

* * * * *

The legate of the Tenth, veteran of numerous wars, recipient of the corona civica, and senior commander in the army of the praetor Julius Caesar, groaned and heaved once more as what was left of his stomach contents disappeared into the roiling waves.

'I feel bloody awful.'

Crispus smiled sympathetically.

'You've gone a very curious colour. I can't decide whether it's green, yellow or purple depending upon the light.'

Fronto glared at him and spat angrily into the water.

'Charming of Varus to offer me a nice fatty piece of pork, just when...'

He stopped talking and threw himself against the rail, making retching sounds.

'Stop thinking about it. He was only doing it for a joke. He didn't know you were as bad a sailor as this. *No one* did. Gods, I don't know whether I've ever *met* a worse sailor. The sea's hardly moving.'

The legate lifted his head once again to glare at his young friend.

'Don't mock your elders.'

The two men fell silent, a friendly smile on the young officer's face as he patted Fronto on the shoulder sympathetically.

'You poor dear.'

Fronto turned to stare in surprise at Crispus and then realised the voice had come from elsewhere. Of course. Feminine.

Lucilia strode along the deck, her gait steady and rolling with the pitch of the deck as though she had been at sea all her life. Fronto grimaced.

'I'm alright. Just a little seasick.'

'I shall leave you in my lady Lucilia's capable hands while I return to the table.' Crispus laughed.

Fronto shot him a desperate glance, shaking his head barely perceptibly, but the man slapped him on the shoulder, grinned, and strode off back toward the wooden housing at the rear of the large merchant vessel that served as dining room for the travellers.

He tried to straighten, but the strength seemed to have flooded from him and instead, he slumped against the railing and wiped his mouth on the back of his wrist.

'You really do appear to be very unwell. You've been vomiting for almost an hour.'

'Thanks for noticing.' Fronto grumbled. 'Crispus is the only one who felt it worth coming to check on me. I could have been turning inside out or thrown up my liver by now.'

Lucilia gave him a gentle smile.

'Don't be so dramatic. It's a little seasickness; bad, yes, but hardly terminal. It may surprise you to hear that strong, unwatered wine, with the addition of ginger, is a traditional cure for the ailment among the Greek sailors in Massilia.'

Fronto glared at her.

'I hardly think I'll be taking the advice of a nation that would bed a goat it if fluttered its eyelashes.'

She laughed.

'You get so very grumpy when you're ill. And intolerant.'

He issued another growl and returned to looking down at the waves for a moment before he had to close his eyes again and concentrate hard on keeping his innards where they belonged.

'I sometimes wonder if you are alone because of your little quirks, or if you have these little quirks because you are alone.'

The legate heaved himself up from the railing.

'I think that officially ends our conversation.'

With difficulty, he sidled along the rail away from Lucilia, but she doggedly followed, a curious and thoughtful look on her face.

'There must be some reason. I asked my father, and all he knows is that you apparently never had time. That's a pathetic excuse if ever I heard one. I'm curious.'

'Don't be.' He said flatly and without a trace of humour.

'You don't have to be quite so guarded around me, Marcus. You'd be surprised just how open and understanding I am.'

She hooked her arm around his as he leaned on the rail and he pulled away angrily.

'Will you leave me be? I'm ill, and there are some things we are simply not going to talk about.'

She smiled.

'Very well. I'm sure your sister will tell me in time.'

She jumped as Fronto wheeled on her and grasped her by the shoulders.

'This is a subject you are forbidden to raise with Faleria, do you understand me?' he growled, furiously.

Lucilia stared at him and nodded her head, a frightened look on her face.

'Of course... I'm sorry, Marcus. I didn't mean...'

He turned his back on her and leaned over the rail.

As she turned away, tears in her eyes, and ran toward the wooden shelter, Fronto growled at the passing waves. Curiously, the anger that had risen in him had completely overwhelmed the illness and left him feeling a lot stronger; physically, at least.

He would have to apologise to her eventually of course, but she could stew for an hour first to discourage any further enquiries in that direction.

'You realise that you'll have to do something soon?'

Fronto turned in surprise toward the prow to find Crassus looking at him with a strange and unreadable expression.

382

'She may look cowed at the moment,' the young officer noted, 'but she's a fiery one. She'll not let this rest, and sooner or later she'll hear the story from your sister if she doesn't hear it from you.'

The legate of the Tenth blinked.

'I wasn't aware that *you* knew?'

Crassus smiled sadly.

'I was at her wedding, Fronto. I don't remember whether Varus was there, but it's entirely possible that he was too. He was certainly in Rome at the time and moved in Faleria's circles. It's hardly a secret, after all.'

Fronto took a deep breath and leaned back.

'Old wounds should not be reopened. You don't have to be a capsarius to know that.'

'I'm not sure any medicus would agree that this particular one ever truly closed.' Fronto grunted and leaned over the rail again.

'She is a prize, Fronto. She looks at you with little less than naked hunger, and that is rare for a man like you.'

'Thanks. That's a charming sentiment.'

Crassus laughed.

'I thought you were supposed to be all practical and pragmatic? I'm on my way back to Rome to a glittering future, Fronto. I'm about to meet my twenty sixth year, I have two successful military campaigns under my belt and, when my father gets a province next year, I shall begin my rise through the ranks of Rome. Quite simply, I am a catch that many respectable fathers will consider for their daughters.'

He smiled as he looked Fronto up and down.

'You, on the other hand, have no interest in politics, which means you will likely live out your days taking on officer positions in the army of whatever praetor is busy warring that season, and face down in a wine mug in the subura the rest of the time. I know why, and I realise that you won't believe me, but I can understand both the allure and the necessity of that for you.'

He straightened.

'But it means that you're not a great prospect for most noblewomen, and you're reaching the age where only the matrons, widows and divorcees will look at you.'

Fronto glared at him silently.

'You know I'm right. And you know that Balbus' life is what you *could* have if only you would just pick yourself up, dust yourself off and play the game a little. You cannot wallow in self pity your entire life, Fronto. Clean yourself up, apologise to Lucilia and use the time with her that the Gods seem to have miraculously granted you, or you will still be doing this when you drop dead in a muddy field in Germania as a septuagenarian.'

Fronto continued to glare in silence as Crassus shrugged.

'Advice is free, Fronto, but I still don't give it often.'

With a nod of the head, Crassus walked off along the deck toward the stern, leaving the Tenth's legate alone at the rail, fuming with himself and entirely unsure why.

* * * * *

Fronto kept his eyes straight ahead. The conversations with Lucilia and then Crassus had ruined what was left of his tattered, sea-sickened mood for the rest of the journey, and he'd felt no relief as the merchant vessel had docked in the port of Ostia and the eager travellers had transferred to one of the numerous barges that ploughed the sixteen miles of Tiber between the great port and the emporium docks by the Aventine.

The curt apology he had planned for Lucilia had never quite come about, and she now moved with a sad and offended look that made it all the more difficult to approach her. The journey along the Tiber, in a great barge hauled upstream by heavy oxen on the bank, had been much the same: quiet and depressing.

In fact, as Fronto stepped onto dry land and stared up at the slope of the Aventine before him, he realised that his dismal mood was constructed partly of the ongoing uncomfortable silence between Lucilia and himself and partly of the nerves gradually increasing as he neared home and wondered what he might now find there.

The group of officers, along with the young lady and the baggage carts, made their way along the waterfront and through the Porta Trigemina into the city proper, though with the crowds and the rickety housing along the base of the hill opposite the docks, the fact that they were now actually in the city of Rome could only be determined by the fact that they had passed through the great triple gateway and the inevitable crowd of beggars that gathered outside, clawing at the hems of the passers by.

At the edge of the Forum Boarium, Crassus and his tribunes, along with Brutus, Roscius, Varus and Crispus separated and went

384

their own ways to family and friends. Galronus fell into position beside Lucilia and the wagon of luggage, while Fronto strode ahead, hardly acknowledging their presence as he walked.

The starting gates of the circus were already busy, preparing for the first race of the day, and the murky, swampy ground around them being churned beneath the feet of the workers was evidence that Rome had suffered heavy rain in recent days. The sky now was a sullen grey that matched Fronto's mood perfectly as he turned and left the great circus, stomping up the sloping street, past the temples of Luna, Minerva and Diana and that drew an unofficial border between the houses of the wealthy and the dwellings of the poor.

A turn to the left and a further one to the right brought the three travellers to the street of Fronto's youth with its gentle slope and wide walkways, the south side marked by high walls that surrounded the gardens of other houses. The city residence of the Falerii, roughly halfway along the street, was relatively modest for a patrician residence, evidence of Fronto's father's modest and frugal nature. The plain walls, almost entirely lacking in apertures, gave an austere impression.

Fronto strode ahead of his companions yet further and reached for the door, rapping hard on the wood.

There was a pause, while the others caught up with him, the wagon squeaking irritatingly as it rolled to a halt.

The door opened slowly to reveal not the disapproving features of the house's chief slave, but those of four men Fronto had never seen before. Two had the distinct look of brigands, the third a massive man wearing the braids and beard of a Celt of some variety and the fourth a small, steel-eyed man bearing scars that clearly marked him as a professional fighter of some note.

'Who are you?' the latter asked plainly.

Fronto narrowed his eyes.

'I am the master of this house. Get out of my way.'

The other three moved forward, effectively blocking the entrance with a wall of muscle.

'Gnaeus?' the man's voice called and, between the bodies, Fronto saw with relief the familiar face of Priscus duck around a corner. The former centurion blinked and stepped out into the hallway.

'Marcus? Thank all the Gods. It's about *time* you showed up.'

He turned to the small, wiry warrior.

385

'Good job, Cestus, but this is the man I work for.'

The four men backed away from the door and fell to one side, nodding respectfully at Fronto. He was on the verge of an irritated outburst, but Priscus, recognising the signs, reached out and drew the legate through the door by the elbow, gesturing to the men.

'This is Cestus. He's my chief enforcer now. Used to be a gladiator… one of the few ex-gladiators in Rome not currently in the employ of Clodius, I might add. These others are Todius, Aranius and Lod; all good men. No bugger gets in here without being cleared by me or Faleria.'

Fronto stopped, an eyebrow raised.

'First name terms now, eh, Gnaeus?'

Priscus looked past Fronto's shoulder and grinned.

'Galronus! Good to have you back.'

He paused.

'You have company too?'

'I'll tell you all about it in good time, when…'

'Marcus?'

He looked up past Priscus to see Faleria, dressed in simple pale green and her hair down and damp, fresh from the baths. Somehow, despite the difficulty he always had with her, something eased inside him. She looked healthy.

'Faleria. How are you?'

She laughed a small surprised laugh and then hurried past the guards and threw her arms around her brother.

'It is far beyond time you were home, Marcus. Gnaeus does a perfect job, but mother has been counting down the days to the Armilustrium. She knew you'd be back before then.'

Fronto smiled with a curious sadness and then looked up at Priscus and gestured with his thumb. The former centurion nodded, limping forward, and gestured to Galronus.

'Come, my friend, I have quarters ready for guests. I presume you'll be staying the winter?'

The Remi officer smiled and bowed respectfully to Faleria as he passed and joined Priscus, the two disappearing round the corner deep in conversation. Fronto turned to the guards.

'Get that wagon through the side gate and unloaded, then secure the front door and gates.'

Cestus jerked a nod and the four men disappeared out through the front door, respectfully sidling around the young lady in the doorway. Faleria noticed the other visitor for the first time and frowned a question at her brother, her arms still tight around his shoulders.

'This is Lucilia, the daughter of my good friend Balbus. I've spoken of him.'

'And of Lucilia, of course' she added with a smile, giving him a final squeeze and then releasing him as she moved on to her new guest.

'Are you here for a time, my dear?'

Fronto turned and shrugged.

'She's here to weigh up a potential match to one of the Caecilii. Balbus asked if we would be good enough to look after her while she was here. Well, in actual fact, he asked if *you'd* be good enough.' There was an unspoken question of his own there.

'Of *course* she must stay here. With Priscus' little army, there's nowhere safer in the city these days.'

She smiled as she reached out for Lucilia's arm.

'Have you been to Rome before?'

'This is my first opportunity to visit, my lady.'

Her hostess laughed.

'If you know my brother, then you'll realise that I expect little in the way of formality in this house. Call me Faleria.'

'Thank you. And I, Lucilia.'

'Perhaps, if Marcus can spare Gnaeus and some of his men as an escort, I can show you some of the glorious sights of the city in the morning, though you must be exhausted from your journey.'

Lucilia gave Fronto a strange look and shook her head.

'Actually the trip was very uneventful and quiet. Almost silent, in fact.'

Faleria gave Fronto a questioning glance and he shook his head.

'If you two ladies can do without me for an hour or two, I think I ought to see Priscus and catch up on events.'

Faleria shook her head emphatically.

'Not until you have visited mother. She's in the tablinum outside.'

Fronto paused for a moment and then, nodding, strode off through the doorway to the rear that led into the peristyle garden. Pausing briefly to note the strange juxtaposition of the carefully-groomed garden and the three wooden dummies at the far side, regularly used for sword practice in army fashion, he turned away and into the reception room doorway.

Faleria the elder reclined on a couch, reading a scribbled note on parchment; a copy of the acta diurna made from the tablets in the forum by the house's chief slave, Posco, for such was the habit of Faleria.

As the light from the doorway dimmed, she looked up and blinked at the silhouetted figure of her son.

'Marcus?'

'Mother.'

Walking slowly in, he wandered across to the couch, where she reached out with her hands. He was shocked to see the trembling in them, but clenched his teeth and reached out to cup them in his own hands and squeeze them.

'I knew you would come home soon. Gnaeus kept telling us you were on your way.'

He smiled weakly.

'I wanted to come earlier, but...'

'I know. Young Gaius needed you too much. He is a drain on your energy, but it is good to attach yourself to a rising star.'

Fronto heaved a sigh and let go of her hands.

'I'm not following him into office, mother, even if he asks me. We've not spoken for half a year, so please let's not launch straight into the old arguments.'

She gazed at him levelly, and he studied her face, dismayed at how much she seemed to have aged in such a short time. There was something about her gaze that...'

He looked down to hide his expression as he realised that one of her eyes was not moving as her gaze wandered. Pausing long enough to be certain of his composure, he looked up again and studied her. The bone around her right eye was bumpy and misshapen, as though it had been badly broken and had set slightly off.

Her wounds from the attack had been worse than Priscus had intimated. Fronto rocked back on his feet, the anger rising in him. Stepping forward again, he embraced her tightly.

'Do not panic, Marcus. I'm fine.'

'Of course you are, mother. And nothing is ever going to happen to you again. I need to go see Priscus. I expect Faleria will be along very shortly with a guest in tow. Quintus Balbus, former legate of the

Eighth has sent his daughter to Rome and Faleria has agreed to look after her while she stays.'

The old woman looked up at her son and focused her good eye on him. Fronto flinched slightly at the lack of movement in the other, but more at that penetrating one-eyed gaze. Since his early youth, Faleria the elder had had an uncanny knack of looking directly into his thoughts and soul and laying them bare.

'I see. Make sure you are kind to her, Marcus. You have a habit of driving off those whom you would have closer.'

Fronto took a deep breath.

'She is the daughter of a friend, mother; nothing more. I must attend to business, but I will see you shortly at dinner.'

As he bowed and turned, he was extremely aware of both the penetrating gaze that remained on his back and of the fact that he wasn't even sure he had convinced himself, let alone his mother.

He was continually assaulted by waves of guilt and anger as he strode purposefully through the house to the quarters set aside for Priscus and his hired thugs. How could he have let this all happen?

As he reached the bunk room, the lame soldier sat on a cot opposite Galronus, watering a jug of wine as he entered.

'Gnaeus?'

'Ah, good. I'm very glad you're back.'

Fronto sank into one of the bunks.

'I've seen mother.'

'She's been waiting eagerly for you.'

Fronto shook his head.

'She was almost killed. You knew that. That blow to her eye could have done for her.'

Priscus nodded sadly.

'Truly, but it didn't. She's a strong woman, Marcus, and it was *her* decision not to give you the full horrible details of the attack, not mine. She knew it would just torture you, 'cause you couldn't come home anyway.'

Fronto glared at him for a moment and then let his gaze fall to the floor before taking a deep breath and straightening.

'This situation needs to be resolved. I'm not having anything like this happening again. We need to *end* Clodius or at least remove his claws. What have you seen of our mysterious ghost?'

Priscus eyed Galronus for a moment and shrugged.

'There's been no sign of him since that day in the mausoleum. I went back the next day and the body was gone. Another visit two days later and there was a new unnamed funerary urn in there. I think I must have left some trace of my presence, 'cause when I went back to his accommodation he'd left. I spoke to his landlord, and he paid the rent in full and left with no further word. No idea where he is now, but I've got everyone being very watchful in case he shows up.'

Fronto nodded.

'And Clodius?'

'He has been buying up all the nasty spare muscle in Rome. You can't lay hands on a good solid thug anywhere in the city, since Philopater's been everywhere. Even the slave markets are down to just the thin and weedy scholars. Any time you see anyone connected with Clodius, they're surrounded by a small army. The man must have more muscle under his control than anyone else in Latium.'

Fronto nodded again and leaned back.

'Then we may have to start trying to hire our own muscle from Ostia, Albinum, Tusculum, or Veii. I want that man toothless or dead.'

Priscus smiled.

'I have a hidden weapon at my disposal yet. See, there's a man called Titus Annius Milo, a former tribune who apparently holds as healthy a dislike for Clodius as we do, and he also has his own private army. Milo's been in touch with me. He's staying very much out of the public eye at the moment, but that means that, as far as we're aware, Clodius knows nothing about him and his men.'

Fronto smiled in return and rubbed his hands together.

'I may need to meet this Milo and buy him a drink. Caesar's back in Rome, now, along with Crassus, Brutus and the rest. I think we need to call a meeting of all those who have a grudge against Clodius and see what we can turn up. Think you can sneak this Milo in for a meeting tomorrow or the next day?'

Priscus shrugged.

'I can try. Are you actually intending to *start a war* on the streets of Rome?'

Fronto's eyes narrowed.

'No point. Clodius already did that. I'm going to *end* the war.'

Chapter 21

(Late Octobris: House of the Falerii in Rome.)

As the door opened, Caesar stepped back in surprise.

'Nam?' demanded the hulking hairy object that blocked most of the doorway.

The general blinked and turned to look in surprise at the younger Crassus, standing next to him. The officer, now dressed togate and with perfect high-class attire, leaned toward the massive doorman.

'This is Gaius Julius Caesar, governor of Cisalpine and Transalpine Gaul and Illyricum, you ignorant oaf. Stand aside: we are expected.'

The man rubbed his chin and shrugged.

'Caesar, yes.' He stepped to one side and straightened. The general was impressed to note the crown of the man's head brushed the ceiling of the hallway. He and Crassus entered and shivered from the cold dampness in the air. With an almost negligent flick of his hand, the general dismissed Ingenuus' group of unarmed and dismounted cavalry who had escorted them across the city.

As the guard closed and locked the door behind them, a small man with muscular arms and a number of fascinating scars rounded a corner and bowed.

'Mighty Caesar; noble Crassus, if you would follow me?'

The two men, slapping along with their wet boots and leaving murky footprints on the marble, followed the servant through the house and to the large triclinium.

The room was occupied by six men, lounging on couches or sitting on chairs, several tables between them laden with simple food, jars of wine, goblets and jugs of water. Fronto and Priscus sat with Galronus as though they were in some way separate from the rest.

Caesar looked around, taking in the faces of the other men. Marcus Caelius Rufus, the defendant that Fronto had protected, Quintus Tullius Cicero, brother of the great orator, and lastly a man that he vaguely recognised but could not put a name to.

'I see that you have begun raising a legion for yourself, Fronto.'

His host smiled humourlessly from the far end of the room.

'Having a gang seems to be the only way to survive in the city these days, Caesar.'

391

He gestured to the seats and the general and Crassus made themselves comfortable, reaching for the water and grapes. To the general's surprise, the man who escorted them to the room also took a seat and helped himself to the food.

'Everyone here is well acquainted I think,' Fronto announced, 'apart from Titus Annius Milo over there, and the excellent and very dangerous Cestus who met you outside.'

Fronto noted Caesar's expression and smiled.

'Cestus is now in charge of the household's 'guard' if you wish to call it that. He's a veteran of seventeen bouts in the arena, recipient of the rudis and a man to stay on the good side of.'

The small man nodded at Caesar, who returned the gesture, frowning.

'Milo I remember, however' the general said, straightening again. 'A tribune of the plebs last year?'

The man bowed curtly.

'Very well.' Fronto sat up. 'Everyone in the room either has good reason to hate Clodius, or is bound by ties to those who do. For the first time in months, we are all in Rome and so is he. In our absence, he's had free rein in the city causing murder and mayhem. The time had come to deal with him. We simply can't leave a snake like that in a position to do further harm.'

There was a general murmur of agreement around them, but Caesar rubbed his brow and leaned forward.

'I have the feeling you are suggesting direct action and even rather illegal violence, Fronto?'

Their host smiled a feral grin and leaned back.

'You are damn right I'm suggesting illegal violence. If I could have thought of a way to get past his constant array of guards, I'd have kicked the man to death myself before now.'

Caesar shook his head.

'Don't think in such narrow terms, Fronto. This is too complex an issue to lunge out like a thug and strike him down. That is *Clodius'* way, not that of reasonable, intelligent men.'

Fronto leaned forward himself, his face filling with angry colour.

'That is the opinion of a man who has yet to feel the full unpleasantness of Clodius. Wait until your little Octavia comes home one afternoon with a broken face, or that pretty niece of yours, and *then* tell me it's too complex an issue.'

The general shook his head.

'I feel for your family, Marcus, but that is still not the way.'

He turned to Milo.

'If I am not mistaken, you are bound to the great Pompey?'

Milo nodded.

'And yet you are here, plotting without him?'

The man shrugged.

'If questioned, I will deny ever visiting this house, but I see no conflict in my behaviour. Pompey charged me with building him a force of very loyal men with low expectations. This I have done and, since Pompey has made no secret of his distaste for Clodius, this could even be seen as a meeting of like minds. As such, I am prompted to enquire as to why the great Pompey himself was not invited to this clandestine meeting.'

He smiled.

'Or even the noble Crassus' father?'

Crassus shrugged.

'It is well for those in such high position to be seen to be uninvolved with such things. I was in two minds as to whether to attend myself as, I believe, was Governor Caesar here.'

'Perhaps. Or perhaps none of you feel comfortable placing your trust in them? Regardless, the fact remains that, yes I am bound to Pompey and yes, I am here. I will not, however, employ my men in any action without the authorisation of my patron. It would be unthinkable to do so, I'm sure you'll agree.'

Fronto swept his hands through the air angrily.

'This waffling is getting us nowhere. Clodius is a plague that needs to be dealt with. I'm sure some of you at least agree with this? Cicero?'

The young officer opened his mouth to speak, but Caesar turned to him.

'Yes, I would be interested to hear the opinion of the noble Cicero, given that he has such a responsible commission in my army and yet his brother, from what I hear, denounces me and my works daily in the senate, supported and urged on by those poisonous dogs Cato and Ahenobarbus.'

He narrowed his eyes at Cicero.

'It has taken me three years to completely pacify Gaul. That is a drop in the ocean of time compared to what it took Rome's greatest generals to pacify Africa or Greece, and yet now the senate of Rome call me names and consider my campaign a failure and a waste; they

393

say that I am unable to keep the place down. Why? Because of Cicero, Cato and Ahenobarbus. Clodius blocks my moves in the senate by the exercise of subtle bribery and corruption, and therefore he is my enemy. What should I make, then, of those who oppose me openly?'

Cicero rounded on him.

'My brother does not attack *you*, Caesar. He is a just and good man and attacks laws and acts that he deems unworthy of the republic, whatever their origin. Do not feel singled out.'

Milo laughed.

'I fear you are being a little blinkered by your brotherly love, my friend. Cicero attacks Caesar because he is an easy target at the moment and your brother is still trying to ingratiate himself to the senate after his exile. He is doing nothing more than sacrificing one ally to make several others.'

The conversation stopped as everyone was aware of a low growling noise. All eyes turned to Fronto.

'This is like *being* at a meeting of the bloody senate! Everyone talking about their own agendas, no one sticking to the matter at hand. Just squabbling like chickens. The point of this whole meeting was Clodius! What are we going to do about the little shit head?'

'If you'll pardon me throwing in my lot'

All heads turned again to face Cestus.

'You are faced with two options. Either you find a way to put an end to Clodius, and this is my speciality, or you work on a method to remove his power. It seems to me that this is a disparate group. Half of us are committed to, and suitable for, one path and the other half to and for the other. The question is which way to go?'

Caesar shook his head.

'If Clodius turns up dead in a sewer, it will merely raise ugly questions, many of which will be levelled at myself, Pompey and even you, Fronto. Careers could be ruined, exiles considered, or even prosecutions made. The solution is to make Clodius trip himself up.'

Cicero and Rufus nodded.

'The first step' the younger officer said 'is to form a faction: a gathering of like-minded people, and to bring all those who waver on to our side. We need to convince my brother to abandon his attacks on Caesar in the senate. I can do this. We need to try and discourage the same with Cato and Ahenobarbus.'

He turned to Fronto.

'We need to make sure of our allegiances. The noble Crassus and the great Pompey should be drawn into the matter and, where their allegiances are shaky, they should be redirected, forcibly if necessary.'

Milo frowned.

'You seem to be edging around saying something about Pompey?'

Fronto leaned toward him.

'Look, it's not generally known and I'm not even sure whether we should be speaking to you about it, but there is considerable, though circumstantial, evidence that Pompey has been having dealings with Clodius in secret, while condemning him publically.'

Milo shook his head and leaned back.

'I have spoken to the man myself. He would rather bed a snake than throw in his lot with Clodius. Whatever he is doing, you can be sure it is not for the benefit of your enemy.'

Caesar glared at Fronto.

'Was that *really* necessary? Is this the time to start levelling accusations among the people who supposedly have a mutual enemy?'

He turned to Milo and made conciliatory gestures.

'I would appreciate it, given the nature of rumour and the uncertainty of everything here, if you would do us the honour of not passing on these spurious accusations to Pompey. I will speak to him myself in due course.'

The other man frowned for a long moment, but nodded.

'If I were to report every unsavoury rumour I heard to him, I would be running in and out of his house like a courier. If you hold your tongues about this and remain open minded until you are in a position to confirm their truth or falsehood, so will I.'

Fronto grumbled irritably.

'This is getting us no closer to a solution.'

'On the contrary, I feel that this little meeting has been of great importance and use' the general smiled. 'I have had certain fears allayed and am satisfied that all here are of a like mind. We all want to see Clodius declawed.'

'Dead' corrected Fronto.

'Declawed... or more if the opportunity arises, yes.'

'Dead' repeated Fronto flatly.

'More important now is to decide how to progress from here. Clearly I will need to arrange a meeting with Crassus and Pompey. Not a great public meeting like the one I attended early in the year, though; a more private affair. In the meantime, Cicero can begin trying to calm things in the senate, though I fear you will have great difficulty with the irrepressible Cato. If you, Milo, will simply keep your own mind open and observe the moves of both Pompey and Clodius, hopefully you will be able to arrive at a definite conclusion as to the truth of any complicity.'

He smiled at Cestus.

'In the meantime, it would be a good idea that no one with a grudge against Clodius go out in public without adequate defensive measures. His enemies do tend to end up bobbing along the Tiber with no head.'

He leaned back.

'Does anyone have any suggestions as to how we can prod Clodius in the direction of tipping his hand and perhaps putting a foot wrong?'

On the far side of the triclinium, Fronto stood, angrily.

'It seems that you all have the situation well under control. I am therefore currently entirely superfluous to this discussion. Please feel free to stay and partake of the food and drink. My mother would be horrified if you left unsatisfied.'

Casting a baleful look around his companions, he strode from the room.

Galronus made to rise, but Priscus put a hand on his shoulder and pushed him back down.

'Leave him to stew. If he has anyone to rant at, he'll just wind himself up even further.'

The two men settled back into their seats as the conversation resumed in depth.

* * * * *

Fronto stormed down the street angrily, ignoring the fine misty drizzle that had begun to fall. He had not even bothered to stop and wrap a toga about him or throw on a cloak, and tramped down the paving in an increasingly soggy white tunic.

It never ceased to amaze him how the cleverest and most powerful people in the world would talk themselves in ineffectual circles without being able to spot the plain truth of the matter, though it was hanging plainly in the air before them.

'Pointless.'

He ignored the questioning look the old woman threw at him from the side of the street.

They would argue for another hour and the conclusion would inevitably be that they should do nothing and simply wait to see if something miraculous happened, and Clodius fell down a sewer and drowned.

He looked up irritably in the drizzle. Ahead stood the temple of Bona Dea, lonely and surrounded by a peaceful garden. Often there would be stalls or at least beggars in the street close by, hoping for a tossed crust from the citizens descending the streets from the Aventine, but the chilling wet had driven them indoors, possibly even into the temple itself.

On a day like this...

Fronto's thoughts whirled in panic as everything went black, a bag thrust over his head and muscular arms were suddenly around his elbows and his midriff.

His mind reeled, but his body was already reacting like the soldier he was. He stamped down hard on the foot of a man and then raked his heel down the shin of another, all the while lunging and struggling this way and that.

Had he been able to free his arms, he might have stood a chance, but the grip on his elbows was spectacularly tight and painful, other hands grasping him as he was pulled sharply to his left.

His mind began to calm despite the circumstances and he noted the creak as an outside gate was opened. Waving his fingers as best he could, he felt the edge of a brick and mortar wall and then felt the brush of a large garden plant with waxy leaves.

Then he was being bundled unceremoniously through another door and out of the weather. A doorway, eight paces within, and then a right turn. Twelve paces along the corridor and then a left. Two paces and suddenly he was thrust violently to the floor.

Before he could find his senses and struggle to his knees, however, huge hands clamped themselves around his elbows and shoulders and pushed him down to what felt like a pile of rough sacking. While he struggled in vain, the bag was whipped from his head and he blinked as his eyes adjusted.

He was in a bare room, reasonably well lit by an unshuttered window opposite. The room was clearly in the process of decoration or restoration from the workmen's detritus around him: piles of brick and plaster, sacks of goods and tools strewn here and there. The shape blotting out a large portion of the window slowly resolved itself into the shape of a tall man in a grey cloak and tunic, thin and bordering on dangerously so. It was not until the figure turned to the side and nodded at the men holding Fronto that he saw the pronounced jaw and hook nose silhouetted against the white.

Philopater.

He drew a sharp breath and bit his lip to prevent crying out as a man unseen to his left grasped his middle finger and snapped it to vertical, breaking the knuckle.

'My employer is inclined to be generous, particularly with the benefit of the doubt.'

'Really?' Fronto panted. 'Funny way of showing it.'

Philopater leaned closer, and his features became clearer.

'You are clearly Caesar's creature. And yet' he said as he stepped sideways and put his finger to his lip, 'it is well known in some circles that you are a disapprover of the maniac and do rarely see eye to eye with him. This prompts my employer to take an interest in you.'

He leaned closer again.

'Sever your ties with the man and stay well out of the way. Be not involved.'

Fronto laughed.

'Caesar may be less than I would hope, but he's a *paragon of virtue* next to you and your master.'

He bit his lips enough to draw plenty of blood as the fourth finger on his left hand joined the middle one with a snap.

'Torture is hardly likely to win me over, you Egyptian faggot' he panted.

Philopater nodded.

'Indeed. You are made of sterner stuff. However, our reach is long. Remember your mother and think about your sister and that lovely little thing you brought back from Gaul. You're not a medical man, so you probably don't know that broken skulls can be extremely catching, very contagious.'

Fronto growled.

'In time,' Philopater continued, 'my employer may make you an offer that even Croesus would be hard put to refuse, but a show of faith by disassociating yourself with Caesar is required at this juncture. This will be your one and only opportunity to decide which side of the coin looks more favourable to you; be careful not to waste it in bravado.'

Fronto nodded, smiling knowingly.

Philopater frowned at him.

'What?'

'You.'

'What *about* me?'

As the man leaned in, Fronto lashed out with his foot, smashing his boot directly into the man's face and sending him flailing across the floor.

'I was wondering what you'd look like with a flat nose' Fronto laughed as the grip on his arms tightened.

The gaunt Egyptian stood slowly, unfolding like some Greek war machine. He reached his full height and turned to Fronto, his face covered in blood, his nose broken in several places above a badly split lip.

'Hold him.'

As the grips tightened further and fresh hands clamped themselves on Fronto's legs, he watched Clodius' henchman reach down among the workmen's tools and pull out a large, wooden mallet of the sort used for removing old plaster.

Steadying himself against what was to come, Fronto smiled and spat at the Egyptian's feet.

'Good night, master Fronto.'

The hammer came round at a dizzying speed, and after the briefest explosion of crimson agony, Fronto's world went black.

* * * * *

Pain.

Pain and white light.

Fronto closed his eyes again.

'What?'

A hand touched his arm, and he flinched.

'Calm, Marcus. It is I.'

399

He opened his eyes again, with all the discomfort and pain that brought and slowly focused on the figure of Lucilia by his side. A second shape beyond resolved into that of his sister.

'I...'

He tried to rise but his world exploded with white pain.

'Lie still.' The voice of Faleria. 'Lucilia here has treated your wounds with the consummate skill of a professional, aided by Posco, but it will be hours before you should sit up, let alone go about your ordinary business.'

Fronto tried to nod, but settled for a painful smile.

'How did I get here?'

Another voice joined the melee, and he turned to see Priscus and Galronus standing to the other side of the couch.

'You were dumped at the front door in a large grain sack. What in the name of seven stupid Gods were you thinking, leaving the house on your own?'

Fronto winced, and Faleria waved a finger.

'He's too weak and bleary for recriminations and anger, Gnaeus. Wait until he's stronger before you beat him with the stupidity stick.'

Lucilia leaned forward.

'What can you feel?'

Fronto laughed sharply.

'Pain.'

'Specifically' the girl said quietly.

'My left hand feels like it's been under the wheel of a cart. My ribs are aching, as are my shoulders and neck. But my face feels like I fell off the Tarpeian Rock head first.'

'Good.'

'Good?' he enquired in astonishment.

'Yes,' Lucilia replied. 'If you can feel the pain then there is no permanent damage to your system. If you *couldn't* feel the pain, I would have panicked. And you have only mentioned the wounds we had already located.'

Fronto sighed.

'Philopater and his gladiators. They really went for it.'

He grinned.

'But I broke the bastard's nose in the process.'

Priscus nodded.

'Well at least that's something. The gathering are long gone, but Milo has stayed on for a while. We've been knocking about a few ideas.'

Fronto clenched his good hand and turned his head painfully to look at them.

'Here's an idea: get out there with a bunch of men and find Clodius and Philopater. Follow them and see if there's any hope of getting them alone. If you get the chance, bag 'em up like they did to me and bring them here.'

Priscus nodded.

'We were planning to do just that, but I didn't want to go before you woke.'

Fronto smiled at him.

'Thank you, the pair of you. I should listen to you more often and not run off on my own.'

Priscus and Galronus nodded to him and then left the room, their voices fading as they moved through the house.

He turned back to the two women.

'I had no idea you were a medicus?'

Lucilia laughed.

'Hardly, but where we live there is not a great deal of access to a proper medicus and I have grown up taking care of the horses at the villa. The shape may be different, but the principle is the same.'

Fronto blinked.

'You're a *horse* healer?'

'After a fashion.'

She leaned closer.

'You had a narrow escape there, Marcus. That blow to your head could very easily have killed you, or at least left you blind, deaf, or a gibbering lunatic. Faleria has told me about what's happening.'

Fronto sighed.

'Has she indeed. Thank you, Faleria. Balbus will not appreciate us drawing his daughter into all of this.'

Faleria approached and waved her finger admonishingly in his face.

'You cretin. *You* drew her into this when you agreed to bring her to Rome. I'm just giving her appropriate warnings. She cannot be expected to look out for herself if she is unaware of the dangers. Really, Marcus; there are times when I wonder how you command a legion, when you don't seem to have even the tiniest fragment of common sense.'

She tapped the finger on his forehead and then stepped back.

'Try and remember that you're home now, Marcus, and you have friends and family around to help.'

Lucilia gently mopped his temple, and he winced at even the faint, whispery touch of her hand.

'It feels like I've been *kicked* by a horse!'

'It looks a lot like it, too' Lucilia smiled.

'Just try and lie still for a while and be calm.'

Faleria, behind her, straightened.

'I must go and speak to Posco about the arrangements for the evening meal. And before you argue, you're eating alone in here, where you can rest.'

Lucilia nodded and patted him gently on the chest.

'Absolutely right. I'll keep you company while you eat.'

The wicked little knowing smile on Faleria's face was not lost on him as she turned and left the room. Fronto sagged and closed his eyes.

* * * * *

Priscus nudged Milo and nodded to Galronus. The three men ducked back behind the temple of the Penates and Priscus glanced around himself once more. Dusk had descended less than an hour ago, and now the last of the light was threatening to vanish, oil lamps, braziers and torches springing to life all around the forum behind them and up on the Palatine hill to their right. The temple was closed now and no lights flickered in the window.

The dozen men they had brought with them as protection lurked between the buildings back down the slope, ready to rush out and engage if needed, but conveniently out of sight otherwise. The occasional passing figure gave them all a curious glance, but no more; too much interest in gangs of thugs in Rome was an unhealthy thing to have.

'What do you think?'

Milo turned to Priscus and shrugged.

'They appear to be alone. It's too easy. Everything about this tells me to stay away.'

Priscus nodded.

'It *is* just a little too convenient.'

The three men, shadowed by their hired help, had located Clodius in the early afternoon outside the entrance to the theatre, a great timber structure in the Velabrum so tall that it almost matched the heights of the Capitol. The man had spent the next few hours visiting a number of houses, spending no longer than a quarter hour in each, most of his large bodyguard remaining outside on each occasion.

His shadowing pursuers had almost given up following him when, beside the house of the Vestals, Clodius and his guards had met up with Philopater and a second gang. Priscus had strained his eyes trying to get a good look at the Egyptian's face. He would have loved to have seen that smashed nose, but the light was too low and the distance too great.

Just as the three men were about to gather their own hirelings and leave, there had been a brief altercation between Clodius and his chief enforcer. The nobleman had sent most of his men with Philopater, who had taken the large force and left toward the subura, heading back to the Clodian residence. The half dozen men that remained with him were the biggest and most disciplined-looking of the bunch, and the group headed off past the slopes of the Velian ridge and away from the forum.

'I'd give good money to know where he's going. Either Philopater disagreed with him going there, or he doesn't want that Egyptian scum with him. Either way, it's an interesting development.'

Milo nodded.

'Then we just follow and observe. No attack.'

Galronus rumbled behind them.

'Fronto wants him dead. There's seven of them. The *three* of us could take them down even without your men.'

Again, Milo shrugged.

'Something feels uncomfortable about the situation.'

'Shit!'

The pair turned back to Priscus, who had peered around the corner of the temple at their quarry but had just ducked sharply back.

'What?'

'He's looking directly up here. How could he have seen us?'

Galronus' jaw firmed.

'He couldn't. He must have known we were here already.'

403

'Oh, shit.'

They became aware that moment of a cacophony of bangs, thuds and shouts back among the buildings on the lower slope of the Velian. Cries of dismay marked the location of Priscus and Milo's gang as Philopater's much larger force fell on them from the rear, clearly intent on murder.

'He's attacking us?' Milo queried in astonishment. 'Now, in the centre of the city? But there are witnesses?'

He gestured to the figures moving along the Via Sacra below, but Priscus snarled.

'As if any passing grocer is going to get in the way of this lot!'

Galronus flexed his knuckles and turned back, but Milo put a hand on his shoulder.

'Are you *mad*? There must be fifty of them.'

Galronus growled angrily, but a voice cut through the early evening air from down by the edge of the marsh beyond the Via Sacra and distracted them.

'Little boys intent on mischief should not be out so late. Your mothers will be worried.'

Priscus sighed.

'Looks like we're in the shit now, lads. Fight or run?'

Milo shook his head. 'Run if we can.'

The situation was worsened with the sound of the brief struggle among the buildings behind them coming to a close. The dozen men they had brought along had hardly bought them enough time to argue their course, let alone pursue it.

Galronus nodded to them.

'I will distract them. You run back.'

Priscus stared at him.

'The only way you have to distract that lot is to let them beat you to a pulp. Come on.'

Without waiting for conversation or argument, Priscus ducked out around the temple and ran down the slope, his lame leg giving him a peculiar and ungainly gait, across the white paving of the Via Sacra, where he disappeared into the shadows around the shrine of Jupiter on the far side.

He stopped, catching his breath, heaving in air, as Galronus and Milo followed suit, pelting down the hill at breakneck speed and across the open ground in between. Priscus looked up, to the left and right, trying to decide what to do, as he rubbed his hip vigorously.

His leg felt as though it were on fire. He could not keep this up for long. He could not tell the other two, but there was no hope of him getting back as far as the house of the Falerii.

Philopater's men were emerging between the buildings on the Velian hill, looking down the slope, trying to spot their prey. Other small groups of men, almost certainly another part of the Egyptian's force, were slowly stalking down the Via Sacra from the forum, converging on their current location. To the other side, Clodius and his half dozen burly thugs were closing the net. The members of the general public had, to a man, vanished, making themselves conveniently absent in the face of such danger.

'We're hemmed in on three sides.'

The shrine in whose shadows they lurked unseen was small, nothing more than an ancient altar surrounded by a brick wall as high as a tall man and with an iron gate; hardly a place to hide or defend against a large force.

'We're going to have to make a break for it and head up the Palatine.'

The others nodded their agreement and, taking a deep breath, Priscus sprang out of the darkness, the other two men hot on his heels, and, ignoring the screaming pain in his hip and thigh, loped in his strange manner as fast as he could up the cobbled street that led up to the heights of the Palatine, closed shops lining it as it ascended into the gloom. Here and there, at the top, lights flickered among the houses of those wealthy enough to afford land on the hill that was the very heart of Rome.

Panting with the ascent, they passed the shattered pylons to either side of the street that marked the ruins of one of the city's most ancient gates, disused for centuries, and finally crested the top. The road led to a wide open space with an ornamental fountain at the centre, ornate decoration around the edges. From here half a dozen smaller roads led off among the wealthy villas, but Priscus focused on the one straight ahead that would take them across the plateau and which opened into the great stairway that led down toward the end of the circus and the Porta Capena.

'That way!'

The three men took a desperate breath, becoming aware in the sudden quiet of the noises of close pursuit back down the street. Sharing a quick, desperate glance, they ran on into the open space. Already, the former centurion's leg was juddering, threatening to collapse under the strain and he was starting to fall behind the others. By the time they crossed the Palatine, he would be flat on his face.

Priscus cursed himself as they ran for underestimating the audacity of the man. They were in the very centre of Rome, just after nightfall. There were fewer people about in the chilly damp air than during the day or on a warmer night, but still there must have been at least twenty people witnessed the attack tonight. The man clearly had no fear of discovery or recrimination. It was said that Clodius 'owned the streets', and Priscus was starting to see how the saying had come about.

He was trying to figure out a way to gain distance on their pursuers and keep himself in the game when a squawk from ahead startled him. A thrown rock connected with Galronus' skull hard enough to knock him from his feet. The Remi nobleman fell with a shout, rolling on the pavement. In former times, Priscus would have leapt lithely over him. Not now. Not with the leg the way it was. He tried to clear the rolling form, but his foot barely left the ground and he came down with a crash, falling over the prone form of Galronus.

Milo skidded to a halt and turned. Priscus waved at him.

'Go on. Get back to the house and tell them what happened.'

Priscus glanced around them in desperation. Only three men had emerged at the top of the slope, one of Philopater's smaller gangs that had approached from the forum end. If he and Galronus could just stand and take them on...

A shout made him turn back. Milo had stopped. Another force of perhaps a score of men was approaching out of the gloom from the direction of the circus, cresting the slope on the very road they were making for. Milo backed toward his fallen companions.

'We may be in trouble.'

Priscus tried to rise, heaving the stunned Galronus as he did. Neither of them had the strength or stamina to stand. Milo backed up to them and ground his teeth. Clodius appeared over the crest of the hill behind them, followed by Philopater and a large group of murderous men.

Briefly, Priscus considered the other exits from the square. They could perhaps have got to the Velabrum and descended the hill there to get lost among the shops and narrow streets. But there was simply not enough time and, even had there been, he had not the strength. There was nowhere to run as the two forces converged on the three men, trapped between the pincers in a vice of mercenaries. Lights in the nearby houses went out as self preservation led their occupants to an expedient ignorance of events in the square outside.

'It would appear that the Gods are favouring you tonight, Gnaeus Vinicius Priscus. And your friends.'

Priscus frowned as he regarded the man who effectively controlled the streets of the city. Clodius and Philopater had stopped at the edge of the square, their followers gathering around them.

Glancing over his shoulder he heaved a sigh of relief.

Cestus strode out of the front ranks of the other force, the hulking figure of Lod, the Celtic giant beside him. The former gladiator bore no blade, according to Roman law, but the wooden stave he carried would be, in his capable hands, better than a sword in most.

The small warrior crouched close to the trio of desperate men.

'It would appear that the lady Faleria is right: master Fronto's suicidal bravado *is* infectious.'

Priscus grinned, heaving in air in deep gulps.

'How the hell did you know where to find us?'

Cestus laughed.

'Good grief! I've had men shadowing you since you left the house. I'm not about to allow a repeat of what happened to Fronto. I have a reputation to maintain.'

Priscus turned again as Clodius shouted to them.

'Be grateful. You've been given a reprieve, but the sky is lowering by the hour and it will fall on you and yours presently.'

The man turned and strode off among his men. Philopater continued to glare at them, lingering for a moment then, grinning, drew a finger across his throat meaningfully and turned to leave.

Milo looked across at Priscus, who had begun to chuckle.

'What's so bloody funny?'

'Did you see the shape of his nose? Like a strawberry!'

407

Chapter 22

(Late Octobris: House of the Falerii in Rome.)

Fronto slipped his legs over the side of the bed in the large room that had once been his father's and let his bare feet fall to the marble floor with a cold slap.

'Get back in.'

'Not a chance in Hades, Faleria.'

'You're in no state to be walking around. Lucilia said at least a day before we were to let you even get up, let alone walk around.'

'It's just bruising and the odd crack, Faleria. I've suffered worse in the stands at the circus. Where are they all?'

Faleria sighed.

'They're in the summer triclinium discussing what to do next.'

Nodding, Fronto slowly pushed himself upright and, wobbling for a moment, began to stretch his arms and gently test his legs. Certain moves with his left arm sent waves of pain through his shoulder and chest, any sharp movement in his neck was excruciating and there was a constant dull pain in his head but, other than that, he appeared to be in working order. Frowning, he took a tentative step forward. No problem there. They seemed to have left his legs alone nicely.

'I'm fine. A bit of exercise and a couple of cups of good unwatered wine to wash away the headache, and I'll be back to normal.'

'You're an idiot, my brother.'

He turned and grinned at her.

'Your insults are getting formulaic, Faleria.'

'I worry about you. Don't do anything stupid.'

He moved toward the door and then stopped, a frown on his face.

'Where *is* Lucilia, anyway? I haven't seen her in hours. I thought at one point she was never going to let me out of her sight again.'

Faleria cast her eyes downwards.

'What?'

'We had a little chat, Marcus.'

His eyes narrowed as he turned back toward her.

'About?'

'About Verginius and Carvalia. Don't be angry with me, Marcus.'

Fronto's eyes hardened, and he began to grind his teeth.

'I specifically forbade her from talking to you about this.'

Faleria nodded.

'It was a long time ago, Marcus. It doesn't pain me to talk about it like it does you.' She smiled weakly. 'And her reasons for enquiring appeal to me.'

Fronto shook his head.

'She's an impulsive girl with idiotic ideas.'

Faleria fixed him with a strange look.

'She's been in Rome for over a week and has not yet even *asked* about the possibility of visiting the house of the Caecilii. Do you really think she has any intention of meeting her proposed match? Are you blind, daft or simply wrapping yourself in clothes of denial, Marcus?'

'I have neither the time nor the inclination to deal with this, Faleria. Go see her and try to persuade her to meet the Caecilii. I have more important matters to attend to.'

Faleria watched him leave the room and turn the corner before smiling that weak smile again.

'I'm not convinced about that, my brother.'

Fronto stormed through the house, grumbling. Since waking with a start to hear about Priscus' near miss in the forum, his mood had slowly slipped from disgruntlement into a deeper anger, but the fresh knowledge that Lucilia was prying into areas that were none of her business and causing Faleria pain, whatever she said, had pushed him into borderline fury. He ground his teeth as he slapped across the marble. Even the very air smelled angry and acrid.

Dithering for a moment, realising that goose pimples were rising on his flesh in the cold of the night and that his bare feet were not helping, he detoured by his room, slipped on his boots and gathered his scarf and a cloak before heading out toward the triclinium.

As he strode in through the door, a heated debate was in progress and the voices tailed off slowly, the occupants looking up at him.

Had his mood been lighter, he would have turned his surprise at the presence of Caesar and young Cicero into a quip. Instead, he continued to issue the low rumble of discontent that had begun back in his room.

'Fronto? I was given to believe you were recovering and would not be joining us?'

He glared at the general.

'Frankly, this is *my* house, Caesar. When plots are being hatched in it, I like to be involved.'

He nodded to Priscus and Galronus, sitting wearily back on a couch next to Milo. The Belgic officer was tending to a patch of bloody, matted hair with a damp cloth.

'I hear Clodius actually had the nerve to attack you in the streets?'

Priscus nodded.

'There were plenty of people about to start with, but I think you'd have trouble finding a witness if you tried. He organised it well: after dark, but during the early lull when most people are indoors eating. I'm afraid we lost some good men tonight.'

Fronto shook his head and then winced at the pain that brought, striding across the room to the flask of wine on the table and taking a swig directly from it.

'I told you we had to deal with him directly.'

Caesar shook his head.

'It's still not the time. Besides, after tonight every gang and private force the senators can muster will be out in the streets. It looks extremely bad for the government if one man's force is allowed to effectively control the streets. They will have to do something about it, and that means fielding their own gangs to try and maintain order.'

Milo leaned forward.

'But that's just asking for trouble; an escalation. Clodius has the edge on the streets. He has the largest gang in Rome and everyone knows it. If other people start trying to muscle him out, there's going to be trouble.'

Fronto smiled.

'And that gives us the chaos we need to deal with him unnoticed.'

Again, Caesar shook his head.

'He has an *army*, Fronto. You'll never get near enough.'

'I'm not having a repeat of the last discussion we had here.'

Caesar sighed.

'The streets are becoming too dangerous for a man to walk alone. The senate cannot keep control, and as soon as there are more gangs out in the night, eruptions will occur. If we sit back out of the way, Clodius is likely to make a slip. With the increase in violence, something will happen, and he will be named. Then there will be a trial, and he can be dealt with in the correct manner.'

Fronto shook his head.

'Banishment is not good enough. I want his head on a spike, pecked by crows.'

'But once he is tried and banished and out of the city, a great many options open up, Fronto. He will lose his land and his money. Without the money he won't be able to pay his thugs.' He smiled unpleasantly. 'And outside the pomerium, there are no weapon laws and soldiers can be soldiers, if you follow me?'

Fronto blinked.

'You would actually consider open war against him?'

'As I said, there are many options out there, but not within the city. He is just too powerful in Rome. Let things progress naturally and wait until he becomes a viable target, Marcus.'

Fronto sighed.

'I...'

He stopped and frowned.

'What time is it? I assume I slept through the evening meal?'

Priscus nodded.

'Hours ago. So what...'

But by now they were all frowning.

'Smoke!' shouted Cestus, and rose hurriedly from his couch, rushing to the door. 'That's smoke. Something's burning!'

As the room burst into activity, Fronto wheeled and ran from the room, stopping in the open peristyle garden outside. Spinning around in panic, he saw smoke rising from the rear rooms of the house, where the wall backed on to another street, a second column from the roof around the bath house, and a third from the atrium area at the front.

He shook his head desperately.

'Priscus? Cestus? Get your men out and check the house over. Get the slaves onto putting out any fires they can find.'

Paying them no further attention, he ran around the corner and into the main area of the house, his head snapping this way and that. The vestibule was filling with roiling smoke and orange flame licked at the front door and danced along the wall, mocking the altar to the

411

house's guardian spirits. The room where he had so recently been indisposed was empty; he could see directly through the doorway.

Ignoring the thumping in his head, he turned to his right and ran toward the apartments. As he entered the darker corridor that led to them and to the baths beyond, Faleria appeared from a side door, helping their mother, who was coughing and shaking.

'Marcus! What's happened?'

Fronto took a deep breath. Without even checking, he knew damn well what had happened.

'The house has been fired, Faleria. The front door's impassable, so get mother out into the garden where she can catch her breath. The servants and slaves will be coming through there too, and Priscus and Cestus are around.'

Without waiting further, he ducked past them and saw a half dozen of Cestus' men come racing around the corner from their bunk room near the baths.

'Try to put the fires out' he yelled at them

Pushing past them, he approached the door at the corner, wondering for a moment whether a polite knock was a good idea before settling on his course of action. He started to run and had to make a sudden adjustment as he realised that his left shoulder was a bad choice and turned, just in time to hit the door with his right, sending it smashing inwards with a crack. Lucilia sat bolt upright at the sudden intrusion.

'Come on!' Fronto yelled and grasped her wrist, hauling her out of bed and to her feet. She was, fortunately, merely resting while fully dressed and made panicky noises as he hauled her out of the room and into the smoke that was beginning to fill the corridors.

'What's happening?'

'*Clodius* is happening!'

As they raced around the corner toward the garden, Priscus appeared.

'The rear entrance is completely ablaze, Marcus.'

'Front too. We're going to have to try the outside gate.'

As they pushed on past the garden corridor, slaves and servants were now rushing around in the increasingly smoky house with buckets of water. Pushing open the side door and gulping down precious fresh air, Fronto glanced left and right. The stable and sheds were already catching alight from the rear rooms and he could hear the horses whinnying in fear and crashing around in their pens. To the right, the outer gate stood firm and solid.

Taking a moment, he stood Lucilia on the step.

'Breathe deep and stay here for a moment.'

She nodded, and he ran toward the gate, where Priscus was already beginning to lift the latch.

Fronto dived on him and pushed the latch back down, cupping his hand to his ear. The two men leaned forward to the crack between the gates. At least a dozen men stood outside, armed in contravention of the law, and the familiar hawklike figure of Philopater stood at the far side of the street, arms folded. As Fronto stared, his heart thumping, the men steadied grips on their weapons and stepped purposefully toward the gate.

'Shit!'

The two men turned and ran back to the side door.

'Come on.'

Grabbing Lucilia, they rushed in, slamming and bolting the door behind them before turning and running into the garden.

Slaves were now at work around the house, trying desperately to quench the flames, but fighting a losing battle. The officers and ladies stood in the centre of the small garden, a small force of Cestus' men with them. The rest would be in other parts of the house, trying to help the slaves put out the conflagration.

'We have company! Armed men are coming in.'

Cestus immediately began giving orders to his men while Faleria helped their mother across toward him, Caesar taking her other arm gently.

'What are the options, Marcus?'

Fronto shrugged.

'Both doors are infernos. The outer gate's alright, but that's where they're coming in. If we can hold the outside for a while, the civilians can climb onto the stable roof and maybe cross it and drop into the next street, assuming he hasn't got men there too?'

Caesar nodded.

'Then we'll have to put steel to steel. Do you have a spare sword in storage, Marcus?'

* * * * *

413

Fronto threw the door open and stepped inside. Behind him, Caesar walked into the room in a strange silence. Priscus whistled through his teeth.

'What sort of a man' Caesar asked quietly 'keeps an *armoury* in a private house in Rome?'

Fronto reached over to a chest against the wall and drew his gladius from its sheath, examining the glinting point.

'There's my campaigning gear here, as well as that that used to belong to my father and my uncle. There's stuff here that was gifts from Verginius and other family friends. You know how it is… one tends to hoard things.'

He turned and threw a gladius, still in its sheath, across to the general, who caught it in a deft hand and drew it, examining the blade.

'This was your father's?'

'Yes. Priscus, Milo, Galronus and Cicero, help yourself to anything you can find. Cestus, get your men armed.'

Priscus grinned, lifting a lengthy cavalry blade from a shelf, decorative and likely never before used.

'This'll surprise the buggers.'

'Come on.'

As Cestus shouted his men and pointed them toward the armoury, Fronto stopped in the garden and looked around until he saw Posco issuing commands to a group of slaves.

'Posco? Get into the stables with a few men. See if there's anyone in the back street. If not, break the wall down and get Bucephalus and the other horses out of there. Start getting the guests out too, beginning with Lucilia and the family.'

Posco nodded and grabbed three of the men gathered around him, running off toward the house's storage and stabling area. A crash outside announced that the attackers had broken down the outer gate.

'Come on! We've got to move.'

Fronto quickly doglegged around the corridor to the exterior door, ignoring the slaves and servants rushing desperately to their tasks, Priscus, Galronus, Milo, Caesar and Cicero at his heels as he ran.

The bolt was thrown back, and the six men burst out of the villa, weapons brandished and yelling defiance. The attacking gang had already spread out in the passageway outside, perhaps seven or eight between them and the stable door, countless others in the yard between them and the gate. The house's occupants, almost entirely military trained, fell into a defensive position without the need for commands and before the milling attackers even realised their victims were among them. Fronto found himself facing the gate, Priscus to his right and Caesar his left, while Galronus, Milo and Cicero formed a line behind them, facing the stable. The open door to the house stood between the rows of defenders and, realising that a means of egress had come available, the thugs of Clodius turned and launched a violent assault on the six men.

Fronto lunged at the first man to close on them, a tall, muscular man with a curved sica blade that suggested his origins lay in the arena. The man grinned, a section of his jaw missing, along with half a dozen teeth, evidence of an almost crippling wound long ago. With a deft flick of the curved blade he knocked Fronto's gladius aside. The man was good, and unconventional.

Fronto took a deep breath, wincing as he reached for the dagger at his belt with his bad hand, two fingers bound tightly to the others in order to heal correctly. Fortunately, despite the pain, the fingers the thugs had chosen to break would not prevent him from holding a hilt.

The gladiator swept a surprisingly fast and odd stroke, the sica dipping down and then coming back up, the concave edge angled perfectly for a lethal strike to the upper leg near the groin. Fronto was forced to leap back, momentarily inconveniencing Milo who stood behind him. His gladius dipped down to catch the deadly stroke, only just turning it away so that the point scored a jagged line across his leg above the knee.

He drew air through his teeth in pain as his bad hand fumbled the dagger's hilt, trying to draw it in the press. Beside him, Priscus was locked in a violent embrace with a man a foot taller than him, both too close to bring their weapons to bear. Caesar parried and struck repeatedly, almost perfectly evenly matched with a man that showed all the hallmarks of a veteran legionary. Had he had time to watch, Fronto would have been impressed with the strength and skill the general was displaying.

Instead, he was forced once again to suck in his gut as that swift curved blade made to hook his liver. Gods, the man was fast. Taking the brief opportunity afforded him, he lashed out with his gladius, but the man somehow had his sica in the way in the blink of an eye, pushing Fronto's blade up into the air. As Fronto marvelled at the sheer skill of this gladiator, the man took the opening he saw, head-butting the wounded legate.

Fronto's world exploded in pain, and for a moment he went completely blind with agony. His skull was already cracked and tender and the man had, likely purposefully, managed to land his blow on the already broken and bruised area.

He staggered, white light suffusing his world, and felt excruciating pain as that sharp point jabbed into his upper arm, slicing into muscle. Only his unpredictable staggering had saved him from the blow's intended fatal target.

His vision began to return, and he could see the broken-jawed man grinning at him as he drew the sica back to repeat his blow, this time with a more certain aim. As the man lunged forward, however, his eyes locked on his opponent, the dagger that Fronto had drawn and just managed to turn outwards slid into the man's belly with ease. The gladiator gasped, his eyes dropping to the hilt in his belly.

To his credit, he came on with the blow, ignoring the fatal thrust to his gut, but Fronto was recovering from the stun quickly now and ducked in underneath the man's sword, ripping the dagger out of the man's gut and then striking again and again, repeatedly hammering the blade into the tunic, the brown linen filling with blood that ran down from beneath and soaked his legs.

The gladiator was dead before he fell back, the curved blade toppling away to fall on the ground. Next to him, he saw Priscus still struggling in a bearhug with his opponent. Caesar was now beginning to lose the edge in his fight and, watching the next man bearing down on him, Fronto took advantage of the opportunity to strike a side blow at the general's attacker, thrusting his gladius into the man's ribs and whipping it back out in time to turn and face the next man.

Behind him there was a grunt, and he felt Milo collapse at his feet, the slumping form almost pushing him forward into his enemy. More men were coming at them from the gate; a seemingly endless supply of hired killers.

The smaller, wiry man before him made a textbook military thrust with a gladius and Fronto turned it with his own blade with only a little difficulty, wincing at the pain in his chest and arm as he did so. Again, his dagger lashed out, but the man danced back out of the way. Suddenly devoid of his target, Fronto took the opportunity

416

to change his footing. Milo, below him, was in a pile and bleeding, but groaning and alive. As the man before him made another strangely acrobatic leap forward and thrust with the gladius, Fronto ducked to the side and brought the pommel of his own sword down on the man's lunging wrist, smashing the bones so that the blade fell away helplessly to the floor.

The man stared at him in surprise, but Fronto had no time to savour the moment as the next man behind thrust with a long sword. Fronto grinned and shifted the prone, panicked and disarmed man into the path of the blow. The small attacker gasped as his companion behind drove the long blade through his back, the tip bursting from the man's rib-cage and coming dangerously close to continuing on and into Fronto.

A quick jerk turned the man by forty five degrees and ripped the impaling long sword from the next man's hand and Fronto let the body fall away, blade still projecting from him, as he lunged at the new target. Next to him he heard a yelp as Caesar, having just dispatched another attacker, suddenly succumbed to a blow from a man he'd not seen at the periphery. Behind, Galronus staggered against a wall, clutching his elbow.

'Get inside and close the door.'

Galronus looked like he might argue for a moment, but nodded, ducked through the door they were defending, and began to bolt it closed from within.

Behind them, the attackers that had become cut off from their main force had been dispatched, Cestus and his men issuing forth from the stables and stores and falling on them from behind. Now they faced only the attackers at the gate, though there were still many of them to come.

Fronto stepped back.

'Fall back. Defend the passage!'

As he stepped back again, Priscus disengaged from the huge man, and the two brought their weapons to bear. Caesar clutched his side and fell back in line with them, his sword point running with blood. The enemy rallied over the bodies of their fallen companions and two men stepped out from the crowd, one armed after the fashion of a Samnite gladiator and massively-built, moving in a crouch, the other lithe and reedy with a sword in each hand, both spinning in circles like the sails of a mill. The pair stalked forward, slowly and menacingly.

417

'Who the hell are *these* two?' Fronto said, almost sneering.

He felt a hand touch his shoulder.

'Those two are *death*, plain and simple. Get in the house.'

Fronto glanced round into the eyes of Cestus and, for the first time, saw uncertainty in the man's eyes. His urge to stay and fight evaporated with that look and he nodded to Priscus and Caesar. As Cestus and the giant Celt known as Lod stepped forward, accompanied by half a dozen other men, Fronto and Priscus hauled Milo to his feet, and half walked-half carried him back toward the stable. Cicero was spattered with blood and held the door open with a hollow expression as they passed through.

The stables had been brought under control, the advancing flames now out, steam and smoke mixing, filling the air with noxious fumes. Fronto caught sight of Posco.

'Have you opened an exit?'

Posco shook his head.

'There are several dozen men waiting in the road to the rear, master. I thought it prudent to concentrate on saving the stables and putting out the fire.'

Fronto nodded.

'Good.'

Gesturing to him, the group made their way into the storeroom and into the house proper. Barrels, sacks and boxes lay around, blackened and charred and now soaking wet. Most of the house's stores were clearly ruined, and structural damage had been done to the building itself.

'Think your man Cestus can hold them?'

Priscus nodded.

'If *anyone* can, he can.'

'Good. Posco? What's the situation?'

The slave shrugged.

'The rear door is still burning. We started getting it under control, but then it occurred that at this point it would just crumble if we put the fire out and then the rest of those men could get in, so we've contained it but let it burn.'

'Quick thinking, Posco. Good man.'

'The fire in the bath house was easy to put out, given... well, it's a *bath house*, sir. The Oecus is on fire, and there is still burning in your father's room, but the vestibule is under control, and the flames are almost out.'

Priscus smiled.

'Sounds like you've done a damn good job there. That could easily have gone the other way.'

Fronto nodded.

'Yes, very good. But the front door is clear, you say?'

Posco nodded.

'The flames are out, master. Everything is hot to the touch, and you can hardly see your hand in front of your face for the smoke, but the danger is past.'

Fronto grinned and turned to Priscus.

'Want to have a little fun?'

* * * * *

Paetus had been forced to move further into the shadows, aware now that Priscus, and therefore Fronto and possibly several others, were conscious that he still lived. He had changed accommodation and cursed himself for letting his activity become too open.

Clodia had ignored his warnings and pushed her vicious agendas until he'd been forced to take matters into his own hands and remove her from circulation. His opinion of Clodius had plummeted further, if such were possible, with the fact that he barely acknowledged the disappearance of his sister. Indeed, the man had been overheard privately stating his relief that she was no longer messing in his affairs.

And so Paetus had pulled back, returning to mostly just observing events and planning and so now he sat on the wall that surrounded the garden of the house across the road from Fronto's and looked down. Things had clearly not gone the way the attackers expected. He had counted forty five men with the Egyptian, and ten of them had split off to move into the street behind, presumably to prevent anyone effecting an escape.

He had initially wracked his brains for a way to warn Fronto or even to help, but such desire had melted away when he watched the attack progressing around the burning house and had seen, among the other defenders, Gaius Julius Caesar step out into the passageway, fighting for his life. At that point it had become a matter of supreme indifference which side won, as one of the two men he most hated in the world fought desperately against the forces of the other.

419

And then things had started to swing toward Fronto's defenders. Philopater, standing beneath Paetus' very position, shaded by the laurel leaves that flowed over the wall top, committed the small group of hardy men that had remained by his side and watched as the two psychopaths, known to the underworld as Castor and Pollux in a most impious fashion, moved in to shred the defenders.

Fronto's guards fought well, especially the one called Cestus. They were losing ground, being pushed back along the passageway, but they were making the attackers pay for every foot, and the Egyptian's force was rapidly diminishing. Every now and then the deadly Dioscuri twins would move to the front of the attack and cause mayhem before stepping back and letting the others do some of the work. Bodies from both sides littered the yard.

And then something happened that would stay with Paetus for the rest of his life.

The kindling and dried wood that had been stacked against the front door of Fronto's house, then sprayed with pitch and set alight had burned down quickly. The door had caught, and the flames had spread within, but the debris around the entrance had turned to a pile of grey charcoal, steaming in the damp night air and discolouring the house's white wall.

There was a faint click. Philopater had not noticed, his attention riveted to the scene of destruction that he had caused. Paetus, however, was in a commanding position, and was continually scanning the roof of the house to see where fire still burned.

The front door of the house swung open silently, a cloud of smoke billowing out of the aperture and into the street, entirely engulfing the façade.

At last Philopater became aware that something was wrong.

'What in the name of…'

The cloud billowed and bulged, carbon filling the air and ash settling on the glistening pavement and, as the haze began to thin in the gentle night breeze, three figures appeared in the gloom, stepping out of the cloud and into the street.

Paetus almost laughed as he realised that the figures were Fronto, Priscus and Galronus, all three daubed in carbon, their faces and hands blackened, their tunics dark grey with ash. They looked like lemures, the spirits of the restless dead. He could only imagine what Philopater saw, but the gasp from below told him the man was not moved to mirth.

As the three figures stepped into the air, carrying a blade in each hand, Fronto's two companions separated and stepped to the side, forming a strange, unearthly barrier between the fight in the yard and the events that were unfurling in the street outside.

'To me!' the Egyptian bellowed, his voice cracking with fear. Had he identified the men yet? Did he care?

The hired thugs paid no attention. They had not heard their master, involved they were in a fight to the death.

'*To me!*' he yelled again, desperation flooding into his voice.

One or two of the attackers at the back turned to look; one even strode across to the gate but, as his eyes fell on the black spirits stalking the street, he began to push the gate closed, wide eyed in panic. Paetus heard the gasp from Philopater as he realised his men had abandoned him to his fate.

The gate shut. Galronus and Priscus stepped to the side, to a position where they could leap to Fronto's assistance if needed, but could make sure that gate stayed closed and the other thugs unable to join them.

'Help me!' Philopater howled, backing away against the wall.

'No man in his right mind will help you, you Egyptian catamite!'

'*Fronto?*'

'In the flesh.'

The legate advanced slowly on his quarry, who backed against the whitewashed plaster, left with nowhere to run.

'I have just done my *job*, Fronto. Surely you understand that? Would you blame a soldier who attacked you? No; you would blame his commander: the man who sent him against you. Your argument is not with me, but with my master.'

Fronto smiled. Paetus was impressed at the effect of that feral white grin in the blackened face. It even sent a chill up *his* hidden spine.

'I think you do yourself a disservice, Philopater. You are known to enjoy your work. In fact you go above and beyond your orders at times. I think, though, that your end has finally caught up with you.'

The Egyptian, breathing fast and heavy, swept a sword from his belt; a short weapon with a strange, wavy blade of an Egyptian design.

'You will find, Fronto, that I do not submit so easily.'

He swept the blade through the air a couple of times with an expert flick of the wrist, creating pretty silvered patterns in the air.

Fronto swung the heavy Celtic blade - a prize from his first year in Gaul - in his right hand with negligent grunt severing the Egyptian's fist and carrying both it and the strange blade off down the street where they bounced and came to rest in a gutter, glinting silver and red.

Clodius' henchman stared at the severed wrist and the arc of blood that hung in the air for a moment before spattering the floor.

'I'm not looking for your submission.'

Fronto threw the heavy Celtic blade behind him, where Galronus, struggling with two swords already, caught it with difficulty. Paying no heed, Fronto swapped his gladius from his bad hand to the good.

'You'll understand if I don't use my left. I had a little accident recently.'

Philopater straightened.

'You are a Roman noblemen. I yield to you. Surely you will not strike down a surrendering enemy?'

Fronto barked a laugh.

'Oh surely you don't believe *that*? You're going to die now, Philopater. It just remains to be seen if it'll be like a man, or like a quivering coward.'

The Egyptian heaved in a deep breath and looked down at his missing hand. Shock was holding off the agony, but he knew that at any time that shock might wear off, and he would start to feel what had happened.

'You will make it quick? And certain? How a patrician would expect to die?'

Fronto frowned.

'Hardly a death you deserve, as I'm sure even *you* would agree?'

Philopater sighed.

'But you are *better than me*, or so you believe.'

Fronto narrowed his eyes.

'A quick, sure death then. On your knees.'

The Egyptian rolled his eyes upwards, muttering a prayer to one of the deities of his homeland, and Paetus ducked back into the shadows of the bushes on the wall top.

The legate stepped forward, his two companions approaching to be sure the Egyptian had no last moment deviousness in mind.

Philopater smiled as he pulled his tunic neckline down to reveal the olive flesh beneath and threw his head back, exposing his neck.

'Does it bother you that you yourself are now wielding a sword on the streets of Rome in contravention of your most sacred laws?'

'Shut up before I change my mind.'

Placing the tip of his gladius at the man's throat, just above the meeting of the collar bones, Fronto took a deep breath.

'Nemesis, my guide.'

As his strength fell behind the blow, driving the gladius down through the man's neck and windpipe, deep into the cavity of his chest, and straight through his heart, Fronto looked up and smiled.

The Egyptian gave a last sigh as the steel cut through his heart and swept his life away, blood fountaining up from the wound and adding to the grisly appearance of Fronto. The legate withdrew the blade and let the body fall away to the floor, gladius dropping to his side while his face remained raised.

'You can come down now. We appear to be alone.'

Paetus dithered for a moment, hanging back in the shadows.

'I know you're there. I saw you from across the street, before I struck the blow here. You have my word I will not stand in your way.'

Paetus shook his head angrily. Even now, trying to remain as uninvolved as he could, he had still failed. Biting his cheek in irritation, he dropped from the wall and landed on the pavement, his knees bent, a few feet from the leaking corpse.

'You look well, Paetus. Funnily enough, now that you're a civilian, or a ghost, or whatever it is you purport to be, you're in better military shape than you ever were as a soldier.'

The former camp prefect straightened.

'You, on the other hand, Fronto, are in the same state as ever: filthy and wounded.'

The other two were approaching across the street.

'Paetus.'

He looked up at Priscus and nodded respectfully.

'Why this strange charade, Paetus? What is it you want? Clodius? Caesar? Me?'

'Hardly you, Fronto. You must know I could have killed you a hundred times now if I'd wanted.'

'Indeed. Priscus tells me you've been something of a guardian spirit to the Falerii? I suppose I should thank you?'

Paetus smiled.

'More happy coincidence, really. My troubles are not with you, yet I did not set out to protect you, but to ruin Clodius. The two goals are happily often in concert, however.'

He cocked his head.

'You knew about me, but you've never mentioned it to Caesar? It warms me to you, I have to say, but I also have to enquire as to why?'

Fronto shrugged.

'Not everything is appropriate to report. You should go now. The fight inside will be over soon, and then the general will come out here. You don't want to be here when that happens.'

Paetus smiled.

'True. You've dealt Clodius a heavy blow tonight. He will seek revenge, and it will come like the breath of the draco, fiery and lethal. Get out of Rome as soon as you can. This will seem like a simple brawl compared to what he will do next.'

Fronto smiled.

'I will deal with it when it comes. Clodius will fall in time.'

'Clodius is mine, Fronto. Do not concern yourself with him. Events are even now in motion. His end is coming. Not immediately, but when it does it will be painful and ignominious. Leave him to me.'

The former prefect smiled at him and clapped a hand on his shoulder.

'It was good to speak to you again, Marcus.'

Fronto smiled in return.

'And you, but Clodius is only yours if you beat me to him.'

The two men stood for a moment in silence, and then the fugitive turned and disappeared down the street, fast and quiet.

'I feel for him.' Priscus sighed.

Fronto nodded.

'He was right about Clodius' reaction, though. Time for the Falerii to beat a temporary retreat, I fear.'

Chapter 23

(Late Octobris: House of the Falerii in Rome.)

Fronto stood in the atrium, gingerly rubbing his aching shoulder and side.

'What's the upshot?'

Priscus glanced across at Cestus, who straightened from where he leaned against the soot-blackened wall.

'We lost twelve men from the guard, two slaves to the attackers and two to fire. Three men are wounded, and one slave, but they'll all mend in time. That leaves the household support at six slaves and Posco, and fourteen guards, not including the seven we have out in the city.'

'And the enemy?'

Now Cestus smiled unpleasantly.

'Twenty eight dead.' His smile became yet more vicious. 'Well, there were twenty four, but we took the opportunity to finish off four more wounded ones we found when it got light.'

Fronto nodded.

'Not bad, given the circumstances.'

'There is one thing' the former gladiator said with a sigh. 'Castor and Pollux, the two assassins, escaped. Don't know how they got away, but they're not among the bodies. Too clever, that pair.'

Fronto frowned for a moment and then remembered the two killers that had come to the fore as Cestus sent the defenders inside.

'Nothing we can do about that. Philopater's body makes it all worthwhile, though.'

Priscus leaned against the wall.

'Have you decided what you're going to do with it? Going to send the skull to Clodius?'

Fronto shook his head.

'No. That's beneath us, Gnaeus.' He turned to Cestus. 'Get all twenty nine, including Philopater, into a cart, take them down to the end of the street, opposite Bona Dea, and dump them in a pile, weapons and all. Let's leave a no-nonsense message for Clodius.'

Cestus nodded and turned to leave, pausing for a moment.

'I'll take six men to help and leave eight here with you. The other lads in the city will be reporting in shortly, so you should be safe.'

As he left, Fronto and Priscus sighed and looked one another up and down.

'Time we hit the baths and got all this soot off, eh?'

Fronto nodded.

'In a moment. Something to do, first. I'll catch you up.'

Clasping hands, he watched Priscus hobble off toward the baths, before turning to stride wearily through the corridors toward the garden.

Faleria and her mother sat in the tablinum, along with Lucilia and Posco.

'Mother?'

'Marcus. Who does this man think he is to invade our house? If your father were still alive...'

Fronto smiled.

'The years he has been gone have somewhat magnified his legend, mother. I fear he would have fared no better than we. Rome is changing. The city he knew is gone, replaced by a lawless labyrinth of intrigues and criminals.'

He glanced across at Lucilia.

'And I brought you into it. I should not have done that. I should have left you in Massilia, and I'm sorry about that.'

The young woman shrugged.

'You are not to blame for the state of the republic, Marcus.'

He sighed and straightened.

'Rome is no longer safe for good people. It's no longer safe for the Falerii. You must leave.'

Faleria bridled and glared at him.

'If you think that a gang of cutthroats is going to frighten me out of the city...'

She faltered as Fronto swept his hand across in front of him.

'Don't be stupid, Faleria. You saw what happened last night. You've become targets now, and I simply won't have that. You are leaving the city; today. Cestus will send a dozen men with you. You need to pack everything you want to keep from here in three carts and prepare to move out. After lunch you will be on the road back to Puteoli. The villa there has many more staff and is a long way from the gangs of Rome. When you get there, Faleria, you will speak to the decurions of the town and hire a large force to 'work' the estate. You need a force of at least fifty men at all times to make sure you're safe.'

Faleria the elder nodded.

'He's right, daughter. Your father would not have blinked before sending us back to Puteoli.'

Fronto smiled.

'The villa has the added bonus that, being outside the city, you can legally support a large armed force and don't have to keep your blade sheathed.'

Faleria frowned angrily.

'You and Caesar should just bring the legions back from Gaul and sweep these scum from the streets once and for all.'

Fronto opened his mouth to speak, but the quiet, measured tone of the general cut in from the doorway.

'Be careful what you wish for, my lady. Remember Sulla, the martial law and the proscriptions? Do you really want to see that happen again? Soldiers in the streets, gutters full of blood and fear in the eyes of all? The legions must not enter Rome, or we might as well say farewell to the republic for good.'

She sighed, and the general smiled.

'Things will not always be like this. There are still men who care about Rome and her institutions: myself, Pompey and Crassus to name but three. Tomorrow we will meet and decide what must be done to put the city back in order, but Fronto is absolutely right to send you away in the meantime. Pompey has sent my daughter to his country estate already and my nephew-in-law has sent my niece and the children to his estate at Velitrae, though I am not convinced that will be far enough from the city for safety.'

'And I?' Lucilia said quietly. 'What is to become of me? Will you send me to the Caecilii, or back to Massilia?'

Fronto shook his head.

'For now, neither. The journey home is too long and unsafe without an escort, and I cannot spare the men. Equally, it is far too dangerous for you to stay in the city. Unless you have any objection, mother, I will send Lucilia with you to Puteoli?'

His mother smiled and reached out toward the young lady.

'She would be most welcome, of course.'

'Good. It is for the best, Lucilia. Depending on circumstances, I will hopefully come and join you all soon.'

As silence descended, Caesar stirred from where he leaned against the doorway.

'I have sent word to Pompey and Crassus to arrange a meeting tomorrow, out of the city and somewhere safe, in neutral territory. I would like you to be there, Marcus, along with several others. In the meantime I have a great deal to do and am short on time and assistance. Could I borrow Posco for a few hours?'

Fronto glanced across at his mother and Faleria, who shrugged and nodded.

'Very well, Caesar. I fear we will be mostly catching up on sleep until lunchtime anyway, while the staff sort the house.'

Faleria turned to the general.

'Shall we see you again before we leave, Caesar?'

The general smiled.

'I would consider it an insult if you left without my seeing you off. I shall return by lunchtime and add my own arm to your escort from the city.'

Fronto rolled his eyes.

'Silver-tongued old devil.'

Caesar gave him a sly smile and beckoned to Posco.

'Come, my friend. I have several tasks for you. Firstly a visit to the records of the tabularium in the forum. Do you have a stylus and tablet? You'll need them...'

As the two men left the room, Fronto walked across to help his mother rise from the couch. Every day she seemed a little older to his tired eyes.

'I think I had better rest a little' she sighed. 'The slaves will know what to pack, if the fires have left us much to take.'

Her son smiled at her sadly, and Faleria stood and took her mother's arm as the two walked from the room, leaving him, coated with thick black dust and blood, alone with Lucilia. He looked wearily around at the house with its charred marks, sooty footprints and general disarray. There would be months' worth of repairs to be done, though it was possible the house would be destroyed entirely this winter while unoccupied. Clearly he would not be staying here now.

'What will you do?'

He glanced round at the young lady who sat on the couch behind him. He had actually forgotten she was there.

'Caesar will arrange somewhere for Priscus, Galronus and myself to stay. Crispus offered us rooms with his family if we needed them.'

'Are you going to kill Clodius?'

Fronto turned and raised an eyebrow.

'I would love nothing more. Caesar is right, though: it cannot be done in the city. The weasel must be forced out of Rome before he can be dealt with. It may be a long job.'

He tapped his lip thoughtfully.

'Though there are other forces abroad that seek his end, and they are not so prey to Rome's laws and traditions as we. A vengeful spirit follows Clodius, and it is possible the man may meet the sunrise one morning lying next to his own head before I ever have the opportunity. For now it is more important to keep those we care about safe than to launch a dangerous war of revenge.'

Lucilia smiled.

'Your sister is more like you than she would like to admit, I think, Marcus. The pair of you argue and fight, spit and fume, but I believe you are closer than most, despite that.'

He sagged.

'Faleria is infuriating, but she is my sister. She is so much like my mother at times that I could almost scream. But then, in fairness, I am truly my father's son, and that cannot be easy on either of them.'

A silence fell over the room, and Fronto was surprised at how comfortable it felt. He suddenly wished he were accompanying them to Puteoli that afternoon.

'I have been unrelenting in my disapproval of you, Lucilia. It has made me a bad host and a bad friend. My apologies have been largely hollow and driven by wine.'

She smiled understandingly.

'Do not underestimate those around you, Marcus. I see nothing in you that I did not already know was there, and what you sometimes see as weaknesses, I can see as strengths. Your sister told me…'

She tailed off, uncertain as to how he would react, but Fronto merely sat back heavily on a couch and sighed.

'I know. She has spent years coming to terms with what happened, and I assumed she was still… unhappy about it. She is far stronger than I gave her credit.'

429

Lucilia smiled sadly.

'What happened to Faleria's husband was not your fault, Marcus.'

He shook his head vehemently.

'Yes it was. Verginius was killed by my inexperience, lack of ability and reckless attitude. I sent him to his death, and I'll never entirely forgive myself for that. And it was that which killed Carvalia too.'

Lucilia leaned forward.

'Faleria forgave you years ago. When the time comes, and you can forgive *yourself*, I suspect a world of opportunity and happiness might just open up for you. I know you're a perceptive man, Marcus, and you know my mind. I will wait for you in Puteoli until the demons stop chasing you.'

Fronto stared at her, a dozen emotions battering him in constant waves, leaving him feeling drained and yet less sure of himself. He watched as she rose, crossed to the door and, with a last, lingering look, walked off to her room, leaving him entirely alone.

Standing slowly, he crossed to the door, but she was already gone. Wearily he stepped across the threshold, around the peristyle, and to the armoury that stored so many memories. With a sigh, he lifted the baldric over his head, uncomfortably, and held the sheathed sword tightly. For a long moment he stared down at the weapon, a quality blade freshly made so many years ago for an eager young tribune heading off to fight with Caesar in Spain.

His finger traced the text picked out on the leather in bronze.

GN VERGINIO

With a last, deep, sigh, he returned the weapon to the rack on the wall before turning and heading for the baths.

* * * * *

Fronto grunted with the release of tension as he lay flat on the bench at the side of the caldarium. He had arrived at the cold bath to find the water a dark grey where first Galronus and then Priscus had dunked themselves. Shaking his head with a smile, he had added his own sooty coating to the slick floating on the surface and then strode through to the hot room to find Priscus standing at the large labrum, washing himself down to remove the last remaining traces of the filth.

430

The presence of a strigil and towel lying in a pile at the room's centre announced that Galronus had been and gone. The Belgic officer had taken to bathing after the Roman fashion, but still held a faint and unshakable distrust of the process.

'I see you decided to skip the full experience and just dip and wash?'

Priscus shrugged as he crossed the room and lay down on the bench opposite, the steam in the room billowing up and making Fronto's face hazy in the cloud of white.

'No slaves around to help scrape, and just too much shit to clean easily.'

Fronto laughed.

'Yes, I saw the cold bath. Looks like a sewer.'

Priscus sighed as he settled back.

'I've got rather used to this, you know? Two years of bathing in weed-infested Gaulish rivers makes you appreciate the simple comforts. Though at least a running river would clean us more thoroughly in this state.'

'We'll be clean enough.' Fronto smiled. 'Once we've seen the family off, we can drop in at the piscina publica on the way back for a swim. That'll get the last off.'

'You sound considerably calmer and more content than I've seen you since you returned to Rome.'

Fronto nodded, unseen in the mist.

'Strangely, despite all the trouble we're having, some things long overdue seem to be falling into place and I'm finding that I'm feeling curiously positive.'

It was Priscus' turn to laugh.

'That has the sound of a woman's involvement. You been cornered by that little morsel of Balbus'?'

A low rumble was Fronto's only answer, and Priscus laughed again.

'Thought so. She's been stalking you like a lion, you know.'

'Oh shut up.'

There was a light metallic clunk and Fronto laughed.

'I thought you were forgoing the scraping.'

'I am.'

Without time to breathe, Fronto rolled off the bench and painfully onto the mosaic floor as the tip of a blade slammed down through the slatted wood precisely where his sternum had been a moment before.

'Gnaeus!' he yelled as he rolled and came up into a crouch, naked but ready. The sounds of desperate movement through the mist and the faint view of shapes moving confirmed that Priscus was also busy.

Ducking back instinctively, Fronto saw the bulk of a large figure loom in the mist and swung his right fist with as much force as he could muster.

His knuckles connected with a helmet and a resounding 'clong' echoed through the vaulted room. Fronto cursed as he withdrew his hand, the fingers numb from the impact, and the gladiator's head became clearer through the clouds.

The helmet, a huge, iron construction, bulkier and far heavier than those used in the army, had a wide brim and a full faceguard, two round holes for the eyes the only elaboration. Two long blue feathers rose up decoratively beside the huge plain iron crest. Fronto's knuckles had not left a dent, unsurprisingly. The same could not be said in reverse.

He had only a moment to see the wide, battle-crazed eyes of the gladiator flashing white in the deep darkness of those two holes before the huge rectangular shield with its dented and marked bronze boss hit him full in the chest and sent him hurtling backward against the huge granite labrum, whose contents sloshed for a moment, slopping water onto the hot floor where it quickly burned off to steam.

Fronto shook his head in a daze and drew sharp breath at both the heat of the floor where he floundered and the pain in his shoulder, ribs and knuckles. Pushing himself up against the granite stand, he reached his full height for only a moment before he had to duck madly to avoid the swung sword that whistled past his ear.

'Shit, shit, shit, shit, shit!' he shouted, unable to concentrate enough to think of anything more useful, hoping that someone would hear the cry.

Quickly recovering, he danced out of the way of where he could see a vague looming shape and suddenly found himself a mere handwidth from Priscus, who pushed him back, just as a long, narrow and sharp sword swished through the air where he had been. Castor and Pollux had clearly marked their own targets.

As he staggered from Priscus' shove, Fronto heard the attack coming before he saw it and threw himself forward into a painful roll across the mosaic floor, the blade passing harmlessly over the top of him as he came back up against the bench where he had so recently been relaxing.

'A hundred denarii just to piss off and bother someone else' he yelled.

His answer came in the form of the gladiator's shield, swung out horizontally so that the dented bronze strip along the edge caught Fronto on the elbow, spinning him bodily and sending him sprawling across the bench.

Across the room he heard a cry of pain and could only hope it was the other gladiator and not Priscus that had issued the sound. There was no time to enquire, though, as, ignoring his throbbing elbow, he jumped up onto the bench, spied the looming shape of the huge man and kicked out as hard as he could.

The gladiator, even suffering such a restricted view, and all but rendered deaf by the huge helmet, pulled back out of the way, and the momentum carried Fronto off the bench and face first onto the floor.

How could the man be this alert and quick in such armour?

He struggled to turn onto his back and once again had to roll out of the way as the gladius slammed point first into the floor where he had been, sending up shards of plaster and half a dozen black and white tesserae.

Fronto scrambled away past the wide granite labrum, desperately trying to plan a useful move, but unable to come up with anything. The forbidding shape of that enormous helmet with its incongruously elaborate feathers appeared out of the enveloping mist, and suddenly the sword lunged across the huge bowl's flat surface, the water slopping this way and that, splashing Fronto's chest as he danced back and right, being sure to keep the huge labrum between them.

As the sword pulled back away, Fronto anticipated the next move and ducked down to his left as the huge shield swept horizontally across the water's surface, smashing the nozzle that fed the fresh water into the bowl and causing the jet to spray out at an angle.

He hardly had time to straighten again before he had to duck back out of the range of that thrusting blade.

And then he saw it coming.

433

Pollux made his mistake and Fronto, every bit as experienced in combat as the gladiator, recognised the opening for the opportunity it was and leapt on it.

Drawing the shield across, the gladiator repeated the sweeping blow, but this time as a backhand, the shield sweeping across the space as Fronto ducked sharply.

For a moment - no more - the shield was swinging harmlessly out of the way, and the sword was pulling back to the right for another blow.

Tensing, Fronto leapt bodily across the wide bowl, his finger tips wrapping themselves around the brim of the helmet and the feather-holder, his bound left hand scrabbling to maintain a grip on the short nozzle, snapping off the blue barb. His feet dangling as he lay across the bowl, his belly submerged in the cold water, Fronto hauled with every ounce of strength, yelping at the pain in his two broken fingers.

The move took the gladiator by surprise and the white eyes widened in their darkened hollows as he was pulled from his feet and slammed down face first into the bowl. The helmet disappeared into the cold water, the torrent running through all the gaps and holes in the iron construction and filling it in moments.

The huge man tried to shout, but the sound came out as submerged bubbles. The shield flailed and the sword jerked, trying to land a blow, but the man was prone, partially submerged and in desperation, bordering on panic. The gladius blow landed harmlessly on the granite edge of the labrum and the blade skittered away while the shield proved too heavy in the circumstances to lift over the top.

Fronto almost lost his grip as the huge, powerful killer struggled to free himself, and was forced to pull himself up and over until he was lying on top of the gladiator, both hands on the helmet, holding the face underwater.

Again and again the man bucked, trying to throw off his assailant until, after a lifetime of moments, the spasms slowed and the jerking stopped. Fronto held the head under the water for a count of forty, just to be sure, and then slid backward until his feet touched the warm floor. The gladiator lay still in the huge, shallow bowl, his heavy helmet keeping him anchored there, bubbles occasionally escaping a join in the helmet.

He stepped back, taking a heavy breath, and suddenly became aware of the continuing grunts and scrapes of fighting across the room in the fog.

'Priscus?'

'Bit busy!' the reply came, sharply.

Fronto squinted into the mist and could just make out two shapes moving in the whiteness. A whirring confirmed which one was the double-bladed Castor.

Grimacing, Fronto stepped back to the slumped figure in the bowl. The sword had gone from the man's hand sometime during the last throes of the struggle and could be anywhere on the floor in the mist. Narrowing his eyes, the weary legate crossed to the far side and worked the shield straps free from the man's arm until the huge, rectangular item was in his hands.

Gritting his teeth, he padded quietly, barefoot, across the patterned floor toward the shadowy shape. Priscus had somehow managed to pull a heavy wooden slat from the bench and was using it like a sword to parry the blows of the gladiator, though the state of the wood and the tinny, acrid smell of blood announced that he wasn't doing very well.

Smiling, Fronto approached the killer and raised the shield above his head.

'Hello' he said warmly.

The man spun round, a sword flicking out, ready to deliver a horrible blow but, as he did so, Fronto brought the huge, heavy shield down hard on the man's unprotected skull, the rounded bronze boss smashing into his forehead just above the eye. The blow was hard enough to send the gladiator flat to the floor, his swords falling away, unheeded, as he passed from consciousness in an instant.

Priscus looked up at him in surprise as he lowered the wooden slat.

'A shield? Really?'

Fronto shrugged.

'You'd prefer I spent some time scouring around for something better?'

Priscus laughed as he reached down and gingerly touched a deep wound on his forearm.

'Thanks. Your style's a bit peculiar, but your timing's excellent as always.'

He paused to deliver a hearty kick, full of feeling, to the unconscious gladiator.

'What do we do? Tie him up and interrogate him?'

'No point' Fronto shrugged. 'We know damn well who he was working for and what he was trying to do. Never leave a vengeful enemy behind you.'

Reaching down, he picked up one of the man's swords and examined it.

'Ever seen one like this before?'

'Nope. Thin and sharp. Some sort of cavalry weapon I suppose. Hurts, though, I can confirm that for you.'

Fronto smiled as his friend fingered another wound on his thigh.

'Get those cleaned up. Lucilia will stitch them for you. If you're lucky, she might give you a carrot too.'

Priscus frowned at him in incomprehension as Fronto leaned over the prone gladiator and carefully positioned the narrow blade over the heart before leaning on the hilt with his full weight and driving the blade home until he heard the point scraping in the mosaic below. The gladiator gave what sounded like a sigh of relief and shuddered once.

'I always love the games. Gladiators are so *exciting*' Fronto said with a grin as Priscus reached the labrum, pushed the body out of the way, and started to wash his wounds with the cold water, drawing sharp breaths each time.

'I personally have had about as much excitement as I can take in one day. Can we just have a little boredom for a while, now?'

Fronto laughed as he dropped the blade and sat on the bench.

'I was contemplating bed for a while after this to catch up on my sleep, but now I'm favouring surveying the damage to the wine store. What d'you think?'

* * * * *

Caesar smiled and gave a tug on the straps that held the baggage tightly in the second cart. With a nod of satisfaction, he stepped back.

'It would seem that you are all set, ladies.'

Fronto rolled his eyes as he leaned against the slightly carbon-stained gatepost. Both he and the stable hand had checked the straps more than once, but Caesar had to give his approval and win the smiles of the three women in the front carriage. It was, to Fronto's mind, born of a pathological need to be lauded for even the smallest things.

436

Turning to look out into the street, he spied Cestus standing at the far side, looking back and forth.

'Are we good to go?'

The former gladiator had a last check, motioned to a few of his men, and then nodded. Fronto smiled at the three ladies in the wagon.

'Time to go. Once you're beyond the Porta Naevia, stick to public places and don't wander out of sight of Cestus and his men. The mansios on your route should be good and secure, but avoid anywhere you suspect might be trouble. Just stay quiet, unobtrusive and safe.'

Faleria leaned over the side of the wagon.

'For the tenth time, Marcus, we know. We'll be alright. It's those of you staying in the city *I* worry about.'

Fronto smiled.

'Let's move.'

At a wave Posco led the carriage out into the street, the other two wagons grinding and squeaking behind as they began to rumble forward. Fronto accompanied the vehicle with the three ladies, Caesar matching his position at the far side. Priscus sat on the bench of the rear cart, saving his leg as much of the walk as possible. It would be only a count of maybe three hundred to the gate, and then the party would continue to accompany the caravan for the next mile or so until they were clear of the urban area.

Slowly, the three vehicles, accompanied by almost two dozen men, rolled out into the street and, turning, began the slow descent from the Aventine toward the temple of the Bona Dea at the junction with the Via Ardeatina. Fronto glanced across at the general. It would have been closer and more direct to leave the city by the Porta Capena and straight onto the Via Appia, rather than this roundabout route that required a connecting road a few miles south, but Caesar had been insistent that this path would be the safest, and the ladies fell over one another to agree with the great orator, whatever Fronto's opinion.

He grumbled irritably as he walked.

Slowly, the group reached the lower end of the street, the edges here lined with beggars, the concentration increasing as they neared the temple. It had not rained now for days, and the streets were beginning to look filthy, coated with animal dung and general detritus. Fronto's grumbling intensified as he trod in something soft.

Out to the front, Cestus and Lod stepped out into the main road, and the gladiator waved a hand. The carts rolled to a halt, and Fronto and Caesar loped on ahead to meet the small warrior. As they reached the junction, the reason for Cestus' gesture became clear.

Off to the left, toward the Circus Maximus, the street was lined to either side with busy stalls, interspersed with beggars, drunks and occasional respectable folk. The open street in the centre was, however, devoid of the general citizenry of Rome. A surly gang of several dozen men, a match for their own force at least, stepped slowly and menacingly toward them, hammers, pick handles and lengths of wood in their grasp.

'Shit. Clodius has absolutely no fear, does he?'

Caesar nodded and made a very subtle hand gesture.

'Keep moving on slowly and purposefully. All will be well.'

'I hope you're right.'

The two men retreated toward the carts and their escort and Cestus returned to his position at the front as the caravan turned away down the street. Lod fell in at the rear, walking backward as six of the guards fell in beside him, carefully eying the sizeable gang that was following them slowly, stalking like a predator cat.

'Why they no fight?'

Fronto, glancing over his shoulder at the huge Celt, was wondering the same thing, and then shook his head in irritation as the answer popped into his head.

'Because there's more of them ahead. We're being herded.'

Caesar nodded.

'That is possible, but here the road is far more defensible than by the Porta Capena should the situation arise. I think we will be fine, Marcus.'

'You keep saying that, but even if that's fully half their force out here, it still means we're outnumbered two to one.'

The two men fell silent as the carts rumbled on along the street, the population thinning out here as they moved away from the temple and toward the gate and the slumlike region that clung to the outer wall like some parasitic sea creature. Certainly Caesar had been correct about the more defensible nature of this route. The less affluent neighbourhoods in the area led to the insulae and walled blocks to either side of the street pressing in and narrowing the thoroughfare.

438

A movement caught Fronto's attention, and he glanced across at a narrow side street. Three men were moving slowly down it toward them, wooden clubs in hand. Every ten steps or so brought them past another side street, each with its own small group of thugs converging on them.

'There's going to be a hundred of them by the time we reach the gate' Fronto noted to Caesar, nodding in the direction of the latest arrivals. The gang following them had almost doubled in size as they moved slowly on.

'It's important we keep moving. The closer we are to the gate, the safer we are.'

Fronto held less certainty about the defensive nature of the area, but there seemed little else to do as they moved slowly on, the tension building constantly.

'Clodius must have an almost infinite supply of thugs. It's almost as if he breeds them!'

On the cart just above and behind them, Priscus pointed ahead.

'There's the gate. We're almost there.'

Fronto glanced past the shoulders of Cestus and his companion. The Porta Naevia with its single arch of heavy travertine blocks crossed the road fifty paces ahead, just coming into view as they rounded a gentle curve in the road.

'We're going to make it.'

The carts rumbled on, closing the distance with interminable slowness, and the huge arch grew ever more tantalisingly near, the heavy gates standing open to either side.

'Why is there no one around?' Fronto said nervously.

Caesar shrugged. 'One armed gang following another? Even the rudest peasant can spot that kind of trouble approaching, Fronto. You expect them to stay around for the show?'

'Crap.'

Cestus stepped into the shadow of the gateway, three more of his men with him, and the lead carriage rolled under the arch. Fronto bit his cheek.

Behind them they could almost sense the tensing of muscles ready to attack. The silence was taught and dangerous.

'Whoa!'

Fronto's head snapped back to the light at the far side of the gate. Cestus, silhouetted in the arch, was holding up his hand and the

439

wagons were quickly slowed and stopped. The gang behind came on at an even slower pace, closing the gap.

Fronto was about to shout a question ahead to Cestus when he saw the rest of Clodius' men, spreading from the sides of the street into the gateway, blocking the path ahead.

'Shit. What now?'

Caesar arched his brow and shrugged.

'Now we see what they have to say.'

The two men strode out forward into the shadows until they fell in alongside Cestus. There were perhaps three dozen men in the road ahead. A fight now would be virtual suicide. Some of the men, being outside the city, had taken the opportunity to arm themselves with real weapons. To the rear, a tall man with a scar down his face that permanently closed one eye stepped up. The mob parted before of him.

'You appear to have reached the end of the road. My master sends his regards. He hopes you will allow us to make this quick and painless.'

'Your master can kiss my hairy pink arse!' Fronto barked.

Caesar cast a sidelong glance at Fronto, and there was a genuine smile there.

'*What*?' Fronto hissed back at him.

'You really must have faith in your general, Marcus.'

He turned to the Falerii's chief house slave, standing by his shoulder.

'Now, Posco, if you would?'

The slave nodded with a smile and drew a small copper horn from the cart beside him. Taking a deep breath, he blew a series of loud, sharp notes and then lowered it. Fronto narrowed his eyes.

'Where did you learn the muster call, Posco?'

The slave merely gave him an enigmatic smile and pointed.

Ahead, beyond the armed gang that barred their way, more men were appearing from the side of the road, falling in to the street and settling in ordered rows.

Caesar smiled at the tall, scarred thug, who was looking over his shoulder in surprise.

'Would you like to kiss Fronto's 'hairy pink arse', or just get the hell out of our way?'

Fronto blinked.

'Who *are* they?'

The men were falling into military formation and, though in plain tunics and cloaks, a number of them bore a gladius or pugio or a solid legionary shield on their arm.

Caesar grinned.

'Sound off!' he bellowed.

From the depths of the large unit, still increasing in strength, voices called out.

'Servius Tarcus, centurion of the Ninth Legion... retired.'

'Aulus Octavius, optio of the Seventh Legion... retired.'

Other voices were announcing their origins among the crowd, and Fronto turned to frown at Caesar, whose grin widened.

'You'd be surprised how many veterans of my legions there are within the city's bounds, Fronto, and most of them hold a loyalty that goes far beyond receiving their honesta mission. Some of them are *your* men, even.'

Fronto blinked again and turned to look over his shoulder. The advancing mob behind them had stopped. Lod stepped forward and crouched menacingly.

'Boo!' he barked, and some of the men at the front of the gang actually jumped.

Caesar stepped toward the tall, scarred spokesman.

'Disperse immediately or pay the penalty for public disorder. Your choice.'

The man stood silently for a moment, clearly weighing up his options, but the decision had been made for him. The men of his gang melted away at the periphery into the side streets and doorways, and he stood at the centre of a rapidly shrinking force.

'Run, then, and don't come back' the man said to Caesar defiantly.

The general grinned.

'Oh, we're not *all* leaving. Some of us have business yet in Rome.'

The man dithered again, fumbling for another pithy retort but, realising there were now less than a dozen men between him and a century's worth of veteran soldiers, he threw an angry glance at them, let out an exasperated grunt, and ran off into a side street.

Fronto shook his head.

'You *do* like to show off, don't you? Did it not occur to you to let me in on it?'

'And spoil the surprise?' Caesar grinned. 'Hardly.'

441

He looked up at the three women, each heaving sighs of relief.

'Well ladies, it would appear that the way ahead is clear. The veterans of my legions will join Cestus and escort you as far as Albanum and the mansio there. I hope the sea air agrees with you and that we will meet again very soon.'

The ladies of the house of the Falerii smiled gratefully at the general and, waving at Fronto, gestured to Posco to move on. As Priscus slipped down from his seat and wandered across to the officers, Lucilia leaned over the edge and planted a difficult and somewhat unexpected kiss on Fronto's forehead.

'Hurry back, Marcus.'

Fronto stared at her as the vehicles trundled on, the legionaries falling into escort positions as he rubbed his head and looked at his fingers suspiciously.

Turning, he realised that Priscus and Caesar were both grinning at him.

'Oh, grow up!'

Chapter 24

(Late Octobris: On the Janiculum, overlooking Rome.)

'I can't see why they couldn't have met in the city' Priscus grumbled, massaging his painful hip as he stumped slowly up the sloping gravel path.

'Neutral ground. They are the three most powerful men in Rome, so I suppose it's symbolic.'

'Sym-*bollocks* is what it is!'

Fronto smiled at his friend. Behind them, Galronus stomped up the path, showing no sign of fatigue. Fronto glared at him and, turning, plodded wearily on. Ahead of them, Caesar walked quietly, as though out for a stroll to enjoy the late autumn air, Aulus Ingenuus striding along beside him, armed now they were well outside the city's pomerium.

Ingenuus had tried desperately to persuade the general, in light of recent events, to allow the entire contingent of his cavalry guard that had returned from Gaul to escort him today, but the general had insisted on a small accompaniment only.

Ahead, a small group of men loitered at the hill's crest, lounging on benches or leaning on the decorative balustrade. Fronto squinted and could make out the figure of the younger Crassus, clad in his dazzling white toga. Fronto mentally dismissed the showy garment; whitening it with chalk was a practice rarely carried out these days, and yet, he could not help but nod with approval when he spotted the tip of a gladius sheath below the hem.

'Looks like Crassus and his men are already here.'

Behind them, Galronus hurried to catch up.

'I still do not understand the importance of this. We should be concentrating on Clodius, surely?'

Fronto smiled.

'In a way, we are. I had a lot of time to think last night, Gnaeus, and every time we've pushed Clodius, he's pushed back harder, and each time it's not us that gets the brunt of it, but my family. I sat chatting to Nemesis last night and came to the conclusion that I had a choice: vengeance against Clodius or looking after those I care about and that simply *has* to come first. The time to deal with Clodius will come, but when there is no chance of the backlash destroying the

443

Falerii. Anyway, these three men can, between them, make almost anything happen in Rome; or stop it happening. The chaos in the city is only rife because these three are not working together and therefore letting it happen.'

He became aware of Caesar watching him with a frown.

'Not specifically because of you' he added wearily. 'But it needs sorting out.'

As the general turned back to face their destination, Fronto glanced ahead and then back over his shoulder. The temple of Janus on the hill's crest had been chosen carefully as the venue for a number of reasons: it was neutral territory for the three men; it was sacred ground, and no true Roman would commit an act of violence within; it offered an unrivalled view to aid privacy and safety; last of all, the two faced Janus was the master of beginnings, changes and choices and the symbolism of the god's shrine would not be lost on any man present.

Behind them, the gravelled path led down the Janiculum hill in a wide arc to the Pons Aemilius that would take them back to the city when this was over. Fronto noted with interest part way back down the path, among the rapidly thinning foliage, Pompey striding up the slope with a certain speed as though he were late, half a dozen men rushing along around him, some carrying goods.

'How long do you expect the meeting to take?' Fronto asked.

'I really have no idea, Marcus. If all goes well and my peers share my vision of the coming year, we could have everything settled within the hour. Rarely, however, do we all see quite eye to eye without some levelling of the ground.'

Fronto grumbled something under his breath.

'What was that?'

'I said we should have brought lunch with us.'

Caesar laughed and sighed, stretching, as he reached the top of the path and stepped out onto the paved walkway surrounding the small temple. Nodding at the younger Crassus, he gestured to the temple's open doorway. Crassus nodded.

'Father is in there, alone. He is waiting for you, general.'

'Thank you.'

With sighs of relief, Fronto and Priscus clambered up the last step and onto the walkway, the latter immediately slumping onto the low, stone balustrade and kneading his leg.

'I am getting bloody sick of hills. Why couldn't Romulus and Remus have gone west instead of north? Rome could have been built somewhere flat with a beach!'

Ingenuus strode off toward Crassus and the two fell into quiet conversation as Fronto and Galronus leaned on the railing next to Priscus.

'Nice day' the Gaul noted, looking at the hazy mauve sky through the sparse trees.

'Make the most of it. It'll be about the last good day of the year, if I'm any judge.'

Priscus looked up, grinning.

'Nice to see you're as optimistic as ever.'

'Sod off.'

The sound of feet tramping on gravel increased and finally Pompey, his strangely chubby, good-natured face rosy from the climb, appeared at the platform.

'Good morning, gentlemen. My hearty apologies for any tardiness.'

Crassus, behind them, spoke quietly and respectfully.

'No tardiness, master Pompey. Caesar and my father await you inside.'

The general smiled warmly at them.

'I had the forethought to have wine and food brought up for you all, in case this goes on too long.'

Behind him, three of his men crested the slope and carried a large basket and an amphora across the paving, laying them to rest near the spot where Fronto leaned on the balcony with his friends.

'Thank you' Crassus nodded, and Pompey gave them a military salute before striding into the temple, turning and closing the door as he entered.

Priscus grinned and slapped his hands together as he watched the basket being opened and spied the array of bread, fruit, meats and cheeses within. One of Pompey's men began removing the contents and arranging them on trays.

'Nice.'

Fronto grinned and, crouching, reached inside.

A sharply-drawn breath and he suddenly paused. His hand withdrew and he stepped back to his friends at the railing. Priscus frowned. The legate's face had slid into an angry grimace.

'What's up?'

Fronto grabbed his arm and turned him round so that the three of them leaned forward over the railing, looking down toward the city, facing away from the crowd.

'I *know* him.'

'Who?'

'That man of Pompey's. He's not actually Pompey's man.'

Priscus sighed.

'Try and make more sense.'

Fronto grumbled.

'He's got two rings on his fourth finger. I saw them together recently, holding down my leg while that Egyptian bastard Philopater beat me to a pulp.'

Galronus frowned at him.

'You're sure? No one else could be wearing those rings?'

The legate shook his head.

'I'm positive. Galronus, no Roman man wears more than one ring. It's tasteless, gaudy and simply not done. But the rings are fairly memorable too. They're both signet rings.'

Priscus narrowed his eyes, and Fronto nodded.

'A lion with a sword?' he said quietly.

'That's Pompey's seal!' Priscus said, his tone incredulous. 'He trusts one of his men with his own seal?'

Fronto waved his hands, trying to warn his friends to lower their voices. He took a quick glance over his shoulder and was irritated to see that, while the man was still emptying the basket, he was also watching the three of them attentively.

'The other one shows a cornucopia. Ring any bells?'

Priscus nodded.

'Clodius. So what do we do?'

Fronto shrugged.

'I favour flattening his face into the floor, myself.'

Priscus nodded his agreement and the pair started violently as Galronus suddenly jumped up.

'He runs!' the Remi officer shouted.

Fronto and Priscus spun around, but the man had abandoned his basket and was already away, disappearing around the rear corner of the temple to the astonishment of the rest of the gathered escort.

Without comment or question, Galronus was already off, his feet pounding on the slabs as he ducked and weaved between the goods being offered around and the gathered dignitaries and servants, heading toward the corner around which the man had run.

Fronto picked himself up and ran after them and Priscus, sighing and muttering about his leg, stood and hobbled at high speed around the near side of the temple in the hope of cutting the man off and saving himself a run.

The panting legate rounded the end of the temple at speed, vaguely aware of the sound of heated debate coming from within as he entered the shade at the building's rear, his head snapping this way and that. The man had vaulted over the balustrade at the far side and was busy speeding away down the hill, away from the city and toward the Via Aurelia, Galronus close behind and running with the speed of a horse and the surety of a mountain goat.

Managing a somewhat graceless and clumsy leap over the railing, Fronto continued his pursuit, Priscus appearing at his awkward pace at the far side of the temple.

There would be little chance of either of them catching the man at this pace; it was all down to Galronus, though that was clearly no long shot, given the strength and speed of the man.

Suddenly Fronto's world spun and blurred as his running foot came down on a fallen apple and slipped, sending him into a forward roll that carried him a dozen paces further down the slope, where he slid painfully to a halt. Angrily, he rubbed his head, brushing the sticks from his hair, and stood, gripping one of the many fallen apples that lay scattered around on the slope. For a moment, he glared at the fruit angrily.

Ahead, Galronus had closed and was almost on the running man. Tensing, the Remi warrior leapt, hurtling through the air and hitting the man just below the waist, his arms wrapping around the target's legs. As Priscus came sliding to a painful halt next to Fronto, the pair watched Galronus and his prey disappear in a flurry of arms and legs, leaves, sticks and dust hurtling into the air and forming a cloud around them.

Moments later, the fugitive managed to struggle free and clambered to his feet, drawing back his leg to deliver a mighty kick to Galronus' ribs when Fronto's thrown apple caught him on the temple with a surprising amount of force, knocking him back to the ground, stunned.

Fronto grinned at Priscus, who shook his head.

'How the hell you pulled off that throw I'll never know. I've seen you at festivals trying to put a ball in a bucket. You couldn't hit the Porta Fontinalis with a rock if you were standing underneath it.'

Fronto's grin widened, but there was an absence of humour in it.

'You forget; Nemesis is my patron, and she's working hard today.'

The two men picked their way down the slope, being careful not to fall and tumble once more. Ahead, Galronus had restrained the fugitive and now had his arms wrenched around behind his back in a painful and restrictive manner. A moment more and the Fronto and Priscus joined the pair. The man had recovered from his stun, but his struggling had died down, pinned as he was. Fronto narrowed his eyes.

'Clodius must value you to let you wear his seal like that? And Pompey too?'

The man merely drew a deep breath and glared, silently.

'I'm sure you remember me?' Fronto asked pleasantly. 'I remember *you*, for certain. Have you *nothing* to say?'

'If you value your life, you'll let me go' the man barked, a hint of menace in his voice. Fronto laughed.

'You're hardly in a position to dictate terms. Clodius can't threaten me any more than he already does. I'm not afraid of him.'

The man snorted.

'It is Pompey Magnus of whom I speak. I am *his* man and he will not take kindly to this treatment of his factor.'

Priscus sighed.

'I think you'll find that Fronto here considers himself beyond and above mere politics. I honestly believe he thinks he's the hand of Nemesis at work.'

Fronto grinned.

'I'm going to start by breaking two of your fingers in return for mine. Then I'll decide on the next move, while Priscus sources a hammer for me.'

The man's eyes widened.

'You wouldn't? You couldn't? My master will kill you!'

'Which one?'

The man opened his mouth and started to babble desperate threats and promises, but Fronto reached to the hem of his tunic, snagged in his fall, and tore a strip from it, balling it up and shoving it forcefully into the man's throat, gagging him.

Galronus frowned.

'Do you not wish to interrogate him?'

'Hardly worthwhile.'

Reaching down, he grasped the man's middle finger and, with a jerk, snapped it to vertical. The man's muffled scream brought a smile to the legate's face.

'Ah, the beauty is truly not in the receiving, but rather in the *giving* of gifts.'

The man's eyes widened again, tears rushing down his cheeks as Fronto grasped his fourth finger, ready to snap it.

'Wait!' Priscus grinned. 'I may have a better idea.'

As Fronto let go of the finger, his head cocked to one side, Priscus drew his pugio dagger from the belt around his tunic. Gripping the same finger carefully, he positioned the blade. The man realised what he was doing and tried hard to struggle free, but Galronus' grip was vicelike.

He screamed into the balled cloth as Priscus severed the finger with the two rings on. Holding it out to Fronto, the former centurion grinned.

'Evidence.'

The legate stared at the finger and slowly broke into a smile.

'I'd best go put this to good use. Could you two do me a favour and break any part of him that's supposed to bend? Careful not to kill him though. I want to send him back to Clodius alive.'

Turning his back on the nods of his two companions, Fronto smiled down at the finger in his hand bearing the priceless seal rings of Clodius and Pompey. With a light laugh, he set off back up the hill toward the temple, ignoring the unpleasant noises behind him.

* * * * *

Caesar shook his head.

'We should be *above* this, gentlemen. We agreed on a course of action at the start of the year at Lucca that should have secured things for all of us in Rome and beyond and provided a solid foundation for our work in the coming year.'

'We did' Crassus agreed, nodding, 'and I have seen no reason to change our plans. You keep Gaul and Illyricum, Pompey keeps Spain, and I get Syria. Our various factors and clients manoeuvre things in Rome for us, and everyone is happy. Why reconsider?'

Caesar shook his head.

'Things are *not* working out, though. Clodius continues to rabble rouse and interfere in Rome. There is violence and almost outright war on the streets. Cicero, Cato and others work to bring me down in the senate and, while that affects *me* directly rather than you, think on how it weakens our alliance. We are interdependent. We cannot allow weakness in any one of us, for fear it brings down the others.'

He sat back against the temple's cold wall.

'No. It will simply not do to have the three of us absent from Rome for at least a year, with mere assistants attempting to keep things moving for us here. Rome needs to be gripped with a strong hand and guided, else the chaos and disruption I have seen in the streets in the past week will simply escalate until we are faced with disaster.'

Crassus was nodding slowly.

'I agree to an extent; things *are* getting out of control in the city. I will be leaving my son in the city in a position of some importance. In *him* I have the utmost trust, but I am not sure about any others.'

Caesar smiled.

'I have seen your son at work, my dear Crassus. He will not fail you, but *we* three are the men who have the strength and the will to push Rome in the right direction and you both know that. Withdraw our direct guiding hand and people like Clodius and Cato will gain the upper hand.'

Pompey, until now largely silent, sat forward.

'We only need one man in Rome. With the governorship of Spain, I have already maintained the province from here the past few years, and I can continue to do so. I may have to visit a few times, but there is nothing to stop me remaining in Rome.'

He smiled.

'Indeed, my theatre will be completed next year, and I would wish to be in the city for its inauguration and the first shows anyway. I could be the man of whom you speak, guiding Rome, while the pair of you deal with Syria and Gaul.'

Crassus nodded again.

'The plan has merit, Gaius. With Pompey in the city keeping control, I can settle in Syria and prepare to move into Parthia. You would be free to consolidate Gaul and consider your next move.'

He smiled sadly.

'I am aware that there is some disparaging talk about your conquest, but with a year to consolidate with no rebellions, you can be sure of the province before moving on.'

Caesar sighed.

'You would need more power than you currently have, Pompey, if you alone were to try and control the heaving hydra that is Rome.'

He pursed his lips.

'We considered the consulship at Lucca but put aside the idea as something that might provoke a negative reaction to our alliance. Since we already *have* that reaction now, let's use the consulship. We can arrange to have the two of you voted into the consulship together. Between you you would effectively have control of the city.'

'What about you?'

Caesar smiled at Crassus.

'I will be far too busy to attend to the duties of a consul in the coming year. You, however, will have at least a year in Syria before you could even consider attacking Parthia. You can stay in contact with Pompey here and the two of you would be able to keep things under control. Is that not the answer?'

There were nods from the other two men.

'It's workable' Pompey smiled.

'But' Caesar added, gesturing with a cautionary finger 'this would be for the benefit of us all, and of Rome itself, and not for personal gain.'

He concentrated his gaze on Pompey.

'I would expect you, in my absence, to maintain my reputation and keep my enemies muffled in the senate as you would do for yourself. I hope we understand one another?'

Pompey nodded, his brow furrowing slightly. Crassus looked back and forth between the two men, an unspoken question in his expression.

'I...' Pompey began, but there was a knock at the door.

The three men exchanged surprised glances, and Crassus, nearest to the entrance, rose from the seat.

'Come in?'

The great bronze portal swung open with a metallic creak and dazzling sunlight invaded the gloom of the temple. The figure silhouetted in the doorway slowly resolved itself into the shape of Fronto, his arms folded.

'Marcus? We were not to be disturbed. This is most discourteous.'

Fronto stepped slowly into the shadow and bowed.

'I apologise for my breach of etiquette, gentlemen. I realise your time and privacy is important, and I shall not keep you, but for a moment.'

'Get on with it, man' Crassus sighed.

Fronto nodded.

'Yes, of course. I have a message for master Pompey that could not wait until after the meeting.'

Pompey smiled at him warmly.

'Indeed?'

Fronto strode across to him, bowed, and withdrew a hinged, folding wax tablet from within his tunic, passing it to Pompey. With a bow, he stepped back and strode toward the dazzling doorway.

'Thank you, gentlemen' he said with a nod and, withdrawing, pulled the door shut behind him.

Silence filled the temple and Pompey turned the tablet over in his hands, examining the seal that crossed the join; it was his own. With a frown, he snapped the seal and opened the tablet.

'Well?' Crassus demanded impatiently. 'What was so urgent that it couldn't wait a half hour?'

In the darkness neither of them could see the colour drain from Pompey's face as he stared down into the tablet. The wax that formed the two pages had been scraped out hastily to make room for the finger that sat in the centre, its two signet rings mocking him and announcing in no uncertain terms that his clandestine dealings with Clodius were no longer merely a rumour.

Swallowing nervously, he looked up and forced a smile, snapping the tablet shut and tucking it away into his toga.

'It seems that my son Gnaeus has suffered a fall while riding. He will be fine. This could have waited... my apologies.'

Crassus nodded.

'No apology necessary, my friend. I know how it is when a son injures himself. It fills the heart with butterflies and pushes it up into the throat. We should be finished very soon, and you can go and see him.'

Caesar narrowed his eyes as he studied the man opposite him.

'Yes,' he said very slowly and deliberately, 'you should certainly look after your own.'

The sun beat down on the Janiculum as the doors of the temple swung open. Fronto stood alone, twenty paces from the door beneath a tree, and it was to him that Caesar strode as his peers returned to their escorts.

'What did you *really* give Pompey.'

'You don't need to know that, Caesar.'

The general eyed him suspiciously.

'I would say that whatever it was gave the man rather a shock. After you left, he hardly said a word other than to hurriedly agree with anything I said. Honestly, I suspect that if I'd suggested he dress as a woman from now on, he would be having his hair curled and pinned up as we speak.'

Fronto grinned.

'Marcus, I want to know what you've done.'

'I've settled things, Caesar. Leave it at that. I think you'll find that Clodius' claws have been dulled. The great Pompey will, I suspect, be very careful to keep control of Rome for you while you're away.'

The general continued to glare at him and finally shook his head in exasperation.

'You are an infuriating man, Marcus Falerius Fronto.'

'I have been told that, yes.'

The two men sighed and stretched. Smiling, Fronto proffered a mug of wine to the general.

'Thank you, but no. I have much to do. Another week or so of planning and organising things with those two and then it will be time for me to return to the provinces.'

Fronto looked across in surprise.

'You leaving so soon?'

'I have a number of matters to attend to in Illyricum and more in Cremona. I need to do something about the Veragri at Octodurus. I'd like nothing more than to lead the legions there and make them pay for what they did to the Twelfth, but that could just cause another set of eruptions in Gaul. So, what I'm thinking of doing is sending Mettius and Procillus with a chest of money and a small escort and buying enough peace and goodwill across the Alps to persuade them to open the trade route I need. It might be simpler and less costly in the long run.'

He smiled curiously.

453

'Also, I am reorganising the legions prior to the next year. Priscus is insistent that there are men in the legions, once of Pompey's army, who are of dubious allegiance, and since Priscus is now my camp prefect, I can hardly ignore his concerns. I will be taking him with me to arrange matters; all my rotten legionary eggs shall be placed in one basket and I may then hand that basket to the Germans or the British when I see them.'

Fronto raised an eyebrow.

'Germania?'

Caesar smiled.

'Gaul is pacified, or will be when I've bought the Veragri, but the German and British tribes are restless. They must be subdued before they have an adverse effect on the settlement of Gaul. Prepare yourself, Marcus. Next spring, we move on to pastures new.'

Fronto sighed.

'Could you not have swapped your governorship with Pompey? Spain is so much warmer and friendlier than the far north.'

The general laughed.

'Make the most of the winter, Marcus. Next year could be a difficult one.'

'Aren't they all?'

The two men fell silent and stared off down through the woods at the city below. Rome glistened in the sun. There were times when the city was simply breathtaking.

Fronto sighed. Britannia meant ships and sea journeys.

'*Great.*'

* * * * *

Posco looked up over the edge of the well where the bucket slopped water this way and that, and balanced it on the brick surface, a smile breaking out across his face. He turned to the slave girl next to him, who was busy lifting a yoke and settling it on her shoulders to receive the water.

'Drop that and run inside. Tell the mistress that the master has returned.'

She looked up in surprise and squinted at the hill, past the outbuildings and the edge of the great sulphurous crater that bounded the eastern edge of the estate and past which the main road ran. A lone figure on horseback was making its way down across the grass from the road.

'Go on, girl. Quickly.'

As she removed the yoke once more and ran back into the front door of the villa and to the atrium in search of the house's mistresses, Posco quickly washed his hands in the bucket and dried them on his tunic before walking out toward the arched gateway with its canopy of crawling vines.

Fronto looked tired, but the smile he wore dispelled the tension Posco had been feeling ever since they had arrived almost two weeks ago.

Standing respectfully aside, he watched as his master approached and finally, as he reached the gate, haul on the reins and slide from the horse before tying him to the fence.

'Posco... am I glad to see you?'

The slave grinned.

'And I you, sir. I have sent word to the mistress.'

Fronto nodded, stretching.

'I am ready for a bath, a meal and a large mug of wine, Posco.'

'May I ask why sir travels alone? We were expecting master Priscus or master Galronus at least?'

'They will not be joining us, Posco. I winter with the family alone this year. Priscus is preparing to return to the legions as their new camp prefect and Galronus decided to stay in the city and try his luck at the circus again. I tried to tell him we have one in Puteoli, but I fear that Gaul has become more of a Roman than I will ever be.'

The slave smiled again.

'I shall have the baths heated ready for you, master. The evening meal is not prepared yet, but if you will allow a few moments, I will arrange something to tide you over, sir.'

Fronto grinned.

'The drink will do in the meantime. I haven't had a local wine in a very long time.'

Another slave appeared and took Bucephalus' reins, leading the magnificent beast to the stable as Posco accompanied his master through the garden toward the villa's door.

As they approached, the figure of Lucilia appeared in the archway, her deep blue chiton emphasising her pale skin and ebony hair, the simple gold earrings and necklace glittering in the afternoon sunlight. She was, simply, breathtaking.

Posco, busy chattering away, realised suddenly that he was alone and turned to find that his master had stopped a dozen paces back. He smiled.

'I'd best get to the baths.'

Grinning cheekily, he scuttled off toward the bath house, mentally cataloguing the tasks he would have to complete before dinner. On the way, he found young Pegaleius watering the garden and, grasping him by the arm, took him along to help.

Lucilia smiled at the weary traveller.

'You rode alone?'

Fronto nodded and started to walk forward again slowly, unable to take his eyes from her.

'Was that wise?' she asked. 'With so many troubles, I mean?'

He grinned.

'I think the troubles are largely past. Clodius will no longer be any trouble. Pompey the great is sweeping Rome clear of all its mess and I have hired workers and artisans to repair the house and left a few men to look after it.'

'So you are here for the winter?'

'I am here for the winter' he smiled. 'At least until spring. I see no desperate reason to return to the city.'

He eyed her questioningly.

'Though *you* may have one?'

She frowned in incomprehension.

'The Caecilii?' he said, an unspoken question in his eyes. 'A young man who has probably been expecting you for some time?'

The smile that flooded her face warmed his heart.

'I expect he has already received a letter calling off the match' she said with a contented sigh. 'I left mother working on father. She can be very persuasive.'

Fronto laughed.

'You are as expert a manipulator as any politician in Rome, Lucilia.'

She smiled as he finally approached her and reached out, taking her in his arms and enfolding her in them tightly.

There was silence for a long moment until finally she loosened her own grip and pushed her head back, looking up into his eyes.

Fronto smiled and leaned down to meet her kiss.

This was going to be a winter to remember.

END

Thank you for reading Marius' Mules III, I hope you enjoyed it. Please consider taking a few moments to leave a review online..

Author's Note

Love it or hate it! It was important to me, with this third year of Caesar's wars, to start broadening the scope of the series. Having solidly set the tone with the military campaigning in books one and two, it was time to begin exploring some of the political and social aspects of the war.

Those aspects come in the form of Clodius Pulcher and the other two members of the triumvirate. I would produce an extremely blinkered view of the war if I were to concentrate solely on the action in Gaul and not begin to draw in elements of the wider world - particularly in Rome, where the political state was becoming extremely taut and having an effect on the famous general and his clients and friends.

This extra dimension has also allowed me to explore more of the character and background of Fronto, which I believe has given our favourite legate a little extra depth and humanity.

In any series, be it novels, movies or television, there is the danger of new episodes becoming repetitive and 'samey'. I hope desperately to avoid falling into that trap and I believe that straight military accounts going on with this series would become slightly tedious for the reader.

Do not worry, though!

I have no intention of turning the Marius' Mules series into a political 'soap-opera' in Rome. Enough writers have covered the situation in the Eternal City - and done it well - that to devote too much time to it would be to rehash work needlessly. All I wish to do is add a dimension to the military tales. Books four and five will reflect this, though there will be future titles devoted more strictly to the military side. After all, everyone's favourite Gallic hero will become active soon enough.

I have, as usual, taken some liberties with characters. I have started to show the strain appearing in Caesar, having cracks appearing here and there. But the strongest characterisation - and possibly the most unfair - is that of the younger Crassus. There is a reason for this - beyond the need for solid antagonists: Crassus is shown in Caesar's writings to be a very able military commander and Caesar has praise for him, even leaving him to completely command the army in the southwest. However, the details of Crassus' activities are a little telling, I feel. Events such as his treatment of the tribes that led to the Veneti's revolt are the actions of a harsh man, given to punishment rather than conciliation and that, added to the portrayals of his father as a somewhat mercenary, selfish and domineering man lead me to believe that for all Crassus' vaunted military expertise, there were some serious negatives to his character.

The reader may by now have noted a theme woven into this tale. There is something in it of the exploration of what it meant to be either Gaulish or Roman - or indeed both - and the ethical considerations on both sides.

For all the general belief that Rome considered the Gauls barbarians, we have to remember that this is a modern concept. To Rome, the Greek word 'barbaroi' simply means foreigners or outsiders. They are 'not Romans'. This does not mean that no Roman could have respect for a Gaul. Indeed, when Rome was still a young republic, the Gauls had sacked the city. Moreover, Narbonensis and Cisalpine Gaul had been part of the republic for many years and a certain understanding of the Celtic world must have informed Roman thought. Thus characters like Labienus, starting to understand the enemy perhaps more than his own people.

Gallia Invicta brings more politics and thought into the series and I hope it captures you the way it was intended.

Simon Turney - March 2013

Full Glossary of Terms

Ad aciem: military command essentially equivalent to 'Battle stations!'.

Amphora (pl. Amphorae): A large pottery storage container, generally used for wine or olive oil.

Aquilifer: a specialised standard bearer that carried a legion's eagle standard.

Aurora: Roman Goddess of the dawn, sister of Sol and Luna.

Bacchanalia: the wild and often drunken festival of Bacchus.

Buccina: A curved horn-like musical instrument used primarily by the military for relaying signals, along with the cornu.

Capsarius: Legionary soldiers trained as combat medics, whose job was to patch men up in the field until they could reach a hospital.

Civitas: Latin name given to a certain class of civil settlement, often the capital of a tribal group or a former military base.

Cloaca Maxima: The great sewer of republican Rome that drained the forum into the Tiber.

Contubernium (pl. Contubernia): the smallest division of unit in the Roman legion, numbering eight men who shared a tent.

Cornu: A G-shaped horn-like musical instrument used primarily by the military for relaying signals, along with the buccina. A trumpeter was called a cornicen.

Corona: Lit: 'Crowns'. Awards given to military officers. The Corona Muralis and Castrensis were awards for storming enemy walls, while the Aurea was for an outstanding single combat.

Curia: the meeting place of the senate in the forum of Rome.

Cursus Honorum: The ladder of political and military positions a noble Roman is expected to ascend.

Decurion: 1) The civil council of a Roman town. 2) Lesser cavalry officer, serving under a cavalry prefect, with command of thirty two men.

Dolabra: entrenching tool, carried by a legionary, which served as a shovel, pick and axe combined.

Duplicarius: A soldier on double the basic pay.

Equestrian: The often wealthier, though less noble mercantile class, known as knights.

Foederati: non-Roman states who held treaties with Rome and gained some rights under Roman law.

Gaesatus: a spearman, usually a mercenary of Gallic origin.

Gladius: the Roman army's standard short, stabbing sword, originally based on a Spanish sword design.

Groma: the chief surveying instrument of a Roman military engineer, used for marking out straight lines and calculating angles.

Haruspex (pl. Haruspices): A religious official who confirms the will of the Gods through signs and by inspecting the entrails of animals.

Immunes: legionary soldiers who possessed specialist skills and were consequently excused the more onerous duties.

Kalends: the first day of the Roman month, based on the new moon with the 'nones' being the half moon around the 5th-7th of the month and the 'ides' being the full moon around the 13th-15th.

Labrum: Large dish on a pedestal filled with fresh water in the hot room of a bath house.

Laconicum: the steam room or sauna in a Roman bath house.

Laqueus: a garrotte usually used by gladiators to restrain an opponent's arm, but also occasionally used to cause death by strangulation.

Legatus: Commander of a Roman legion

Lilia (Lit. 'Lilies'): defensive pits three feet deep with a sharpened stake at the bottom, disguised with undergrowth, to hamper attackers.

Mansio and **mutatio**: stopping places on the Roman road network for officials, military staff and couriers to stay or exchange horses if necessary.

Mare Nostrum: Latin name for the Mediterranean Sea (literally 'Our Sea')

Mars Gravidus: an aspect of the Roman war god, 'he who precedes the army in battle', was the God prayed to when an army went to war.

Miles: the Roman name for a soldier, from which we derive the words military and militia among others.

Octodurus: now Martigny in Switzerland, at the Northern end of the Great Saint Bernard Pass.

Optio: A legionary centurion's second in command.

Pilum (p: Pila) : the army's standard javelin, with a wooden stock and a long, heavy lead point.

Pilus Prior: The most senior centurion of a cohort and one of the more senior in a legion.

Praetor: a title granted to the commander of an army. cf the Praetorian Cohort.

Praetorian Cohort: personal bodyguard of a General.

Primus Pilus: The chief centurion of a legion. Essentially the second in command of a legion.

Pugio: the standard broad bladed dagger of the Roman military.

Quadriga: a chariot drawn by four horses, such as seen at the great races in the circus of Rome.

Samarobriva: oppidum on the Somme River, now called Amiens.

Scorpion, Ballista & Onager: Siege engines. The Scorpion was a large crossbow on a stand, the Ballista a giant missile throwing crossbow, and the Onager a stone hurling catapult.

Signifer: A century's standard bearer, also responsible for dealing with pay, burial club and much of a unit's bureaucracy.

Subura: a lower class area of ancient Rome, close to the forum, that was home to the red-light district'.

Testudo: Lit- Tortoise. Military formation in which a century of men closes up in a rectangle and creates four walls and a roof for the unit with their shields.

Triclinium: The dining room of a Roman house or villa

Trierarch: Commander of a Trireme or other Roman military ship.

Turma: A small detachment of a cavalry ala consisting of thirty two men led by a decurion.

Vexillum (Pl. Vexilli): The standard or flag of a legion.

Vindunum: later the Roman Civitas Cenomanorum, and now Le Mans in France.

Vineae: moveable wattle and leather wheeled shelters that covered siege works and attacking soldiers from enemy missiles.

If you enjoyed Marius' Mules III why not also try:

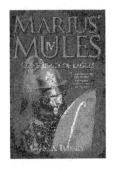

Marius' Mules IV: Conspiracy of Eagles

55 BC and Caesar's army gathers in the north of Gaul, preparing to drive invading Germanic peoples from Gaul and to traverse the dangerous northern ocean bringing punishment to the tribes of Britannia for their assistance of Gaulish rebels. But Fronto's troubles don't stop there. As his burgeoning relationship with Lucilia steps to a new level, so do his responsibilities at home, a situation exacerbated by the disruptive influence of the villainous Clodius in the city, causing trouble and endangering those about whom Fronto cares most.

With two troublesome new centurions, a selection of worthless and argumentative senior officers and the suspicious deaths of a number of notables, Fronto's year is about to take a turn for the unexpected.

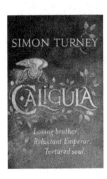

Caligula by Simon Turney

The six children of Germanicus are cursed from birth. Father: believed poisoned by the Emperor Tiberius over the imperial succession. Mother and two brothers arrested and starved to death by Tiberius. One sister married off to an abusive husband. Only three are left: Caligula, in line for the imperial throne, and his two sisters, Drusilla and Livilla, who tells us this story.

The ascent of their family into the imperial dynasty forces Caligula to change from the fun-loving boy Livilla knew into a shrewd, wary and calculating young man. Tiberius's sudden death allows Caligula to manhandle his way to power. With the bloodthirsty tyrant dead, it should be a golden age in Rome and, for a while, it is. But Caligula suffers emotional blow after emotional blow as political allies, friends, and finally family betray him and attempt to overthrow him, by poison, by the knife, by any means possible.

Little by little, Caligula becomes a bitter, resentful and vengeful Emperor, every shred of the boy he used to be eroded. As Caligula loses touch with reality, there is only one thing to be done before Rome is changed irrevocably.

Praetorian by S.J.A. Turney

Promoted to the elite Praetorian Guard in the thick of battle, a young legionary is thrust into a seedy world of imperial politics and corruption. Tasked with uncovering a plot against the newly-crowned emperor Commodus, his mission takes him from the cold Danubian border all the way to the heart of Rome, the villa of the emperor's scheming sister, and the great Colosseum.

What seems a straightforward, if terrifying, assignment soon descends into Machiavellian treachery and peril as everything in which young Rufinus trusts and believes is called into question and he faces warring commanders, Sarmatian cannibals, vicious dogs, mercenary killers and even a clandestine Imperial agent. In a race against time to save the Emperor, Rufinus will be introduced, willing or not, to the great game.

Made in the USA
Monee, IL
18 October 2021